Praise for Leigh Greenwood

D0049722

Praise for Leigh Greenwood's Night Riders series

Heart of a Texan

"An emotional, fast-paced Western tale, full of realistic characters, authentic settings, nonstop action, back-stabbing villains, and rough justice."

—*RT Book Reviews*

"Another excellent Western romance to add to the ever impressive list of novels penned by Leigh Greenwood."

—*The Romance Reviews*

"Strap yourself in for a wild ride with this cowboy and the stubborn love of his life."

—*Fresh Fiction*

"Rip-roaring, fast-paced high adventure...a delicious romance."

—*Historical Hilarity*

Texas Pride

"[An] entertaining high-stakes adventure."

—*Booklist*

"Another powerful, yet poignant saga in his Night Riders series...saddle up and read on!"

—*Fresh Fiction*

"A breathtaking Western romance."

—*The Romance Reviews*

"Greenwood is a word master."

—*Long and Short Reviews*

Texas Homecoming

"What more could we want? More cowboys!"

—*RT Book Reviews*

"Few authors provide a vivid, descriptive, Americana romance filled with realistic, angst-laden protagonists as this author can."

—*The Midwest Book Review*

"Greenwood's plot flows like paint across the canvas of a master. He reveals his characters with the skill of a diamond cutter, one facet at a time."

—*Rendezvous*

When Love Comes

"Complex and compelling. Full of cowboys and characters from the Old West, this book is like watching a John Wayne movie."

—*RT Book Reviews*

"Leigh Greenwood NEVER disappoints...always, always, a guaranteed good read!"

—*Heartland Critiques*

Someone Like You

"Greenwood never disappoints. Continuous action, sharp intrigue, and well-rounded characters captivate."

—*RT Book Reviews*

"This is a love story that will keep your interest from the first sentence until the last page. Enjoy!"

—*A Romance Review*

Born to Love

"The characters are complex and add a rich element to this Western romance."

—*RT Book Reviews*

"[Greenwood] has a nice sense of place, and his ability to write interesting, flawed characters dealing with real issues is admirable."

—*Rendezvous*

To Have and To Hold

LEIGH GREENWOOD

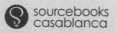

sourcebooks
casablanca

Published by Sourcebooks Casablanca, an imprint of Sourcebooks,
Inc.
P.O. Box 4410, Naperville, Illinois 60567-4410
(630) 961-3900
Fax: (630) 961-2168
www.sourcebooks.com

Printed and bound in Canada.
MBP 10 9 8 7 6 5 4 3 2 1

To Imogen Ayne Villeha, my first granddaughter
May 25, 2012

One

The Santa Fe Trail, 1865

Colby rode with a loose rein.

It didn't matter where he was going or when he got there. No one was expecting him and there'd be no welcome when he arrived. But that didn't bother him. That was the way things were, and Colby had learned to accept life as he found it.

His eyes narrowed to slits to keep out the glare of the blazing June sun. The dry air absorbed the perspiration as soon as it dampened his shirt between his shoulder blades. It was more than a hundred degrees on the plain, too hot to hurry.

There was no breeze. Nothing moved except the shimmering heat waves. Even the grass protested the heat. A wet spring had produced luxuriant growth, but the searing summer sun had turned green and gray to gold and brown. Stiff stalks brushed against his boots with the dry rattle of seedpods while the grass's rough edges tugged at the underbelly of his long-limbed Appaloosa stallion.

But Colby's thoughts weren't on his surroundings. He was entering a land of ghosts, the land of his past.

His destination was a rocky bend in a shallow tributary of the Cimarron River. Two graves lay hidden deep in the shade of a cottonwood grove, his parents' graves, parents he had never known, parents whose love and kindness hadn't been there to lessen the pain of growing up. A childless couple had taken him in, but they hadn't liked the boy he became. He left home at fifteen.

Eight years of drifting had earned him little beyond a horse, gear, and a distrust of women. Things hadn't been any better in the army. He had been too open in his contempt of incompetent men unfit for the ranks they held. He left the day the war ended.

Now he was drifting again.

The only place he'd ever felt at home was a cottonwood thicket, his only family the mounds of stones. He had had two brothers, but he'd never been able to find any trace of them. He would stay a few days, sleeping under the trees by day, walking the river by night. The graves had no past and no present, no hope, no expectation. They could mean anything he wanted them to mean, what he needed them to mean.

One corner of Colby's mind—the part always busy receiving and digesting information gathered by his alert ears, constantly moving eyes, and acute sense of smell—never forgot to be vigilant. He was in Comanche territory.

It had been a Comanche raiding party that killed his parents.

Colby glanced down at wagon ruts cut through the buffalo grass. He'd been following them for two days.

It was a small train of just over a dozen wagons, but they had taken the Cimarron Cutoff. Did they know Comanche raids had closed the cutoff during the war? Nobody traveled this route without army protection. Colby scanned the horizon from north to south. He could see no sign of movement, but he didn't expect to see the Comanches until they were upon him. He grasped the reins more tightly, and the powerfully muscled horse between his legs snorted in protest.

"Easy, Shadow."

Colby slowed his mount to a fast walk. The stallion sniffed the air and snorted. Apparently the scent of the train animals was still strong. They couldn't be more than a few miles ahead. As he studied the thin line etched into the dry sod of the plain, Colby felt his skin contract and the muscles in his stomach flutter. An odd foreboding settled over him. Senses honed through years of fighting told him something was amiss.

The crack of a rifle shot caused him to pull up. In the vast quiet, the sound was unmistakable. The wagon train was under attack!

Colby didn't stop to ask himself what one man could expect to do against a band of Indians. He thought only that some other child might be deprived of his family, might be forced to live a life of bitter loneliness.

Gripping the reins firmly and digging his heels into Shadow's flanks, Colby let out a yell that sent the powerful stallion into a flat-out gallop.

≈

Naomi Kessling stumbled over a gopher hole as she walked beside the lead yoke of oxen. Muttering angrily as she regained her balance, she raked the back of her hand across her forehead to wipe away the drops of perspiration that seeped through her eyebrows and lashes to sting her eyes. She jerked her yellow gingham sunbonnet farther down, but it didn't help relieve the glare from the relentless sun. Stifling another curse she wouldn't have wanted her father to hear, she pushed her way through the dry grass that snatched at the hem of her dress, crushing it beneath her boots to clear a path for those who followed.

Her father dozed inside their wagon. He'd been up all night with Wilma Hill, who was expecting her first child in a matter of days. Ben, Naomi's younger brother, walked before her, beating the grass to scare away rattlesnakes. Mr. Greene, their guide, had ridden ahead to find a suitable stopping place for the night. His son drove the lead wagon while his son's wife and small son slept inside.

The Kessling wagon was second. Fourteen other wagons followed close behind, men and boys guiding the oxen and mules or herding the livestock, women and children huddled inside to escape the merciless sun. The journey had turned into a nightmare punctuated by the preparation of tasteless meals, fruitless attempts to rest, and one crisis after another. Tempers flared, anger burst from between compressed lips, and fear-haunted eyes searched the horizon for their familiar forested and well-watered hills. But every morning the ruthlessly unforgiving prairie stretched before them—flat, dry, and empty.

Until today.

There was no warning of the attack. The Indians

seemed to rise out of the ground like morning mist from the surface of a pond. The first arrow knocked Abe Greene backward off the seat. The second buried itself in the ground at Ben's feet. The third missed its target because Naomi had already turned back to reach for her father's rifle.

So swift and unexpected was the attack that the Indians might have slaughtered them at once if Ethan, Naomi's seventeen-year-old brother following in the train's wake hoping to bag a sage hen for supper, hadn't knocked the leader off his pony with his first shot.

"I'll get the Greenes' wagon!" Naomi shouted to her father. She yanked Ben from where he stood paralyzed with shock, staring at the arrow buried in the ground, and shoved him behind the Greenes' wagon. Using the oxen as a shield, Naomi turned the wagon to start forming a circle.

Inside Cassie Greene screamed over and over again.

Somehow, despite the hail of arrows, the cries of the wounded, the gaps in the ranks, they completed the circle. Men crouched under wagons. Some lay flat on the ground; others shot from behind flapping canvas. Ethan, wide-eyed and breathless, came running up to join Naomi. Kneeling back-to-back in the grass under their wagon, they fired as rapidly as they could reload.

Naomi knew nothing about fighting Indians. She had listened to the stories Mr. Greene told of surprise attacks, but she hadn't taken them seriously. Thousands of wagons had traveled the Santa Fe Trail for nearly forty years.

Yet here they were, in the middle of a searing hot plain, some of their friends dead or wounded, she and her brother fighting for their lives from underneath a wagon.

The agonized moans from various parts of the train threatened to draw Naomi's attention from the attackers, but she couldn't worry about them now. Their wounds wouldn't matter if they didn't come out of this alive.

But would they? There could be as many as fifty Indians out there. She couldn't see through the thick grass to count them. She didn't know if any of them had been killed besides the leader. Even before the acrid smoke cleared, she aimed her rifle and pulled the trigger.

Medicine bag in hand, her father jumped down from their wagon and climbed into the Greenes'. A moment later Cassie began to cry with high keening wails. Naomi's father left the Greenes' wagon and turned his attention to other wounded.

Naomi knew Abe Greene was dead.

Suddenly the Indians pulled back. Accurate shooting and the constant boom of Morley Sumner's repeating rifle had enabled them to break the first attack. Now the train might have a chance.

Ben came running around the corner of the wagon to join them in the grass. "Abe's dead as a mackerel," he said, the pallor of his skin betraying the fear he tried to hide. "He's got an arrow sticking out of his eye. There's blood and goo all over his face. Cassie's gone crazy."

Naomi pushed Ben down in the grass. "I don't want to hear about it," she said, fighting off nausea. "Can you load a rifle?"

"Sure," Ben said, proud of his skill.

"Then load for Ethan and me. And keep down. Those Indians could come again any second."

Norman Spencer stuck his head under the wagon. "Where's your father?" he asked.

"I don't know," Naomi answered.

"We've got people hurt."

Mr. Spencer had been the most important man in their hometown of Spencer's Clearing. Back in Kentucky he'd seemed like the natural choice to lead their community, but Naomi doubted he knew any more about crossing the prairie or fighting Indians than she did.

"Abe's dead," Ben announced. "Got an arrow sticking out of his eye."

"Toby Oliver, too," Mr. Spencer said.

Toby! He was only nineteen, fresh home from the war and hanging around Polly Drummond with more than stealing kisses in mind.

"Will they attack again?" Ethan asked.

"I don't know," Mr. Spencer said.

"I think they will," Naomi said. "If they hadn't been meaning to, they'd have left by now."

"Your sister's probably right," Norman agreed. "You'd better keep your guns loaded."

"You think they're just waiting?" Ethan asked after Norman had left.

"Yes," Naomi answered. "I expect they'll attack again any minute."

But they didn't. The minutes crawled by and the attack still didn't come. She had heard that sometimes if the defense was strong enough, Indians would go away rather than lose braves. But she was certain they weren't going to let them escape. The Indians meant to kill them.

The heat under the wagon was stifling. The tall grass prevented the breeze from reaching them. Bits of dried stalk, ground to a powdery dust under the feet of the restive oxen, coated her skin. Drops of perspiration washed furrows as they raced down her face or burned into her grazed knuckles. Naomi wiped the sweat from her eyes, her unwavering gaze on the circling Indians.

"How much ammunition do we have left?" she asked Ethan.

"We've used a lot already."

"Don't shoot unless you have to."

One of the Indians suddenly spurred his pony in the direction of the wagon, zigzagging as he came. Black hair flying behind him like the mane of a wild stallion and his face distorted by rage, he looked like a monster out of a nightmare. Naomi struggled to hold her fear at bay at the sound of his maniacal screams.

She fired and missed.

The Indian loosed an arrow that buried itself in the flesh of one of their oxen. As the animal bellowed in pain, the Indian turned and galloped off.

Furious at the attack on the team he cared for with such pride, Ethan crawled from under the wagon. Standing, he took careful aim and fired at the retreating Indian's broad, muscled back. When the smoke cleared, the pony was riderless.

The wounded ox bellowed and lunged against the traces. Worried the brake would come loose and they'd be crushed under the wagon's iron-rimmed wheels, Naomi thrust an ax handle through the spokes to lock the wheels.

The arrow had sunk halfway up the shaft just behind the ox's left shoulder. Naomi was certain it had entered his heart. One leg folded beneath the animal's weight. The ox fell to the ground and rolled on his side. He lifted his head to deliver a final bellow of protest, but the sound that came out was a death rattle from deep in his throat.

"The bastards!" Ethan's voice was thick with emotion. "The heartless, stinking bastards!"

When he started forward, Naomi yelled, "Stay back!" and pulled on the straps of his overalls. "You can't do anything now."

She wondered if the Indians intended to kill their oxen so the settlers would be stranded and die of thirst. It had been two days since they crossed the Arkansas River—it would take them nearly a month to cover the remaining four hundred miles to Santa Fe—and the water in their barrels was low. They had to do something, but what?

"We've got to get away after dark," she told Ethan. Her throat was so choked with dust her voice was little more than a whisper.

"Where can we go?"

"I don't know. But they'll kill us if we stay here."

Suddenly, the air was rent by earsplitting yells and the Indians charged from all four directions.

"Get behind me," Naomi shouted to Ben.

Their shots turned away three attackers, but the fourth came on, jumping down from his pony to get a better line of fire at the people under the wagons. Chalky colorings of black, white, and blue turned his face into a mask of terror. He had colored his body with a red stain, streaked his chest with a dark brown that made Naomi think of dried blood. More than a dozen strings of beads hung around his neck. Two scalps dangled from the string that held up his loincloth.

The Indian ran a few strides toward them, dropped to his knee, and loosed an arrow at Ethan. It found its mark with a sickening impact. With a cry of rage, Naomi snatched up the rifle Ethan dropped and thrust it up toward the Indian now only a few feet from her.

She fired, and the savage fell to the ground clawing at the gaping hole in his throat.

Fighting against the waves of nausea rolling through her, Naomi turned to her brother. Ethan lay huddled in the grass, his face ashen, his body motionless, the arrow protruding from his leg.

"Is he going to die?" Ben asked, rigid with fear. His eyes seemed to be entirely white.

"No." Ethan struggled manfully not to give in to the pain. "I just got hit in the leg."

Naomi wondered if the Indians had more arrows than everyone in the wagon train had bullets. She counted the boxes of shells. Six left. The sun was still high in the sky. Night was several hours away.

The Indians stopped to regroup. Once more Naomi was forced to watch and wait.

How long? A minute? Half an hour? Time seemed to stop. It was so hot under the wagon at times she could hardly breathe. The images before her eyes grew faint and indistinct, but she fought off the dizziness that threatened her.

The smell of blood from Ethan's wound filled her nostrils and made her sick to her stomach. She shooed the flies away.

A cry from Cassie Greene riveted Naomi's attention.

She looked out on the plain. The Indians had lined up for another charge. How many were still out there, twenty? Thirty?

It didn't matter. There was no more suspense. No more fear. They would all die. She could face the certainty of death, but her pride wouldn't let her face it cowering under a wagon. She would meet them on her feet, a rifle in her hands.

"Load for me," she ordered Ben. Her voice was hoarse now, barely an intelligible whisper.

"They'll kill you," Ethan protested, pulling her back as she started to crawl from under the wagon.

Naomi turned on him. "They're going to kill us anyway." She heard her voice as though from a distance. She sounded slightly hysterical, but she felt utterly calm. Her gaze bored into him, and her voice dropped to a rasping whisper. "Don't let them take me alive. I can stand anything but that."

Ethan turned his eyes away. "You know I can't do that."

She grabbed him, made him look at her. "Promise me." It was no longer a request.

He averted his face. "Christ!"

She seized his chin and forced him to look at her. "I know what they do. I'd go mad."

It was an awful thing to ask of a man. It was especially cruel to ask of a seventeen-year-old, yet Naomi didn't hesitate. Her gaze, intense and resolute, locked with Ethan's. "You've got to promise me."

"All right," Ethan replied, but he didn't look at her.

"Swear it! I'll haunt you if you don't."

"I said I would." This time Ethan looked straight into her eyes, and Naomi knew he meant it. She rose to her feet.

At almost the same moment, the Indians charged along a broad front. Naomi lifted her rifle, but before she could bring it level, a series of thundering shots rang out and Indians fell from saddles like toys knocked over with the back of an angry child's hand. Naomi stared dumbfounded as the attackers divided into two groups, wheeled in panic, and galloped off in opposite directions.

"What's happening?" Ethan asked Naomi.

"Over there!" Ben cried, pointing.

In the distance Naomi could see a man's head above the grass. Then he burst into full view. A rider on a great Appaloosa was galloping toward them.

No one followed him. He was alone. He had attacked the Indians all by himself. He had to be crazy.

Naomi looked to where she had seen the Indians disappearing, but they weren't running away any longer. Attacking from opposite directions, they formed a semicircle around the rider. His only chance was to reach the wagons before one of their arrows buried itself in his back. His horse was magnificent. Such an animal could easily outrun the Indian ponies, but could he outrun the Indians' arrows?

The whooping and screaming warriors loosed their arrows to no avail. Naomi was hopeful he would reach the wagons when she saw the closest Indian draw his bow. She fired at him but missed.

"Shoot him!" she shouted to Ethan, who had dragged himself from under the wagon to kneel next to her. "Hurry before it's too late!"

Ethan didn't hit the Indian, but he caused the brave to drop his bow. Before she could sigh with relief, an Indian rose out of the grass not thirty yards away.

The Indian leader she thought Ethan had killed! He drew his bow and aimed for the stranger's back. Before she could shout a warning, she heard the twang of the bowstring, the zing of the arrow through the air, and the sickening thud as it buried itself in the man's back.

Rifle fire burst from all around her, and the Indian fell to the ground, truly dead this time.

With a tremendous leap, the Appaloosa jumped over the Kessling oxen and landed inside the ring of wagons. The stranger toppled to the ground virtually under the hooves of the frightened, milling animals.

Two

Before Naomi could overcome her shock, the man jumped to his feet, snatched the rifle from her, stumbled to a position at the end of their wagon, and sent a bullet into a brave who was about to use his hatchet to kill another ox. The stranger thrust her rifle back at her. "Load it, then bring me my rifle from my saddle." He shouted to Ethan, "Give me your rifle!"

The sight of the blood staining the stranger's shirt made Naomi dizzy. When she remained rooted to the spot, Ethan grabbed the rifle from her slack grip. "Get the rifle from his saddle. I'll load for him."

Finally able to force her legs to move, Naomi hurried to the Appaloosa. She caught up the reins, then led him back to the wagon, pulled the rifle from its scabbard, and handed it to the man.

"Can you load this rifle?" he asked.

"No." She had never seen a rifle like that.

Without looking at her, he emptied two rifles, which he handed to Ethan and Ben. Still keeping his gaze on the Indians, he snatched the rifle from Naomi's hands. He took a handful of large, long shells from his pocket and started forcing them into a slot halfway down the stock. Naomi watched, fascinated.

Once finished, he leapt to his feet and stepped around the end of the wagon so he had an uninterrupted field of fire at the attacking Indians. They had an equally uninterrupted field of fire at him, but the barrage of rifle fire that erupted from his weapon had a devastating effect on the Indians. As fast as he could pull the trigger, fifteen bullets exploded from the rifle. The Indians had no time to attack while he reloaded. There were a half dozen empty saddles when the stranger slumped back to reload.

"Where did you get that rifle?" Ethan asked in shock.

"In the army," the stranger replied, busy thumbing bullets in the chamber. "In a few years, the Indians will have a thousand just like it."

The thought of what could have happened if they'd had them today turned Naomi's blood to ice.

"Do you think they'll charge again?" Ben asked. The twelve-year-old was on the cusp of maturity, young enough to be excited but old enough to understand the finality of death.

"We'll see in a moment," the stranger replied.

"You're wounded." Naomi pointed to the bloody shirt.

"I've had worse," the man said. With that, he reached around and pulled the arrow out of his back and tossed it away.

Naomi gasped in horror. How could he do that like it was no more than extracting a splinter?

"You'd better see about that leg," he said to Ethan.

Apparently feeling he couldn't be outdone without calling his courage into question, Ethan yanked the arrow from his leg. He turned so white Naomi was afraid he was going to faint.

Willing herself not to be sick, Naomi said, "I'll get something to bind your wounds, but you need to see Papa."

Naomi ran to their wagon, but when she returned with a roll of flannel a moment later, the stranger was using Ethan's shirt to bind his leg.

"Save that for people who need it," he said.

"Like you?" She couldn't understand how he could ignore his wound. It had to be extremely painful.

"I've been hurt worse, but I'll let you bind it if it will make you feel better." Before she could object, the stranger removed his shirt and turned his back to her.

Ever since the nightmares began, Naomi had struggled to keep from being sickened by the sight of blood. Faced with a ragged, oozing wound, she could only remain steady by focusing on the rest of the man's back. That was nearly as dangerous. Compared to her brothers' youthfully thin bodies, his shoulders were broad, the smoothness of his skin disturbed only by the heavy cords of muscle underneath, scars from old wounds, and something that looked like welts. Good heaven! Had the man been beaten?

Her father shoved Naomi aside. "The man could bleed to death before you stopped staring at him. I know how you feel about blood. See if you can do something to calm Cassie."

"I can't leave until we're sure the Indians won't attack again."

"I'll call you if they do." It was the stranger who spoke.

He looked at Naomi over his shoulder, his expression

one of amusement mixed with curiosity. His nearly black eyes seemed to pin her in place. She hesitated a moment before nodding in acknowledgment and turning away. Once her feet were in motion, they moved so fast she was almost running. She had to slow down before she collided with the Greenes' wagon. When she climbed inside, she found Cassie holding her husband's body as she rocked from side to side, her face streaked with tears, her infant son's cries unheeded.

Naomi barely knew Cassie. Unwilling to be part of a large caravan, their group had hired Roy Greene to lead them to Santa Fe. They'd seen no reason to object when he said he needed to bring his son's family along. Abe Greene had been friendly, but Cassie kept to herself, rarely leaving their wagon. Only fifteen, she seemed more child than bride and mother. Unsure of what to do or say, Naomi picked up the baby. He looked so much like his father it made Naomi want to cry.

"He's dead," Cassie wailed. "What am I going to do?"

"We'll take care of you and your baby."

But would they? The twelve families in the train represented the entire population of Spencer's Clearing, a small Kentucky community near the border with Tennessee. Something had forced them to leave their homes and head west. No one would tell Naomi the real reason, but they kept away from other people and went out of their way to avoid contact with the army. She was sure someone had committed a terrible crime.

When the nightmares started, she was afraid *she* had.

"No one likes me," Cassie moaned.

"We don't know you." At least that was true.

Cassie's sense of wrong abated her crying. "I've seen the way you look at me and Abe. It's like you can't wait until you can get rid of us."

"It's not that," Naomi insisted. "We're a small community. Most of us are related. It's like we're one, big family. We don't know what to do with outsiders."

"You don't want to know outsiders," Cassie accused.

The baby was nuzzling Naomi. "I think the baby's hungry."

Cassie looked down at her husband. "He wanted to stay in Alabama, but his father insisted there was nothing left after the war. He said the future was in the West." She looked down at her husband. "He doesn't have any future now."

Naomi wondered about her future. Why hadn't they stayed in Kentucky? Would they end up like Abe?

❧

"What's your name?" Dr. Kessling spoke without looking up from bandaging Colby's shoulder.

"Colby Blaine."

"I'm Roger Kessling. You've already met my daughter, Naomi, and my sons, Ethan and Ben. I don't know what you were doing out here, but I don't know if we'd have survived if you hadn't shown up."

"I can't be sure we're out of the woods yet," Colby replied. "Those damned Comanches have been known to spread their attack over several days. How much ammunition do you have?"

"You'll have to ask Roy Greene. He's leading this outfit."

"Where is he?"

"He went ahead to look for a camping spot."

Colby didn't know a guide named Roy Greene, but he didn't think much of any man who'd leave his caravan in the middle of Comanche country. "This is a dangerous route for a small train. Why didn't you stick with the trail to Bent's Fort? You'd have had army protection most of the way."

The change in the doctor's demeanor was subtle but unmistakable. "We're a close-knit group. We're more comfortable traveling by ourselves."

"Even in the middle of Comanche country?"

"We were told that attacks were unlikely now that the war's over."

"Most of the army is still stationed in the Southern states. There're only enough troops to cover the most dangerous parts of the most popular trails. This isn't one of them. An experienced guide would know that. Where did you find this Greene fella?"

"You'll have to talk to Norman Spencer or Tom Hale. They hired him. There, you're all bandaged." The doctor stood. "You'll have to take it easy for a while, but you look healthy enough for it to heal soon."

"Where'd you get those streaks on your back?"

It was the younger of the two boys who asked, the one who looked like Naomi.

"You shouldn't ask questions like that." The older boy turned to Colby. "Ben doesn't know when to keep his mouth shut."

"I do, too," Ben insisted. "He doesn't have to tell me if he doesn't want to."

"I don't mind," Colby said. "The man who adopted me after my parents were killed was a mean son-of-a-bitch. When he didn't like something I did, he took his strap to me."

"Gosh! My father would never hit me."

"You're lucky." Colby studied the horizon for a full minute. "I don't think the Comanches will come back today, so we'd better decide what to do about your ox."

Both boys turned their gazes to where the ox had sunk in its traces. "They didn't have to kill it," Ethan said.

"We've got to butcher it to save as much meat as possible," Colby said. "Can you walk well enough to help us get it out of the harness?"

"I can do it." Ben stretched to his full height and squared his shoulders. "I'm strong."

Colby grinned. "I'm sure you are, but I need both of you. That's a big ox."

"I've never seen anyone butcher an ox," Ben said. "How are you going to do it?"

"Just like you would a pig," Colby said.

Before they could get the ox out of the harness, they had to unhitch the other five oxen. After that, it was a simple matter to remove the harness from the fallen ox. Colby had just made the first cut when he heard a voice behind him.

"What are you doing?"

He turned to see a tall man probably in his mid-forties regarding him with a frosty glare. "We're getting ready to butcher this ox."

"That's not your ox. Who said you could butcher it?"

"The doctor is busy trying to make sure nobody else dies, and his daughter is sitting with the woman whose husband was killed. The boys are helping, but you can take over for me if you want." He held out the bloody knife.

The man recoiled.

"Round up as many people as you can so we can get this done quickly. This place will be thick with wolves by nightfall."

"I haven't seen any wolves."

"You didn't see any Indians, either."

The man clearly didn't like being spoken to in that fashion. "I'll speak to the doctor."

"Who is he?" Colby asked after the man stalked off.

"Norman Spencer," Ethan told him. "He was the richest man in Spencer's Clearing."

"I guess he would be if the town was named after him."

"It was named after his grandfather, even though *our* grandfather helped found it."

"Norman is only nice to us because he married our cousin," Ben added.

Before Colby could return to butchering the ox, he heard a galloping horse approaching. He tossed the knife to Ethan, grabbed his rifle, and stepped around the corner of the wagon.

"That's Mr. Greene." Ben had followed him. "He's our guide."

"I heard gunshots," Greene said as soon as he dismounted. "What happened?"

"Indians," Colby said.

Greene looked around. "Anybody hurt?"

"Abe got an arrow in his eye," Ben told him. "He's dead."

Greene paled, turned, and ran toward his wagon. The moment he disappeared inside, Cassie's wails grew in a steady crescendo. Less than a minute later, Naomi emerged from the wagon. She glanced toward the family's wagon, blanched, and turned in the opposite direction.

"I guess she doesn't want to help with the butchering, either," Colby commented.

"Naomi gets sick at the sight of blood," Ben told him.

"She was fine until a couple years ago," Ethan said.

"What happened?"

"Nobody knows. It came on real sudden."

Colby figured it wasn't that simple. Things like getting sick at the sight of blood didn't just *come on real sudden*. Something had to happen to cause it, most likely something really bad. He wondered what it could have been. Naomi didn't seem like the kind of woman to give in to something like that. But he couldn't be sure what kind of woman she was as long as she avoided him like he smelled bad. Which he probably did. Taking a bath hadn't been much of a priority recently. It was hard to defend yourself against an Indian attack when you were naked, up to your waist in water, and your rifle and horse were twenty feet away. If he had to be scalped, he wanted to have his pants on.

Several people helped butcher the ox, but it was hard to concentrate with Cassie's hysterical demands to go back to Alabama coming from the next wagon.

"Can't say I blame her," one woman said as she lifted the heart from the carcass and dropped it into a bowl. "She's lost her husband and has a new baby. How's she going to find another husband out here?"

"This country is full of men without wives." This from a woman cutting meat into strips for drying.

"Considering what most of them are like, I'm not surprised. I wouldn't marry a man with no more than a horse and rifle to call his own."

The woman Colby had hoped to marry had felt the same.

When the carcass had been stripped of everything that could be used before it spoiled, Colby stood and stretched. "You can bury the carcass and offal if you want, but I suggest you move to a new camp and leave everything to the wolves. They've been cleaning up the prairie for thousands of years."

"I'll have to confer with Mr. Greene."

That from Norman Spencer, who had watched while others worked. Colby figured Norman thought he had too much money to have to work like everybody else, but that wasn't what bothered Colby.

People seemed willing to help with the butchering, but they spoke to him only when necessary. When he spoke to them, they mostly responded with a nod or shake of their heads. Only Ethan and Ben seemed comfortable talking to him. Naomi wouldn't even look in his direction.

Then there was the way the people acted toward one another. During the butchering, they broke into three distinct groups. They exchanged looks filled with unspoken anger and resentment as though bitter over a long simmering disagreement. Colby had been in trains where people kept their distance because they didn't trust strangers, but these people came from the same small community. If they disliked each other so much, why had they agreed to leave Kentucky and travel together?

Roy Greene climbed down from his wagon and walked over to Norman Spencer. His normally ruddy complexion was pale and drawn.

"I need to speak to you," Norman said to Mr. Greene. "This man says we need a new campsite for the night."

Mr. Greene looked at the remains of the ox. "That's what I'd recommend. I'll find one for you, but only because I need a place to bury Abe. After that, I'm taking Cassie and my grandson back East."

Norman exploded. "You can't do that. We've already paid you to—"

Greene withdrew a sack from his pocket. "Here's the money you paid me. All of it."

Norman pushed the purse away. "I don't want the money. I want you to honor your agreement."

"My son is dead, and I fear for his wife's sanity if I don't turn back."

"It looks like the only alternative is for all of us to turn back."

Colby turned to see Naomi behind him. "Why would you think that after you've come so far?" he asked.

"We don't know where we're going, and we don't have a leader," she replied. "I'm not even sure why we're here in the first place."

Colby didn't bother to hide his surprise. "You've come a thousand miles, and you don't know why?"

"We decided as a town," Norman said.

"You mean, the men decided," Naomi grumbled.

Norman glared at Naomi. "Naturally our wives would leave such a determination up to us."

Colby took a harder look at Naomi. She looked about nineteen or twenty. Dark blond hair down to her shoulders and bright blue eyes in an oval face added up to a vision any man would be glad to find on the pillow next to him each morning. If he'd had any desire to become involved with a woman, she would have appealed strongly to him. But after Elizabeth's heartless betrayal, he couldn't bring himself to trust any woman.

"I'd be curious to know why she thinks your group ought to turn back," Colby said to Norman.

"Your curiosity is of no concern to me," Norman replied. "We're grateful for your help in fending off the Indians." Glancing at the remains of the ox, his face showed disgust. "You made a quick job of butchering the ox. You can stay with us as long as it takes your wound to heal."

Colby hadn't made up his mind what he wanted to do. They were headed in the same direction so it would be nice to have a little company. And the Indians could attack again.

Besides, he liked Ethan and Ben. Maybe they could take the place of the two brothers who had been adopted by other families after his parents had been killed. He'd always wanted a family, a whole mess of kinfolk stretching to aunts, uncles, cousins, and grandparents. He didn't think of the couple who'd adopted him as family. They were just people who provided for him until he was able to take care of himself. They didn't have any kin he knew of. As far as he could tell, they hadn't wanted any.

Then there was Naomi. He was attracted to her—no red-blooded man could ignore a woman who looked like she did—but that's not what interested him. She was different. He couldn't tell why just yet, but he had felt it from the moment he handed her his rifle. Even in the midst of a battle, she stood out. He'd never met a woman who could do that. He was curious to know more about her.

"Thanks for the offer," he said to Norman. "Now if you'll take my advice, we ought to start looking for that new camp. Any time now you're going to see the Indians coming to collect their dead. As soon as they're gone, the wolves will come. They won't attack the wagons, but they'll kill any livestock that wander too far from the camp."

"The man knows what he's talking about." Mr. Greene introduced himself to Colby, and shook Colby's hand. "If you hadn't been here, I might have lost more than a son."

"And I might have lost one or more of my children." Dr. Kessling shook Colby's hand as well. "I'd like you to travel in my wagon."

Out of the corner of his eye, Colby noticed Naomi didn't appear happy about her father's offer. He wondered why she should have taken a dislike to him so quickly.

"We ought to get moving," Mr. Greene said.

Everyone headed toward their wagons, leaving Colby with Dr. Kessling and his family.

"My wound isn't bad," Ethan insisted.

"Maybe not," his father said, "but it could become infected or you might develop gangrene. I don't think you'd like going through the rest of your life with just one leg."

When Ethan started to argue, Colby said, "I know an easy way to make sure it doesn't become infected or gangrenous."

"How?" Ethan asked.

"Heat an iron poker until it's red hot, then thrust it into the wound. That will cauterize the flesh and prevent infection."

Ethan blanched.

Dr. Kessling smothered a smile. "I don't think we need to go that far. Get in the wagon, Ethan. You can drive. Ben, you can help him."

Ethan objected, but his father overruled him. When the wagons started to move, Colby found himself walking alongside Naomi.

"You don't like me, do you?"

She seemed unsettled by his blunt question. "I don't know you." She wouldn't look at him. "I can't dislike you."

"Of course you can. People dislike other people for all kinds of unaccountable reasons. Sometime for no reason at all."

Naomi turned to face him. "I don't know where you came from, who you are, or anything about your family. I'm not in the habit of offering friendship to people who just happen along."

Colby had expected something like that. "Where are you headed?"

"What do you mean?"

"Where are you looking to settle? Santa Fe? California? Somewhere in between?"

"Norman thinks we should settle somewhere beyond Santa Fe. Why do you ask?"

"The West is nothing like back East. There aren't many settled communities. People come and go. Most want to leave their pasts behind. You'll have to decide who to trust without that information."

"Why should anyone want to hide his past if it's honorable?"

"Because it's none of your business…or mine. Are you going to tell everybody you meet where you came from and why you left?"

Naomi looked away. She seemed to be attempting to put the same kind of separation between them that the others had.

"You don't have to answer me," Colby said. "Everybody can have perfectly honorable pasts without wanting to share them with the world."

"Does that go for you?"

"Definitely."

She had been watching for gopher holes, rocks, and snakes as they walked through the rough grass alongside the wagon, but now she turned to him. "You don't look like an honest person."

Colby was amused rather than angry. "You don't look like the kind of woman to let a man make decisions for her."

From the look on her face, he'd succeeded in surprising

her as well. "My father decides what's best for the family. Setting myself against him would mean setting myself against the good of the family."

"I expect your mother may have felt that way, but you've got the look of an eagle in your eye."

"I don't know what you mean by that, but I doubt it's a compliment. I need to look in on Cassie." With that she lengthened her stride and left Colby behind.

❧

"I don't know how you can stand the thought of living out here," Cassie said to Naomi. "I don't see why anybody would want to go to a place where savages kill people for no reason."

Naomi knew the Indians had good reason for what they did, but Cassie was in no frame of mind to appreciate them. Even though he had fought them, she suspected Colby might even be sympathetic. He was a strange man, and she didn't trust him. But what really upset her was that she found him attractive. Magnetic. Fascinating. Mysterious. She wouldn't have felt any of that back in Spencer's Clearing. Why should she feel that way now?

"I don't know how anyone could think I could find a husband out here," Cassie complained. "They're probably all like that Blaine fella."

"What's wrong with him?" Cassie had never left her wagon. What could she know about Colby?

"Mr. Spencer told Abe's father how he killed half the Indians with no more bother than if he was shooting ducks. Not that I care about that, but he got himself covered with blood cutting up that ox and didn't seem to mind." She shuddered. "How could any woman think of marrying a man like that?"

"I admire a man who doesn't hesitate to do what needs to be done."

"He looks as wild as those savages."

That wasn't true, but Naomi figured it would be useless to argue with Cassie. "I have a feeling we're going to have to get used to a different kind of man from now on."

Cassie shook her head. "I'm glad Papa Greene is taking me home. I think I would kill myself before I married a man like that."

Many men might covet Cassie's youth and looks, but Naomi was certain Colby wasn't one of them. That's part of what fascinated her about him. She got the feeling he would marry a homely, penniless woman if he found her worthy of his love. Naomi wasn't homely, penniless, or interested in marrying anyone, but she found that concept intriguing. Could a man *really* be like that?

The wagon came to a stop, and Cassie froze.

"What's wrong?" Naomi asked.

"I don't want to watch them bury Abe."

"All you're expected to do is be at the graveside when they bury him."

Cassie held her baby so tightly he cried in protest. "I can't. I can still see the arrow sticking out of his eye. It was horrible. I can't look at him."

"He's wrapped in a blanket."

Cassie shook her head. Deciding there was nothing she could do to change the woman's mind, Naomi started to climb out of the wagon only to come face to face with Colby. Having him appear so unexpectedly was a shock.

"How is the young widow doing?"

"She's still too upset to attend the burial."

Colby's arm was like iron as he offered to help Naomi down from the wagon

"It's good he's taking her back East. We don't need women like that out here."

Naomi released his hand the moment she was balanced on her feet. "What kind of women do you need? Or is it a personal preference?"

Colby didn't appear affected by the sharpness of her words. "We need women as strong as the men they marry. This isn't a land where a man can do all the work while a woman stays inside. It takes husband and wife working together to survive. Sometimes that isn't enough."

"I suppose you think cooking and caring for children isn't work?"

"Of course it is, but men out here learn to do that, too. Some women give up and die. Others go back East. You wouldn't. You'd stick until the end."

Naomi could hardly have been more surprised if he'd said she had two heads. "Why would you think that? You know nothing about me."

"Out here, you learn to take a person's measure right quick. You're scared of something, but you haven't run away. You've got backbone."

Naomi didn't know what to say. It was like he could see inside her head, and she didn't like that.

She didn't understand why Colby felt compelled to help them. They were strangers, people he would never see after he left the train. Was it because he wore a Union Army uniform? Was he here to find out why they left Kentucky, to force them to go back? She wouldn't feel safe until he'd gone. She didn't know why their whole community was headed for the Arizona Territory by way of Santa Fe, but she was sure it had something to do with the Union Army, with something *she* had done. There had to be some reason for the nightmares. And all that blood.

&

"I hated to see Roy Greene leave," Naomi's father said.

"At least we don't have to listen to Cassie's screaming anymore," Ben said.

"Burying your husband has to be a terrifying thing for a young woman, especially one with a new baby."

"Naomi wouldn't have carried on like that. She's got backbone."

Naomi wondered why Ben chose those words. He'd never said that before.

"I'm proud of your sister, too, but that's no reason to disparage the character of someone else."

"I'm not dis-parg-ing her,"—Ben stumbled over the word—"just saying Naomi wouldn't have carried on like that."

"You can stop talking about me like I'm not here," Naomi told her father and brother.

Ben wasn't ready to give up. "Polly and Toby were planning to get married, but she didn't throw herself on his grave."

Naomi hadn't been surprised when Cassie changed her mind about attending the burial, but she hadn't anticipated such a display of emotion. Mr. Greene had had to carry her back to their wagon.

Norman Spencer approached her father. "We're having a meeting to decide what to do."

"What choices do we have?"

"That's what we're going to talk about."

Twelve men gathered around the dying embers of a small fire. The women and older children formed a second circle. The younger children stayed in the shadows.

Within minutes, the discussion devolved into three separate camps throwing accusations at each other.

"If my wife loses her baby, I'll break you in half with my bare hands," Paul Hill shouted at Norman.

Given the size, apparent strength, and barely contained fury burning inside the young man, Naomi hoped Norman would take the threat seriously. From her position on the second row, Elsa Drummond, Polly's mother and sister to Frank Oliver's wife Mae, cast burning looks at Norman, his brother Noah, and his father-in-law, Tom Hale. What a tangled mass of inter-family relationships! At the rate they were going, it would be midnight, and they'd still be blaming each other.

Without warning, Frank Oliver jumped to his feet and punched Norman in the face with so much force blood spurted from the broken skin. The impact of the blow knocked him backward where he lay on the ground holding his face.

"You god-damned son-of-a-bitch!" Frank shouted. "It's your fault Toby's dead."

Colby jumped to his feet a fraction of a second after Frank. He locked Frank's arms behind him and pulled him away from Norman.

In seconds everybody was on their feet, men shouting threats and waving their fists at each other, women attempting to pull their husbands and older sons from the fray, the younger children filled with excitement or fear. Naomi had been aware of the fault lines that had developed within their group, but she felt helpless to do anything to prevent the shattering of their small community. How could they survive in a hostile land when they hated each other so much? Their only choice was to turn back.

Colby forced his way into the tangle of shouting men. "Stop!" His shout carried over the collective voices. "If the Indians were to attack right now, you'd all be dead in five minutes."

Naomi hadn't believed anything would quell the furor, but that did.

"There are ways to settle your differences," Colby said when he could be heard without shouting, "but this isn't one of them."

"There's nothing that will bring Toby back." Frank Oliver didn't attempt to hit Norman again, but his eyes blazed with pain and rage.

"No more than anything can bring Abe Greene back," Colby pointed out. "You need to mourn for your loss, but right now you have to decide what to do. You have only two options, stay here and hope to hook up with the next train that comes along, or go back to the Arkansas River crossing and hook up with one of the caravans taking the route to Bent's Fort."

Both suggestions had stumbling blocks, but the only point on which there was general agreement was the group's desire to avoid contact with outsiders.

"We can follow the river on our own," Haskel Sumner suggested. "Mr. Greene said it wasn't more than fifty miles from the Arkansas to the Cimarron."

"If you confuse the Cimarron with Sand Creek, you'll be headed south instead of west," Colby said.

"Why would we do that?"

"If you strike it below the normal route, it will be dry like Sand Creek."

"Why should we strike it below the normal route?"

"The trails that were there before the war have been washed out and overgrown. If you make a wrong turn, you won't reach the Cimarron before your water runs out. Your livestock are so thirsty now, they'll stampede at the first smell of water."

Naomi's father looked up from where he'd been tending to Norman's lacerated face. "I think we should go back to the Arkansas. It will only take a few days. With all the caravans passing that way, we're bound to find one we can follow."

Virgil Johnson objected. "We might as well announce who we are and where we're from."

"What do you suggest?" Dr. Kessling asked.

Virgil directed an angry glance toward Norman. "I *suggested* we not leave Kentucky, but that was overruled."

"We're a thousand miles from Kentucky, so there's no point in bringing it up again," Dr. Kessling said.

Though he had been excluded from the inner circle, Ethan spoke up. "I think we ought to ask Mr. Blaine to be our guide."

"No!" The unexpected force of her objection caused everyone to turn astonished gazes on Naomi.

Three

A SENSE OF GUILT WASHED OVER NAOMI, BUT SHE refused to let it take hold. She had nothing against Colby, but she wanted him to leave as soon as possible.

Norman Spencer was annoyed she had dared voice an opinion. "What's your objection? It must be important for you to have practically shouted it at us."

Naomi felt her face flush with heat. "I didn't mean to shout. I just think we ought to choose someone else, a professional."

"I know this trail as well or better than anyone you'll find," Colby said. "I've traveled it most years since I was fifteen."

"That makes him a perfect guide," Ethan said.

"I'm not looking for a job." He glanced from Ethan toward Naomi. "And I don't want to upset anybody. I'll leave first thing in the morning."

"You can't leave," Ethan said. "You're the best shot we have. What if the Indians attack us again?"

"Your wound still needs looking after," Naomi's father said.

"How much would you charge?" Norman asked.

"Why would I charge anything when I'm already going in that direction?"

It was Tom Hale who spoke up. "Because you'd be responsible for finding water—food in case we need it—deciding when and where to camp, for making sure every wagon gets across every stream and river, and for protecting us in case of another attack."

Colby glanced at Naomi, then back to Tom. "Can't say I want that much responsibility."

"Is your conscience willing to take the chance that we might perish if you don't help us?"

"It not fair to put a man in a corner like that," Colby said.

"Look at us," Tom said. "We're townspeople. We don't know anything about this country. We need you."

"You could wait here or go back. There's bound to be a caravan you could join."

Tom paused before answering. "There are reasons why that's not possible."

"He's wearing a Union Army uniform," Naomi reminded everyone.

"We can see that," Norman said, "but he says he's not in the army anymore."

"How do you know? You said somebody might come after us."

A strained silence followed Naomi's outburst. Ethan elbowed her, but she stood her ground. If they refused to tell her what had happened—what *she* had done—to force them to leave Kentucky, they had to expect her to be afraid of anyone wearing an army uniform.

"I'm wearing this because I don't have anything else," Colby explained. He paused. "I don't like the sound of *somebody might come after us.* Especially if that somebody is wearing a Union Army uniform. What kind of trouble have you people gotten yourselves into?"

"It's nothing like that," Tom assured Colby. "Our community was on the line between Kentucky and Tennessee. Neither side trusted us. With all the hard feelings after the war, we decided it was best to leave."

That's what Naomi had been told whenever she asked. It sounded logical, but something didn't quite ring true. Everybody had been different since her nightmares had started. The men met in secret; people who had been friendly suddenly stopped speaking; people whispered and looked over their shoulders. Rather than welcome visitors, they were nervous until they left.

"I don't like the feeling I'm getting about this," Colby said, "but I couldn't square it with my conscience to abandon anybody on this trail."

"Will you take us to Santa Fe?"

"I'll get you to La Junta. That's where this trail hooks up with the one from Bent's Fort."

"Let's talk about money," Tom said.

"Where's he going to stay?" Ethan asked. "He doesn't have a wagon."

"He can travel with us," Dr. Kessling said. "After what he's done, that's the least I can do."

Naomi turned and rushed from the gathering. They couldn't have hired Colby to guide them, but they had. They couldn't expect her to trust anyone in a Union uniform, but they did. Worst of all, her father had invited him to travel with them. Ethan was delighted. Ben probably would be, too. How could she explain that she was frightened because she found herself attracted to the man she was certain had come after them to take her back to Kentucky to face punishment for some unnamed crime?

Ethan caught up with her. "What is wrong with you?" he demanded angrily. "You act like Colby is our enemy."

"He could be. We don't know anything about him."

"That's nonsense. We don't have any enemies."

"Then why did we leave Kentucky?"

"You know why we left."

"I know what everybody says, but there's something else, something about me they aren't telling."

"You've let those dreams spook you," Ethan said.

"You'd feel the same way if you dreamed you were standing over two bodies covered in blood."

"It's probably the war. It's hard to ignore when it's all around you."

Hearing Colby's voice behind her was a shock. She spun around to face him and was victim once more to the attraction that was as powerful as it was unexpected and unwanted.

"I know you're not happy your father invited me to travel with his wagon."

"I'm glad he did," Ethan said. "Maybe you can teach me to shoot like you can."

"I'll be happy to," Colby replied, "but I want to assure your sister I'll do my best to stay out of her way."

"She's just upset about the attack and Abe and Toby being killed. She'll be okay by tomorrow."

Colby directed a wry smile at Ethan. "It's been my experience that a woman's sensibilities are more delicate than a man's. If you don't want to spend the rest of your life as a bachelor, you'd best remember that."

"Naomi's not like Cassie," Ethan assured Colby. "She's as tough as any man."

"Maybe so, but I expect she would enjoy a little pampering now and then."

Ethan turned to Naomi, puzzled. "Would you?"

Naomi itched to smack him. "Both of you are talking nonsense." She directed her attention to Colby. "I'm too old to want or need pampering, and you don't have to stay out of my way. You have a job to do that is more important than my feelings."

"There's no reason I can't do my job and still consider your feelings." His gaze narrowed. "I wish I knew why you disliked me."

"I don't dislike you. I don't even know you."

"Then why do you distrust me?"

"For the same reason."

"Did you know Mr. Greene before he was hired?"

Naomi wasn't about to be backed into a corner. "I expect you'll want us to start moving soon. Will we travel into the night?"

Colby's smile said he'd accepted her decision, but this wouldn't be the end of it. "We need to cover as much ground as possible. We often get violent storms in June. We don't need water-starved livestock dragging us into a swollen stream."

"My father's wagon will be ready to leave when you give the command."

Naomi turned away, but Colby's voice caused her to halt.

"I have my own grub."

Naomi turned. "As long as you're my father's guest, you'll eat with us."

Unwilling to strain her self-control any further, she hurried off. Somehow between now and tomorrow she had to learn how to stop being attracted to Colby Blaine. Now that he'd shown an unexpected depth of understanding, that was going to be harder than she expected.

❧

Colby didn't like the look of the sky. He wanted to make at least five more miles before they stopped for the night.

"Gosh. The breeze is picking up real fast."

Ben Kessling had begged to ride alongside Colby. He had always wished he could have found his brothers, but now he was reconsidering. The youth had pummeled him with questions from the moment the caravan started moving.

"It's doing more than picking up fast," Colby said. "It's building up to a storm. Ride back and tell everybody to make sure everything is tied down. Inside and out," he called back to the boy who had taken off at a gallop, delighted to have something important to do.

Colby had experienced many storms over the years, but never one that built up this fast. Ben wasn't out of sight before he saw a wall of water coming at them with the speed of a train. This was the kind of storm that could spawn a tornado. He wheeled his horse and galloped back to the following wagons.

"Circle up!" he shouted as he rode from one wagon

to another. "Unhitch the stock and herd them in the middle."

They took too long and didn't do it the right way, but this was no time to try to teach proper circling. The most important thing now was keeping everybody safe. Seeing one team of mules on the verge of breaking from the circle, Colby grabbed the bridle of the outside mule. Using his Appaloosa's body, he forced the mules back into the circle.

By the time the circle had closed up, the storm was upon them. Rain came at them in horizontal sheets, slamming into the wagons and blinding anyone who didn't turn his back. Despite the onslaught, Colby went from wagon to wagon telling everyone to put out buckets and pans to catch water for cooking and watering the livestock. Just then a bolt of lightning lit up the sky and sent several mules bucking in their traces.

Men fought the rain to get their teams unhitched before they broke the traces or got tangled up in the harnesses. The rain was coming down so hard that within minutes everyone was sloshing through water up to their ankles.

"Get inside," Dr. Kessling called to Colby.

A bolt of lightning struck the ground practically under his feet. A woman screamed, and an ox bellowed in fear. Within moments the lightning strikes were so numerous it was practically like daylight. Raindrops struck with stinging force while the wind threatened to throw Colby off his feet.

That didn't help when hail as big as pigeon's eggs started plummeting to earth. Over the wind Colby could hear it bouncing off the canvas coverings of the wagons and pinging as it landed in pots and pans. It was as though the elements were furious he had invaded their domain and were determined to drive him out.

"Come inside!" Ben Kessling urged.

Colby didn't bother answering. The wind would have ripped his words away before they could reach the boy. He needed to make one more circuit.

Once he was sure everyone was inside their wagons with both front and back flaps secured, he turned his attention to the animals milling about inside the circle of wagons. Colby didn't like oxen. Not as strong or as temperamental as mules, they were generally placid animals easy to control—except during a storm. They didn't mind the wind and rain, but the lightning dancing all around caused their eyes to bulge and their placid nature to turn skittish. Having someone around generally helped to calm them.

Crossing between two wagons, he was surprised to see a rain-drenched figure moving among the restless animals. He was shocked when he realized that figure was Naomi. "What are you doing out here?" he shouted when he was close enough for her to hear.

Naomi spun around, her eyes wide with shock.

"You're drenched," Colby shouted. "Get back in your wagon."

Naomi pulled the rain slick lower to shield her face. "Mr. Greene said oxen can get frightened during thunderstorms, that they sometimes run off."

"I'll make sure they don't stampede. Now get back to your wagon."

"There's no reason you should be the only one to be cold and wet."

"I'm paid to get cold and wet."

Yet Naomi didn't leave. Colby didn't know when he'd met such a stubborn woman—or one who was willing to take on a man's job and act like there was nothing unusual about it.

"It's my job to take care of the livestock. It's your job to stay safely in the wagon so I can do my job."

Naomi didn't answer.

"If you don't go, I'll carry you."

The rain and the slick made it impossible to see her expression even with the constant flashes of lightning, but anger mingled with surprise in her voice. "You have no right to force me to do anything."

Colby admired her courage, but this was not the time or place to display it. He scooped Naomi into his arms and headed toward her father's wagon. She wasn't a small woman, but he was surprised how light she felt. He suspected she hadn't been eating well for quite some time. He'd have to talk to her father about that.

"Put me down!"

He didn't bother answering. It should have been obvious he wouldn't have picked her up if he'd been willing to put her down the moment she objected.

"I'll have you fired for this."

He laughed. It would be a relief to have only himself to worry about rather than a dozen families who should have stayed on the other side of the Mississippi River.

"I thought you had a streak of decency, but you're just as barbarous as every other man I know."

When he reached the Kessling wagon, he shouted, "Open up. Naomi wants to get in."

"I do not."

He ignored her protest.

The canvas cover opened and Dr. Kessling's head appeared. "Where have you been?" he demanded. "Ben is looking for you."

Colby set Naomi on her feet. "Get inside. I'll find your brother."

"Make sure you do." Naomi accompanied her command with a fist to his jaw.

"Naomi Annabelle Kessling," her father exclaimed. "Apologize immediately."

"I'm very sorry I'm not strong enough to hit you harder." With that she turned and climbed in the wagon.

"I'm very sorry for my daughter's behavior," Dr. Kessling apologized. "I don't know what's gotten into her. She was never like this back home."

Colby rubbed his sore jaw. That woman packed a powerful punch. "Just make sure she stays inside until the storm is over."

"You can be sure I will." Dr. Kessling drew back inside the wagon and closed the flap.

For a few moments Colby didn't move. His jaw still stung, but he was barely aware of it. It had been a long time since he'd had a woman in his arms. After Elizabeth's betrayal, he practically had to be hogtied to deal with them. That was pretty much how he expected to feel when he scooped up Naomi.

But it wasn't.

Despite the raging elements, his own irritation, and the several layers of clothing between them, he'd been startlingly aware he held a woman in his arms. More worrying than that, he thought she was attractive. Most important and almost frightening, he'd liked it. Added to that was the physical response. Warmth spread through him despite the cold wind and rain. For the first time in years he felt tempted to linger.

He had to be crazy. He was in the middle of one of nature's hissy fits. He had to find Ben and calm the oxen. How could he be so lost to common sense as to be affected by a stubborn woman who didn't like him and had underscored that fact by punching him in the face? Maybe the lightning had unsettled his brain. He would find Ben. Then he would stay out in the rain until the chill drove every trace of unwelcome warmth from his body.

∽

Naomi was furious, and the fact that she knew she'd behaved badly did nothing to ease her anger. It wasn't all her fault, however. Norman Spencer and Tom Hale had no business hiring Colby to be their guide. How did they know he hadn't been sent to find them? He'd been following them. He was wearing a Union Army uniform.

"I'm appalled by your behavior," her father said. "I can't believe you struck a man who's shown us nothing but kindness."

The inside of the wagon seemed spacious enough when she was free to walk alongside. However, when three adults were crammed inside—two of whom she wanted to get as far away from as possible—it felt like they were practically cheek by jowl.

"He had the effrontery to pick me up."

"That's because you didn't have sense enough to come back to the wagon on your own."

"I wasn't in danger."

"You put your brother and Mr. Blaine in danger looking for you."

"No one had to look for me. I can take care of myself."

A gust of wind struck the canvas covering with so much force it tipped the wagon to one side. The double covering of osnaburg cloth flapped noisily against the hickory bows. The lantern suspended from the central bow swayed so wildly her father took it down and blew out the flame.

In the dark, the storm seemed even more threatening. Raindrops and hail struck the covering with pistol-like cracks. The shrieking wind sounded like a wild animal dying in agony while the crashing thunder made the earth tremble.

Ethan spoke in the darkness. "I don't know why you dislike Colby so much."

Before she could respond, the wind lifted the wagon far enough off the ground that the metal pots suspended from the bows clanged noisily against each other. Naomi was flung against the side of the wagon hitting her shoulder.

"I wouldn't have believed a wind could be this strong," her father said.

"Colby said there are spring storms like this all the time out here."

The muffled sound of Ben's voice came from outside the wagon. "Let me in!"

Groping for the buttons in the dark, Naomi managed to open the flap.

Ben crawled inside, dripping water all over Naomi and the bottom of the wagon.

"The next time you decide to go out in a raging storm, I'm not going to risk my neck to find you," he complained through chattering teeth. "Colby thinks you're crazy."

"Did he say that?" Naomi wanted to know.

"Of course not, but what else could he think?"

Something cold and wet landed on Naomi's foot. Ben was changing out of his wet clothes. He was no longer a little boy. Even in the dark, she was uncomfortable at the thought of being next to a naked male.

"It's horrible out there. I begged Colby to get in the wagon with us, but he wouldn't."

Another piece of wet clothing hit the floor.

"He said it was his job to make sure everyone else stayed warm and dry."

More wet clothing. Did he have anything else to take off?

"I told him anybody out in this mess deserved to be wet and cold."

She supposed the piece of clothing that hit her in the face was intended to hit the floor, but Ben's aim was off because a tremendous gust of wind lifted the left side of the wagon off the ground and tipped it over. A half-dressed Ben landed atop his sister.

The noise, the chaos, the confusion of raised voices contributed to the sensation that the world had gone crazy and taken her with it.

Naomi shoved at Ben. "Get off me. I can't breathe."

"I'm trying, but something's on top of me."

"Is everybody okay?" her father asked over the noise of the storm.

Ethan groaned. "Something landed on my leg. It hurts like hell."

Naomi decided this was not the time to tell her brother not to cuss.

"We've got to go outside to set the wagon back up," her father said.

Ben objected. "I'm barely dressed."

"I don't think anybody will care about that," his father said.

"*I* care."

"Stay here," Naomi said. "I'll help Dad."

"It'll take more than the two of us," her father said.

"Oh hell, I'll come even if I am half-naked."

"Me too," Ethan said.

Naomi was the first to crawl out of the wagon… right into Colby's arms.

"Is anybody hurt? I saw the wagon go over."

Naomi was too shocked to speak. She hadn't been in the arms of a man since she was a child. Now she'd been in Colby's twice. She couldn't take a deep breath until he put her down. Even then she felt dizzy. "Nothing serious, but I expect we'll find a few bruises in the morning."

"Several of the men are coming to help set the wagon to rights."

"We can do it ourselves."

"The more people helping, the quicker it'll be done. You may think yourself indestructible, but Ethan is wounded, your father isn't a robust man, and Ben is young. This wagon probably weighs close to three thousand pounds. If you break the bows, you'll be exposed to the weather for the rest of the trip."

If she had had any desire to argue with Colby, the raging storm would have prevented it. She watched as he positioned the men, explaining to each exactly what he was to do. She might not trust him, but he knew what he was doing. When he gave the signal, each man bent himself to his assigned task. The wagon resisted before being slowly lifted up to settle back on its wheels. An affirmation of their success was the metallic jangle as the contents of the wagon tumbled over each other.

"You can't stay in there tonight," Colby said.

"Naomi can stay with my wife," Norman Spencer offered. "Sibyl is her cousin."

Norman offered to let her father and two brothers bed down in his third wagon.

"Come on," Noah said to Naomi. "You need to get out of those wet clothes."

Naomi turned to Colby. "Thanks for your help." She ought to say more, but the raging storm and the presence of every grown man in the caravan, each one soaked to the skin, paralyzed her brain. Apologies would have to wait.

❧

Naomi wasn't surprised to find Colby up when she crawled out of Norman's wagon. It was barely light, but she was relieved the storm had passed. The ground was soggy under her feet. She panicked when she saw the animals were gone. Before she could raise the alarm, Colby rounded the end of her father's wagon.

"I put them out to graze," he said, apparently guessing her unspoken question. "They should have been out all night. We'll have to leave later than I want, or they won't have time to eat enough to keep up their strength."

"Do you always know what to do before anyone else?" She didn't know why that irritated her. She ought to be thankful.

"I grew up out here. What are you doing up so early?"

"I couldn't sleep. Besides, I need to put our wagon in order."

"Some of the oil leaked out of your lantern, but everything else looks okay."

"How can you tell? It's barely light enough to see outside."

"I can see in the dark." His smile was unexpected and boyish. "All wild animals can."

She felt herself flush. "I never said anything like that."

"I know, but you act like you're afraid of me. No, that's wrong. You're not afraid of anything. You treat me like I smell bad. You stay as far away as possible."

She knew she should apologize, but she was feeling too irritated. "How is your wound? The way you keep busy, it's hard to remember you got an arrow in your back yesterday."

"It hurts like a son-of-a-bitch, but it would hurt just as much if I did nothing, so I keep working. It helps me forget it."

She couldn't imagine how he could forget a hole in his back, but she was learning that Colby Blaine wasn't like other men. "I guess that's what makes you the perfect man to live in this brutal land."

"I gather you don't like it here."

"Why would anybody want to live here?" Her mouth tightened and she frowned. "I never wanted to leave Spencer's Clearing, but talking won't change anything. I'd better see about setting the wagon to rights."

"I'll help."

"You have more than enough to do. Besides, I don't think my family would like a stranger going through their things."

"You really don't like me, do you?"

She had turned to leave, but his words froze her in place. "As I said, I don't know you."

"That hasn't stopped you from disliking me. Why? What have I done?"

She turned, forced herself to look him in the eye. "My family is in your debt."

"*Your family* doesn't hate me. Just you. Is it my looks? My clothes? The way I talk? I probably smelled bad yesterday—it's hard to take a bath when you can't find water—but last night's storm should have left me smelling fresh and clean."

She didn't know why that image should have made her laugh. "I don't dislike you, but I can't trust you."

"That's a little hard to understand without an explanation."

"You don't have to understand. You just have to take my word for it." She didn't like the way he was looking at her, like she was a spoiled brat in need of discipline.

"If you're afraid I might be sweet on you, you don't have to worry. I fell in love when I was twenty."

Naomi flushed. "I'm not so full of myself that I believe every man I meet will fall in love with me."

"Good. I just wouldn't want that to be a worry."

"It's not. Now I have work to do." She headed for her wagon. When she reached it, she was dismayed to find he'd followed her. "Why are you following me?"

"It's not time to wake up the camp, and I've taken care of the livestock, so I have nothing to do for the next twenty minutes. Offering to help seemed like the neighborly thing to do."

He made it sound like only a heathen would refuse him. "I would be grateful if you would find our stove and put it back in the wagon. I can't lift it. Everything that was under the wagon needs to be found, dried, and put back. I don't know what goes where. The boys always take care of that."

She started to climb inside the wagon, but a distant sound caused her to pause. Colby must have heard it, too, because he was listening intently.

"It sounds like a wagon," she said. "How is that possible?"

Both moved from behind the wagon. He motioned for her to be silent. "It's coming from behind us."

The land wasn't flat enough to have an unobstructed view of their back trail, but the sound of a wagon being driven at a gallop was unmistakable. Naomi started to ask if Colby thought it was someone being chased by Indians, but he was no longer standing beside her. Instead, he was running to his horse, which he mounted without a saddle.

At that moment, a wagon topped a rise. It was the Greenes' wagon, and Cassie was driving.

Four

By the time Colby escorted Cassie's wagon into the camp, everyone was awake. Naomi hurried to meet them. "What happened?" Cassie's eyes were wild, her appearance deranged.

"Indians." She repeated the word over and over.

"Roy Greene was killed," Colby said.

"Indians." Cassie seemed incapable of anything beyond the mindless repetition of that single word.

"I have to go back for the body," Colby told Naomi.

"You could be killed. Then where would we be?" Norman Spencer said.

Naomi had never been fond of her cousin Sibyl's husband, but he had just sunk to a new low in her estimation.

"I'll take care of Cassie," Naomi volunteered.

Sibyl offered to take care of the baby until Cassie was better.

"I'll go with you," Frank Oliver told Colby. "I'd like a chance to pay those Indians back for what they did to Toby."

"It could be dangerous," Colby said.

"That's why you shouldn't go by yourself."

Zel Drummond and Morley Sumner also volunteered.

"If they get you, they're liable to get the rest of us," Morley said. "I don't aim for that to happen."

"Bring Cassie to my wagon," Sibyl said to Naomi. "We have more space."

Not only had Norman brought three wagons, he'd purchased extra large wagons that were so heavily loaded they require four yokes of oxen each.

Cassie seemed paralyzed in body as well as mind. Colby had to lift her out of the wagon. Once on her feet, she wouldn't take a step unless forced.

"We'll never get her inside the wagon," Sibyl said.

"She needs to lie down," Naomi told her cousin. "We'll make a pallet under the wagon. We can lay the baby next to her. Maybe he'll bring her out of this state."

"I hope so, but I'd probably go crazy, too, if I saw my husband and my father-in-law killed right before my eyes."

With no husband to take care of her and her baby, Naomi knew Cassie would have to face difficulties far beyond anything she could imagine. It was time to put all personal opinions aside. Cassie would need all the support everyone could give her.

It took several minutes before Naomi could coax Cassie to crawl under the wagon and lie down. Naomi sat on one side, rubbing and patting Cassie's hand in hopes it would soothe her, while Sibyl sat on the other side with the baby between them.

"Indians."

"Don't talk," Naomi said. "You're safe, and your baby's sleeping next to you."

"They came in the night. Papa Greene said Indians never attacked at night."

Naomi guessed the Indians had attacked at first light, which must have seemed like night to Cassie.

"I couldn't sleep with all that rain and lightning. The thunder kept the baby crying half the night so we decided to leave as soon as it was light enough to see."

Naomi couldn't imagine what it must have been like to feel lost in a wilderness during a horrific rainstorm with a crying baby.

"Papa Greene had finished harnessing the mules and had gone to get the milk cow when I saw him. He had painted his face to look so awful I screamed. Papa Greene reached for his rifle, but the Indian's arrow got him first. Papa managed to stand long enough to shoot the Indian before he fell to the ground."

Cassie had grown so agitated Naomi wished she would stop, but the girl continued.

"I ran to him, but he wouldn't get up. The arrow was here."

Cassie pointed to her chest. Naomi figured the arrow had entered Mr. Greene's heart or punctured his lung.

"I don't remember anything until I saw that man who killed all the Indians coming toward me." She started to cry. "I thought I was going to die. My baby, too."

Naomi didn't know what to say. Nothing she'd ever experienced came close to what Cassie had endured during the last twenty-four hours. Words of sympathy seemed useless, assurances that things would get better like outright lies.

"You don't have to worry about that now. You're safe with us."

"But what if they come back?"

"Mr. Blaine won't let anyone hurt you or your baby."

Naomi was surprised Sibyl would make such a promise. Was she the only one who didn't have implicit faith in Colby?

"Try to get as much rest as you can before we have to leave," Naomi said.

Cassie turned to Naomi, gripped her hand hard. "I want to go home." No sooner had she uttered those words than she burst out crying. She must have realized that with Abe and Mr. Greene dead, she had no home.

Naomi could think of nothing to say, so she returned Cassie's grip hoping it would provide some comfort.

The three of them hadn't changed positions when Colby and the other men returned. Mr. Greene's body was draped over the back of a horse. There was no question that he was dead.

"You go," Sibyl said. "I'll stay with her."

"I need volunteers to dig a grave," Colby said. "It needs to be deep enough that the wolves can't dig him up."

While a grave was being dug, everyone else worked to cook the first meal of the day in preparation for resuming their journey. It took Naomi all of that time to get the family's wagon put to rights.

"I brought you some breakfast. You need to eat."

Colby was standing at the rear opening holding out a plate of food to her.

"I haven't had time to fix anything for my father and the boys."

"Your cousins took care of them. I didn't know you had two cousins in the train."

Naomi took the plate of food from Colby, sat down, and started to eat. She hadn't realized she was so hungry. "Spencer's Clearing was a small community. Most of us are related in some way."

"Is that why everybody decided to leave at the same time? Ethan says no one stayed behind."

"Ethan talks too much."

"He has to make up for you talking too little."

He smiled at her. Naomi was certain it wasn't because he was happy with her, yet the smile wasn't sarcastic, accusatory, or unfriendly. Maybe it didn't mean anything. Much to her dismay, it had a strong effect on her.

Wandering around in this horrible wilderness by himself, Naomi doubted Colby had reason to know his smile transformed his face. An attractive man at any time, he now looked quite handsome despite a beard that badly needed shaving. His dark, almost back, eyes danced with the energy of a man who acted like the world offered no challenges he couldn't meet. It was difficult to appreciate the richness of his chestnut brown hair because most of it was covered by a hat with a wide brim to shield his eyes from the sun and the rain, but the rest of his imposing physique was there for anyone to see. Naomi decided it would be safer to keep her attention on her food.

"We're a small community unused to strangers. When they did come, they were from one army or the other and cared little about our safety or what we thought. They wanted only our cooperation and our food and threatened our lives if we withheld either. You can't blame us if we prefer to keep ourselves to ourselves."

"Out here everybody needs help to survive. People won't leave you to stand and fight alone even if you aren't family or distant kin. If I was willing to risk my life for a bunch of strangers, don't you think it's only fair at least to *act* like you like and trust me?"

He had turned things around so that Naomi felt small, petty, ungrateful, churlish, and about a dozen other unflattering words. Of course he was right. Everyone else had managed to appear civil and appreciative. "I'm thankful you helped us survive the Indian attack. It's just that I know nothing about you."

Colby leaned on the tailgate of her wagon, a lazy smile across his face. "There's not much to tell, but you're welcome to all of it."

"You don't have to—"

"My parents were killed by Indians. Their graves are along this trail. That's where I was headed when I ran into you. I had two older brothers. Each of us was adopted by a different family. A childless couple adopted me. God knew what He was doing because they should never have been allowed within a mile of any child. They hated what I became. When I got tired of the beatings, I ran away. After bouncing around a bit, I got a job working on caravans traveling up and down the Santa Fe Trail. After eight years, I joined the Union Army. I hated it, but I hung in until it was over. Now I'm heading back to my old stomping ground."

"You didn't have to tell me any of that."

"Yeah, I did. I'm tired of being treated like I have a disease."

"Sorry. I didn't know it was that bad." He'd left out one thing. "You said you fell in love at twenty. Did you get married?"

His reaction wasn't what she expected. Colby closed down just as effectively as a shop owner locking the door and pulling down the shades. He straightened up, tipped his hat.

"I got to get busy. I hope to make it to Sand Creek before we stop tonight. The stock got a bit of water from the pans we set out last night, but they'll be really thirsty if they don't get a drink before tomorrow. I don't want them stampeding at the smell of water. If you're finished with your breakfast, I'll take that plate. Better get your coffee before they put out the fires."

Puzzled, Naomi watched him walk away. She wouldn't have thought much about it if he'd said they fell out of love and his sweetheart married someone else. Or she was too young, that her family moved away, that they'd been separated by the war. All of those things happened hundreds of times, probably thousands of times, a year. It was the way he reacted that made her believe there was pain behind his refusal to answer her question.

Much to her disgust, that made him more intriguing than ever.

❧

"I don't know what I'm going to do when I get to Santa Fe," Cassie said to Colby. "I don't know anyone there."

"You don't have to know anybody to be able to

contact your family back east so they can make arrangements for you to go back home."

Colby had agreed to drive in Cassie's wagon because she insisted she didn't feel safe with anyone else, but he wasn't happy about it. Neither was Norman Spencer.

"You were hired to guide all of us, not babysit Cassie." The bandage that covered Norman's battered face didn't cover his black eye.

"She gets hysterical if I leave her," Colby had said. "You have to remember she's buried a husband and a father-in-law within twelve hours. She'll be much better in a day or two."

Over the last several hours that hope had begun to wane. He'd asked Ethan Kessling to ride along one side and Naomi to bring their wagon up on the other. He hoped that with three Kesslings being attentive to her—Dr. Kessling had given her something to calm her nerves—he could transfer responsibility to them. But Naomi didn't look happy about it.

"I can't go back where they killed—" Cassie wasn't able to say the words.

"Most of the caravans take a different route," Colby told her. "Some are so large and well-armed there's no danger of an Indian attack."

"But I have no one to help me."

"You'll have no trouble finding someone to take care of you."

"Could you take care of me?"

"I'm not going to Santa Fe."

"Why not? I don't trust anyone but you."

Naomi made a derisive sound, but Cassie appeared oblivious.

"I'm sure you can depend on Mr. Spencer or Mr. Hale to make arrangements for you."

Cassie pouted. "They don't like me. They think I'm too young to be married or have a baby."

Colby thought they were probably right, but it wasn't his place to judge. "There are others here who'll be equally willing to help. Now I'm going to have to leave you with Ethan. It's time to stop for the nooning."

Within minutes, the wagons had circled, the teams had been unharnessed and turned out to graze, and the fires for the midday meal had been started. Colby organized a hunting party led by Reece Hill and Zel Drummond to look for fresh meat.

"You're to eat with us," Ben said, out of breath from running over. "Naomi says don't drag your feet, or everything will be cold."

Dr. Kessling had offered his wagon to Colby because of his wound, but he'd never received a personal invitation to eat with them. He wondered why the change. He wondered even more why the invitation had come from Naomi.

As he walked around the camp, checking to make sure the wagon wheels were still in good shape after the morning drive, he couldn't take his mind off the way Naomi had looked at him when he was sitting next to Cassie. She didn't appear angry or jealous. The closest he could come to describing it was exasperation, but why should she feel that way? And who was she exasperated at? Cassie? Him? Herself? And why should it bother him what she felt? He'd sworn off women.

He wasn't interested in any relationship no matter how brief or casual. He wanted to get these people to La Junta then disappear into the wilderness. The only times he'd ever been content had been when he was alone. He didn't have any family now and he didn't need one.

He didn't even know his real parents' names. His adopted parents had refused to tell him. When he finally found their graves, only stones remained to mark the site. His adoptive parents thought the less he knew about his real parents, the less he would be like them. They told him how much they loved him, how much they'd longed to have children, how happy they were to welcome him into their family. They had given him a new name and a new home, but neither the relentless lectures, the harsh punishments, nor the cruel beatings had been able to make him into a new person. His father had tortured his body, but his mother had tortured his soul. It was either run away and take his chances on survival, or stay and be destroyed.

Being on his own hadn't been as hard as he'd expected. When he found Elizabeth, he thought he'd found a reason to live. When she abandoned him, he decided love was an illusion. It had failed him twice. He wouldn't give it a third chance.

"How long are we going to rest here?" Elsa Drummond asked as he passed.

"About two hours. We'll have to drive late into the night to reach Sand Creek."

Elsa looked up at the bright sun. "It's hot inside the wagons."

"Make a pallet underneath. The wagon will shade you and the ground will keep you cool. Make sure the children rest. They'll be the first ones to get tired."

"Do you intend to make it your personal responsibility to make sure every woman is properly cared for?"

Colby turned to see Naomi approaching from behind.

"I came to see what was keeping you," she said. "The boys are eager to eat."

"You shouldn't wait for me. I never know when I'll have time to stop."

"I realize you have important duties, but it's essential to keep up your strength. Otherwise, how can you be an effective leader?"

Colby didn't know what she was really thinking, but he was certain it was more than concern for his empty belly.

"Dad said you haven't let him look at your wound today. What will we do if it gets infected, or you get sick and die?"

"I thought you wanted to get rid of me. Having me get sick and die would be one way to do it." He'd hit a nerve. She looked angry and embarrassed. What was going on with this woman?

"Wishing you weren't part of the train isn't the same as wanting to get rid of you."

"It sounds like it to me."

"I've never wanted you to get sick or die, either. I'm not cruel."

Now he'd upset her. "I never thought you were. What have you fixed to eat?"

She was only slightly mollified. "Beans cooked with pork, but I fixed spiced apples for dessert."

"It sounds good. If the men have a successful hunt, you'll have fresh meat for tonight."

She thawed a little more. "I've never tasted antelope or buffalo. Is it good?"

"After a diet of beans and pork, it tastes wonderful. I'll show you how to cook it."

"I've never met a man who knew how to cook."

"There are probably ten men to every woman out here. If we didn't know how to cook, we'd starve."

She couldn't hide the hint of a grin. "Maybe I should be the guide, and you do the cooking."

"Maybe I should let you help me guide, and Ethan can cook."

She laughed easily. "The men in my family think it's an insult to be asked to do anything in the kitchen except eat."

"I thought you'd never get here," Ben called out to Colby as he approached where the three Kessling men were having their midday meal. "Dad said we'd better not wait, that you had a lot of things you had to do. What were you doing?"

"Checking the wagons to make sure they didn't need any repairs before our afternoon drive."

"Why do you have to do that?"

"One broken-down wagon delays everybody."

"See, I told you he'd make a great guide," Ethan said to Naomi.

Colby turned to Naomi. "You thought I wouldn't?"

Naomi was flustered. "That's not what I said. I said we didn't know whether you had the experience you said you had."

"You think I would lie?"

She directed a nettled glance at Ethan. "One's opinion of one's own abilities can sometimes be exaggerated. And we know so little about what's required to be a guide."

"After a month on the trail, I'd say we know a good bit," Ethan insisted.

"I'd say we'd all be a lot happier with more eating and less talking," Dr. Kessler said.

"I haven't said a thing," Cassie whined. "I haven't been given a chance."

Colby had decided that everyone in the caravan should have joint responsibility for Cassie and her baby, each family taking her for a day in rotation. Naomi had volunteered to take the first day.

"You'll have plenty of time to say whatever's on your mind during the drive this afternoon," Colby assured her.

"I want you to ride with me."

"I have to ride ahead to find a suitable camp for the night. I've asked Ethan to ride with you."

"He's wounded."

"So am I."

"I forgot." Cassie giggled. "You don't act like it."

"I doubt Colby has forgotten." Naomi sounded out of patience. "He said it hurt like a son-of-a-bitch."

"Naomi Kessling!" her father exclaimed. "I never thought to hear such language from you."

Naomi grinned at Colby. "I'm just repeating what he said."

"That's no excuse." He turned to Colby. "I'd appreciate it if you refrained from using such language around my daughter."

Colby threw an accusatory glance at Naomi, but she responded with a smirk. "She caught me at a moment when I wasn't in a charitable mood."

"She'd probably been telling you why she didn't want you here," Ben offered.

Colby pounced on the chance to give Naomi back some of her own. "She had. Quite pointedly, in fact."

"Once again, I apologize for my daughter," Dr. Kessling said to Colby. "She doesn't always know when it's best not to share all of her thoughts."

"Don't waste your time apologizing for me," Naomi said, any trace of amusement gone. "You can't change what I said. However, I will apologize to Colby for doubting him. According to everyone's judgment, including mine, he's doing an admirable job."

"It's only been one day so far," Colby said. "I have plenty of time to reinforce your original opinion."

"I think he's wonderful," Cassie said. "I'm going to try to talk him into taking me home."

Finding himself the recipient of curious glances from all four Kesslings, Colby decided it was time to focus on eating. "I'll have some of those beans, if you don't mind," he said to Naomi. "I'm looking forward to the spiced apples."

"I don't know how to make spiced apples," Cassie said, "but Naomi has promised to show me."

Colby decided that was something he'd do well to miss.

❧

Naomi was out of charity with herself, her family, Colby, and everybody in the caravan except Cassie.

That's because she was furious with Cassie. Every time Colby came within ten feet of that girl—Naomi refused to call her a woman—Cassie made an overt and inexpert attempt to convince Colby to take her husband's place.

"She acts like a strumpet," she'd said to Ethan when they stopped for the night. "I can't believe she would throw herself at a man with her husband dead less than two days."

"She's got no one to take care of her," Ethan had said. "Colby would be perfect for her."

Ethan sounded miserable at the prospect, and Naomi wondered just what her brother though of Cassie. She was young and pretty, which likely outweighed her callowness with Ethan. He was seventeen, young enough to become infatuated with the most inappropriate female of his acquaintance. Naomi was glad Norman and Sibyl would be responsible for Cassie tomorrow.

Despite the torrential storm of the previous night, when they reached Sand Creek it was dry. Colby set the boys old enough to handle a shovel digging for water. "We will reach the Cimarron tomorrow," he'd told them, "but that might be dry, too."

They'd driven until past eight o'clock, but no one had objected. The hunting party had shot a buffalo. Everyone was looking forward to fresh meat for supper. The teams had been unharnessed and put out to graze for the night. Already fires were going alongside every wagon.

"Buffalo meat is very lean," Colby had told everyone. "Don't cook it as much as you would beef, or it will be dry and tough."

Naomi had held him to his promise to show her how to cook it properly. "I don't want to take a chance of doing it wrong. The boys will never let me hear the end of it."

"I'm not sure I can eat the meat of a wild animal," Cassie said.

Naomi's patience was running very low. "Cows, pigs, and chickens were wild animals before we locked them up in pens."

"But that would make them taste different, wouldn't it?"

Fortunately for Naomi's evaporating patience, Cassie's baby started to cry. She took him to her wagon to nurse.

"I need to look at your back," Dr. Kessling said to Colby, "but don't let that stop you from making sure Naomi doesn't ruin the meat."

"I'm not going to ruin it," Naomi said.

"I hope not. I'm looking forward to my first taste of buffalo."

"So are we." Naomi looked up to see both her brothers had returned.

"We dug a long trench," Ethan told Colby. "The water wasn't far below the surface, so there ought to be plenty for the stock by morning."

Ben came to watch Naomi. "Are you doing it right?" he asked. "It doesn't smell cooked."

"She's doing fine," Colby assured the boy. "Your sister is a great cook. We'll have the best buffalo steaks of anybody."

Naomi was sure Colby said that for Ben's benefit, but she hoped he meant it. She'd given up trying to pretend she wasn't intrigued by him. It infuriated her to see him succumb to Cassie's whining at the same time it impressed her that he would make such an effort to help her endure tragedies that would have devastated any woman regardless of age. She was also impressed with his easygoing style of leadership despite being meticulous in every detail. He didn't shout, threaten, or bully. He merely stated what needed to be done, designated who he wanted to do it, then moved on to the next issue. There was something about him that made people respect him. Even Norman Spencer, who normally questioned every decision that wasn't his own, had accepted Colby's authority.

Then there was the fact that he didn't seem to be attracted to her. She wasn't a vain woman, but she was used to having an effect on men. Colby treated her much like he did her brothers. Compared to the effort he made for Cassie, that piqued her vanity. Watching her cook buffalo steaks while her father tended his wound didn't do much to settle her feathers. She still felt ignored. That wouldn't have been so bad if she could have ignored *him*, but she couldn't.

Drat. If she didn't pay more attention to what she was doing, she was going to ruin this meat.

"I think they're done," Colby said.

"I was about to take them off," she told him.

"I know." He winked. "I just said that so Ben would think I knew what I was talking about."

Why did he wink? What did it mean? He'd never done that before.

"Hurry up," Ben said. "I'm hungry."

"Hold out your plate."

"Don't let him grab the biggest steak," Ethan warned. "Colby ought to have it."

Naomi served six plates. "I'll take Cassie's to her," Ethan volunteered.

"This is good," Ben said, chewing vigorously. "When can we shoot another buffalo?"

"We have plenty of food without trying to slaughter all the wild animals," his father said.

"One a day is not a lot," Ben said.

Naomi appreciated Ben's approval, but she needed to see Colby's reaction before she could feel like she'd been successful. "Okay," she prodded when he didn't say anything. "Is it as good as Ben thinks?"

"It's perfect. I knew it would be."

"It had to be with you watching to make sure she didn't burn it," Ben said.

That took some of the shine off her pleasure, but it didn't matter because Colby winked again. Heat suffused her face, and her stomach flipped over. All thoroughly uncomfortable.

"That wasn't very generous of you," Dr. Kessling said to his son. "We're fortunate Naomi is a good cook. You'd be very unhappy if you had to survive on my cooking."

"Colby could cook for us." Ben fixed his adoring gaze on Colby.

"I'm sure he would," his father said, "but he wasn't around during the six years since your mother died."

"He's promised to leave us after La Junta," Naomi reminded Ben.

Only after the words were out of her mouth did Naomi realize what she said.

"He didn't *promise*," Ben corrected. "He said he'd take us that far. He didn't say he wouldn't go any farther."

"That was implied," Naomi insisted.

"You could change your mind, couldn't you?" Ben asked Colby.

"There'll be plenty of trains from La Junta to Santa Fe. You could join one, or just follow."

"Why won't you take us to Santa Fe?" Ben asked.

"That's none of our business," his father said.

"But I like Colby. I don't want him to go away. I—"

"Indians!"

The cry sent everyone scrambling for their weapons.

Five

THE CRY CAME FROM ETHAN. CASSIE WAS HAVING hysterics. Naomi grabbed her rifle and followed Colby to Cassie's wagon.

"Where are they?" Colby asked.

"Over there." Ethan pointed to a distant rise where Colby could see the head of an Indian above the tall grass that rippled in the breeze.

"Is he the only one?'

"No. I could see more before I jumped down from the wagon."

"Hold your fire," Colby called out.

"Why should we wait until they get closer?" someone asked.

"If these Indians had meant to attack us, we wouldn't have seen them until they were on top of us."

"I can see a lot more of them now."

"They're coming toward us."

"They're keeping their horses to a walk," Colby pointed out, "so they don't mean to attack. Keep your weapons ready," he called out to the others, "but keep them out of sight."

"What are you doing to do?" Naomi asked.

"Find out what they want."

"Can you understand them?"

"Enough. If you work in Indian country, understanding what they want goes a long way toward avoiding conflict." Colby turned to Ethan. "Can you do something to quiet Cassie? She's liable to set folks' nerves on edge."

"I'll try."

"She's lost her family to Indians," Naomi reminded Colby. "You can't expect her not to be frightened."

"I understand, but she could make someone so nervous they'll shoot one of these Indians. If that happens, they'll come back with a war party and try to wipe us out."

"I'll go," Dr. Kessling offered. "If necessary, I'll give her a sedative."

All the Indians were in plain sight now.

"I'll go meet them," Colby said to Naomi.

"If there is trouble, they'll kill you first."

"I'll be okay as long as no one shoots. I'm depending on you to make sure everybody remains calm."

Depend on her to make sure everyone remained calm! Her heart was in her throat. How could she calm the fears of anyone else? Suppose this was a trick to get them to relax, let down their guard. What if more Indians were waiting out of sight? They were staring hard at the wagons as though trying to see something out of sight. That made Naomi uneasy. What did they have that the Indians were so curious about?

"Ben, run and tell everybody what Colby said. They're not to shoot no matter what happens. If they do, they'll kill Colby."

Ben took off like a shot, shouting his message as he sprinted past each wagon.

"What's Colby doing?"

Norman Spencer had come up behind her. His rifle was leveled at the closest Indian who was sniffing the air.

"Colby says there won't be any trouble unless someone shoots one of these Indians. If they do, Colby says the Indians will come back determined to wipe us out."

"How can he know that?"

"He's lived in this part of the country his whole life. He said he could understand some of their language."

"How can a decent person understand their heathenish gibberish?"

Naomi was surprised by how much Norman's words offended her. "I suppose our language sounds like gibberish to them, or the French, the Germans, the Italians, the Span—"

"What he's doing is irresponsible. What will happen to us if they kill him?"

Naomi turned away from Norman and looked to where Colby had come to a stop in front of the nearest Indian. The man was speaking to Colby, making expansive gestures, pointing in first one direction and then another. Most often, however, he pointed straight at Naomi's wagon.

"It looks like he's asking Colby something about us," she said. "He doesn't seem upset, just curious."

Norman's grip on his rifle tightened. "He's probably trying to get close enough to see how many of us there are. Then they'll come back and kill us."

Naomi didn't answer because Colby was talking. She couldn't understand anything he said, but he was pointing down their back trail.

"What's he saying?" Norman asked.

Naomi didn't bother to explain that she couldn't understand what Colby was saying any more than Norman could. "He'll tell us when he gets back."

"If he gets back."

Ben came running up, breathless with excitement. "I told everybody. I said I'd shoot them myself if they got Colby killed."

"Don't be ridiculous," Norman said.

"Colby's my friend," Ben insisted. "I won't let anybody hurt him."

Naomi didn't bother to listen to Norman's response. He was acting just as immature as Ben. With his bandaged face and black eye, he looked comical. Two more Indians came up to Colby. He lowered his rifle enough to indicate their back trail then added a sweeping motion to the north. Naomi didn't know how he could appear so calm. He could have been talking to anybody.

"Why's he taking so long?" Norman asked.

"It doesn't matter how long he takes as long as it means all of us will be safe."

Only a short time had passed, but the tension made it seem longer. No one had told her Indians could be friendly. All she'd ever heard was that Indians were savages who wanted to kill all white people. The Indian attack two days ago had reinforced that lesson in a manner that was impossible to forget. She couldn't convince herself that these men wouldn't suddenly transform into maniacal killers like the ones who'd killed Abe and Toby.

How could Colby find the courage to walk out there and talk to them like it was nothing out of the ordinary? What kind of man was he? She had underestimated him, but how could she have known? The leaders in Spencer's Clearing had been Norman Spencer and Tom Hale. Next to Colby, they looked like mere imitations.

The Indians had finished talking. They exchanged signals she didn't understand. When Colby stepped back, the Indians turned and headed off to the northeast. Colby didn't turn back to the wagons until the last Indian was out of sight.

Norman Spencer didn't wait for Colby to speak before he asked, "What did they want?"

"Why did they keep pointing at us?" Naomi asked.

"I've heard they like to capture white women," Norman said. "They could have been pointing at you."

"Don't let gossip cause you to make a dangerous mistake," Colby said. "They were pointing at us because they were attracted by the smell of the steaks we're all enjoying. They wanted to know where we found the buffalo. They've been hunting without success."

"What did you tell them?" Norman's tone and expression indicated suspicion.

"I told them we sent a hunting party north about ten miles back. It was only a small herd so it was easy to miss it. I also warned them about the Comanche war party."

"You warned Indians about Indians?"

"Not all Indian tribes are friendly with each other.

They don't want to get killed any more than we do. Now everybody ought to get back to their food before it gets cold." He suddenly smiled. "They also wanted to know if one of our women was having a baby. I don't think they've ever heard a woman having hysterics."

Norman turned and stalked away. Everyone else returned to their wagons, but the mood wasn't as lighthearted as before.

"What's wrong with Norman?" Colby asked Naomi as they returned to food that hadn't completely gone cold.

"He's not used to having someone else know all the answers, especially when he doesn't know most of the questions. Having his face smashed by Frank Oliver makes his pretensions look even more ridiculous."

Colby laughed. "You have a sharp tongue when you want to use it. How do I get on your good side?"

"You ought to hear her when she gets mad at me," Ben volunteered.

Naomi felt herself grow warm. "You're not on my bad side. I just had my reasons for questioning whether you should be our guide."

"At the time, it didn't sound like a question to me. It seemed very definite."

"If it makes you feel any better, I no longer have any doubts about your knowledge of the trail or your ability to keep us out of trouble."

"But you still have the other objections?"

How did she answer that? She had passed the point of merely finding him attractive. In a remarkably short time, she'd come to admire him, be intrigued by him, want to know more about him. He seemed to have a solution for every problem. Nothing threw him off stride, not even when she refused to go back to her wagon during the rainstorm. He'd simply picked her up and taken her there. She could still remember the strength of his arms, the heat from his body despite the cold rain and fierce wind. How could she regain her peace of mind as long as he was around?

The army uniform still worried her. She didn't know the real reason they had had to leave Spencer's Clearing, but she was certain it had something to do with the Union Army. Someone in their small community had done something that had put everybody else in danger. She couldn't discount the possibility that Colby had been sent by the Union Army to discover who'd committed the crime. It had to be something truly dreadful to force all twelve families to leave their homes and livelihoods behind and start for the newly formed Arizona Territory, which they knew nothing about. At least three families were still bitter. She didn't know if that wound would ever heal.

"I admit it's unfair," Naomi said, "but I'm not going to explain my objections."

"Do others share your concerns?"

"I expect so, but they're too afraid of being abandoned to say so."

"But you aren't afraid of being abandoned."

"Of course I am. I think we ought to go back. We shouldn't have left in the first place."

"Why did you leave?"

There was no way around this question. Either she could ignore it, or she could answer him truthfully. "I don't know, but I'm sure it's not the reason I was given."

"It's no use asking Dad or Ethan," Ben said. "Ethan doesn't know and Dad won't say."

"Is this about the person you're afraid might be following you?" Colby asked Naomi.

"Yes."

Ben lifted his gaze from his food long enough to state quite casually, "Naomi thinks it might be you."

Colby stared at Ben for a moment before slowly returning his gaze to Naomi. His eyes were stormy, his lips tightly compressed. "I told you I'm no longer in the army, that I'm wearing this uniform because I don't have any other clothes, and that I'm not following you. Do you think I'm lying?"

"Of course she doesn't," Ben said.

"No one but your sister can answer that question."

He had reduced the issue to one simple question: did she believe he was telling the truth?

Oddly enough she believed him despite being unable to get rid of her fears. "I'm sure you would lie if you thought it was necessary—"

Ben didn't let her finish. "Everybody does that."

"—but I don't think you've lied to us…or to me."

Colby's grim expression gradually relaxed. "A fair evaluation."

"I don't see anything so special about that," Ben observed. "Can I ride next to you tomorrow?"

❦

"I don't know how to ride a horse," Naomi told Colby the next morning. "I wouldn't know how to get on one."

Colby looked at Naomi in disbelief. "You've never even been on a horse?"

"There was no need. If something wasn't in walking distance, one of the men would go after it. If I had to go a long distance, I'd go in the wagon or a buggy."

Coming to a decision, Colby said, "Leave the driving to Ben. You have to go with me."

"That's boring," Ben complained. "Those dumb old oxen don't need me to tell them to follow the wagon in front of them."

"Well it's not fair to make Naomi do all the boring jobs."

"How about Ethan?"

"He's helping Norman with Cassie and her baby. Do you want to change with him?"

Ben showed a typical twelve-year-old's horror at having anything to do with a young mother and her baby. "I'll drive today, but I want to ride tomorrow."

"That depends on how Naomi's riding lessons go. Out here a woman has to know how to ride. Her life could depend on it."

Ben made a disgusted sound but didn't argue. "I guess I'd better see to the oxen," he said. "A man's got to be sure his team's harnessed good and proper." He strode away with a swagger that brought a smile to Naomi's lips.

"He seems an easygoing boy," Colby said.

"Most of the time. It's not really necessary that I know how to ride," she insisted. "One of the boys is always around."

"The boys will grow up and move away. You'll get married and have your own family."

"Then my husband will do the riding for me."

"What if he's injured? Or he's away and one of the children gets sick?"

"I'll have a buggy or a wagon."

"Some of the country is too rough for either one."

"I expect I'll live in town. I probably won't need to ride at all."

Colby gave her an appraising look. "Are you afraid of horses?"

"Of course not."

His eyebrows arched. "Are you afraid of me?"

His question surprised her. "Why would I be afraid of you?"

"I don't know. That's why I asked."

The breakfast dishes were wiped clean and everything put away. There was nothing to keep Naomi from looking at Colby when she answered. "I'd rather not spend a whole day with you. I don't want to give people a reason to gossip."

"I spent half of yesterday riding next to Cassie with her making eyes at me. As far as I know, no one is gossiping about her."

"I'm the oldest unmarried woman in this train. That's all the reason anyone needs to start a rumor."

"I'm surprised you'd let idle chatter keep you from doing something that might one day save your life. I thought you had more backbone than that."

Naomi knew he was goading her, but she couldn't back down from the challenge. "I've never let gossip keep me from doing what I thought was right or important. If you think it's essential that I know how to ride, then I'll learn. I don't have a horse, and I don't have a sidesaddle. What are you going to do about that?"

"You can use Ethan's horse, but you don't need a saddle. Indians never use one, and they're the best horsemen I've ever seen."

Naomi bridled. "I hope you aren't intending to teach me to ride like an Indian."

Colby chuckled. "I won't. Now I have to make sure everybody is ready to move. I hope to make a long drive today."

Naomi watched him stride away. She had no idea why he insisted that she learn to ride. Mr. Greene had said the Arizona Territory was nearly empty except for the Spanish town of Tucson. Where would she be going in such a hurry if there were no towns or substantial settlements to look to for help?

Then there was the matter of her attraction to Colby that continued to grow stronger. How could she risk spending several hours with him? She wasn't sure it mattered. She was going to be in his company for at least twenty days. If she couldn't survive a single afternoon with Colby, she'd never survive the next three weeks. Now was probably a good time to see what she was up against. If she failed, she could always volunteer to stay with Cassie for the rest of the trip.

❧

When Mr. Greene was leading the caravan, his wagon had always been first in line. Colby had announced that the wagon at the head of the line one day would move to the rear the next day. That way no wagon would be stuck at the end catching the dust stirred up by dozens of hooves or be the most exposed to a possible attack. Cassie's wagon had led yesterday so the Kessling wagon was leading today. Having made sure that all the teams were properly harnessed, all the wagons ready for travel, and the horse for Naomi saddled and ready, Colby went in search of Ben.

"Time to get started," he told the boy. "Head to the right of that tree on the ridge ahead."

"Where are you going to be?"

"I'll be busy trying to teach Naomi how to get on a horse and stay there. I'm depending on you to lead the caravan until I can take over."

Colby could practically see Ben swell with pride. He had no doubt the boy was capable of handling the three yokes of oxen, but his father would be walking alongside the lead pair just in case.

Colby asked himself why he was so determined to overcome Naomi's objections to him. It would be easier to do his job if he just forgot about her altogether. It bothered him that he didn't know why he couldn't. She was undeniably attractive, but so were Cassie and at least three other women in the train. She had made it abundantly clear she wasn't interested in him, so was this a question of not being able to endure having a woman be indifferent to him? He'd never acted that way before. He'd always been the one who was indifferent. Why should that change now, and why with Naomi?

There were many reasons why this was a bad idea, and they didn't include that he didn't believe in love, that he didn't intend to get married, and that he was going to stay with the caravan only as far as La Junta. Yet here he was preparing to do something stupid. No, not *preparing* to do it. He'd *insisted* on it. Had he gone crazy? When he set out on this journey, all he'd wanted to do was visit his parents' graves, then find a place where he could get lost for the rest of his life. He'd never planned to travel with anyone, much less guide a caravan. He'd felt obligated to help them, but his duty didn't extend to teaching Naomi to ride. Yet he was inexplicably looking forward to the lesson. Some things didn't have a reasonable explanation.

Naomi watched the family wagon as it pulled away. "I hope you realize that asking Ben to lead the caravan has convinced him he's only a step removed from taking over."

"I'm depending on your father to make sure he doesn't steal my job." A weak effort at humor to ease the tension, but why was he feeling tense? There was no attraction between them that wasn't casual and therefore unexceptional. And if there had been, Naomi's dislike of him would have stamped it out.

"Don't worry," Naomi said. "Ethan will do that for you." She eyed the horse with surprise. "Where did you get that sidesaddle?"

"Norman brought one for his wife. He agreed to let me borrow it."

Naomi sniffed. "Norman always did have to prove his wife was better than the rest of us."

"I thought you liked your cousin."

"I love Sibyl. It's Norman I could do without. She wouldn't have married him if her father hadn't forced her."

Naomi immediately looked like she'd said more than she wanted. Colby decided to act like he hadn't heard it.

"If you can manage the courage to go against convention and split your skirt, I can teach you to ride astride."

"I've never heard of a woman doing such a thing."

Her expression showed so much consternation Colby had to laugh. "You'll get used to a lot more shocking things before long. Riding astride with a split skirt is a practical solution when using a wagon or buggy isn't possible."

"I'll stick to the sidesaddle, but I'd prefer that we wait until every wagon has passed us. I don't like being stared at."

"Then you shouldn't be so pretty." Good God! What was he thinking to let something like that slip out? She'd either suspect he had some romantic notions or some ideas that weren't so commendable.

Naomi appeared to have been taken off guard, but she recovered quickly. "If you think I look pretty in the conditions this trek across the wilderness has reduced me to, then all I can say is you haven't seen any attractive women. I'm surprised I don't scare your horse."

"I'm sure my horse would agree with me that you're a very attractive woman. However, I didn't mean to get started in that direction."

He tried to assume a businesslike tone, but it was unexpectedly difficult. It was almost as though he hadn't noticed she was attractive until he said the words. But having said them, he couldn't stop thinking about it. She was a damned pretty woman. If she thought she was dowdy now, heaven help the male gender if she ever got turned out to her satisfaction.

He was determined to control his wandering thoughts. "I don't know how much you know about a sidesaddle, but since you don't ride astride, you need a way to keep yourself in the saddle even when a horse jumps over some obstacle. That's what these two pommels are for."

Naomi looked dubious. "They look dangerous."

"It's the way women have been riding for centuries."

Naomi eyed the saddle with disfavor. "I'd rather walk."

"Don't lose your courage now."

"Look at that thing!"

Naomi turned to see Reece Hill's youngest boy pointing at the saddle and laughing. His father jerked him up and said some sharp words that wiped the grin off the boy's face.

"I agree with the boy," Colby said, unable to hide a grin. "Are you sure you don't want to try riding astride?"

"Watching me make a fool of myself with this saddle is more than enough. Come on. Let's get it over with."

"When I lift you, you have to throw your leg—"

"When you lift me?"

"The proper way, I'm told, is to have a set of steps so you can climb up and settle yourself in the saddle without assistance. Since we don't have any steps, I have to lift you into the saddle."

Naomi didn't look pleased.

"I could ask someone else. Do you want me to call your father?"

"No. Just tell me what I'm supposed to do with those *things*."

Colby stifled the impulse to chuckle. "You have to

throw your right leg over the upper pommel, and tuck your left leg under the lower one letting your foot rest in the stirrup."

"That sounds terribly uncomfortable."

"I'm told it's not."

"Who told you all this?"

"You're not the only woman I've known in my twenty-seven years."

Naomi got an *I'm trying hard to keep a rein on my temper* look. "Never mind. Lift me onto that thing, and don't dare let go until I tell you."

"I promise. Now stand next to the horse and let me know when you're ready."

Naomi took her position, closed her eyes for what Colby expected was a moment of prayer, then said, "I'm ready."

Colby placed his hands around her waist. It felt too small, too fragile, for a woman of Naomi's height. "It'll be easier if you bend your knees and jump as I lift you." He wasn't used to lifting women into a saddle or anywhere else. If there was a proper way to do it, he didn't know it. Dammit! He was nervous. He never got jittery about anything so he didn't understand why this time was different. Okay, he had his hands around the waist of an attractive young woman, but he was immune to women. Done with them. Would never trust them again.

"What are you waiting for?" Naomi asked.

To stop feeling like a fool he told himself. "I'm ready. Lift."

As he guessed, there had to be a certain way to do this because nothing seemed to go right.

"How do I get my leg over this pommel?" Naomi asked. "My skirt is in the way."

How the hell was he supposed to know? He'd never worn a skirt or used a sidesaddle. "Lift your leg up," was all he could think to say.

"Set me down in the saddle but don't let go."

That wasn't as easy as he expected. In order to place her squarely in the saddle and hold her there, he had to lean forward until his chest pressed against her left leg. She may have been too involved with arranging her skirt so she could get her right leg over the pommel to be aware of what was happening, but he wasn't. His entire body suddenly became keenly alive. From his upper chest to his waist, he could trace every point of contact from the heat generated. Someone might as well have taken a hot poker and traced a line down his body. He started to tremble. It was embarrassing, but he couldn't stop it.

"I think I got it," Naomi said, "but if you don't do something about my left leg, I'm going to fall off."

Breathing a sigh of relief, Colby let go and stepped back. "You'll be fine once I adjust the stirrup. Just let me know when your leg rests comfortably between the lower pommel and the stirrup."

Hell! The man who invented this damned contraption must have been senile. How was he supposed to concentrate on adjusting the stirrup when her bare ankle was practically in his face? There must be something wrong with the way she was sitting that kept her skirt from hanging low enough to cover her ankle. Fumbling with the buckles, he finally got it adjusted to what he hoped was the correct length. "How is this?"

She swung her foot forward but missed the stirrup. She couldn't lean over far enough to see without losing her balance. "You'll have to put my foot in the stirrup. I can't find it."

Colby gritted his teeth. This would teach him to tease a woman into doing something she'd rather not do. Next time, she'd have to convince him. Only he'd make sure there was no next time. What was it about a woman's ankle that had the power to turn a normal, sensible, coordinated man into a mindless bumbler? He was being ridiculous. Everybody had ankles. He should hardly notice Naomi's. Thank God it was encased in a boot. If her foot had been bare, he'd probably have keeled over in a dead faint that would have mortified him beyond hope of recovery. Telling himself not to be an idiot, Colby guided Naomi's foot into the stirrup and stepped back.

"Is that a good length?"

"No. It's too long."

Damn. He had to go through it again. There was no point in backing down now. His only option was to get it over as quickly as possible and get on his own horse. Admitting that it was a cowardly thing to do, he closed his eyes and readjusted by feel. When he had time alone to reflect, he would figure out why he was behaving so foolishly, but right now he had to get through any way he could.

"How's that?"

"It's too high."

"It's on the next hole. There isn't one between."

"I can't help that. It's too high. If I rest my foot on it, I feel like I'm about to fall over backwards."

"Which is better, too high or too low?"

"Too low I guess."

"Then you'll have to make do with that until I can find a punch to make a new buckle hole."

"I don't understand why any woman would want to ride a horse. How am I supposed to keep my balance?"

"The top pommel will keep you from falling to the left, and your foot in the stirrup will keep you from falling to the right."

Colby readjusted the stirrup length, placed Naomi's foot in the stirrup, stepped back, and took a long slow breath to release some of the tension. Nothing like this had happened to him since the early days of his courtship of Elizabeth. Embarrassed by this unforeseen show of weakness, he stepped away. Maybe if he didn't look at Naomi for a few moments, his senses could return to normal. He walked over to his own horse and fiddled with his stirrups. Next he readjusted the cinch. Once that was done, he looked for something else, *anything* that would give him time to regain his senses. He'd assumed he would have his usual reaction to an attractive woman—polite interest that would fade when she was out of sight. He was sure that would be the case with Naomi. He'd just had a weird reaction, a momentary—

A frightened whinny snapped his thoughts. He spun around to see Naomi's horse bound away from three wolves that followed close behind.

Six

COLBY CURSED HIMSELF. NAOMI WAS ON A RUNAWAY horse she didn't know how to ride and was struggling to stay in a sidesaddle that offered no handholds. How could he have been so affected by her that he could miss the approach of three wolves? He turned to where his own horse had been ground hitched, but the Appaloosa had snorted and dashed off.

Colby whistled softly. "Steady, boy." He had trained his horse to come whenever he heard that signal. The stallion snorted loudly and trotted in a half circle facing Colby. Looking wildly about, he shook his head and caracoled nervously.

Colby refused to let himself think of what might be happening to Naomi. Instead, he concentrated on catching his horse. He kept talking, hoping his voice would soothe the horse enough that he could catch up the reins. He approached slowly until he was able to grab the trailing reins. In the time it would take the average person to take a deep breath, he was in the saddle, yelling, and jabbing his heels into the Appaloosa's flanks. Within five jumps, the stallion was in full stride.

Naomi's horse was running *away* from the caravan. She was still in the saddle, but she lurched from side to side. Colby was thankful the grass was tall and thick. It had little effect on his mount's speed, but the wolves, powerful predators that they were, labored through the grass. Colby closed on them quickly. Once within range, he drew his rifle from its scabbard, took aim, and fired at the closest animal. The wolf stumbled and somersaulted through the grass before coming to a stop, blood oozing from a wound in the back of its head.

The two remaining wolves turned, snarled with bared teeth, but Colby swept by them. Now that one of them was dead, the others wouldn't follow.

Colby's stallion was powerful and swift, but Naomi's mount appeared to skim over the grass on winged feet. She was still in the saddle, but he knew that couldn't last. Her strength would give out, the horse would make a sudden change of direction or stumble.

The horse jumped some small obstacle Colby couldn't see. Naomi pitched forward on her mount's neck before being thrown backward, but by some miracle she managed to stay in the saddle. Colby was gaining ground, but not fast enough. He wanted to shout for her to hold on. He wanted to apologize for forcing her to ride against her will, for being so affected by her physical presence he failed to notice the wolves. Teaching her to ride wasn't part of his responsibilities. If he managed to rescue her, he'd keep his mind on his job—and not on Naomi.

Fortunately, Naomi's horse had either begun to tire or had realized the wolves were no longer following, for it began to slow. When it came to a dry streambed and its hooves sank into the soft sand, it slowed even more. Colby caught up when it climbed the opposite bank. The sensible thing to do would have been to grab the reins and lead the horse back to the wagons, but Colby suspected Naomi had had enough challenges for one day. He lifted her out of the saddle and onto his lap. He might as well have hauled in a wildcat.

"Put me down!"

"Relax, we're nearly a mile from the wagons. No one will see." She struggled so hard he had to hold her more tightly against himself.

"Good. Then no one will see me haul off and hit you. And then I'll *walk* back to the wagons."

Colby laughed. What a woman! Was she frightened? Not that he could tell. Was she thankful he'd rescued her? Not in the least. Was she proud she'd survived a dangerous ride on a runaway horse? He doubted the thought had crossed her mind. All she wanted to do was hit him as hard as she could. "I think I'd better hold on to you."

She punched him in the chest, but she couldn't draw back far enough to make the blows effective. "In the future stay as far away from me as you can."

"Why are you so angry? You stayed on that horse when half the men I know would have bailed out or fallen off. You're not hurt, and you certainly aren't frightened. You're a natural rider. Give yourself a week, and I doubt there's any horse that could unseat you."

"Save the flattery." She punched him again. "I'm never going near a horse again."

"I guess that means you'll be driving Cassie's wagon from now on."

She punched him again. "It's just like you to think of that."

"Just doing what I'm paid for. Ethan will need his horse so he can help with the stock, look for game, or search for wood."

"I can do that."

"Not on foot."

She stopped fighting. "You mean I can do all those things if I learn to ride a horse?"

"That's not all, but—"

She didn't give him a chance to finish. "Put me back on my horse."

"What?"

"You're not deaf. Help me catch my horse. I intend to ride the rest of the morning. If I haven't learned to ride by then, I'll ride this afternoon and every morning and afternoon until I am good enough."

Colby took a moment to catch his breath. He hadn't foreseen this turn of events. He doubted her father would allow her such free rein, but he wasn't going to be the one to stop her. She had grit. The question was whether she understood how to use it.

It took several minutes before he was able to catch her horse, but each time he looked back at her sitting astride Shadow her gaze was locked on him.

"Are you sure you want to ride him?" Colby asked when he returned with her horse.

"How would I get back to the wagons other-wise?" When he didn't answer immediately, her gaze narrowed. "You can't believe I would be seen riding in your lap."

That's exactly what he had been hoping.

"Can you imagine what people would say? They would say it to my face, too. That's one thing about family. Everybody feels free to disapprove of anything you do and to make certain you know it."

Colby couldn't imagine people feeling free to make his business theirs. "Let me help you into the saddle." Determined to avoid a recurrence of his earlier reaction to touching her, Colby lifted her into the saddle and immediately stepped back. "Can you find the stirrup?"

Naomi settled herself in the saddle and hooked her leg around the pommel. "I can't see it. How can I find it?"

Steeling himself against the inevitable, Colby placed her foot in the stirrup and backed away. "Is that okay?" Why did he sound out of breath? This was absurd. The woman didn't even like him, yet he couldn't touch her without his heart racing. He wasn't sure what was going on, but he didn't like it. He'd acted like this with Elizabeth, but he'd been young and foolish then. A lot had changed since.

Naomi flashed a daredevil grin. "I'm just waiting on you."

The cheekiness of it enabled him to regain his equilibrium. He swung into the saddle and turned to face her. "Is that a challenge?"

Her brash grin retreated until only a friendly smile remained. "Definitely not. Staying in the saddle when this horse went crazy was challenge enough. What happened?"

"Your horse was panicked by three wolves. I'm sure they were attracted by the remains of the buffalo we killed yesterday and have been following us hoping for more."

"Would they have attacked my horse?"

"They can bring down a full-grown buffalo. I doubt a horse is much different."

"I'll feel a lot better when we catch up with everyone else. How do I make this horse go?" Her mount was cropping grass. "He won't lift his head."

He'd forgotten that he'd just settled her in the saddle when her horse ran off. She didn't know the first thing about riding, yet she'd managed to stay in the saddle. She'd probably end up a better rider than anyone in her wagon train.

"Pull gently on the reins. If he doesn't lift his head, pull a little harder."

Responding to the first attempt, her mount raised its head, still chewing a mouthful of grass.

"You tug the left or right rein to change direction. To make him go faster, you can cluck to him, nudge him in the flank with your heel, shake the reins, or use the end of the reins to whip him on the flank."

"Wouldn't that make him mad?"

"No. He would run faster, but we're not going to gallop today. I think a gentle canter would be best."

She eyed him suspiciously. "That sounds like you're trying to baby me."

It amused Colby that she was determined not to be treated differently just because she was a woman. "Trotting can be very uncomfortable unless you know how to do it, and you've had enough galloping for one day. A canter is in between those two."

"How will I know the difference?"

Colby found it difficult to understand how anyone could grow up knowing so little about horses.

"Don't look at me like I'm an idiot," Naomi snapped. "We had mules in Spencer's Crossing for pulling a plow or a wagon. Norman was the only one with enough money to own a riding horse."

"Once you've cantered, you won't forget. Horses are herd animals so your horse will probably stay close to mine. The main thing I want you to do now is learn to relax in the saddle."

Naomi eyed his saddle. "It looks a lot easier for you."

Colby grinned. "Want to change horses?"

Naomi laughed aloud. "If I thought you'd ride up to the train in this saddle, I'd do it."

"Forget it. I'm not as brave as you."

Her horse kept alongside Shadow without urging. After a few hundred yards, the tension left her body. It wasn't long before she broke into a smile. "Why didn't anybody tell me this was fun? Can we go faster?

Colby was proud of her courage and ability, but he cautioned, "Let's wait until tomorrow. There's more to riding a horse than just staying on his back."

Naomi scowled at him. "You sound like my grandmother. She could take the fun out of anything."

"It's best not to try too much the first day."

Naomi made a face at him but didn't urge her mount to go faster. However, when they rejoined the wagon train, she didn't get the reception either of them anticipated. Her father was furious.

"I've always known you were strong-minded," he said to his daughter, "but I never thought you were completely lacking in intelligence. Get down from that horse now," he ordered. "What possessed you to leave Colby and set off at a mad gallop the first time you were on a horse? If he hadn't managed to catch up with you, you'd probably be lying somewhere out there with a broken neck."

"Just a minute, sir."

"Don't try to excuse her behavior," Dr. Kessling said to Colby. "I've depended upon her so much since her mother died that I've forgotten she's still a young woman capable of making some ill-considered decisions."

"She didn't this time," Colby interrupted. "Her horse was spooked by wolves. She did a brilliant job of staying in the saddle. I don't know any woman, and few men, who could have done what she did."

Her father seemed at a loss for words, but Ben wasn't similarly affected.

"Wolves!" he exclaimed. "I wish I'd seen them. How many of 'em were there? Did they howl and try to bite your horse? Did they have fangs this long?" The distance he measured with his hands was at least a foot. "Raymond said they drool something awful and have huge, blood-red eyes."

Colby had no idea who Raymond might be, but he obviously enjoyed entertaining young boys with tall tales. "They're a lot like large dogs, but they're very dangerous."

Ben looked disappointed, but his father was chagrined. "I guess I overreacted, but I nearly had a heart attack when I saw her horse take off like that. I could see her lying dead somewhere out there."

"I don't think we'll have any more trouble with wolves," Colby said.

"Good, but I don't think she should ride anymore."

Her father's sharp rebuke had shocked Naomi, but now she spoke up. "Colby said women out here have to ride. He says it's often necessary to their survival. And the survival of their families," she added.

"There are few roads, and distances frequently make the use of a wagon unlikely," Colby explained. "Walking isn't a consideration."

"Will you teach me to ride?" Ben asked.

"You already know how to ride," his father said.

"A mule that wouldn't go faster than a walk," Ben said scornfully. "I want to gallop like Naomi did."

"You'll have to wait a little longer," Colby said. "We're approaching the Cimarron River. We'll stop to eat and fill up the water barrels."

But when they reached the river, it was dry.

❧

"Are we going to have to dig for water every time?" Norman asked Colby.

Colby wondered why the man had the gall to use the term *we* when he had yet to pick up a shovel. "Much of the river bed is made up of sand or gravel, which allows the water to run below the surface. There's a bend up ahead that's usually a torrent of rushing water with green, grassy glades. We shouldn't have any trouble after that. We're likely to run into more water than we want in the form of storms."

"I thought we were done with that."

"You're never done with storms on the plains. A

northerner can blow through and drop the temperature thirty degrees in less than ten minutes. On occasion, it can turn into a blizzard."

He could tell from Norman's expression that he didn't want to believe him, but Colby didn't care.

"Have we dug enough?" Reece Hill and his brother had been willing volunteers.

Colby looked at the several pits, some as deep as a man. "That's more than enough. Get something to eat and rest. We'll fill the barrels when it's time to leave."

❧

After the midday meal, Naomi had insisted on riding with him when he went in search of a camping spot for the night. *Consider it my second riding lesson* she had said. She didn't need lessons, just a few tips and some experience.

Naomi shielded her eyes and looked up at the cloudless sky. "If every day was like this, I could understand why people might want to live here, but what would they use to build houses? There are no trees."

The weather had turned cool after a heavy rain the night before. A strong breeze and warm sunshine had dried the grass and turned the colors vibrant.

"Prairie fires kill off most of the trees, but there are enough to build sod houses."

"You mean people build houses of dirt?"

Colby laughed at Naomi's look of astonishment. "It's not as bad as you think. You'll see large homes built of adobe in Santa Fe."

"What's adobe?"

"Dried clay. And don't make another face. The bricks

people use back east are nothing more than baked clay. For that matter, so are the dishes on your table."

Colby didn't know when he'd had a more enjoyable afternoon. Naomi was like a child who absorbed everything new with a look of wonder and amazement. Instead of being bored, he found himself looking at his familiar world with the eyes of someone who'd never seen anything like it. It must be as strange for Naomi as it had been for him to find himself fighting a war in Virginia, a state with deep forests and rivers that never ran dry.

Naomi gave him a questioning look. "You have a way of making everything seem ordinary, uninterestingly familiar, even dull. Why?"

"I don't know what you mean."

They were walking side by side, leading their horses. Naomi bent down to pluck a small blue flower that was nearly hidden in the tall grass. She brought it to her nose, but apparently it had no fragrance. "You don't seem to get excited by anything. Or like anything. Or even want anything. It's like you're here, but you could be anywhere else just as easily."

Colby was pleased Naomi seemed to have gotten over her fear that he was a danger to her, but he wasn't comfortable with this examination of his character, especially when she appeared to find it lacking depth. "Why would you say that?"

"It's not a criticism."

It felt like it.

"You treat everybody the same even though Norman is an arrogant bully and Ben bombards you with questions. You're never angry or upset, tired or frustrated." She looked up at him. "Even when you caught me out in the storm, you didn't get upset when I refused to go in or angry when I hit you. You don't like anything or hate anything."

"I like my buffalo steaks cooked properly, and I hate having arrows in my back."

Naomi laughed. "I don't mean that."

Did this woman have any idea how beautiful she was when she looked up at him and laughed? She couldn't, or she'd know the damage she could do to a man's self-control. He would have given anything he possessed—well, not Shadow—to make love to her at this very moment. It wouldn't have been mere sex. Nothing about this woman was ordinary. It would have been an experience to savor, something by which to measure every woman in his future.

"The only time I've seen you feel strongly about anything was insisting that I learn to ride," she said.

Teaching himself to feel nothing was the way he'd survived. Learning to need no one, to depend on no one, had turned the ache of loneliness into an evenness of spirit that enabled him to accept the world as it was without anger or resentment. How did he explain any of this to a woman who'd been loved, valued, and protected her whole life?

"I have feelings like anyone else. I just don't allow them to control me."

Yet in the moments when his defenses were down and the pathway to his heart was thrown open, there were two things he wanted. Love and a family. Having accepted that he would never have either, he'd worked to build a wall around those desires, to enclose them so tightly not a single ray of hope could escape.

"Do you think I allow my feelings to control me?" Naomi asked.

"No, but you can't feel anger, frustration, dislike, or disgust without influencing your ability to make good decisions."

She stopped and turned to face him. "You said people out here had to be able to sum up a person in a matter of minutes. You've known me four days. That ought to be time enough to know everything about me."

He touched her elbow and started her walking again. "I think you make good decisions despite the fact that you might wish to do otherwise."

Her peal of laughter surprised him as much as it startled her horse. He was sure that whatever had caused her to laugh wasn't flattering to him.

"I've never heard a more diplomatic answer. You would get along fine with my father. No matter what he says, he does it without offending anyone. As a consequence, he's the only one everyone trusts."

"I take it you would prefer I be more straightforward."

"Of course. I don't like wishy-washy opinions."

Colby decided to give her what she wanted and see if she liked it. "I think you're a beautiful young woman of spirit who will make some fortunate man an uncomfortable wife."

Naomi hissed with exasperation but didn't interrupt him.

"You're kind, so you'll spare your friends by keeping your most severe criticisms for those you love.

Those judgments will show both the depth of your love and the height of your ambitions for them. You expect a great deal of yourself and will demand no less of others. You'll forgive them if they fail, but you won't be able to hide your disappointment."

Naomi looked shocked. "You don't like me at all, do you?"

"You didn't ask me whether I liked or disliked you, just what I thought of your character."

"But you couldn't possibly like the person you just described."

"Of course I can. I don't expect anybody to be perfect."

"But you are."

Colby couldn't have been more surprised if she'd said she was in love with him and wanted to marry him on the spot. His laugh was without humor. "You should have heard what my parents had to say. Besides, you dislike that I don't display emotion."

"Okay, that's a flaw, but only a small one. You're kind, handsome, strong, smart enough to know everything about traveling in this miserable country, and you've managed to make everyone respect you enough to do what you ask without arguing. Even Norman, and he doesn't respect anyone but himself."

"You think I'm handsome?" Maybe it was vanity that made him latch on to that first, but he'd spent too many years being told he was an ugly little savage. His parents had wanted an obedient, unquestioning son with untanned skin and perfectly combed hair who kept his clothes neat and clean. Their disappointment became a daily litany.

Naomi cast him a scornful glance. "You know

you're handsome. Why do you think Cassie has been fawning over you?"

"Because she's alone, scared, and I'm the oldest unmarried man here. She'd cling to me if I looked like a lobo wolf."

"I don't know what lobo wolves look like, but if they looked like you, people would probably sacrifice half their livestock just to have them hang around."

"You *really* think I'm handsome?" Colby was alarmed that Naomi's thinking he was handsome could have such a powerful effect on him. He'd never worried about what anyone else thought of his looks, not even Elizabeth.

"Yes, I do. So do Sibyl and Laurie. We've talked about it." She favored him with a sly smile. "You didn't expect women to ignore the presence of a handsome man, did you?"

"Just a few days ago you made it clear on more than one occasion that you didn't trust me and wanted me to leave as soon as possible."

She looked away. "I never felt that way about *you*, just about what I thought you represented. Since I don't think you represent that any more, I feel differently."

"How do you feel about me?" He had always made it a point never to ask questions like that, it only led to hurt and disappointment, but she had thrown him off guard.

She still refused to meet his gaze. "I'm not sure yet."

"Not fair. I gave you a direct answer so it's only fair that you give me one."

She looked up, met his gaze fair and square. "I really *don't* know beyond what I've already told you.

You appear to be an unusual man, one I admire and would like to know better."

Colby felt a sudden tightening in his chest, the feeling of being pressed too close, of having no room to move. He didn't want anyone admiring him or wanting to know him better. That inevitably led to them wanting something from him, to *expecting* certain kinds of behavior in return for their good opinion.

Yet he'd opened himself to this invasion by asking her opinion of him. Having done that, did he have the right to cut her off without an explanation? What explanation could he give? That he was a loner, that he didn't trust people, especially women, that he didn't want to be close to anyone? He could say all of those things, but were they true? If so, why had he insisted that Naomi let him teach her how to ride? Why had he gone to such lengths to understand her objections to him? Why was he even interested in her opinion of him?

He couldn't be sure of the answer just yet, but one of the possibilities scared him right down to his toes.

"You wouldn't find anything very interesting about me. I'm no different from hundreds of other men who've grown up out here."

Naomi studied him for a moment. "I don't know anything about where you grew up or the people around you, but you're different, and I'm going to find out why."

As the wagon train came into view, Colby could feel the fetters tighten around him. In a short while, he would be consumed by his duties and Naomi would be involved with her family. Later they would all go to sleep and leave him to make sure the camp was secure. Then, in the silence and the stillness, he'd try to figure out why he'd let himself become infatuated with Naomi when he didn't want anything to do with women.

❦

The rest of the day had passed without anything more threatening than Paul Hill's wife saying she was worried the bumping and bouncing of their wagon was going to cause her to have her baby early. Her sister-in-law had stayed with her until it was time for everyone to go to bed. Dr. Kessling would sleep next to their wagon in case he was needed.

The women and children were asleep. A guard was responsible for watching the livestock that had been put out to graze. No wagons needed repair and they had enough water for two days. There'd be no shortage of fresh meat because Frank Oliver had worked off some of his anger and bitterness by killing two antelope. The night was clear with enough breeze to keep the mosquitoes away. Colby had to make one more circuit of the wagons. Once that was done, there was nothing left for him to do but seek his own rest.

Yet he was too restless to sleep.

He'd always preferred night to day, dark to light. In the daylight he was forced to share himself with the world. In the quiet that filled the night, he was able to reclaim himself *for* himself. His parents had said that was selfish, that it showed he was unworthy of the love they longed to share with him. It had been the only way he could survive their idea of love, the only way he endured Elizabeth's treachery, the only way he survived the horrors of war and knowing he had brothers he would never see.

Yet tonight he was unable to achieve that inner peace, to find the place inside where all parts of him came together.

"You still up?" Dr. Kessling asked as Colby approached Paul Hill's wagon.

"Just checking one last time."

How could he sleep when his mind was filled with unanswered questions? No matter how alluring and interesting, no matter how strong the physical attraction he felt for Naomi, he had no interest in a relationship. He wanted to visit his parents' graves, get this wagon train to La Junta, and then head off into the wilderness where he could gather the familiar loneliness around him. Loneliness was a remorseless companion, but it shielded him from the folly of hope, the pain of broken dreams.

His steps slowed as he approached the Kessling wagon. Ethan was standing the first watch, Ben was sound asleep under the wagon, and Naomi slept inside. He didn't understand how, after having known them only a few days, this family could have started to feel like a part of his life. They were essentially strangers. He liked them, but that didn't mean—

A moan from inside the Kessling wagon claimed his attention. He stopped and listened, but he heard nothing more. He was about to move on when it came again, only louder and more pain-filled. The moans changed to words so muffled he couldn't understand them.

Naomi was becoming more agitated. He was about to turn back for Dr. Kessling when she screamed—

"Blood!"

Seven

WITHOUT EVEN THINKING ABOUT IT, COLBY JUMPED into the Kessling wagon.

"Blood!"

The single word was filled with such horror Colby knew there had to be more than a simple dislike of blood. He didn't know whether to wake Naomi or wait to see if the dream would subside. It was difficult to see her in the semi-dark inside the wagon, but he could tell she was truly terrified.

"No!"

Naomi thrashed about so wildly Colby was afraid she would hurt herself. Overcoming his reluctance to wake her, he reached for her hand. The moment he touched her, Naomi came awake and threw herself at him sobbing.

"It was worse than ever this time."

She pulled him down until he was kneeling on the bed of the wagon next to her, wrapped her arms around him, and rested her head against his chest.

"I saw Grandpapa lying on the floor," she mumbled. "Why would he be covered with blood? And who was that other man?"

Colby knew the proper thing to do was to wake Ben and send him to bring their father. But having Naomi's arms around him felt too good.

"But it can't be Grandpa," Naomi said. "He died in bed."

Colby patted her back and tried to soothe her. But once she fully came to her senses, he knew there'd be hell to pay. Naomi would never want to be caught so vulnerable.

"Why do I keep having these dreams?"

He couldn't explain that, but it seemed odd she would dream of a violent death for a man who had died in his bed.

"I want my mama," she moaned.

Those words drove an arrow straight to his core. It's what he'd always wanted, a mother and father to love him, to comfort and protect him until he was old enough to comfort and protect them in return. He'd spent years trying not to think of that, yet a single sentence had shattered all the barriers and opened the pathway to the part of him that he had spent years trying to ignore.

"Your mother is dead."

"I know. You've told me—" Her body stiffened. She released him and sat up. "What are you doing here?"

"You were having a bad dream. You were starting to get hysterical. I was afraid you'd wake the whole camp if I didn't do something."

"I *never* get hysterical."

"You were becoming *very upset*. You said something about seeing your grandfather and another man covered in blood. You didn't understand that because your grandfather died in bed."

Naomi's stiffness melted away. "This dream has haunted me for two years. It started after my grandfather died. In the beginning I didn't see anybody, just blood smeared over the floor and the walls, even the windows. I would wake up shaking. It was like I was drowning in blood. I was sure I'd done something terrible no one knew about. But that's impossible. You couldn't do anything in Spencer's Clearing without everybody knowing about it."

"Was anybody killed in Spencer's Clearing?"

"No."

"Do you have any idea why you'd dream something like that if nothing like it ever happened?"

"No."

"What does your father say about it?"

"He says it's a reaction to two deaths in the family. My mother died from consumption. During the last year she often spit blood. My father was frequently away tending patients from neighboring towns, even troops on occasion, so I was left to take care of her. But I never dream about her that way, only the way she was before she got sick. I didn't start seeing anybody until about a year ago. Papa said it was because my uncle had just died from a shotgun accident that left him covered in blood. I tried to tell him my dream was different, but he didn't believe me. Now I know it was. My grandfather was one of the men. That's got to mean something."

Colby agreed with her, but since he didn't know anything about her grandfather or his death, there was no explanation he could offer. "You'll have to ask your father."

"He'll just say I'm imagining things." Naomi seemed to pull herself together. "Thank you for waking me, but you can go now. I'm all right."

"What if you can't go back to sleep?"

"I always do."

"What if you have the dream again?"

"How could you stop the dream?"

"I couldn't, but I could wake you before it got to be too awful." He couldn't see her expression, but he could sense she paused to consider.

"Suppose I stay until you go to sleep," he offered. "Then I'll bed down underneath the wagon with Ben."

Naomi laughed. "You'll wake up with bruises over half your body. That boy throws himself about like he's in a wrestling match."

"I'll take my chances. Now go back to sleep."

"I can't go to sleep with you so close. It's not you. It would be anybody."

"Okay. I'll sit on the wagon seat, but I won't go farther than that."

"You could hear me from under the wagon."

"Not if I went to sleep."

He could hear her sigh. "You're not going to leave, are you?"

"Nope."

"Did anybody ever tell you that you're a stubborn, frustrating, and often annoying man?"

He chuckled. "You'll have to go a far piece before you get close to the things my parents said about me. Now stop trying to run me off and go to sleep. We'll be climbing some hills tomorrow so it'll be easier on the oxen and mules if everybody walks."

He didn't want to go, but he needed his sleep as well.

Yet sleep wasn't the only reason he needed to leave. Naomi was taking up too much of his thoughts. He knew this wasn't a momentary interest fueled solely by lust. Lust was there. How could it not be with a woman as alluring as Naomi? Still, how could he have known that merely holding her in his arms would ignite a fire in his loins? It didn't matter that he knew nothing more would happen. He couldn't stop thinking of holding her, of kissing her, making love to her. He was sure her skin would be soft and warm. He could almost feel its silkiness beneath his fingertips as he explored every part of her body, seeking out the places that would fuel her need for him. He was certain her lips would be as soft and welcoming as her smile. He could imagine kissing her—*had* imagined kissing her—until they were swollen with desire.

He tried not to think of what it would be like to make love to her, but he couldn't stop himself.

Yet there was something more than lust happening here, the kind of something that caused men to start thinking of building houses and sleeping in a comfortable bed every night, the kind of something that caused him to want to go home to the same woman every night, the kind of something that changed the thought of having a houseful of children from a man's worst nightmare to a wistful dream.

When that kind of *something* showed its face, it was time for a sensible man to saddle up and ride like the devil himself was after him.

❧

Naomi breathed a sigh of relief when Colby climbed down from the wagon seat. She had tried to sleep, but she could practically *feel* him watching her. It was unnerving…but exciting too.

She hadn't been concentrating so hard on learning to ride that she'd been unmindful of Colby's presence. That would have been impossible even if he hadn't lifted her into the saddle or placed her foot in the stirrups. She wasn't used to being in a man's embrace—any type of embrace—but having been in his arms twice before, she was no longer so shocked she couldn't appreciate his strength or his sheer magnetism. It didn't matter that she didn't *want* to be attracted to Colby. Sensuality radiated from him like heat from the sun making her want to reach out and touch him. She had attracted the attention of several soldiers during the war, but none of them had caused her to give them more than a few moments' thought. She was still reeling for the shock of discovering Colby's affect on her was entirely different. After seeing two cousins forced into marriages against their wills, she'd thought a lot about the kind of man she would marry. It shocked her to find that Colby came uncomfortably close to fulfilling all her requirements.

୶ఄఁ

"Wake up, sleepy head. The day has already begun. You'll have to hurry to catch up."

Naomi came awake with a start. She struggled to sit up, but her body felt heavy and sluggish. "What time is it?" She rubbed her eyes vigorously before opening the flap at the end of the wagon. She found herself staring into Colby's smiling face. "What are you doing here?"

"Coming to wake you up. Your brothers will be shouting for their breakfast before you have time to get a fire started."

The stars were still out, but the first rays of light could be seen sliding their slender fingers into the far horizon. She wanted to fasten the flap and go back to bed, but she had to get up. It wasn't her brothers' fault that she'd lain awake for half the night thinking about Colby.

"Did you sleep well?"

"Okay." She doubted she sounded convincing.

"Did you get any sleep at all? I know you were pretending so I left."

It was unnerving the way he could see through her, and she didn't like it. If her thoughts weren't her own—okay, pretending to sleep wasn't a thought, but it was close—what was?

"I didn't get as much sleep as I wanted, but I got enough. Now go away so I can get dressed." No matter how hot it got during the day, it was cold on the prairie at night. She slept in a nightgown under a quilt.

"You weren't so shy last night."

"That doesn't count. I thought you were Papa."

Colby's chuckle as he walked away was just what she needed to set her nerves on edge. And just when she had started to think there might be a warm, thoughtful, maybe loving person hidden under that hard-glazed exterior. She muttered several uncomplimentary observations as she slipped out of her nightgown and put on her chemise and a heavy cotton dress of dark blue. He had no right to treat her like a little sister. Just because he was older and had traveled over half the world didn't mean he knew more than she. It just meant they knew different things. As far as she could tell, most of what he knew wasn't worth much unless you intended to live as far from other humans as possible. She pulled on her socks and shoes. She didn't have time to waste on Colby Blaine. He could do whatever he wanted. She didn't care.

She hurried to open the flap and climb down from the wagon only to find Colby had already started the fire...and was frying bacon.

"I thought you'd never get up," Ben said when he saw her. "I got the wood for the fire *hours* ago. Colby said it was my job. I have to eat in a hurry if I'm to help with the harnessing."

Naomi would have said something rude if her father hadn't come bustling up in a cheerful mood.

"I'm hungry as a bear," he announced. "Wilma Hill didn't have any labor pains last night. I thought I would hate sleeping on the ground, but I slept better than I have in years." He glanced at his sons. "Why didn't you tell me it was so relaxing? I'll have to try it more often."

"You can have my bed," Ben offered. "I'll be happy to sleep in the wagon with Naomi."

Naomi was measuring out cornmeal, but she turned to her brother. "You can't sleep in a bed, a wagon, or any other confined space with another human being until you learn to stop kicking like a colicky calf."

She reached for the milk someone had ready for her use. Probably Colby. He'd done everything else. No reason he shouldn't have milked the cow, too.

"I could tie his feet together," Colby offered.

"Don't forget his hands," Ethan added.

"Nobody's tying me up." Ben took the precaution of edging closer to his father.

"Got any coffee?" her father asked.

Before Naomi could formulate an excuse, Colby reached for a pot nestled in a bed of coals.

"I expect it's ready now. I know it's hot."

She was going to kill that man. She hadn't decided when or how, but she was definitely going to do it.

"Save a little of that milk," Naomi's father said to her. "The cream off the top would be even better."

Naomi had learned long ago how to pour fresh milk without losing the cream. Everyone knew of her father's fondness for it. At least that was one thing Colby hadn't done.

"Good coffee," her father murmured appreciatively. "Naomi always did know how to make it better than anyone else."

Ben started to speak—undoubtedly to tell his father Naomi *hadn't* made the coffee—but Colby clamped his hand over the boy's mouth.

"Ethan needs help filling the water casks," he said to Ben. "Why don't you help him?"

"Wait a minute and I'll help," their father said. "I want a few more swallows of coffee."

"Don't take long," Colby said to Ben. "Naomi has breakfast nearly ready."

The boy glared at Colby before stomping off. Her

father saluted with a smile and a wave of his coffee cup. "Don't drink it all before I get back."

Naomi managed to hold her temper in check until her father was out of hearing range. She whirled around to face Colby. "Why didn't you tell my father you made that coffee? He'll figure it out tomorrow if Ben hasn't told him by the time they get back. And that doesn't include starting the fire, milking the cow, and putting the bacon on. You should have woken me up earlier."

"You had a rough night. I figured you needed to sleep a little longer. Besides, Ben gathered the wood and Laurie milked your cow. She was up before I was. Come to think of it, that's not the first time it's happened."

Naomi decided not to tell Colby about the situation between Laurie and her husband. Some things were better kept within the family.

"Don't let me sleep late again, not even if I have a nightmare. I don't want anybody to think I'm shirking my responsibilities."

Colby studied her a moment, which made her so nervous she nearly forgot to take the corn cakes out of the pan before they burned.

"Everybody falls a little short now and then," Colby said. "Someone will take up the slack for you. You'll do the same for them later."

"Who takes up the slack for you?" she snapped. "Nobody, because you're perfect. You never fall short. You know the answer to every question. You can cook. You even make better coffee than I do." She knew she sounded ungrateful, but too much perfection was irritating.

"I've been on my own since I was fifteen. I've had to learn to do everything for myself. Besides, this is my part of the country. If I were back in Spencer's Clearing, you'd be the one telling me how to do everything."

Naomi doubted that was true. He probably could darn socks, repair a tear, and sew on a button faster than she could. She doubted he could crochet, knit, or spin cotton into thread, but she wasn't very good at those herself.

"You must have other duties," she said. "I can take care of everything now."

"Are you trying to run me off?"

"I don't want to monopolize all your time," she said from between teeth that were perilously close to being clenched, "but there are twelve other families."

"Nobody's doing anything besides filling the water containers and getting ready to eat. Besides, your father promised me you'd feed me breakfast."

Naomi swallowed her pique. "I'm sorry I'm in such a bad mood. I'm never my best in the morning, but it's particularly bad when I've had a nightmare and didn't get much sleep."

"Does it happen often?" The caring in his voice made her feel even more like a selfish ingrate.

"More and more recently. Seeing my grandfather was a shock. If he weren't already dead, I'd be afraid it meant something awful." She couldn't bring herself to tell Colby about the man in a Union Army uniform who was also part of her dream. If he thought she'd killed a soldier, wouldn't he be honor bound to tell somebody in the army, a sheriff, a marshal, *anybody* who could bring her to justice? No man of character could overlook a murder.

"I know this doesn't sound very helpful, but try not to think about it. If there is any meaning behind the dream, you'll figure it out. Maybe something happened that was so terrible you repressed it. That happened to some of the men during the war, especially the ones who'd led a conventional life and had no way to cope with the carnage they witnessed. Maybe it's just one of the weird dreams we all have sometimes."

"What are you, some kind of head doctor?"

"No, but during the war I saw men do things I would never have believed if I hadn't seen them. Maybe it's a manifestation of your fear of coming west."

"I'm not afraid of coming west. I just didn't want to. There's no desirable place to live and bring up a family."

"So you hope to marry?"

That was a strange question. Every woman hoped to marry. Life as a single woman meant you were a widow or a maiden aunt, both of whom ended up being a burden on her family.

"Of course, but I won't marry just anybody. He'll have to be a man of character and honesty, kind and thoughtful yet strong enough to support his family. Brave enough to face hardship, trustworthy enough to be a man other men respect."

"Rather high standards, aren't they?"

"I don't think so."

"Do you know anyone other than your father who possesses all those qualities?"

She came very close to saying *you*, but she managed

to withhold the word at the last moment. Instead she avoided the question. "I'm sure there are such men, even in this godforsaken part of the world."

He laughed, and she wondered why that always made her feel like it was because he knew something she didn't.

"Aren't you afraid a godforsaken world will produce only men who have forsaken God?"

She sighed in exasperation. "Here, your breakfast is ready. Now I want some of that wonderful coffee. I need to know my competition."

When he laughed this time, she laughed, too.

❧

"I never knew there were so many rattlesnakes in the whole world," Naomi exclaimed. "How does anybody live out here?"

They had passed through the hills that surrounded the Middle Springs of the Cimarron, an area known for its abundance of rattlesnakes and tarantulas. During one hour, Colby shot two snakes, one directly in front of Shadow and one about to slither between the hooves of Naomi's mount. "No one lives here except the Indians. But we're out of the worst area now. This is a good place to camp."

A barrier of tangled brush surrounded the springs, but low riverbanks offered easy access to the Cimarron and its steady flow of clear water. A nearly flat flood plain covered in thick grass reaching for nearly a hundred yards out into the prairie afforded abundant graze.

"Time to tell everyone to circle up for the night."

Naomi was riding her father's horse until Ethan's

leg recovered enough for him to ride again—or until he got tired of driving Cassie's wagon, which didn't seem likely at this point. Making sure the wagons were properly circled each night wasn't difficult, but assigning that duty to her was an indication of Colby's growing respect. She rode outside the circle making sure the rear right wheel of the first wagon was up against the front left wheel of the next wagon until a near circle was formed leaving only an opening for livestock to pass in and out.

While Colby oversaw the unhitching of the teams and putting them out to graze, Naomi went about warning everyone to make sure there were no snakes or spiders near their wagons before they went to sleep.

"I'm not afraid of any old snake," Ben insisted, but after she left to warn Sibyl, she could hear Ben beating the grass around their wagon.

"I always sleep in my wagon," Sibyl told her. "I'll make sure Elaine doesn't set foot on the ground until we're well clear of this horrible place." Sibyl's two-year-old daughter was perched on the seat next to her mother. She rarely spoke, but her enormous brown eyes took in everything around her. Naomi often wondered what went through that child's mind.

Norman's brother, Noah, and his wife owned the next two wagons. Naomi was sure Laurie would be safe. Noah never let her out of his sight. It was harder for the families that had children. After having been confined to the wagons all day, the younger children were bursting with energy.

"I couldn't keep my boys in a wagon a minute longer without tying them up," Paul Hill's wife told Naomi. "I just hope they don't go looking for snakes. I can't make them understand how dangerous they are."

"Colby says as long as they stay near the wagons, they should be okay."

When Naomi reached Haskel Sumner's wagon, Pearl was fixing dinner.

"Where are the girls?" Naomi asked.

"Gone to the spring for water."

"Colby said we should get water from the river. He said snakes sometimes—"

A scream brought activity in the camp to a standstill. Pearl's face went white. She dropped the bowl in her hands and headed toward the spring at a run.

Eight

NAOMI WAS THE FIRST TO REACH THE THREE GIRLS running from the spring. "What happened?"

"A snake bit Opal on the cheek," the oldest girl answered. "She was bending over to dip her bucket in the spring when it came out of the grass."

The moment Pearl saw the fang marks in her seven-year-old daughter's cheek, she wrapped her arms around the girl and broke out into loud wails. "She's going to die!"

By now people were running from all directions. All asked the same question that was answered by Pearl's repeated lament that her daughter's death was inevitable.

Haskel Sumner pushed through the gathering. The implications of the scene hit him with numbing force. Drawing his two remaining daughters into his arms, he looked into the crowd. "Where's the doctor?"

As though conjured by the question, Naomi's father forced his way through the crowd.

"What happened?" he asked.

Pearl was too hysterical to be coherent.

"A snake bit Opal on the cheek," Naomi said.

"What kind of snake?" her father asked the child.

"It had to be a rattlesnake," someone said. "Haven't seen anything else all day."

"You've got to do something for her," Haskel said to the doctor. "You've got to save her."

"I'll have to incise the wound and hope we can suck the poison out," the doctor said.

Naomi's heart sank. That meant deep and painful cuts in the child's cheek. She didn't know if Pearl or Haskel would be able to endure their daughter's screams.

"A child's cheek is very thin," the doctor said. "The incision may cut all the way through her cheek. If that happens, she'll bleed into her mouth and the scar will be more pronounced."

"Will it be a terrible scar?" Pearl asked. "She has such pretty white skin. That's why I named her Opal."

"Do what you have to do," Haskel said.

"Let me through."

Those gathered around moved to allow Colby to enter the circle. He had a pair of saddlebags over his shoulder.

"Who got bitten?"

"Opal, on the cheek," Naomi told him. "Papa is about to incise the wound and try to suck the poison out."

Colby walked to where Opal was nearly enveloped by her mother's embrace. "Can I see the wound?"

"The doctor's already told us what he's going to do."

"Your daughter is much too beautiful to go through life with a badly scarred cheek," Colby told Pearl.

"It's better than being dead," her father shouted in his misery. "The doctor is going to try to save her."

Colby had been chewing something. Now he took out of his mouth what looked like a blob of chewed grass. He turned to the doctor. "I want you to let me do something different."

"What?" he asked.

"Make a plantain poultice to draw out the poison."

"I've heard of that, but I've never seen it done."

"It's a method the Indians have been using for centuries."

Haskel bridled. "I won't have you using any savage rite on my daughter."

Ignoring the child's father, Colby placed the poultice on Opal's cheek. He pulled some wide leaves from a nearby plant and placed them over the poultice. "I need someone to hold this against her cheek."

Her sister Amber volunteered.

Pearl was undecided. "He's the one who has spent his life out here," the doctor said. "He ought to be able to help her better than I can."

The doctor's words didn't reassure the distraught parents.

"What if that poultice doesn't draw out all the poison?" Pearl asked.

"There's no assurance that incising the wound will get all the poison," the doctor responded.

"I have one other thing I want to do to make sure she has no ill effects from the venom," Colby told Haskel.

"Is it another Indian trick? I won't have any more of those."

"No. Does anyone have any whiskey?"

A couple of men turned and ran to their wagons. One of them was Morley Sumner, Opal's uncle.

"I'm not going to let you treat my daughter if you're going to get drunk," Haskel said.

"It's not for me. It's for Opal."

"Not a single drop of the devil's brew will cross my daughter's lips!" declared Pearl.

"Are you crazy?" Haskel thundered.

"Alcohol can counteract the poison," Colby said. "I've seen it."

Both parents were firm in their objection.

"Rattlesnake venom enters the body almost immediately," Colby explained. "Its purpose is to paralyze the snake's victim quickly so it can eat it. Even if you incise the wound immediately, you won't be able to stop all the poison from entering Opal's body. But alcohol, especially taken on an empty stomach, will enter the body fast enough to counteract the effect of the poison."

Opal's parents were still set against it. Even her father was dubious, but Naomi had been around Colby long enough to be certain he wouldn't do anything that would harm a child.

"Why don't you try it?" Naomi asked. "The worst that can happen is that she will be drunk."

"She's a child," Haskel said. "It would be a sin to force her to drink until she was drunk."

"Is it better that she be sober and dead than drunk and well?"

"Why are you supporting him?"

Naomi turned to find Norman Spencer scowling at her.

"I'm not *supporting* anybody," she told him. "We know nothing about this terrible part of the country, but the Indians have lived here for I don't know how long with the snakes and spiders. If anybody knows how to cure a snakebite, they would. The same goes for men like Colby. If they say whiskey works, I say we ought to try it. Some of us may consider it an evil drink, but it's not poison."

Morley Sumner muscled his way through the crowd and handed Colby an earthenware jar. "I was keeping this to use in case I caught the ague."

Pearl turned anguished eyes to her brother-in-law. "I thought you loved our girls. How can you do this?"

"I know you hate whiskey but Opal won't get a taste for it this one time. We can't take a chance that this might be the one thing that would make the difference." When Pearl couldn't bring herself to agree, he turned to his brother. "You've got to take every possible chance," he said to Haskel.

Seeing Haskel waver, Colby didn't wait. "Let me have her," he said to Pearl.

Pearl didn't want to let go of Opal, but Haskel took his daughter from his wife. "I'm as scared as you are," he said to her, "but we've got to try anything that might work. Let me have the jug," he said to Colby. "I'll be the one to give her the whiskey."

"She's going to choke on it," Colby warned. "She'll probably spit half of it up, but keep pouring it down her throat. When she gets drunk, you'll know the whiskey has destroyed the venom."

Haskel tried to coax Opal to open her mouth, but the child was too frightened to respond. Amber's hand holding the poultice shook so badly Naomi expected she'd lose it.

"Maybe I can help," Naomi volunteered.

"How?" Haskel looked doubtful yet hopeful.

"I will hold her."

"She's my daughter. I ought to hold her," Pearl objected.

"You're distraught," Dr. Kessling said. "You'll upset her more."

Haskel handed his daughter to Naomi.

"Don't be frightened," Naomi crooned to the little girl. "We're going to make sure this doesn't make you sick. You don't want to be sick, do you?"

Opal's eyes grew wide, but she didn't answer.

"Your father is going to give you some medicine. Whenever my father gives me medicine, it doesn't taste good but it makes me better. Do you think you can take a big swallow?"

Opal's gaze searched for and found her father.

"That's a brave girl. Now open your mouth."

When Opal choked and spat out half of what she'd tried to swallow, Haskel was so badly shaken he dropped the jar. Colby scooped it up before more than a few swallows of the liquid were lost.

"Maybe I'd better do this for you."

Haskel sagged with relief.

"Are you sure you can hold her still and keep the poultice in place?" Colby whispered to Naomi as he knelt down next to Opal.

"I'll do my best."

Colby's gaze turned steely. "That's not enough. Are you *sure* you can—"

"Yes," Naomi hissed. "Can you give her the whiskey without pouring it all over me?"

Colby's answer was a half smile. "Okay," he said to Opal. "It's going to burn a little."

Taking the child by the chin, he opened her mouth

and poured a quantity of whiskey down her throat. Opal coughed, but Colby pressed her mouth closed forcing her to swallow the whiskey.

"Good girl," he crooned. "It wasn't as bad as the first time, was it?"

Opal just stared at him. Naomi figured the child was too traumatized to have any idea what she felt.

"One more swallow," Colby said, "then we'll take you back to your wagon. Ready?"

Without waiting for a response, Colby opened her mouth, poured some whiskey in, and forced her to swallow it.

Opal didn't cough so badly this time.

"I'll carry her," Colby offered, "if you'll keep the poultice in place."

The process of handing her over to Colby while keeping pressure on the poultice was awkward, but they managed.

"Everyone ought to get back to work," Colby said. "We have meals to prepare, livestock to keep from wandering away or being run off by Indians."

The women were reluctant to return to their work, but the men hurried away. Everyone could miss a meal, but the loss of the mules and oxen would leave their survival in doubt.

"What are you going to do now?" Haskel asked Colby as they walked toward the family's wagon.

"As soon as we get her settled, I'm going to give her some more whiskey."

"She's had enough," Pearl insisted.

"I won't give her too much, but we can't stop until we can see the whiskey take effect."

Pearl continued to voice her objections, but Haskel didn't back her. When Colby asked him to bring his saddlebags, Haskel did it without hesitation.

"Try not to worry about her," Naomi said to Pearl. "I'm sure Colby knows what he's doing."

"How can you know?" Pearl demanded. "Nobody had ever heard of him before that Indian attack."

"I think the fact that he came to help us rather than stay away and keep himself safe speaks well of his character."

"I'm not concerned about his character," Pearl snapped. "I'm worried he doesn't know what he's doing."

"That's where we can depend on his character," Naomi replied. "A man who would risk his own life to save strangers wouldn't knowingly put a child's life in danger."

When they reached the wagon, Colby lowered himself into a sitting position.

"There are some more plantain leaves in my saddlebags," he said to Pearl. "Crush some so I can make a fresh poultice."

"How can I do that?" Pearl asked. "I don't have a mortar and pestle."

"I do," Sibyl Spencer said. "I'll get it."

"I'd have one, too, if I had three wagons," Pearl grumbled. "I'll wager she has a lot of things none of the rest of us has."

"Where did you find plantain?" Naomi asked Colby. "Why did you know to have it?"

"It's a common weed," Colby replied. "I always keep some powdered root with me, but I picked a fresh supply of leaves in case anyone was bitten."

"When can I find some more?"

"I'll show you as soon as I'm sure Opal is better."

The little girl was beginning to appear glassy-eyed, but she wasn't drunk.

Sibyl returned with the mortar and pestle. "I'll grind the leaves if you want."

"I'll do it," Pearl said rather ungraciously. "She's my daughter."

While Pearl turned her attention to grinding the leaves with such force Naomi feared for the survival of the mortar and pestle, Colby poured some more whiskey down Opal's throat. The child offered so little resistance Naomi feared she might be sick, but she rested quietly in Colby's arms, her head leaning against his chest.

"Is this mixed enough?" Pearl asked.

Colby looked at the pulverized leaves. "That's good. I don't need to give Opal any more whiskey so why don't you find something to hold the poultice in place. Amber can't sit holding it until morning."

"I'll stay up all night if necessary," the teary-eyed girl assured him.

"I know you would, but now we should let your sister sleep. I'll check on her later."

"Do you have a place where I can lay her in the wagon?" Colby asked.

While Pearl hurried to prepare a bed for her daughter, Colby explained to Naomi how to make the poultice and put it in place. Once that was done, he secured it with a strip of cloth then handed Opal to her father who had watched Colby with eagle-eyed keenness. "If she gets restless, send someone to find me."

"Where will you be?"

"I don't know, but I won't be far. I'll hear if you call."

Haskel looked down at his daughter. "Are you sure she's going to be okay?"

"There's no swelling, and the skin around the punctures hasn't turned black." He handed a plantain leaf to Amber. "I want you and your sisters to know what this looks like. When you think you've found some, come show them to me."

"Am I going to be bitten by a snake?"

"I hope not, but it's best to always have a remedy on hand."

"Thank you for what you've done," Haskel said. "I don't know what I would have done if we'd lost our little girl."

"All you need to do now is watch her. I'd better get back to my job."

"Are you as sure of what you did as you seem?" Dr. Kessling asked Colby once they were out of earshot. "I've never heard of treating a snakebite with whiskey."

"I've seen it work, and the Indians have used plantain leaves for ages."

"Maybe you should be the doctor."

Colby laughed. "Not a chance. I know a little about herbs and how to set broken bones. Other than that, I'm as ignorant as anyone else."

Dr. Kessling shook his head. "Not sure I agree, but I'd better go check on Wilma Hill."

"Will she have trouble with the baby?" Colby asked Naomi after her father left.

"Not that I know of, but she's upset and angry."

"Several families are. Why?"

Naomi had hoped Colby wouldn't ask this question, but it had been inevitable that he would.

"There's a lot I don't know about why we left Spencer's Clearing, but some families were forced to leave against their will. Norman has some hold over everybody, but I don't know what it is." She kicked at a thistle in her path. "Nor do I know why Sibyl and Laurie married men they don't love. I'd never do that." She looked up at Colby. "Ethan is convinced I'll end up an old maid."

Colby's mouth formed a crooked smile. "The West is chock-full of men looking for wives. Once they get a look at you, there'll be a line of hopefuls half a mile long eager to convince you your life would be incomplete without them."

She grinned up at Colby. "Are they all like you?"

"Naw. I'm the best of the bunch." When they stopped laughing, Colby continued. "Some will be gimpy legged, missing half their teeth, old enough to be your father, and smelling of the beer hall. A few will be about two steps ahead of the law. Some will be so young they haven't started to shave. The rest will be honest, dependable, upstanding men who'll work hard to be a good husband."

They had reached her wagon. Rather than look for the pot she needed to prepare the antelope stew, she turned to Colby. "And where will you be?"

The change was drastic and immediate. "Far away from Santa Fe."

"We're not going to stay in Santa Fe."

"It won't matter where you settle. Now I'd better

get back to work before Norman starts saying I'm not earning my money."

"After what you did for Opal, I doubt even Norman would complain."

"I still have work to do, and you have a supper to fix."

He tipped his hat and was gone, but he spoiled the whole effect by winking just before he passed out of sight. Naomi was shocked by the sudden change in him, but that wink made her more determined than ever to find out why Colby was determined to avoid people...especially her.

❦

Colby was as good as his word. He checked to make sure the livestock were well pastured and that a schedule of guards was set up for the night. He inspected each wagon to make sure the wheels were tight against the iron rims and all the hubs well greased. He supervised the filling of the water barrels and made sure everyone got their share of antelope. He organized the younger boys and girls into a line that beat the grass around the camp to ensure there were no snakes left to wiggle their way into a warm bed during the night. Yet none of that could drive Naomi's question from his mind.

Where will you be?

He didn't know where the hell he would be, but he was damned certain of where he *wouldn't* be. He didn't intend to set one foot in Santa Fe no matter what the provocation. Elizabeth lived in Santa Fe with a child Colby had never seen, a child who thought its father was Haman Stuart, a child who would never hear of Colby Blaine.

Colby could forgive Elizabeth for not loving him as much as he loved her. He could forgive her for bowing to her father's demand that she marry a man with enough money to support a wife and family. What he *couldn't* forgive was her denying him the thing he wanted most in the world—a family. His child would have loved him even though Colby's parents couldn't, would have wanted to live with him even though Haman Stuart had more money. His child would have learned to value a person according to what he was, not the quantity of his possessions.

In no mood to answer questions or solve problems, Colby turned away from the wagons and headed to where Shadow was cropping the rich grass that grew between the spring and the river. The powerful Appaloosa had been his loyal companion for nearly eleven years. He'd bought him as a colt with the first money he'd managed to save. They'd only been separated during the years Colby spent in the Union Army. He'd left him with a farmer in Illinois rather than risk him in the war. The horse lifted his head when Colby approached, a generous mouthful of grass between his teeth.

"All the food and water you need and a slow ride during the day. Don't have much to worry about, do you?"

Shadow acknowledged his master by shaking his head.

"Rest up while you can. In a few days we'll strike out for parts unknown. I don't know what we'll be facing."

He didn't mind the thought of an unknown future. That's pretty much all he'd ever had. He didn't have anything of a material nature beyond a few guns, a good saddle, and a magnificent horse, but that's all he needed to find a quiet corner of the world he could call his own. There were hundreds of uninhabited valleys and canyons in the Sangre de Cristo Mountains above Santa Fe. It didn't matter what he did, run a few cows or raise horses. He might even do a little trapping. He could hunt for his food, grow a few vegetables, or live off the land.

That plan had appealed to him after Elizabeth's betrayal nearly destroyed him. It didn't sound so attractive now. He'd never go back to Santa Fe, but he no longer wanted to live in complete isolation for the rest of his life. Naomi had changed him.

But he wasn't going to let himself become romantically involved. He didn't believe in love. Okay, maybe he *did* believe in love. He just didn't think it was possible for two humans to find the only kind of love he thought worth seeking.

But what kind of love was that? He'd spent so many years thinking love was impossible he hadn't defined the kind of love he could believe in, the kind that was so impossible he didn't believe it could exist. But if it couldn't exist, why should he try to define it?

"Be glad you're a horse," he said to Shadow. "You don't have to worry about parents, brothers and sisters, wives, or children. As long as you have enough to eat and drink, you're happy."

How did he know Shadow was happy? Just because the horse came when he whistled and allowed himself to be ridden didn't mean he didn't want more from life. If he'd been left to run wild, he'd have joined a herd, maybe become the head stallion and sired lots of foals. Maybe he missed having a family, of *belonging* somewhere, as much as Colby.

"I must be going nuts," Colby muttered. "I'm not just talking to my horse. I'm trying to think like one. What has that woman done to me?"

Finding the conversation was no longer directed at him, Shadow lowered his head and continued to graze.

"That's right, leave me to figure this out on my own," Colby said when Shadow moved to a more appetizing patch of grass. "You'll end up wherever I do. Don't you want to have some say about it?" Colby raked his hands through his hair. "I'm arguing with my horse. What is wrong with me?"

He turned toward the wagons. Somehow, in ways he never expected, he'd become attached to those people. They were quarrelsome strangers who had no idea where they were going or what they would do when they got there. He had no intention of following them beyond La Junta, yet he felt responsible for them, even a kinship with them.

They'd given him a kind of acceptance he'd never experienced before. The adults still kept their distance, but that seemed to be more out of habit or shyness with strangers. The younger ones weren't a bit standoffish. Ben looked at him in awe while Ethan was trying to emulate him. Dr. Kessling treated him like a son, and Norman depended on him though he would never admit it.

Then there was Naomi. No matter where his thoughts might wander, they always came back to her. He'd met beautiful women before who he had no trouble forgetting, yet his attraction to Naomi continued to grow. She wasn't like any woman he'd

ever met. She seemed unimpressed by her looks and
didn't make any attempt to attract his attention. She
didn't seem interested in getting married or worried
about the kind of husband she might find. She was
definitely stubborn, preferred to make up her own
mind, to exercise her own intelligence. She wasn't shy
about stepping forward when something needed to
be done or in stating her opinion, yet she seemed to
prefer being out of the limelight.

The more contradictions he discovered, the more
intrigued he became. It was a good thing he would be
gone in a few weeks. Much more than that, and he
might never be able to forget her.

❧

The eastern sky had barely begun to lighten when
Opal's mother, tears streaming down her face, came
running to where Colby lay sleeping next to the
Kessling wagon. Scrambling to his feet—fortunately
he slept in his clothes—he was nearly knocked over
when Pearl threw her arms around him.

"It's a miracle," she cried, threatening to soak his
shirt with her tears. "Opal acts like nothing was ever
wrong with her. I can hardly tell where the snake bit
her. Just two tiny spots on her cheek." Pearl looked
slightly embarrassed at having flung herself on Colby.
"I'll never be able to thank you enough. Her father
would be here, too, but he cried when she woke up
and her first words were *I'm hungry*." She smiled shyly.
"He's so embarrassed he won't show his face." She
laughed softly. "He's a proud man, a good man, but a
little foolish sometimes."

"I can't think of a better reason to shed tears," Colby said.

"I'm so thankful you knew exactly what to do."

"Everybody out here learns how to treat snakebites. Even the Indians who wanted to know where we found the buffalo could have helped."

Pearl sobered. "I could never have trusted my daughter to an Indian."

"I'd rather trust an Indian than die."

It was clear Pearl's trust boundaries didn't go that far. "I'd better get back. I left Amber to start the meal, but she hasn't learned how to cook on an open fire."

"I think you've just been elevated to sainthood."

Colby turned to see Naomi climb out of the wagon. Slightly embarrassed for her to have heard the excessive praise, he scolded, "You shouldn't eavesdrop."

Naomi gathered her hair in a ribbon so it hung down her back rather than cascaded over her shoulders. "She was barely six feet away. Osnaburg canvas can keep out the sun, wind, and rain, but sound comes right through." She grinned at him. "You're even more important than Norman. Your every word will be akin to divine revelation."

"You're laughing at me now," Colby protested. "You'd better be careful the next time we cross a river. You might find yourself tipped out of the saddle."

She did laugh then. "You wouldn't dare."

Nine

COLBY CLEARED HIS THROAT. AS NAOMI GATHERED their breakfast makings, she wondered what could have turned him suddenly so serious. "Have you changed your mind about me?" he asked.

"What do you mean?"

"You said the fact that I came to help you during the Indian attack rather than stay safely away spoke well of my character. You didn't think much of my character in the beginning, did you?"

Naomi hoped Colby couldn't guess just how radically her opinion of him had changed. She was uncomfortable just thinking about it.

"Well now I've started to get to know you."

"Would you stop fixing breakfast for one minute and look at me? This will only take a minute. I'll help. Just stop."

He put his hand on her arm. There was no force, no effort to turn her to face him. For that reason, it was impossible not to turn around.

"I'm not talking about the Indians, the snakebite, me leading the train. I'm asking about *me*. Has your opinion changed about me?"

Naomi felt ambushed. Irritation caused her to strike out. "Why do you care? You're going to leave us in a couple of weeks, and we'll never see you again. You could be the devil himself, and it wouldn't matter."

His hand fell away and he stepped back, his expression revealing a medley of emotions. Disappointment was there, so was surprise verging on disbelief, but it was the hurt that convinced Naomi she had to reveal at least some of the truth.

"I like you," she confessed. "I didn't at first, but I do now."

Some of the tension left his expression, but he didn't relax. "What made you change your mind?"

"Dozens of things. The way you worry about Cassie. The way you tolerate Ben's questions when I was sure he'd exhaust the patience of a saint. But you are a saint now, aren't you?"

He didn't appreciate her humor. Why was it so hard to tell him how she really felt? She was a woman, and all women were supposed to be spilling over with emotions they couldn't wait to share.

"There's a kindness in you that I'm not sure you know you have," she said. "I see it in so many things you do but especially when you're helping someone younger or less capable. With us that means just about everybody. I also like the way you accept people the way they are. Despite what you say about wanting to live by yourself, you care about people."

He looked like he had gotten more than he expected, which served him right for pressing her so hard.

"Now I have to finish breakfast." She pointed

toward the bag of coffee beans. "You can start by grinding the coffee."

A voice from under the wagon startled her. "I'm glad you're done talking about mushy stuff. I'm tired of pretending to be asleep."

Naomi rounded the end of the wagon and glared underneath at her brother. "You are a rotten little boy, Benjamin Kessling. I hope you end up with a wife who nags you and gives you seven little boys just like you."

Ben was unperturbed by her severity or Colby's laughter. "I'm not getting married unless I can find a woman as pretty as Cassie but who's not silly like her. If I had that many boys, I'd send half of them to stay with their old maid Aunt Naomi."

"With two old maids in the family, your papa had better hope Ethan gives him some grandchildren."

Ben pulled on his pants and crawled out from under the wagon. "Men can't be old maids. They're called bachelors."

Dr. Kessling strolled up looking cheerful and well rested. "What's all this talk about grandchildren, bachelors, and old maids when you ought to be talking about my breakfast?"

"They're talking about feelings," Ben complained. "Before that Opal's mother slobbered over Colby like he was some sort of god."

"You are the most heartless little wretch," Naomi said. "Pearl was thanking Colby for saving Opal's life."

"Papa could have done it."

"But it was Colby who did the saving," Dr. Kessling told his younger son, "so he's the one who should get the credit."

Ben was caught between his admiration for Colby and his loyalty to his father. "But you *could* have done it."

"Colby managed it without leaving any scars. That will be very important to Opal when she grows up into a beautiful woman." Their father grinned. "It might even be important to you when you grow up to be a handsome young man."

Ben's disgust at the implication that he might be sweet on Opal someday amused Naomi.

"I'm going to be like Colby and fight Indians."

That promising conversation was forced aside by the arrival of Ethan with Cassie and her baby.

"Cassie wants you to look at her baby," Ethan told his father. "He's been fussy all night."

"I fed him," Cassie said, "but he won't stop fretting."

Dr. Kessling tenderly felt down the baby's sides and peered into his mouth. "Looks like he's teething. He's going to be fretful for a while, but there's nothing wrong with him."

"I'm hungry," Ben announced.

Forcefully reminded of her duty, Naomi turned her efforts to finishing breakfast while Colby offered everyone fresh coffee.

"I don't want your old coffee," Ben stated. "I bet it tastes like bull pee."

"I've got to hand it to you," Colby said. "I never had the courage to taste bull pee."

Everybody got a good laugh except Cassie, who looked horrified. "I thought you were a nice boy," she said.

"I'm not a nice boy," Ben said proudly. "But nobody's stupid enough to taste bull pee. What's wrong with you?"

Ethan came to her defense. "Nothing's wrong with her. She's just not used to people who exaggerate."

"She's used to herself, isn't she?" Ben retorted. I never saw anybody carry on like she does."

Before the brothers could come to blows, Naomi handed Ethan a plate and Colby took Ben by the collar and pulled him behind the wagon. "There are times when it's not a good idea to utter every thought that pops into your head."

"Cassie does."

"She's a young mother who's lost her husband and father-in-law. She's entitled to get carried away. How would you feel if those Indians had killed your father, Ethan, and Naomi?"

Ben swallowed.

"That ought to give you some idea how Cassie feels."

"Do I have to apologize?"

"Yes."

"Okay, but it's not fair. She *is* silly."

"Life isn't fair," Colby said.

"Don't I know? Ethan was born before me."

"Ethan got an arrow in his leg."

Ben scowled at Colby. "Do you have an answer for everything?"

"No, but some answers are easy. Now go apologize."

Ben looked aggrieved, but put a brave face on it and marched up to Cassie.

"Colby says I have to apologize for saying you carry on something awful." He cast an accusatory glance at his father. "I guess I didn't understand when I was told I'd never get in trouble for telling the truth."

"If that's your idea of an apology—" Ethan sputtered.

"It's not a very good one," their father said, "but it's better than nothing. Now everybody needs to eat their breakfasts. We'll never get to Santa Fe if we sit around talking all morning."

Ben opened his mouth—probably to mount a defense—but his father forestalled him.

"Not another word until the wagons are hitched up and we're rolling."

Apparently Cassie didn't think that applied to her. "I think it was a very nice apology. Nobody has ever apologized to me before."

"I'm sure they never had reason," Ethan said.

Naomi wanted to slap that mooncalf expression off his face. She had seen other boys go loco over a pretty girl, but she'd never expected him to be one of them.

"I didn't have many girlfriends, but all the boys were very nice."

Naomi was starting to wonder if Cassie was as silly as she seemed. She had certainly captivated Ethan, and Virgil Johnson's two boys hovered around when they could find a free moment.

A gurgle from the baby drew their attention.

Cassie looked down and smiled. "He looks so much like Abe, I'll never be able to forget him."

She started to tear up, which made Naomi feel crummy for her uncharitable thoughts.

"You shouldn't forget him," Colby said. "Your son will want to know all about his father when he gets older. Do you have a name for him?"

"I thought about naming him Abe, but I cry every time I say his name." She heaved a sigh of resignation. "I guess I'll stop crying someday."

Cassie might be a little shallow and a lot clingy, but it was apparent that she had loved her husband. From now on Naomi decided to make an effort to be more charitable.

As long as Ethan didn't ask Cassie to marry him.

Colby set his plate down. "Time to round up the stock, hitch up the wagons, and get moving." He looked to where the first rays of the sun had begun to edge over the eastern horizon. "Looks like it's going to be a hot day."

Cassie sighed. "It's always a hot day inside the wagon. The baby gets fretful."

"Maybe I can take him for a while this afternoon." Naomi didn't know where the words came from. It was certain her brain was appalled to hear them come out of her mouth.

"That's very generous of you," her father said.

She couldn't take it back, not with Colby looking at her with approval in his eyes. She'd gotten spoiled riding with him each day. She was going to miss that.

"Do you know how to take care of a baby?" Cassie asked.

"It's been a while, but I took care of Ben." She grimaced at her younger brother who returned the favor. "I remember it all too well."

"I never had a younger brother," Cassie said. "My mama said I was all the children she could handle."

Seemed like Cassie was even more alone than Naomi had thought.

"Come on," Colby said to the boys. "Time to go to work."

"Want me to help clean up?" Cassie asked Naomi after the men left. She laid her baby in a basket. "I guess I have to learn to take care of a baby and a house at the same time."

"It's not so hard. The older he gets, the more time he can spend on his own."

"I guess so, but I like to hold him. He's all I have left of Abe." Cassie gathered up the dirty plates. "I have to learn to put him down and leave him. I have to marry as soon as I can find a husband. He won't want me spending all my time with another man's baby." As Cassie walked away, she said, "Men aren't much interested in babies."

Naomi had been embarrassed about her feelings before, but now she was disgusted with herself. Nearly every word out of Cassie's mouth made her feel like a selfish woman with no concern for anyone but herself. If she ever lost her husband, she wouldn't be alone with no one to turn to. Her sons would have a grandfather and two uncles to initiate them into the secrets that for centuries had been turning perfectly reasonably young boys into quarrelsome, self-centered, and unfathomable creatures called *men*.

What if she were to marry a man who already had children? Could she love them as deeply as her own? Wasn't that too much to expect? Naomi was struck with the sudden question of how Colby felt toward babies. Did he ever think about a son of his own?

She shook her head to dislodge the unwelcome thought.

Ben ran up to the wagon. "Papa told me to help Ethan hitch the mules. As soon as I finish, I'm to come back and help him with our oxen." He scampered away without waiting for Naomi to respond.

"I'd better go," Cassie said when she returned. "I like to get settled before we start."

"You don't have to hurry."

Cassie looked at her with bird-like curiosity. "Why are you being so nice to me? You invited me to eat breakfast with your family, you offered to take care of my baby, and you've talked to me like I'm a normal person. Nobody else has."

Naomi had underestimated how isolated and alone Cassie felt. "I'm sorry everybody has been so stand-offish. We're such a close community we have trouble opening up enough to include other people."

"I've never had a baby before. I wish I had some-body I could talk to."

"Why don't you talk to Pearl Sumner? She has three girls. The oldest, Amber, is about your age."

"She doesn't like me."

"When we started, we didn't think of your family as part of our group. Mr. Greene was just a stranger hired to take us to Santa Fe. Now you're one of us. I'll take you over and introduce you at the midday break."

"I'd like that. Now I'd better go. I see your father is coming with the oxen. I wish I had oxen. Mules are so big. I think Ethan is very brave. He doesn't act scared at all."

Naomi watched Cassie walk away and wondered what kind of life she had led before she came west. Neither Ethan nor Ben would any more think of being afraid of a mule than they would of a pig or a cow.

Ben came running up just as their father was ready

to put the yoke on the first ox. "I wish we had mules," he said, slightly out of breath. "Oxen are so boring."

"The last thing we need is exciting oxen or mules," their father said. "Now stop chattering and help me with these harnesses."

Having put everything away, Naomi went to join them.

"We can do this by ourselves," Ben announced.

"I'm always glad of a little help," their father said.

"Harnessing the team is a man's job."

"Who told you that?" Naomi asked.

"Ethan. He said he'd never ask Cassie to help him hitch up the mules."

"That's because she has a baby and she's afraid of big animals," their father said. "Naomi doesn't have a baby, and she's not afraid of big animals, even Colby."

Naomi was shocked her father would make such a comment.

"Nobody's afraid of Colby except Indians." Ben pantomimed Colby using his repeating rifle.

"If you don't back that ox into the traces, you're going to have more to worry about than Indians."

Ben took his father's remonstrances with good grace. "When I'm grown, I'm going to have nothing but mules."

"As long as you can pay for them, you can have anything you want."

They'd almost finished when Colby came up leading an ox.

"Whose ox is that?" Ben asked.

Colby looked unusually solemn. "I don't know. It joined our livestock sometime during the night."

"Why was it wandering around out here?" Naomi asked.

"I expect it's because of some tragedy."

"You mean Indians?" Ben asked, subdued.

"It could be that a wagon broke down so completely it couldn't be repaired and they let their oxen loose."

"Cholera has been reported all across the country this year," Dr. Kessling said. "It can wipe out whole families."

"Can that ox make us sick?" Ben asked.

"No."

"Can we have it?"

"If you want it," Colby said.

"It would be nice to have three full yokes," Dr. Kessling said. "I've been worried we might be asking too much of the ones left to pull this heavy wagon."

"I've been watching them," Colby said. "They're still okay. I was going to stop for a day if they needed more rest."

"That wouldn't have been fair to everybody else," her father protested.

"The best interest of the train is served by making sure everyone's stock and equipment is equally fit. You wouldn't have left anyone behind who suffered a broken wheel, would you?"

"Of course not."

"Then we wouldn't overwork any single team."

The ox preferred freedom to the harness, but it didn't take Colby long to get it yoked and hitched to the wagon. "Think you can handle three teams?" he asked Ben.

"You bet."

"I'll make sure he does," his father said.

"Is there anything else?" Colby had turned to Naomi when he asked that question.

"I need to talk to some of the women about making Cassie feel she's a part of this group. I didn't realize no one was talking to her."

"I can help with that," her father said. "There's nobody like a doctor for giving advice. They're used to us telling them things they don't want to hear."

Ben had no interest in Cassie or her baby. "Can I have Papa's horse?"

"Maybe this afternoon," his father said. "This morning you have to teach this ox how to be part of our team."

"I'll tether the horse to the back of your wagon," Colby said.

"That's a mighty thoughtful man," her father said to Naomi after Colby left. "I wish he were going all the way to Santa Fe with us."

"Me, too," Ben said. "I like him."

"Everybody likes him," his father said. "Considering our group, that says a lot."

Naomi wondered if her father would be so sanguine if he had any idea how much she liked Colby.

❧

"Are you sure you want to take care of the baby the whole afternoon?"

Colby was grinning at Naomi.

"You looked like you were about to swallow your tongue when you offered. I'd have sworn you spoke before you thought."

"I did," Naomi confessed. "I was feeling so guilty about an uncharitable thought I overcompensated."

"What uncharitable thought?"

"Never mind."

She had cleaned up after the midday meal. The men were either watching the livestock as they grazed or trying to catch a nap in the shade of the wagons. There wasn't a tree in sight.

Rather than stay in Cassie's wagon, Naomi had brought the baby back to her wagon. She was sitting in the shade cast by it. "Why aren't you taking a nap?" she asked Colby

"I'd rather watch you take care of this baby."

"Are you waiting for me to make a mistake?"

"Would I do that?" He could keep a straight face, but he couldn't hide the merriment in his eyes.

"Don't you believe every woman is a natural mother?"

"I don't believe everybody is a natural anything."

"Okay, do you believe every woman should be a mother?"

"Definitely not. My mother should have been barred from going anywhere near children."

"Let me try once more. Do you believe every woman should be married?"

"No more than I believe every man should be married."

"Everybody in Kentucky expected to be married and have a family."

"There are several times as many men as women out here. In some places, there are no women at all, nice or otherwise."

"Then why do the men come out here?"

"Adventure and excitement. Freedom from traditional

restraints. To make their fortune or just find a place of their own. Some intend to go back. Others left something behind they hope won't follow them. Still others are bad men who would be dead or in jail if they'd stayed east of the Mississippi."

Naomi settled the baby into a more comfortable position. "You don't make the West sound like a very attractive place for a woman."

"It's a perfect place for a certain kind of woman. I think it might be the perfect place for you."

Unsure how to interpret that, Naomi asked, "Why do you say that?"

"We need women with the strength of character and independence of spirit to match the men who are trying to tame this wild country. At the same time, we need the civilizing influence and settling habits of women who want to have families and build something permanent. I think you have just the right combination of those traits."

Naomi didn't know what to say. She'd never attempted to analyze herself in the manner Colby obviously had. While she was sure he meant it as a compliment, it reduced her to a list of impersonal traits, much the same way you would list the strengths and faults of a horse you were thinking about buying. She'd always viewed herself as a single personality, not a collection of traits that may or may not mesh into a satisfactory whole.

"I'm not sure I like the West. Even without the Indians and snakes, it's not a pleasant place. It's hot and dry, water is scarce, and trees are virtually nonexistent. The land is flat and the wind blows all the time. I've hardly seen any birds or flowers, while wolves lurk in the tall grass. I haven't seen a town or village in more than a month, and there's no such thing as a house, school, or church. People are free to indulge in violence without fear of retribution. If you can't grow it or make it, you have to do without it. Strength rather than virtue is respected, and force rather than right rules the day."

"I can see why you wanted to go back to Spencer's Clearing. Do the others share your opinions?"

"I can't see how they could feel otherwise. You've lived your whole life here, and what do you have to show for it?"

She hadn't meant to be so blunt, but there was something about holding Cassie's baby and seeing the world as Cassie must be seeing it that caused her to feel vulnerable. What about this miserable land could make her want to settle here, induce her to squander her *strength of character and independence of spirit* in an effort to build a life in a land that lacked nearly everything she considered good about being alive?

His faint look of surprise and disappointment told her she'd offended Colby, but she didn't know what else he could have expected her to say.

"I didn't mean there's anything wrong with *you*, but you have only the clothes on your back. How could you support a wife and family?"

Before he could answer, the baby made a grunting sound and a frightful odor assailed her nose.

Ten

Naomi held the child away from her body.

"What's wrong?" Colby asked.

"What do you think? There's nothing wrong with your nose."

Colby laughed. "Want some help?"

Naomi looked at him like he was crazy. "I've never met a man who wouldn't rather do the roughest, most dangerous and disagreeable work he could find rather than change a baby."

"Give me the baby."

"You might drop him."

"I've held newborn calves and foals. I expect a baby is a lot easier."

Naomi reluctantly handed the baby to Colby who wrinkled his nose.

"The sooner we take care of this the better. Come with me."

"Where are we going?"

"Down to the river."

Colby held the baby out in front of him and Naomi followed. What would have been an innocuous and uninteresting ritual became embarrassing when every person they passed knew exactly what had happened. The men laughed, but the women and children, hungry for anything that promised to be entertaining, abandoned their naps and followed. Soon Colby was leading a noisy parade to the river.

"You going to toss him in?" Bert Hill, Reece's oldest boy, asked.

"He's going to build a boat like it says in the Bible and let him float away," said another.

"I can't wait to see this," Elsa Drummond said to Mae Oliver. "In more than forty years, I have yet to see a man change a diaper."

"I'll lay you odds he sticks his fingers with both pins," Alma Hale said to Alice Vernon.

"Is he really going to change the baby's diaper?" Sibyl asked Naomi.

"That's what he said."

Colby took no notice of the loud, curious, and disrespectful audience. "I never realized changing a diaper could be so interesting."

"It's not," Pearl Sumner told him. "Seeing you change a diaper is."

Naomi was relieved to see Opal was one of the laughing children gathered around.

Colby joined in the fun. "As you see," he announced, "the problem is a baby with a stinky diaper."

"You don't have to tell us that," Bert called out. "We all got noses."

"So what are we going to do about it?"

"Toss him in the river," Bert suggested.

Colby laid the baby down on the riverbank. "I can

see why your mother would have been tempted to toss you in the river, but we actually like Little Abe."

Bert's little brothers pounced on him with glee, the three of them roughhousing like frisky puppies.

"The idea is to get rid of the stink and keep the baby," Colby said, "but first I take off the diaper."

"Watch the pins," one of the women cautioned.

Colby managed to remove the diaper without doing damage to himself. "You youngsters should observe while Naomi rinses the diaper so you'll know what to do when you have your own kids."

Ted Drummond looked toward Amber Sumner. "I'm not washing any diapers. That's for my wife."

"If you can find any girl desperate enough to marry you," Amber replied.

The chorus of laughter didn't dent Ted's spirits any more than the noisy teasing and shouted responses bothered Colby.

"Being on the lazy side, I like to take the easy way out." Colby waded into the river and lowered the baby until his bottom was submerged. "Once the diaper is off, the river makes a quick job of it."

Some people laughed while others jeered. Little Abe slapped the water with his hands. After swishing him around a bit, Colby lifted the baby from the water and announced, "All clean. Once he's dry, he'll be as good as new."

Nearly every female above the age of two converged on Colby. One took the baby while another dried him. Once he was diapered, everyone wanted to hold him.

"They act like they didn't know he existed until

now," Colby said to Naomi. "What did they think Cassie gave birth to, a groundhog?"

"You did that."

"What?"

"*That.*" She indicated the women and children around the baby. "I don't know *how* it worked any more than I know *why* it worked, but you made Little Abe a part of our community."

"By washing his butt in the river? It's got to be more than that."

"He's a baby without a father and a mother who's little more than a child herself. Everybody knew that before, but he wasn't *ours.* Now he is."

Colby stared at Naomi, then the women, then back at Naomi. His expression was one of complete bafflement. "I think every woman in the train has bats in her belfry," he said finally.

"Careful," Naomi said when she stopped laughing, "or you'll destroy your image of a rough, untutored man of the wilderness."

"We have churches with bell towers in Santa Fe," Colby retorted. "Even untutored men like myself know what they are."

"Don't tell Ben. He likes to imagine you were reared by wolves."

Colby scowled. "More like a snarling mountain lion and a two-faced coyote."

"Do coyotes have two faces? It must be hard to keep two mouths fed and two faces clean."

Colby burst out laughing. "You're as crazy as the rest of your crowd."

Suddenly the Hill boys burst from the group and

headed back toward the wagons at a run. Colby grabbed Bert by the collar. "What's the hurry?"

"Mama started talking about when we were babies."

"That made all the girls laugh," complained his brother. "I was never cute."

"You forgot adorable," his brother reminded him.

"I wasn't that, either."

"I'm sure you were a pesky little urchin with dirt behind his ears and a rip in his pants," Colby said.

"Did that happen to you, too?" the youngest boy asked.

"Got my head dunked in the horse trough I don't know how many times."

The boys grinned at the thought of a big man like Colby getting dunked.

"Now you'd better finish your nap," Colby said. "It'll soon be time to hitch up the wagons."

"I don't need no nap," Bert insisted.

His brothers were equally adamant they didn't need naps.

"Why don't you watch the mules to make sure nobody steals them? If you hide under the wagon, nobody will see you."

"Morley Sumner is watching the mules," Bert said. "Ain't nobody going to steal anything from him."

"You'd better watch just in case someone sneaks up behind his back."

The boys trudged off trying to decide who would watch first.

Naomi turned to Colby. "I never heard such nonsense come out of your mouth. And you had me thinking you were serious all the time. First you sweet-talk every female in the camp into being nutty over Cassie's baby, then you gull those boys into thinking they need to guard the mules."

"They'll be sound asleep in less than ten minutes. I was a boy at one time, you know."

"Somehow I find that hard to believe, at least not a boy like Reece's boys."

"No, I wasn't like these boys, but I knew some who were. We got into trouble together then had to think of a yarn that wasn't so far from the truth nobody would believe us."

Naomi shook her head. "I'll never be able to look at you the same way after this."

"Considering what you used to think of me, that's a relief."

The easy, relaxed feeling disappeared immediately.

"I've already told you that my feelings have changed."

"But you haven't told me what they are now."

Naomi was saved from having to answer by a gaggle of women and girls heading toward Colby. "Get ready for a little halo polishing."

"What are you talking about?"

"They do have churches attached to those belfries, don't they?"

"Of course. I've even been inside one or two."

"Then you know saints have halos. You earned yours by saving Opal. Changing Little Abe's diaper warrants a polishing. You also gave him a name. He's going to be Little Abe no matter what Cassie decides."

"You can't be serious about that halo thing."

"Wait and see."

Within moments Colby was surrounded. Having

proved himself adept at handling medical and everyday emergencies, they bombarded him with a multitude of questions that would have caused an ordinary red-blooded male to turn tail and run. Naomi was amused at first, but gradually her amusement turned to admiration. It wasn't that Colby could answer the questions. He couldn't. It was the way he encouraged them to evaluate the problems and come up with their own answers. The whole community, he said, was more likely than any one person to come up with the best answer. He said there was rarely one answer for everybody, that each person should look for the best answer for them.

Pearl Sumner and Mae Oliver were the first to leave the group. "He's a remarkable young man," Pearl said as she placed Little Abe in Naomi's arms. "You should convince him to stay with us once we reach Santa Fe."

"Why would he listen to me?"

"He likes you," Mae said.

"And you like him," Pearl said. "Don't try to deny it," she said when Naomi opened her mouth to object.

"He's not the kind of man I would have wanted for you if we'd stayed in Kentucky, but he's what a woman like you needs out here." Mae was Naomi's mother's second cousin, but she treated Naomi like a daughter after her mother died.

"He is interesting," Naomi admitted.

"And attractive," Pearl said. "Just what any woman would want."

Mae wasn't in total agreement. "Maybe after a fashion."

Pearl motioned Sibyl and Laurie to join them. "Do you find Colby attractive?" she asked.

"Sure," Sibyl said then laughed. "He hasn't a penny

to his name or a change of clothes, but he's completely outshone Norman."

Pearl turned to Laurie. "What do you think?"

She looked stricken. "I haven't thought about it."

"You don't have to pretend with us," Mae said.

"I really *haven't* thought about it," Laurie insisted. "I sometimes swear Noah can see inside my head."

"Well think about it now," Mae said.

Laurie turned to where Colby was talking to Elsa Drummond. "I think he's perfect. If I weren't married, I'd chase him down and tie him up." She laughed, a little hysterically. "If you hear Noah shouting at me tonight, it'll be your fault. Now I'd better go." She hooked her arm in Sibyl's and the two cousins walked back to the wagons.

"I'll never understand why her father insisted on marrying her to that dried-up shell," Mae said.

"Money," was Pearl's succinct answer.

"Money wouldn't have been enough to get me to marry him, and he's my age."

"With that body, her parents were afraid she might get in trouble."

Naomi envied the lush curves and blond prettiness that compelled the attention of every man who laid eyes on Laurie. Unfortunately nature's bounty hadn't brought her happiness.

"Colby is coming this way," Pearl told Naomi. "You can change his mind. I know you can."

"The only reason that would give me the right to try would be that I wanted to marry him. He fell in love some time ago, which I gather didn't end well."

"Why would he tell you about that?"

"I was trying to avoid him in the beginning. He told me so I wouldn't be afraid he might make improper advances."

Pearl subjected Colby to a moment's scrutiny. "He doesn't look like a man suffering from unrequited love to me."

"He wouldn't be if he was interested in Naomi," Mae said.

"He's not interested in me, and I won't try to talk him into changing his plans."

Pearl sighed. "It seems such a waste to let some other female get him."

They couldn't say more because Colby and Elsa Drummond came to join them.

"He's a perfect baby," Elsa said of Little Abe. "I've never heard him cry."

"Hopefully he won't until I take him back for Cassie to feed him," Naomi said.

"Why isn't he with his mother?" Elsa asked as they headed back to the wagons.

"She needed a break. She's had a horrible week and no one to help her with the baby."

"We can help," Elsa offered. "There are a dozen females with nothing to do most of the day."

By the time they reached the wagons, the women had organized a week's help for Cassie.

Colby shook his head. "At this rate, Cassie will barely have time to feed him."

"And all because of you."

"It's you," Colby said. "You're one of them, and they trust you. You reached out to Cassie so they felt free to follow your example."

Naomi was distantly related to a third of the people in Spencer's Clearing, but that had never given her any influence. She couldn't imagine why that should have changed now. "It doesn't matter who did what or why things changed. I'm just glad they have."

"Maybe it will give people something to think about other than why they hate each other."

"Nobody hates anybody."

"Have you seen the way Frank Oliver looks at Norman? That's hate."

"He's just upset over Toby's death."

"Everyone's *upset* over Toby's death. What Frank feels is something else."

"Do you think he'll go after Norman again?"

"I don't know, but if I held a man responsible for my only son's death, I'd want to kill him in the slowest and most painful way I could devise."

The coldness, the biting edge to his voice, caused Naomi to stare at Colby. "Could you kill a man in cold blood?"

"I wouldn't hesitate."

She shuddered. "It's a good thing you don't have a child." When something inside Colby seemed to go dead, she asked, "You don't have a child, do you?"

He answered between gritted teeth. "You know I'm not married."

"That doesn't mean—"

"I know what it *doesn't* mean, but I don't have a child. Do you think I'd leave it if I did?"

"I don't think you would. No, I *know* you wouldn't."

"Now that we've settled that, let's forget it. You

need to get out of the sun, and I need to check on the livestock."

Okay, he didn't have a child, but there was more to his having fallen in love than he'd told her. She told herself to stop trying to come up with answers. It was none of her business. Yet she couldn't stop wondering if Colby was still in love with that woman.

❧

Except for Paul Hill, whose turn it was to watch the livestock, everyone was taking advantage of the opportunity for a nap. For the last three days, a cloudless sky had allowed the sun's rays to beat down on them unmercifully. Colby had announced that they were to take a longer midday rest and drive later in the evening when it was cooler. Naomi had tried to sleep, but she was too restless.

"Make use of that energy and see if you can find some wood in those trees along that wash," her father suggested when her fidgeting kept him awake. "My appetite fades when I know you cooked with buffalo chips."

Naomi didn't like it, either, but wood was so scarce the collection of buffalo chips had almost become a daily ritual.

"I'm asleep," Ben mumbled, "so I can't help."

Naomi left her pallet, pulled a sunbonnet from her trunk to protect her from the sun, and started toward a grove nearly half a mile away that looked to be made up of cottonwoods. She wondered where Colby had gone. Usually he rested near their wagon.

The tall grass pulled at her dress as she pushed through.

By the time she reached the edge of the trees, she was hot and irritated. She didn't understand why Colby hadn't had the wagons draw up under the trees. It would have been cooler than the open prairie. She was about to walk through a gap in the trees when she came to an abrupt stop.

Colby was there, kneeling beside two mounds of stones. Beside two graves.

There were markers at the head of each grave, but she didn't need to read them to know they were the graves of Colby's birth parents.

She still missed her mother after all these years, but she was certain that couldn't compare to Colby's loss. He had no family to comfort him, no community to support him, no history to give him a sense of belonging. The loneliness had to weigh heavily on his soul to drive him to travel so far to visit the graves of parents he couldn't remember.

"Come under the trees. It's too hot in the sun."

Naomi didn't respond because she didn't know what to say.

"It's all right, Naomi."

Naomi moved closer, the dried cottonwood leaves crunching under her feet. "How did you know who it was?"

"You packed lavender in the trunk with your clothes. I can smell it."

She moved closer until she stood next to him. "How did you find them? You said you were a baby when they died."

"All my adoptive parents would tell me was that my parents had been buried in a cottonwood grove alongside a creek on the Cimarron. For years I asked everyone who traveled this trail about graves they passed. Finally I found a man who told me he'd passed fresh graves here late in the summer twenty-six years ago. When I got here, I knew this had to be their graves. The mounds were so small I almost missed the graves. I covered them with stones I brought from the river. I carved the markers myself."

The markers read: *Mother, Died 1839. Father, Died 1839.*

"I don't know which is my mother and which is my father. I don't even know their names. *My name.* My adoptive parents wouldn't tell me the name of anyone who was with them. It was early years for settlers. Many people were killed by Indians, the weather, and each other. Others gave up and went back east. I had two brothers who were adopted by other couples, but I've never found anybody who knew what happened to them."

Naomi couldn't think of anything to say.

Colby stood. "It may seem foolish to visit the graves of people I never knew, but it's the only link I have to anyone I feel must have loved me just as I was." He turned to her. "It probably seems like a weakness for me to be so sentimental over graves."

"I visited my mother's grave regularly. I'm going to miss doing that."

"You've got your father, your brothers, your cousins. You'll never feel like you could disappear from the face of the earth and no one would notice."

"I would notice."

After a long moment, he said, "You ought to go

back. It'll soon be time to leave, and you won't have had any rest."

"What about you?"

"I'll stay here a while longer. I always feel better afterwards."

She wanted to stay, but she understood he was asking her to allow him some moments of solitude to draw what strength he could from his parents' graves.

"I don't think it's foolish to be sentimental about parents you can't remember. It shows strength of character not to forget them and strong loyalty to tend their graves. If you can love them so much without being able to remember them, think how much more they must have loved you when they could see you, hold you, make you part of their lives. You'll never be alone because you've never lost their love. I know because that's how I feel about my mother after I visit her grave."

Colby stared at her so long she started to worry she'd said something that hurt him.

"Thank you. That was a kind thing to say."

She was spared the need to reply when he turned back to the graves. She left the grove and headed back to the wagons. This time she wasn't aware of the clinging grass or the stifling heat. Her mind was filled with the image of Colby kneeling before those graves. Never before had she seen such bone-deep sadness. It would take a lot of love to lift that burden.

❧

"Is this rain ever going to stop?"

Ben was huddled inside the wagon with Naomi and their father. They had stopped for the midday break.

It was too wet to prepare food so they settled for cold stew eaten directly from the pot. The women and children tried to stay dry while the men put the livestock out to graze. Some of them huddled on the lee side of the wagons to avoid the worst of the wind and rain. Some crouched under the wagons, water up to the ankles and wet grass up to their knees. Others gave up the battle and wandered about in the rain with their slicks pulled tightly around them.

"I've never seen so much water," Naomi said. "Why do people call this a desert?"

"Colby said it only rains like this in the spring," her father explained. "The rest of the year is dry with a limited amount of snow."

"Don't talk about snow," Ben said. "I'm freezing."

The weather had made such an abrupt change from hot and dry to cold and wet that several members of the train were suffering with bad colds. Naomi's father had done his best to make sure none of them came down with pneumonia or bronchitis, but there was little he could do as long as they had to march through the rain day after day. Only those too ill to walk rode in the wagons because the soft ground was taking its toll on the mules and oxen. Colby had said they'd have to take a day of rest if the weather didn't clear.

"Give me your rain slick," Naomi said to her father. "I'm going outside."

"Are you crazy?" Ben asked.

"I will be if I stay cooped up in here any longer." She wasn't about to tell him that she was wondering what Colby was doing. She had hardly set eyes on him for three days. She didn't want to admit she'd missed him, but he was a challenge in a way no other man had been. She would have sworn he was no longer in love with the woman from his past, but something was holding him back. Her father would say she ought to keep her nose out of Colby's business, but she couldn't accept that a man like Colby would turn his back on life unless something was terribly wrong.

"I don't want you getting sick," her father said.

She opened the flap at the end of the wagon. The rain continued to fall, but the wind no longer blew it against the canvas. The clouds racing by overhead had yielded to a sliver of blue sky in the distance. "It's clearing."

"I'm not getting out until it stops," Ben said. "I got soaked driving."

The bad weather had prevented the other women from helping with Little Abe so Naomi had taken him each morning, which left the driving to Ben. Her father spent his time doing what he could to make everyone comfortable. Naomi thought his patients depend on him to raise their spirits rather than do it for themselves.

Once her father had satisfied himself that the rain had eased up, he agreed to let Naomi use his rain slick and boots. "Don't be gone long. I'll need them soon."

"Your patients can wait for a change. You've been out in this rain for three days."

"That's a doctor's duty."

"It's your duty to your family to stay warm and dry so we won't find ourselves orphans."

She'd barely set her feet on the ground when Colby came bustling up. "What are you doing outside? It's still raining."

"I got tired of being cooped up having to listen to Ben complain."

"Well now that you're in the rain with the rest of us, what do you intend to do?"

She hadn't *intended* to do anything beyond get out of the wagon. "Just stretch my legs. They got cramped from sitting still all morning holding Little Abe." Even Cassie had begun to call her son by that name.

They were walking past Cassie's wagon. She could hear the murmur of Ethan and Cassie's voices inside. She wasn't aware that she'd frowned until Colby said, "You're worried about him, aren't you?"

She was glad the rain gave her an excuse not to look up at him. "He's too old for me to worry about."

"You're his big sister. You'll worry about him for the rest of his life."

"How do you know? You don't have any brothers or sisters."

"I know because that's what I would do, and you're much nicer than I am."

"That's absurd. Every female adores you. Not a morning or afternoon goes by that you don't speak to each one of them. Papa says he doesn't know who they depend on more, you or him."

"I don't do anything."

"Nothing except give them nasty recipes that make them feel better."

"I learned a lot from—"

"I know. The Indians."

"Not just them. We don't have many doctors out here. Everybody has to know something about taking care of sick people. During the war, the doctors were too busy chopping off limbs and fighting dysentery to concern themselves with anything as harmless as a fever or a bad cough. All of us shared what we knew."

"Is that where you learned so much about people?"

"I learned that growing up. That's why I know you don't have to worry about Ethan asking Cassie to marry him."

"I'm not worried Ethan will marry Cassie."

Colby stopped. "Look at me and say that."

"No. I'll just get a face full of rain."

"You won't look because you know you're not telling the truth."

"All right, if you're so smart, how can you be sure Ethan won't ask Cassie to marry him?" Naomi asked.

"He doesn't love her."

She scoffed. "Boys his age don't know anything about love. Let a pretty girl look at them like they're the most wonderful guys in the world, and their brains cease to function."

"Ethan is too much like you. His brain never ceases to function. Has Ethan ever had a sweetheart?"

"No."

"I expect Cassie is the first girl to treat him like he knows all the answers," Colby said. "It's every man's dream to meet a beautiful woman who thinks he is perfect and can do no wrong. Ethan craves it so badly he'll come to Cassie's defense regardless of who criticizes her."

"I can understand why he likes being adored, but why can't he see she says some silly things?"

"If he thought she was silly, he would have to

accept that her opinions were silly. What would that say about her opinion of him?"

"That he might not be so wonderful after all."

"Exactly."

It annoyed her that he was probably right. It was especially humbling because he'd known Ethan less than a week while she'd had his whole life to figure him out. Had she become so used to seeing the same people year after year that she didn't really *see* them any longer?

When they approached Haskel Sumner's wagon, she was surprised to see Ted Drummond and Amber Sumner standing together on the lee side of the wagon.

"That boy's not serious," Colby said. "Fortunately, Amber isn't either. She's got her eye on the Johnson boy who drives Noah's wagon."

"Cato? You can't be serious! Ted is twice as good looking."

"Not every woman chooses a husband based on his looks."

"Then why do men?" Naomi said.

"There are a few exceptions."

"Are you one?"

"No. I was the most stupid of all," Colby said.

Bitterness and anger fought for supremacy in his tone. Despite the rain, which had started to pick up again, she looked up at him. He was staring off into the distance. For a moment she wondered if he was aware she was there. She was thankful that Vernon Edwards climbed out of his wagon as they approached.

"How long before we hitch up the wagons?" Vernon asked.

Colby looked to the west where the piece of blue sky had disappeared. "From the looks of that sky, I'd say we were in for a night of it."

"My team is getting worn down," Vernon said. "I don't know if they can hold up under another day of driving over soft ground."

If Vernon hadn't loaded his wagon with everything he could manage to squeeze inside, his six oxen might be holding up better.

"We can make a short trip tomorrow and hope the rain will stop, or we can stay here for another day."

"I don't like stopping. It gives the Indians a better chance to find us."

"If they wanted to find us, they would no matter what the weather." Colby pointed to the horizon. "Those clouds are approaching fast. Unless I miss my guess, they'll bring heavy rain."

"I'd better talk to Norman."

Naomi waited until Vernon was out of earshot to say, "Norman doesn't know anything about keeping teams healthy, how long to pasture them, or whether it's best to leave now or wait until the weather clears."

"It won't do any harm to let him talk."

"Once he hears himself talk, he thinks anything he says is a good idea."

"You don't like the man much, do you?" Colby said.

"No, I don't. He thinks he's better than everybody else. I dislike him most for the way he treats my cousin."

"He's a cold man."

A sudden gust of wind as they passed the second of Noah Spencer's wagons caught Naomi off guard, and she stumbled against Colby. His arms closed around her.

The feel of his arms around her—the sense that she would always be safe there—was mesmerizing. She'd had so much responsibility from an early age that she'd never felt the need for a sheltering pair of arms. She didn't *need* them now, but it felt good to have them wrapped around her. Their strength was comforting. Did women always want to feel enfolded in a strength that would protect them from adversity even though they knew that was impossible? She couldn't speak for anyone else, but she liked the feeling. It didn't mean she didn't want to stand on her own two feet. It didn't mean she wanted to be *told* rather than *asked*. It did mean that she wasn't alone.

She was heading toward an uncertain future beyond Santa Fe, and Colby was off to find a corner of the world free of people. It was foolish to allow herself to want something she couldn't have. It would be the height of folly to start to depend on it. She tried to push away, but Colby didn't release his hold on her.

"Are you going to let me go?"

"What if we get another gust of wind?"

"I'm sure I won't—"

A flash of lightning was followed within seconds by an earsplitting crack of thunder. A sharp gust of wind whipped the rain into their faces.

Colby released her. "It looks like the storm is going to be worse than I thought. You'd better get back to your wagon."

The rising wind and heavier rain made it unnecessary for Colby to tell her it was time to take cover.

"If you pass anybody, tell them to get inside and tie the flaps down tight."

As Naomi turned, a flash of lightning so close she could feel the heat in the air split the clouds and lit the landscape in an eerie, blue light. A simultaneous roll of thunder made the ground shake.

"Hurry!" Colby shouted over the sound of rain that was now coming down in drops so large they sounded like hail hitting the canvas.

"You've got to get out of this rain, too," Naomi shouted back at Colby.

"I will as soon as I know everybody's safe."

Naomi took hold of his arm and pulled. "Anybody who hasn't gotten back in their wagon is too stupid to live. Come on. There's room for you in our wagon."

Colby hesitated only a moment before allowing Naomi to pull him after her. They had only covered half the distance when Cato Johnson galloped out of the gloom.

"Stampede!" he shouted. "Lightning killed two oxen."

Eleven

"GET BACK TO YOUR WAGON!" COLBY SHOUTED to Naomi.

"How many men were on guard duty?"

"Just Cato. We never need more than one in the daytime."

"I can help."

"Not riding sidesaddle. Get your father." Colby turned to Cato. "Get every man who has a horse. We need to round up the livestock before they get lost."

Lowering his head against the rain, Colby looked for horses that had been kept within the circle of wagons. He found only one—Morley Sumner's. Cato didn't find any. Counting Dr. Kessling who was a poor rider—Morley Sumner wasn't much better—that meant only four men on horseback. He'd have to see if the doctor would lend his horse to someone else, but by the time Colby got back to the Kessling wagon, the horse was gone. He scratched on the flap at the back of the wagon. He was surprised when Dr. Kessling's face appeared at the opening.

"Where is your horse?"

"I don't know," the doctor shouted back. "Have you seen Naomi? She hasn't come back."

"I'll find her." And if she was on that horse, as he suspected, he'd drag her off and deposit her in the wagon. She'd been riding for barely more than a week. How did she think she was going to round up stampeding animals in a driving rain?

Morley Sumner appeared out of the gathering dusk. He was a powerfully built man, which was necessary in a blacksmith but of questionable value in a horseman. Cato Johnson had all the enthusiasm of youth without much skill to go with it. Colby didn't see Naomi or her horse, but he didn't have time to look for her. Every second was important. With Cato leading the way, the three men headed into the gloom. They hadn't gone a hundred yards when a horse and rider appeared through the curtain of rain.

Naomi! She had ridden ahead on purpose to make it difficult for him to force her to go back. If he could've spared the time, he would've pulled her from the saddle kicking and screaming.

"What's she doing out here?" Cato questioned.

"The same thing we're doing," Colby shouted back. "Spread out. You take the far side with Morley next, then Naomi with me on this side. Try not to lose sight of each other."

"I can't see a hundred yards in this rain," Morley yelled.

"Neither can the livestock. I doubt the milk cows have gone far. The oxen will be next with the mules and saddle horses having gone farthest. When you find one, head it back toward the wagons."

Over the next half hour, they found all the cows

and about half of the oxen. Colby tried to convince Naomi to go back with the gathered stock, but he wasn't surprised when she refused.

The farther they got from the wagons, the more anxious Colby became. He would have no trouble finding his way back, but the other three could become disoriented if they lost contact with one another. He called the riders together.

"Cato, you and Morley take the stock we've gathered back to the wagons."

"What is Naomi going to do?" Cato asked.

"She's going with me," Colby said.

"But she's a woman."

"She's doing just fine—and she has the advantage of a horse. Once you get the stock secured inside the circle of the wagons, send the horses back with other riders. You've done enough for today. We'll gather the stock we find in this area so tell whoever comes how to find it. Stay close to me," he called to Naomi. "If you get lost, you'll never find your way back to the wagons."

As they headed out again, they found more oxen and a few mules, but rounding them up and driving them to a central point was tedious. The oxen were slow and stubborn while the mules were skittish and quick on their feet. Their horses would be exhausted long before they found all the missing animals.

"You okay?" Colby shouted over the noise of the wind and rain after driving three more oxen into the growing herd. He'd had to bring his horse alongside Naomi's before she could hear him.

"I'm fine. Where do we look next?"

His irritation at her had died long ago. She wasn't an accomplished horsewoman, but she had been as much help as Cato, more than Morley. Nor did she appear tired. She smiled like she was enjoying herself. It was hard to understand her enthusiasm. He was miserable.

"There's got to be a streambed somewhere near here. With all this rain, maybe the water is high enough to discourage the mules and horses from crossing."

The rain continued to lash them with numbing force. Turning so the wind was at their backs, Colby led off.

As they rode farther from the wagons, the terrain was crisscrossed by small rivulets of water. He could either follow them until they formed a stream that flowed into the river, or he could continue upland. He decided to follow the water. He was rewarded when several rivulets joined to form a stream of foaming water rushing over and around anything in its path.

"There!"

Colby indicated a point where the stream made a sharp turn against a rocky bank. Gathered in the bend, their backs to the rain, were nearly a dozen oxen, half a dozen mules, and two saddle horses. Driving them to the rendezvous spot took every bit of expertise and patience he could summon. The oxen wanted to stay where they were, and no two mules wanted to go in the same direction. The saddle horses, more accustomed to the company of humans, followed without being driven. By the time he and Naomi had gathered the animals in the chosen spot, his horse was winded. He was certain Naomi's mount must be near exhaustion.

"You ought to go back," he called to her.

"We haven't found all the stock yet."

"We won't find the last of them until tomorrow."

"There's still time today."

"Your horse is exhausted."

"Yours is too."

"Go back."

"Only if you do," she insisted.

The longer the animals were loose in the storm, the farther the storm would scatter them. It could easily take them two or three days to round up the stragglers. He made up his mind to keep looking.

"I'll saddle one of the horses for you."

The horses were so skittish it took several minutes before he could get close enough to grasp one by its bridle.

"You'll have to get down by yourself," he told Naomi. "If I let go of his bridle, he'll be off again."

Naomi threw her leg over the pommel and slid to the ground.

"Here, hold this horse."

While Naomi held the fresh horse, Colby stripped the sidesaddle from her father's horse and put it on the other. The saddlecloth was soaked, but there was no help for that.

"What about Shadow?" she asked when she was settled in the saddle.

"He's had a breather so he'll be okay. Stick close until you get a feel for the new horse."

"This is Norman's horse," Naomi said. "He's beautiful, but I don't know if he has any spirit."

Colby led off toward the upland. The wind and rain

in his face made it impossible to look straight ahead. He would have to be almost upon a stray before he could see it, but he was more worried about Naomi. They had been in the saddle for hours. She had to be nearing exhaustion. Had he made a mistake in not taking her back to the wagons?

As the land rose to what Colby expected would be a plateau some miles ahead, the ground grew more rocky and less fertile. With less grass to feed fires, any trees that took hold along the edges of streams or depressions that carried runoff would have a better chance of surviving. One such clump appeared ahead.

"Head for the trees," he gestured to Naomi.

As he hoped, when they reached the small clump of stunted trees, he found several mules gathered on the lee side.

"I'll go to the right and you go to the left," he instructed Naomi. "Once they're in the open, head them toward the wagons."

It was the bellow that caught Colby's attention. He whipped around just in time to see a bull buffalo break from the trees and charge Naomi's horse. The frightened animal leapt into the air, twisting its body in the process, and coming down on the haunches of the equally alarmed buffalo.

Naomi was thrown into the air to land among the trees.

Colby was off his horse and running toward the spot where she disappeared almost before the branches came together over her. He dived among the trees, pushing the branches out of his way until he found her lying in a heap, rain dripping on her pale face, and her clothes splashed with mud.

"Naomi."

It was a cry of fear as much as of relief. Dropping to his knees, he crawled under the low hanging branches. She lay so still he thought for a moment she might be dead, but a groan relieved his worst fears.

"Don't move," he said. "Let me see if anything's broken."

"Nothing but my pride, which is thoroughly shattered."

Colby didn't know whether to laugh or give Naomi the worst tongue lashing of her life. Relief flooded over him in great waves that left him feeling too weak to do either.

Naomi struggled into a sitting position, pushed her hair out of her face. "I don't suppose that stupid horse was thoughtful enough to wait around to see if he killed me."

She had to be crazy if she thought he was going to let her keep looking for strays. As soon as he found her horse—hopefully his own horse hadn't been scared off by the buffalo—he was taking her back to camp. And he wouldn't leave until her father had tied her up so she couldn't leave the wagon until he said so. Which might not be until they reached La Junta.

"Can you crawl out, or do you need me to carry you?"

"I can get out if you'll hold back the branches."

Colby had seen many men thrown from a horse get up and climb back in the saddle. Still, Naomi was lucky to have come away without a serious injury. She crawled out between the two largest trees. Once on her feet, she would have started looking for her horse if Colby hadn't taken her by the shoulders and turned her to face him. There she stood, rain cascading down, her hair plastered to her scalp, and her dress to her body despite the protection of her father's rain slick. She looked up at him, a question in her eyes, and he was certain he'd never seen a more beautiful woman in this life.

"If you ever do that again, I'm going to break your neck."

Rather than be intimidated or apologetic, Naomi laughed. "Talk to that buffalo. Being thrown into a bunch of trees wasn't part of my plan."

"What was your plan, to get yourself killed or drive me crazy worrying about you?"

"My *plan* was to help round up the strays. I haven't been riding long, but I'm as good as anybody except you. Did you see Morley? He looked like he was riding a hobby horse."

"That isn't the point. I told you to get your father." He had to shout to be heard over the wind and rain, but he would have shouted without that. She didn't seem to understand she could have been killed.

"You *told* me? When did I become a child who needed to be told what to do?"

"When you came to a part of the country were people like you die in Indian attacks, where they get bitten by rattlesnakes, chased by wolves, or drowned trying to cross swollen rivers. Where people lose their way and die of thirst or go mad."

"You act like no one from the East has ever come out here and survived."

"Thousands have, but thousands have died."

"Well I won't be one of them."

"Only because I'll be here to save you when you pull some harebrained stunt."

Naomi pushed the sodden hair out of her face. "*Harebrained!* Now I'm stupid as well as a danger to myself."

"Not stupid. Just so all-fired sure of yourself you think you can do anything that comes into your head."

"Let me remind you that I didn't want to learn to ride, but you insisted. You said it was a requirement for every female west of the Mississippi. Well, I learned, so what better use could I make of that than round up stock we need in order to reach Santa Fe?"

"You're a fine rider when it comes to flat ground during sunny weather. This is *hilly* ground during a *raging* thunderstorm."

Rain streamed off the end of her nose. "I did notice that, but did you notice that I was doing just fine until that stupid buffalo didn't have the sense to stay under the trees where it was out of the rain?"

"Anybody can ride when nothing goes wrong. It's knowing what to do when it does, having the skill and experience to handle trouble."

"I suppose you'd have grabbed that buffalo by the horns and told him it was rude to run into your horse, that he should be punished for his lack of courtesy."

A strangled sound escaped Colby. "You are the most infuriating woman I've ever met. You just about get yourself killed, and you're making jokes."

"Let me go. You're hurting me." She shrugged out of his grip and folded her arms across her breasts. "My horse is probably half a mile from here by now. You'll have to let me ride double until we find him. And don't think you're going to leave me here," she said when he started to speak. "I can put up with the rain and the cold, but that buffalo looked as big as a horse and twice as mean."

"He was frightened."

"Am I supposed to care about that?"

"No. You're supposed to *know* how wild animals react when they're cornered."

"I didn't *corner* him. He had miles and miles of empty prairie to rampage in. He could have attacked your horse. What would you have done then?"

"Don't try to change the subject," Colby said.

"I'm tired of this one. Let's pick on you for a while."

"I'm not picking on you. I'm trying to—"

"Trying to show me I can't do anything without your help and permission, but you're wrong. I can do anything I want, and I don't have to consult you. I don't have to depend on you, and I don't have to ask your advice or—"

It wasn't planned. If he'd thought for even the smallest part of a second, he wouldn't have done it. He didn't know when the thought entered his mind. Maybe it hadn't. Maybe it was just an age-old instinct responding to an opportunity. Whatever the reason, he kissed her.

It wasn't an *oh my god, what have I done, jump back in horror* kind of kiss. It wasn't even an *I can't believe I'm kissing her in the middle of a rainstorm, but I've been wanting to do this for a long time* kiss. It was a *no holds barred, torrid to the point of steamy, tongue down your throat* kiss that obliterated everything in the universe except the two of them. No wet, no cold, no thunder or lightning.

Then it was over.

Mouth open and eyes wide in shock, Naomi stared up at him. "Did you mean to do that?"

He didn't dare tell her she couldn't be more surprised than he, not if didn't want her to shoot him the first time she got her hands on a gun. He couldn't tell her he'd thought about it as an abstract event because it wasn't true. He couldn't be strongly attracted to a woman and not want to kiss her even though he knew his remaining time with her was less than two weeks. There was only one answer he could give.

"Yes."

"Why?"

He equivocated. "Does a man have to have a reason to kiss a beautiful woman?"

She wiped the water from her face only to have the rain drench it again. "We're both soaking wet, shivering with cold, and I was thrown from my horse. I can think of a hundred other reasons why you shouldn't have kissed me, why you shouldn't have *wanted* to, but not one good reason why you did."

A man didn't really need a *good reason* to kiss an attractive woman, certainly not a good reason as a woman would see it, but that was the kind of reason Naomi expected. He hadn't met many good women in his life, but he knew they didn't scatter their kisses without thinking of the consequences. Since the consequences were marriage or ruin, he'd been careful to limit his attentions to women who expected nothing beyond the time that had been paid for.

His feelings for Naomi weren't like that. Yet they weren't the kind that would lead to marriage. They occupied a space somewhere between those two extremes, but he wasn't sure where that space was or how to describe it in a way that would make sense.

"I wanted to kiss you. I've been thinking of it for a long time."

"You haven't known me a long time."

"Ten days is a long time out here."

"Do you have special clocks? Mr. Greene didn't say anything about that. Where would I purchase one?"

He ignored her sarcasm. "Things change quickly. Life can be very short. If we wait a week or a month, the chance may never come again."

"So now that you've taken your chance, what comes next?"

"I'm not going to ask you to marry me, if that's what you're asking. I think you're beautiful and a remarkable young woman, but I don't believe in love or marriage. I've too much proof that it doesn't exist."

"I've had quite a lot that it does, but don't take that to mean I'm expecting you to propose. When you said you intended to find a corner of the world where no one would find you, I gathered that excluded a wife and children."

He hoped the pain that twisted his heart into a knot didn't show in his face. Naomi didn't know he had a child he'd never seen. He'd done everything he could to forget it. It was the only way he could keep from storming into Santa Fe and doing something that would send him to jail or the gallows. It's why he never let himself get within fifty miles of the place.

"I don't do well with people," he said.

"Everybody in the wagon train hangs on every word you say."

"That's not what I mean. I don't do well with feelings."

"So you had no feelings when you kissed me?"

That was too much. He grabbed Naomi and kissed her again, only this time he was agonizingly aware of every moment, every sensation. She would know he wasn't without passion or feelings. It's just that he didn't let them become his master. He would control everything about the kiss.

Until the tension left her body, and she melted into his arms. When that happened, he was lost.

In a flash of understanding, he realized he'd never known the fiery embrace of real passion, never suspected anything as seemingly innocent as a kiss had the power to render everything he'd ever known as meaningless as dust, a puff of smoke, a tendril as weightless as a spider's web. He felt as helpless as he must have been the day he was born. The fervor that encompassed him wrapped itself tightly around him until he felt shaken to the core.

Nothing compared to the feel of Naomi in his arms, her arms around his neck, her lips pressed against his in a kiss that drove the memory of every other embrace from his mind. None of them had packed a punch so powerful it could be life-changing. None had made him feel helpless, had wrapped him in the toils of emotion so intense he felt engulfed in flames. He barely had enough control of his mind to wonder how this was possible, to be amazed that he'd never suspected such powerful emotion could exist between a man and a woman. Even a woman as amazing as Naomi.

She had to be the reason for this mind-numbing experience. Up until now, his kisses had been shared with two kinds of women: youthfully shy Elizabeth, and women he paid for. There was nothing shy or businesslike about Naomi's kiss. She was kissing him because she enjoyed it. She had her arms around his neck because she didn't want to end quickly. She had pressed her body against his because that's where she wanted to be.

It was probably the survival instinct that had saved his life on more than one occasion that warned him someone was coming though he couldn't hear them and could barely see them through the sheets of rain.

Breaking off the kiss and pulling away from Naomi was like being denied oxygen. He felt paralyzed before his body relaxed and he gulped in a lung full of air. Naomi felt equally disoriented. She gaped at him, her expression a combination of shock, hurt, and curiosity.

"Someone's coming."

She regained her senses and looked around. "I don't see anyone."

"There," he pointed through the curtain of rain in the direction from which they'd come. "It's a rider leading a horse."

The rider remained a shadowy figure until he seemed to materialize right in front of them. It was Cato Johnson and he was leading Naomi's horse.

"I was on my way back when I saw your horse," he said to Naomi. "I was afraid you were hurt."

"I was unseated when a buffalo burst out of those

trees and frightened my horse. Thanks for bringing him back."

"I told you to send someone else," Colby said to Cato.

"What kind of man would I be if I stayed behind in a wagon knowing only Naomi was out here with you?"

"A sensible one," Naomi said. "And you'd be dry."

"I was already wet. No sense in giving anybody else pneumonia."

"Let me help you into the saddle," Colby offered. The horse had calmed down enough for Naomi to mount safely.

The saddle was slick with water, but Naomi settled herself quickly, took the reins, and proceeded to give the horse a piece of her mind.

Colby and Cato exchanged smiles.

"I'm ready now," she said. "I think he understands that if he does anything like that again, I'll feed him to the wolves."

"Let's head back with this bunch," Colby said of the mules that were still sheltering among the trees.

"That's not all of them," Naomi said.

"We won't find the rest today. Before long it'll be too dark to see."

It took several minutes to convince the mules to leave the shelter of the trees and face into the storm, but with the three of them working, they finally got them moving. Colby was anxious to get back to camp. He wasn't nearly so worried about getting warm and dry as he was about putting some distance between him and Naomi. Despite the rain and the mules, all he could think about was kissing her again.

                                  ❦

Naomi hadn't listened to most of her father's stern lecture, but she heard enough to know it centered around three points: shock that she would do anything so unsuitable for a daughter of his beloved wife; disappointment that she had such a high opinion of herself that she'd ignored Colby's directions and what she knew her father would have said if he'd been given a chance; her complete disregard for her own safety and health. She didn't offer a defense because she knew he wouldn't have listened. Instead, she thanked him for borrowing an additional lantern from Sibyl in hopes it would provide some needed warmth.

By the time her father finished berating her, the rain had stopped so he and Ben left so she could change into dry clothes. She wondered what Colby would do. He didn't have any extra clothes or a wagon with two lanterns to provide heat. The more she thought about it, the more it bothered her. Finally, she opened the canvas flat and called her father. "Where is Colby?"

"He's checking to determine which animals are missing."

"He doesn't have any dry clothes. Ask Norman to give him some. He brought enough for everybody."

"I'll ask one of the Sumners. Colby is bigger than everybody else."

"Tell him he can change in our wagon. It's warm inside."

Her father peered at her through the night, attempting to read her expression. "Why are you so concerned about Colby? He strikes me as a man who can take care of himself."

"I'm sure he can, but he doesn't have a change of clothes. If it's not good for me to stay chilled, it's even worse for him to sleep in wet clothes."

"I'll ask," her father said, "but I wouldn't be surprised if he turns me down. He's the only person I know who's more independent minded than you."

"What about me?" Ben had been hanging around the wagon, hoping Naomi would let him back in.

"You're twelve," his father said. "At your age it's more ignorance than independent thinking."

"I'm not ignorant," Ben protested.

"We're all ignorant." His father glared at Naomi. "Some of us are just ignorant about more things than others."

Naomi pulled back inside the wagon and closed the flap to keep the heat in. She was worried about Colby but not the way she'd led her father to believe. The first kiss had shocked her. The second had bowled her over because she'd returned it. What did he mean by those kisses? What did she *want* him to mean?

She still hadn't figured out if she meant what she said to Opal's mother the day the rattlesnake bit the child. She had said what she thought Pearl and Haskel needed to hear, but why had she been so confident Colby was the best one to treat the bite? Why hadn't she insisted that her father, the only doctor in the group, was the only one qualified to deal with a snakebite? She could tell herself she'd done it because Colby was familiar with the West and probably knew many folk cures her father didn't, but that wasn't the entire answer. Maybe not even most of it.

The wagon was too small and too crowded to allow her space to pace off some of her agitation, and seating herself on the trunk containing her clothes didn't help.

She felt confined, inhibited, under lock and key, but she couldn't leave the wagon.

She had been sure Colby was right about his treatment for snakebites. She had wanted him to stand out, to inspire confidence. What she didn't understand was why she was so eager for him to show his superiority. Colby wasn't interested in proving he could do everything better than everybody, so why was she trying to do it for him?

He irritated her at times, made her mad nearly as often, but that didn't alter her conviction that he was the most remarkable man she'd ever met. It annoyed her that he seemed to think so little of himself. Not of what he could do, but of what he was worth as a human being. She could only suppose his parents had criticized and punished him so much that he had come to believe what they said of him.

Then there was some mystery about this woman he used to love. It wasn't merely that he didn't talk about her. He withdrew within himself. If he'd been smiling, it disappeared. If he'd been enjoying a conversation, it stopped. If they'd been walking together, he went off on his own. It was obvious the relationship had ended unhappily, but she would have expected a person as strong-minded as Colby to deal with his hurt, chalk it up to making a bad choice, and look for someone who was worthy of his love. Instead he'd decided to isolate himself for the rest of his life.

What about his reaction to her comment about a wife and children? The rain had made it nearly impossible to read his expression, but she was certain she saw a flash of what looked like pain. Not anger and not hurt. Pain. Had there been a child that died? That didn't seem right because he was able to talk about visiting his parents' graves without looking like someone was cutting his heart out.

What was keeping Colby? If he had been here, she wouldn't be torturing herself with these questions. Had her father delivered the message? Had Colby refused the offer of clothes, or was he trying to avoid her? The kisses couldn't have been that shocking to him. He'd initiated them. Unable to sit still, she got up. Finding nowhere to go, she sat again.

She was avoiding the real issue. What were her feelings for Colby, and what did she hope his for her would be?

She had thought she knew the answer to both questions, but the kisses had washed away all her assumptions and left her sinking in a quagmire of indecision. She liked him, but would he have been interested in her if another woman her age—no, a dozen other unattached women—had been part of the wagon train?

She was certain it was more than an idle attraction, but she didn't know if it could develop into something permanent. Did she want it to? He was a remarkable man, but he lived by a set of values quite different from what she'd been taught. Could they find any common ground, or would he always be saying *we do things different out here*?

A scratching at the rear flap interrupted her thoughts.

"Who is it?"

"Colby. Your father said I could change in your wagon. Can I come in?"

Twelve

COLBY HAD BEEN RELUCTANT TO ACCEPT CLOTHES from Haskel Sumner, but the man was so grateful for what he'd done for Opal, it would have been unkind to refuse. In any case, Morley Sumner threatened to strip him himself if he didn't take the clothes. Colby wasn't a small man, but he had no desire to test his strength against a man who'd been a blacksmith for more than twenty years.

Accepting Dr. Kessling's offer to change in his wagon had been more difficult, but Morley said Colby had to be in the saddle most of the next day looking for the missing animals. He also said he had no intention of letting Colby get sick and die, leaving them to wander about the desert like the Israelites in the Bible. When he started talking about manna from heaven and being led by pillars of fire, Colby owned defeat and followed the doctor to his wagon. He had known the doctor wasn't happy with him. It didn't take long for him to find out why.

"I don't blame you for Naomi's wanting to help

round up the missing livestock, but I do blame you for not making her come back."

Colby blamed himself as well. "I would have had to drag her off the horse and bring her back by force."

"I know she can be difficult, but she's—"

"She's more than difficult. She's very intelligent and extremely capable, but she's gotten her way for so long she expects it. I can't make her understand this isn't like Kentucky."

"Then you shouldn't have insisted she learn to ride. That gave her one more way to show her independence. How is knowing she can do everything better than half the men in the wagon train going to help her get a husband?"

"She'll have no trouble getting plenty of offers. The question is whether she'll accept any of them."

The doctor favored Colby with a less than friendly look. "I want her to live long enough to get the chance."

"So do I." They had reached the Kessling wagon.

"Scratch on the flap," the doctor said without warmth. "She's expecting you."

Colby wasn't sure what he was expecting to see when Naomi opened the flap, but he'd been certain he'd see a change in her. He felt transformed, but she looked as she always did. Maybe a little uncomfortable in her father's presence. He wasn't comfortable himself. He usually didn't allow the opinions of others to affect him, but he liked and respected the doctor. He didn't enjoy knowing the doctor thought he'd acted irresponsibly.

"Did you get some dry clothes?" Naomi asked.

"He got some from Morley," her father said. "Now

climb down and let Colby inside. I won't be surprised if he gets an inflammation of the lung from traipsing around in this weather."

Colby didn't see how the doctor could equate looking for stampeded animals with traipsing around, but the prospect of warm clothes and a bit of heat to warm him up destroyed any desire to argue. He put the clothes on the wagon seat. "Let me help you down," he said to Naomi. She looked for a moment like she might refuse, but a glance in her father's direction changed her mind.

"I've left both lanterns burning." She held out her hand but didn't meet his glance. "If you're not warm enough, I'll borrow another one."

"Dry clothes are more than I expected. Heat is a luxury."

When she placed her hand in his, he could feel the electricity. Whatever had overtaken them out there on the prairie was still there.

"Take as long as you need," she said. "I'm going to check on Cassie."

"It won't take but a minute to change."

"Get some warmth in your bones," the doctor advised. "I'm going to see if Wilma Hill is still having labor pains. Don't worry about using too much oil. Norman brought enough for a year."

Colby wondered how Norman would feel about that, especially after he learned the two dead oxen were his.

"What are you waiting for?" Ben wanted to know. "The sooner you get done, the sooner I can get back inside where it's warm."

"I thought you were tough enough to stand anything."

"I am," Ben insisted, "but I don't see any point in doing it until I have to."

Colby couldn't argue with that logic. "Why don't you go see what Reece Hill's boys are up to?"

"They're too little. Bert is only nine. The others are younger."

Not having had any brothers, Colby didn't realize that three years would make so much difference. It hadn't to the rowdies he'd hung around. As long as the kid could keep up, wasn't squeamish, and didn't back down from a dare, he was okay. "How about Cato Johnson? He's older than you."

"Now that he's driving Noah's wagon, he thinks he's too grown-up for me." Ben looked dejected. "Now that he's helped you with the stampede, I bet he won't even talk to a little kid like me."

"You're not a little kid."

"I know that, but nobody else does. Now are you going to get in that wagon, or am I going to climb in and close you out?"

"I'm going in and locking you out."

Colby could remember being twelve, but it was hard being too big to be a child yet too young to be considered an adult. He should spend some time with Ben, he decided as he climbed inside the wagon.

He knew four people occupied that wagon, but Naomi's presence was stronger than the rest combined. He felt closer to her now than at any time except for the kisses in the rain. Was it because she'd just been there? Was it because the things that belonged to her were in the various boxes and trunks, or was it because being in the wagon was like being in her home, the most intimate space a woman could inhabit outside her bedroom?

He was letting the kisses get to him. He had to get dressed and get out of the wagon as quickly as possible.

He sat down to remove his boots and sodden socks. His feet were nearly frozen. He held them close to the lanterns, thankful for the heat. Meanwhile he unbuttoned his shirt, took it off, and removed the cotton shirt underneath. His skin was white from being exposed to cold and wet, but his body heat and the heat from the lanterns combined to evaporate the water. His head brushed against the ribs when he stood to remove his pants. It took an act of will to talk himself into removing his soaked long underwear.

Yet once he was naked, he was reluctant to put on the dry clothes immediately. Now that he had shed his wet clothes and his skin was dry, warmth suffused his body. His muscles relaxed so much he was tempted to luxuriate in being warm and dry, but he reached for the clothes Morley had lent him.

The long underwear fit okay, but the clothes were loose on him. Still, they were better than the sodden army uniform he'd been wearing for weeks. Once they reached the Rabbit Ear Mounds, he'd have to use some of the money Norman was paying him to buy clothes from the *ciboleros* if they had anything to sell besides strips of dried beef and coarse bread.

Ben's voice interrupted Colby's wandering thoughts. "Have you gone to sleep in there?"

"I think I might," Colby replied. "It's warm and dry."

"Open that flap. I'm coming in."

"Hold your horses. I'm coming out as soon as I get my boots on." He hated to put his feet back into cold, wet boots, but it was the only pair he had. Once he was fully dressed, he opened the flap and tossed out his wet clothes.

"Hey, you almost hit me."

"You shouldn't stand so close. I told you I was coming out."

"I wasn't sure. You've been in there forever."

Colby climbed down from the wagon and picked up his wet clothes. "Put out those lanterns. No reason to waste oil." The end of the storm had brought in dry, unusually cold, air. "Put on an extra layer of clothes. It'll be cold tonight."

Ben scanned Colby from head to foot. "Those clothes don't fit."

"It doesn't matter. They're dry. I'm going to look for wood. Want to go with me?"

"Anything out there will be soaking wet."

"It'll dry, and we're down to almost nothing."

"Do I get to ride Papa's horse?"

"Sure. You don't think I want to walk, do you?"

"Hotdog. I was beginning to think Naomi was glued to that horse."

Considering some of the things she'd done, it might have been better if she had. At least she wouldn't have pitchforked them into an argument resulting in two kisses that posed a serious challenge to nearly every decision he'd made since he ran away from home.

❧

"You don't have to sit with me," Cassie said to Naomi. "You must have other things to do."

"Not at the moment. My father is angry with me so keeping some distance between us for a while seemed like a good idea."

"Why is he upset with you? You never do anything wrong."

Naomi laughed. "I don't know who you've been talking to. It certainly wasn't my family."

"Ethan says they never would have survived after your mother's death without you."

If this had been anyone else, Naomi would have been certain she was teasing, but Cassie didn't know how to tease. "He never said anything like that to me."

"You're his sister. He wouldn't. He's very proud of you for learning to ride. He's jealous you could go with Colby while he had to stay here."

"Well he can go tomorrow. I doubt I'll be riding for a while yet."

"I don't think I want to learn to ride. It looks very uncomfortable. I'd rather stay with Little Abe." Cassie looked down at the child asleep in her arms. "I stare at him all the time. I think it's because he looks so much like his father I can imagine Abe is still here."

When she looked up, Naomi saw tears swimming in her eyes. "You loved him very much, didn't you?"

"I didn't know how much until he was gone." Tears ran down her cheeks, which she brushed away with the back of her hand. "Mama always said you could never know how much you valued something until you lost it. I wish I had valued Abe more. I don't think I was a good wife to him. I'm terribly spoiled."

Rather than let Cassie get mired in that dismal train of thought, Naomi asked, "Tell me about him."

"What do you want to know?"

"I don't know. Little things. How you met. What you liked about him. The little things he did to make you happy. How you felt when you first realized you were in love."

Cassie smiled. "We met at a party. I was wearing a yellow dress I'd been after Mama to make for ages. I had bluebells in my hair and a brand new pair of slippers. He was visiting some cousins and only came to the dance because everybody else was going to be there." She sighed. "I didn't want to be left out so I arrived early before all the boys had picked their partners for the dances. I saw Abe when he came in." She smiled in memory. "He was so handsome. He told me later he had to borrow clothes from his cousin because he hadn't brought any party clothes." She sighed again. "He didn't dance with anyone else all night. It was so romantic, just like Mama told me it was going to be."

Naomi's first meeting with Colby could hardly have been more different. Still, Colby probably made an even stronger impression on her than Abe made on Cassie. Abe only danced with Cassie. Colby saved Naomi's life.

"Abe was supposed to go home the day after the dance," Cassie continued, "but he stayed for another week. That's when he proposed to me."

"He asked you to marry him after knowing you only a week?"

"He said he knew he was in love the moment he set eyes on me."

"Did you feel the same?"

Cassie giggled. "I thought he was the most handsome man I'd ever met, but I'd already gotten three proposals. I was trying to make up my mind about them."

Naomi hadn't received even one offer of marriage and she was four years older than Cassie. She could tell herself that was because there were no men of an appropriate age in Spencer's Clearing and all the men from surrounding villages were away at the war, but Cassie had managed to find four men who wanted to marry her despite the ravages of war. Why couldn't she have found just one?

"What caused you to decide to marry Abe?"

"I fell in love with him."

"How did you know you were in love?" Naomi asked.

Cassie shrugged. "I don't know. I just *knew*. I thought about him all the time. When I thought about the others, I only thought of the things I didn't like about them. They were nice men, Frank was charming and Orly's father owned a general store, but there was always something that wouldn't let me make up my mind."

That didn't help at all. She thought about Colby most of the time, too, but he wasn't rich, he wasn't charming, and she had a long list of reasons why she was crazy to be asking these questions.

"But you didn't know Abe. He might have been a drunkard or a wife beater."

Cassie hugged her baby to her bosom. "Abe looked at me like I was the only person in the room or the house or the whole village. The other girls didn't even try to get his attention because they knew he couldn't see anybody but me."

That didn't help, either. Naomi was the only woman of suitable age in the wagon train. Would Colby have paid her any attention if Sibyl and Laurie had been unmarried and Polly and Amber were older?

"He came back the next week and brought his father to see me. Later he told me he'd have married me even if his father hadn't approved."

Naomi knew her father had great respect for Colby, but she had no idea what he might think of Colby as a potential son-in-law. Would she marry despite her father's disapproval? She didn't know. How could she consider cutting herself off from her family?

"When did you know you wanted to marry Abe?"

"The day before he asked me." Little Abe stirred. Cassie rocked him and crooned to him until he went back to sleep. "We were walking along a path that ran beside a stream through the woods. We weren't talking about anything important, just looking for fish in the water and picking wild strawberries. All of a sudden this feeling came over me that this was what I wanted for the rest of my life. I knew he'd never say a cruel word to me. Everything was so peaceful, I was so happy, felt so safe."

Cassie hadn't gotten any of that, yet she still loved her husband.

"What are you going to do when you get to Santa Fe?" Naomi asked.

"I have to find a new husband."

"I'm sure Colby would help you find a way to go back home."

Cassie shook her head vigorously. "I'm not going back where those Indians killed Abe."

"There are other routes. You could travel in a train too big for Indians to attack."

Cassie still shook her head. "Colby says there are lots of unmarried men in Santa Fe. He says I won't have any trouble attracting attention."

"But how will you live until you meet someone you want to marry?"

"Colby said it wouldn't be a problem. He promised to take care of everything."

"Colby told us he wasn't going to Santa Fe."

"He must have changed his mind."

"Why would he do that?"

"Because I asked him."

It was a moment before Naomi could trust herself to speak. "I hope you find a husband who will make you as happy as Abe."

"I don't look for that," Cassie said. "I'm an older woman now, and I have a child."

Naomi decided it was time for her to leave before she said something she would regret. "I don't think we'll travel tomorrow. Colby says it will probably take most of the day to find the rest of the mules."

"Pearl says she and the girls will take Little Abe tomorrow."

Naomi realized Cassie wasn't ignoring the problem of the lost mules and the delay in the trip. She didn't think it concerned her because someone else would take care of it. Naomi couldn't imagine being so unconcerned. Whenever anything went wrong, she felt compelled to do whatever she could to fix it. She couldn't sit back and wait for someone to take care of it. She wondered if that was the reason Cassie had no trouble attracting suitors. She never did anything that would place her in competition with men. It wouldn't occur to her to think she was superior to a man. Naomi wondered if Colby would prefer a woman like that.

He must if he'd agreed to go to Santa Fe so he could take care of Cassie.

❧

Colby was tired and perilously close to losing patience with every person in the wagon train above the age of twelve. They had spent the entire day looking for the remaining livestock. Since they only had mounts for six people, almost everybody had to walk. His plan had been to cover as much ground as possible with the people on foot keeping the person on either side in sight at all times. Once they started finding strays, one of the riders would drive them back to the wagon train where the younger children could watch them. When they found a horse, they would bring him back saddled for the owner to ride. Gradually all the men and older boys would have a mount, which would make the work go faster.

The first problem occurred when it emerged there was too much animosity between some of the families for them to walk next to each other. It took half an hour before Colby achieved an order that everyone would accept. Next came the complaining. The grass was too high, the ground too wet, it was too dangerous because of snakes, the sun was too hot, some people were walking too fast, others too slow. What nearly undid him was being told Norman expected his second horse to be found first. It was such a stupid notion Colby didn't bother responding. Norman had been upset and angry since last night when he was told two of his oxen were dead. The way he talked, you'd think he believed the lightning bolt had been aimed at his team intentionally. Seeing what wolves had done to the carcasses overnight made it worse.

It was all Colby could do to keep the line moving, which resulted in inexperienced riders taking the lead. Cassie Greene's horse was found first, which meant Ethan, who insisted his wound had healed enough for him to walk, could ride. Dr. Kessling was riding his own horse because Naomi stayed with the wagons. She said she'd slept badly and didn't feel well enough to fix breakfast. Colby was certain she was avoiding him. It would have been hard to think otherwise after the way she behaved last night when he and Ben returned with the wood. She took one look at him, climbed inside the wagon, and didn't come out again.

Having been put in a bad mood before the day started, it didn't take much to rub Colby's temper until he was ready to snap. The only way he managed to keep it from erupting was by delegating his job of keeping everyone working together to Dr. Kessling. Released from his bondage, Colby was able to work with the men on horseback, pointing out the most likely places to find the missing livestock. It wasn't until nearly every man was in the saddle that they managed to find the last of the missing animals.

By the time everyone returned to camp, they were tired, hungry, and in no mood to be friendly. People who'd neglected to wear hats or long sleeves had sunburn. Walking miles in wet boots and shoes resulted in numerous blisters on heels and toes. The razor-sharp edges of the tall grasses inflicted small but painful cuts on arms and legs. Insect bites only added to the general misery.

Once in camp, the trouble continued. The children who'd been left in charge of the livestock were tired and cranky. The wood they'd gathered last night was too wet to burn. All the fires smoked—one person's smoke seemed invariably to settle around the wagon of their neighbor sending them into a fit of coughing—and food ended up underdone. By the time Colby was sure everything was back to normal, he was ready to abandon the whole crowd to their fate.

He might have if Naomi hadn't welcomed them home with a pot of bubbling beef stew heated by wood she'd thought to put in the wagon overnight before laying it out in the sun during the day. Though she didn't hide from him, she acted like he didn't exist unless he spoke to her.

"How did you get a fire hot enough to make the stew?" he asked.

"I used the smallest branches that were quickest to dry. Nobody wanted them when you and Ben brought them in last night. I'm going to take some stew to Cassie. She hasn't been feeling well today."

"Ethan didn't say anything about that," her father said. "You think I should look in on her?"

"She's just feeling depressed because of Abe."

"She might feel less depressed if she got out of that wagon more," Colby said.

Naomi left without responding.

"What's wrong with her?" Ben asked his father. "Ever since last night, she's been acting like she hates everybody."

"I don't know," her father said. "I asked, but she said it was nothing."

Ben shoveled a spoonful of stew into his mouth. "As long as she cooks like this, she can be as mad as she wants."

"Cassie said Naomi was fine when they talked yesterday," Ethan said. "Cassie says she's the best friend she has."

"I'm glad to hear that," Dr. Kessling said, "but I agree with Colby that she'd be a lot happier if she was around people more."

Raised voices in the distance caused the doctor to glance in that direction.

"I'm going to suggest that everybody go to bed early," Colby said. "They're tired and we need to get an early start to make up for lost time."

The voices rose higher before falling silent.

"Do you think Norman's losing a yoke of oxen is going to be a problem?" the doctor asked Colby.

"It shouldn't unless we get a lot more rain. From the ruts his wagon leaves, I know he's carrying more than he needs. He can discard something."

The doctor laughed. "You don't know Norman if you think he's going to throw out a single thing. According to him, everything in his house was essential to his comfort. Why do you think he needed three wagons?"

"Sibyl wanted to leave half of it," Ethan said. "It's his mother's stuff, and she doesn't like it."

When the doctor and his sons started enumerating items they thought were unnecessary or downright ugly, Colby's mind wandered back to Naomi. Why was she treating him like a pariah? She'd been worried enough about him to ask her father to find dry clothes and then offered to let him use their wagon to change. What happened after that to change her attitude? She was visiting with Cassie when he and Ben left to get the wood. By the time they got back, Naomi had turned into a block of ice. He couldn't imagine that Cassie had said anything bad about him. The girl didn't always show a lot of common sense, but there wasn't a mean bone in her body.

A sudden escalation of voices caused Colby to set his plate down. "I'd better see what's going on."

"I'll go with you," the doctor said.

"You're not leaving me," Ben said.

Ethan caught his brother by the back of his shirt. "Stay here. If there's trouble, they don't need you making it worse."

"How could I do that?"

Colby didn't hear Ethan's reply because it was drowned out by the sound of gunfire.

Thirteen

A SECOND GUNSHOT FOLLOWED BY A SCREAM CAUSED Colby to break into a run. Across the circle he saw Norman race around a wagon, cut between two, and disappear. Frank Oliver wasn't far behind, and he carried a rifle. Colby didn't know what the trouble was about, but the first thing to do was stop Frank before somebody was hurt. He hoped the scream didn't mean he was too late.

Frank and Norman were about the same age, but Frank was fast and angry. Frank disappeared between the wagons following Norman. Almost at the same time, Norman emerged from between the next two wagons, running in a zigzag to keep the wagons between him and Frank.

Colby shouted, "Stop!" That sounded foolishly inadequate…and useless.

Without breaking stride, Frank dived between the next wagons.

When Frank came around the wagons again, Colby grabbed hold of the rifle. Frank was caught off guard so Colby was able to wrench it out of his grip without it going off. Frank *wasn't* so surprised that he didn't turn on Colby.

It wasn't a long struggle. Frank's anger wasn't enough to overcome Colby's advantage of youth, size, and greater strength. In less than a minute, Colby had Frank pinned to the ground.

"Goddamn you! Let me up! I'm going to kill the bastard!" Frank struggled in vain against Colby's superior strength.

"I don't know what Norman did, but you can't go around shooting people."

"I can damned well shoot Norman. The world deserves to be rid of him."

Frank fought to get away, but he gave up because Colby wasn't going to let him up. Much to Colby's surprise, the man burst into tears. Colby was relieved when Mae Oliver ran up and dropped down next to her husband. He released Frank, and the man and his wife embraced.

Now that the danger of being shot had passed, people started to gather. "Does anybody know what happened?" Colby asked.

Mae Oliver spoke without changing her position or loosening her hold on her husband. "Norman asked Frank if he would sell him two of our oxen. Frank said he wouldn't."

Colby looked through the gathering to see if Norman was present but didn't see his face in the crowd.

"When Frank kept refusing, Norman said now that Toby was dead, we didn't need to keep his things. If we threw them out, the wagon would be light enough that we wouldn't need all six oxen."

Frank had stopped sobbing, but he made no move to get up.

Mae continued. "If anybody needs to throw stuff out, it's Norman. Everybody knows he insisted on bringing practically everything in his house even though Sibyl hates most of it."

Colby couldn't understand why people would continue to live together when they clearly hated each other. There was enough land in the West to move away from anybody you wanted to avoid. There were enough small towns to choose from if you wanted to be close but not *too* close. Out here if a man got mad enough to shoot at you once, he was going to shoot at you again as soon as he got the chance. Colby had to make sure that didn't happen.

"Everybody go back to your suppers before they get cold. Mae and I will see to Frank."

Some were reluctant to move, but Elsa Drummond was a woman to be reckoned with. In less than a minute, the area inside the circle of wagons was cleared.

"How are you feeling?" Colby asked Frank.

"Like I want to blow Norman's head off. I'd have done it if I hadn't been so angry I couldn't remember where I'd put my shotgun."

"I'll talk to Norman."

"It won't do any good," Mae told him. "Norman doesn't have any feelings. Just ask his wife. I don't know where the money came from, but he's so rich he thinks he can tell everybody what to do."

"Are you ready to go back to your wagon?" Colby asked.

Frank nodded.

"You're not to go looking for Norman."

"I won't go looking, but if he comes near me, I won't be responsible for what I do. If he tells me I should throw away Toby's things, I *will* kill him. I hope lightning strikes all his oxen."

"Frank, dear, you can't wish that on Sibyl. She's my first cousin once removed," she explained to Colby.

He had no idea what she was talking about.

"She shouldn't have married Norman. She knew what he was like," Frank said.

"It wasn't her choice, and you know it. Now forget about him," Mae replied.

Frank got to his feet, but his eyes were full of anger. Colby just hoped his wife had enough influence over him to calm him down. He didn't want to charge him with murder.

"I'll go with them," Dr. Kessling said. "I've got something that might help to calm him down."

Once he was sure Frank was in capable hands, Colby went in search of Norman. Sibyl appeared to have been waiting for Colby. She pointed to their first wagon then walked away.

"Come out," Colby called.

"Frank tried to kill me."

"If what they said is true, you deserve it. If you don't come out, I'll go in there and drag you out."

"I'm the head of this wagon train. I can fire you. I *will* fire you."

"Good, I quit. Now come out, or I'm going in there and beating the hell out of you."

"You can't tell me what to do. I'm the richest man in Spencer's Clearing. I can do—"

Colby reached for the back flap, took a firm grip, and pulled hard. Seams ripped and buttons went flying. Colby grabbed hold of the sides of the wagon and heaved himself inside. A thoroughly frightened Norman cowered at the other end.

"I'll come out," he cried. "Just don't hit me."

Colby itched to have a reason to plant his fist in the face of this cowardly bully.

"It's probably best to talk inside. I don't want anyone to hear what I'm about to say." Colby took a moment to get his temper under control. It had been years since he'd been this angry with anyone. "I don't give a damn how much money you have or what your father and grandfather may have done. To me you're just another member of this wagon train who needs to get to Santa Fe. Everybody's need to arrive safely is as important as yours. Everyone's welfare is just as important as yours."

"You can't talk to me like that. I pay your wages—"

Colby covered the few feet separating them so quickly Norman didn't realize what was happening until Colby had grabbed him by the front of his shirt and shaken him so hard his eyes rattled in his head.

"You're lucky I'm *talking* to you. I'd rather drag you into the open and beat that over-exaggerated opinion of yourself out of you one punch at a time. Instead I'm going to give you a chance to prove you're not as big a bastard as it appears. Do you understand me? If not, I can stop talking and start slugging." Colby hoped Norman could see the anger in his eyes. "I like fighting a lot more than talking."

"I understand," Norman stammered.

Colby knew he didn't. He was just afraid for his hide.

"It's unfortunate that lightning killed your oxen, but that's *your* misfortune, not anybody else's. You can either continue with two fewer oxen and hope they keep up their strength, or you can lighten your load by throwing away some of the heaviest items."

"It's impossible to—"

Colby tightened his hold on Norman so that he had to gasp for air. "I'm not through. When I'm done, you can say anything you want. It won't make any difference, but you can say it. Whatever you decide, I will *not* slow up the train for you. You keep up, or you're on your own. That means you and your wife would have to drive three wagons. Since that's not possible, you would have to leave one behind. Now the idea of throwing out that heavy sideboard doesn't seem so bad, does it?"

"That's my mother's sideboard. She had it brought all the way from Boston."

Mentioning a sideboard had been a shot in the dark. Colby had never seen one, just heard them talked about. "Your mother is dead. She doesn't need it anymore. It doesn't feel so good when someone says that to you, does it?"

"Don't talk about my mother like that."

Colby tightened his hold until Norman could barely manage to breathe. "I didn't say you could talk. Your mother probably died in bed after a long and comfortable life. Can you even begin to imagine how Frank feels about seeing his only son killed by Indians while the boy was fighting at his side? The boy was nineteen, engaged to a pretty girl, with his whole life ahead of him. By speaking the way you did, you reduced him to no more importance than a piece of livestock."

Norman's body started to shake. Colby decided his hold on the man's throat must be too tight so he relaxed it a little. Norman strained for a big breath.

"You're going to apologize to Frank," Colby continued. "I'll tell you exactly what to say, and you'll repeat it word for word. If Frank tells you to get the hell out of his sight—which he has every right to do—you will respond only by repeating your apology. In case you've forgotten what to say, I'll remind you. Understand so far?"

Norman nodded.

"After that, you are not to go near Frank unless he invites you. If Frank comes near you, you are to be polite. Since you don't appear to know how to talk to people in a civilized manner, it would be wise to say as little as possible. Preferably nothing. I expect your wife can say all that's needed. Understand?"

Another nod.

"One further set of instructions. Stop telling people what to do. I'll take care of that for you. You're not to mention your money, and you're not to mention your grandfather. I expect everyone already knows more than enough about both. If I think of anything else, I'll let you know. Now I want to make sure you understand before we go to speak to Frank."

When the nod didn't come immediately, Colby tightened his hold, which produced the desired effect.

"One last thing. You might be thinking I can't *force* you to make an apology, and you're right. I can beat the hell out of you, I can choke you—I've spent enough time with Indians to know some rather nasty ways to torture you—but I can't actually force the words out of your mouth. I can, however, call a meeting of the group and get them to vote you out. Your brother and father-in-law might not vote against you, but after what you did today, everybody else will. Are we clear?"

Norman nodded.

"And you will make the apology?"

He hesitated, but he nodded again.

"Good. Now let's go."

Since the Kessling and Spencer wagons were next to each other, Colby wasn't surprised to find Ben lurking outside the wagon. "I've got a job for you," he said before Ben could scuttle away. "Ask everybody to join Norman and me at the Olivers' wagon. He has something he wants to say."

Ben's eyes grew big and his mouth dropped open, but he recovered in a flash and was off, his summons delivered at the top of his voice as he ran.

"Do you think this is wise?" Naomi asked.

Colby was so glad Naomi spoke to him, he didn't mind that she didn't appear pleased to see him. "I think it's necessary if there's any chance of healing the divisions in this group."

"What's he going to say? Papa said he's never seen a man closer to a breakdown."

"Nothing he can say will make losing Toby easier, but he can apologize for being such an insensitive bastard."

"I'm not sure that will help."

"Things won't get better if we don't try. Come

out," he called to Norman. "I don't want to have to go in after you."

Norman's head emerged from the wagon. He hesitated when he saw Naomi.

"It's not going to be any easier if you put it off," Colby told him. "Let's go."

They walked together, Norman on one side of Colby and Naomi on the other. Ben came running up.

"I told everybody. Mr. Oliver said he wants to kill Norman. He said he doesn't care if he hangs for it."

Norman looked ready to bolt.

"He's not going to kill you," Colby said. "It's just his anger speaking."

"He's tried it already."

"You're going to apologize to make sure he doesn't try again. Not another word from you," he said to Ben. "You've said enough."

Ben started to defend himself but thought better of it.

By the time they reached the Oliver wagon, people were gathered three-deep around Frank and Mae. A look of shock came over many faces when they saw Norman.

"Norman has come to apologize," Colby announced. "That's why he wanted all of you to be present."

Colby pulled Norman forward until he was facing Frank and Mae at the center of the circle. Frank started to jump up from his seat. Mae's restraining hand caused him to sink back, but it didn't change the look of black fury on his face. Colby hoped it was more anguish than hatred. Mae faced Norman squarely, her gaze steady and challenging.

"Norman wants to say that he's sorry for Toby's death. He knows Toby died so that the rest of you could be safe. That was a heroic sacrifice, and he wants to acknowledge it."

Norman's first words were mumbled.

"Frank can't hear you," Colby said. "Start again, and look at Frank and Mae so they'll know you mean it."

When Norman finished, Sibyl came to stand next to him.

"I want to join Norman in saying how sorry I am for Toby's death." She turned her glance to Polly Drummond. "He would have made a wonderful husband and father." Somehow she managed to convey the impression that her standing next to Norman was a duty but that her words were sincere.

"Norman is particularly sorry for his thoughtless and insensitive words to Frank and Mae," Colby continued. "He didn't mean to be cruel. He was just too busy thinking of himself, which is a habit he is going to work very hard to break."

There was an audible intake of breath, and all eyes turned to Norman.

Norman managed the first two sentences. It took some prompting from Colby—in the form of a jab in the side—before he managed to repeat the last one.

"He realizes his loss is no one's responsibility but his own. If he can't keep up, he'll choose something to leave behind."

Norman's gaze had dropped to the ground.

"Frank and Mae aren't going to believe you if you don't look at them," Colby prompted.

Norman stumbled through the words, but he did lift his head.

"Norman thinks some recognition should be made of Toby's sacrifice. Once you have found a place to start a new town, he wants everybody to decide on a fitting memorial. You're not to consider costs. He'll pay for everything."

Colby didn't know whether Norman had given up resisting or if he didn't object to a memorial for Toby, but he repeated those words with more energy than any of the others.

"One more thing. Norman realizes everyone is of equal importance to this community, that the differences in wealth or social standing don't change that. As of now, he's giving up his position of leadership. From now on, decisions will be made by a committee of three chosen by everyone present."

Every eye became riveted on Norman. They had to be wondering if he would say those words…and if he would mean them.

"You have to speak a little louder," his wife prompted him. "They can't hear you."

Everyone knew Norman hadn't said a word.

Norman began, "I realize everyone is of equal importance in the community," but appeared unable, or unwilling, to go on.

Colby prompted, "And that the differences in wealth or social standing don't change that."

"Speak up," his wife said.

The words burst from Norman's mouth in an angry torrent.

"Go ahead and finish," Colby said. "You're almost done."

Norman repeated the last sentences in a nearly

normal voice, but it was clear the words would never have passed his lips if he'd had any way of preventing it.

Colby decided to take advantage of the gathered crowd. "Since everybody's here, it's a good time to choose your committee. A couple of rules. Every wife is to have a vote equal to that of her husband, and all unmarried children above fifteen should have half a vote."

Tom Hale protested. "We've never done anything like that. Back in Kentucky—"

Colby interrupted him. "You're not in Kentucky. Out here women are required to make an equal contribution to survival. For that they deserve an equal voice in what happens to them. If Toby was old enough to die for you, he was old enough to have a say in the decisions that would affect his life. The same goes for Polly, Naomi, Virgil's boys, and all the others who work as hard as any adult. Anybody else got a problem with that?"

Morley Sumner spoke up. "No, they don't. We think it's a good notion."

Colby knew his novel arrangements wouldn't go down well with everyone, but he didn't care. "Dr. Kessling would be a good choice to run the meeting." Murmuring and head nodding indicated general agreement. "I'll leave you to your deliberations."

With ground devouring strides, he left the circled wagons and went to where Ted Drummond was posted to watch the grazing livestock. "They're meeting to choose a leadership committee," he told the boy. "Join them. I'll watch the animals."

"There's no point," Ted grumbled. "I can't vote."

"Women and all unmarried children above fifteen can vote. Hurry. You don't want to be left out."

Ted's disbelief didn't stop him from heading toward the wagons at a run. Colby laughed. It would probably be the first time the boy had been asked to give his opinion rather than being told what to think.

He'd chosen the age of fifteen because that's when he ran away from home. If he could survive on his own and be treated as an adult in a world of adults, then others could, too. He would have liked to stay behind to see what effect the women and older children would have on the discussion, but he wasn't part of their community. He was hired just to get them safely to La Junta.

He needed to be thinking about what he would do when he left. It wouldn't be as easy as he'd thought. Despite the inner conflicts that kept them divided into separate camps, he'd become attached to them. He had a special liking for the kids. For them the West would be more of an exciting change than a difficult challenge. It would ask more of them, but it would offer greater rewards. He just hoped they would be able to see that and not become discouraged because their new lives were so different from the old ones.

The night was calm with a cool breeze that ruffled the grass and dissipated the heat of the day. The ground was still soft, but it would dry enough by tomorrow to make traveling easier. With a day's rest, he doubted Norman would have any trouble with only six oxen. Considering the weight of his wagons, he wondered why he hadn't bought mules.

He didn't want to think about Norman, but he was impressed by his quiet and dignified wife. He knew she'd been forced into an unhappy marriage. That was one thing that never seemed to change. Elizabeth had been forced to marry a man she didn't love.

He'd promised himself he wouldn't think about Elizabeth. He just got angry about something he couldn't change.

He whistled to Shadow. The Appaloosa lifted his head out of the grass and started toward him. His attention was so focused on the stallion he failed to hear Naomi's approach.

Fourteen

"Seeing how well you've trained Shadow, I shouldn't be surprised that you were able to get Norman to make that apology. Still, I'm wondering how you did it. I wouldn't have believed it if I hadn't heard it."

"Why aren't you at the meeting? You get a vote in what they decide."

"You certainly stirred things up. Vernon Edwards and Tom Hale tried to change the rules after you left, but Morley Sumner told them to sit down and be quiet or he'd set them down." She laughed again. "I've never seen Tom Hale look so astonished."

"You'll lose your vote by not staying."

"My half vote, you mean. I gave it to Ethan."

"So why are you here? You've avoided me since last night."

"I wanted to thank you for what you did. Forcing Norman to apologize was an important step. However, it was the words you forced him to say that were more important. Norman will do his best to weasel out of them, but nobody's going to let him forget he said them."

"He can only weasel out if all of you allow it."

"That's hard to do when we know he takes it out on Sibyl, but that's not your problem. What made you force the men to let the women and older children have a vote? The men have been adamant that only they would make decisions, and that they would be made in secret."

"I know what it's like to be ignored when you make more of a contribution than a lot of adults."

"Do you intend to let your wife and children help you make decisions?"

"I won't have a wife or children." He stumbled over the last word. He could see that she was about to question that statement so he headed her off. "Why are you talking to me? You haven't even looked at me since yesterday."

Her gaze faltered, but she looked him in the eye. "Because I'm grateful for what you did and admire you for having the courage to do it."

"But you still don't want to look at me."

She did look away. "That's all I had to say."

He reached for her arm when she started to turn away. "What happened after we got back yesterday? You can't be angry I kissed you. You kissed me back the second time."

Naomi jerked her arms out of his grip and turned to face Colby. "I don't know why I did that. I'm sorry."

"You weren't sorry then. Why are you now?"

"I wasn't thinking."

"You were thinking plenty before that. You weren't at a loss for words. Don't try to tell me that my kiss paralyzed your mind."

"That's just what it did," Naomi said.

"I don't believe you."

She reacted like she'd been slapped. "It's not very gallant to call a lady a liar."

"What choice do I have when you won't tell the truth?"

"It's not very gallant to press for the truth when a lady doesn't want to give it."

"A *lady* would have enough courage and class to spit it out. She wouldn't try to hide behind her gender."

"Okay, but don't say you didn't ask for it. A *gentleman* wouldn't kiss one lady when he'd already promised to take care of another one. A *gentleman* wouldn't lie to the first lady because he'd changed his mind because of a second lady."

"What are you talking about?" Colby asked. "That's complete gibberish."

"I'm talking about you swearing you wouldn't take us to Santa Fe, but telling Cassie you would take care of her when she gets to Santa Fe until she finds a husband."

"Where did you hear that?"

"From Cassie herself. Can you deny it?"

Colby could feel some of the tension leave. After a moment, he smiled. Naomi was not merely influenced by their kisses. She was so jealous she'd pounced on every word Cassie uttered. He was a fool to think she didn't care for him as much as he cared for her.

"How dare you laugh at me?" Naomi was enraged.

"I'm not laughing at you."

"I can see your face despite the setting sun, and I know a smile when I see it."

"Do you recall Cassie's exact words?"

"She said you were going to *take care of her*."

"Did she tell you how?" She couldn't have because he hadn't told her.

"No, but she said you had changed your mind about going to Santa Fe because she asked you."

"Cassie is a beautiful young woman who's always had everything she wanted because of her beauty. She assumes if she wants it, it will happen."

"That's the most ridiculous thing I've ever heard," Naomi said. "She's silly but not an idiot."

"I did tell her I'd make sure she had a place to stay in Santa Fe, but it'll be in a convent."

Naomi stared at him in disbelief. "You plan to put her in a convent?"

Colby laughed. "She won't be *joining* a convent, just *staying* there. "There's a group of nuns who take in women with children and no husbands. They will let her stay there as long as she needs."

He waited several moments for what he'd said to sink in, for Naomi to decide if she believed him.

"She didn't actually say you'd agreed to go to Santa Fe," Naomi admitted. "She assumed you had because she asked you."

"Did she tell you she'd asked me to marry her?"

Naomi was aghast. "She *couldn't* do that, not with Abe barely cold in his grave."

"Cassie will be faithful and loving to the man she marries, but she's incapable of the kind of commitment you would give a husband. When one man disappears, she'll have no trouble transferring her affections to another. I don't say that to be judgmental. It's just the way she is. That's why I was drawn to you. When you tell a man you love him, it will never change."

"What about you?" Her voice was so soft it was almost drowned out by the rustle of the grass.

"I believe in commitment but not love. That's why I'll never get married or have children." This time he managed to say the word without stumbling.

"But there's love all around. You can see it even here."

"I see commitment but not love."

"What do you think love is?"

"I don't know. I loved my parents, but they didn't love me because I couldn't be what they wanted. I loved Elizabeth"—he hadn't meant to let her name slip out—"but she didn't love me because I wasn't rich."

"If you knew that in the beginning—"

"She said I was the only man she'd ever loved, the only man she ever *could* love, until"—he did manage to stop this time—"until her father told her I was too poor, so she married a rich man of his choice."

"What do you think love should be?"

He wasn't sure. Maybe he'd just *thought* he loved his parents because that's how children were supposed to feel. Maybe he didn't truly love Elizabeth. If he had, would he have allowed her to turn her back on him? He thought he'd fought for her, but wouldn't he have fought even harder if he'd loved her as truly and deeply as he thought?

"I thought I knew, but now I'm not sure. What do you think it should be?"

"I can't speak from experience, but I think love requires a deep trust that's not based on facts so much as it is what you know of a person's character. I think it requires commitment that doesn't falter during hard times. It requires respect, honesty, a sense of fair play, an ability to compromise, to put yourself second."

"That could describe a business relationship. I want to know what would make you marry a man against your father's wishes, against your friends' advice, maybe even despite common sense."

Naomi favored him with a half smile and a shake of her head. "I hope I never do anything like that."

He was insistent. "But if you did, what would it take?"

Naomi sobered, regarded him thoughtfully for a moment before speaking.

"I'd have to believe I saw something in him that was hidden from everyone else, something that maybe only I could see because of the special relationship between us. There'd have to be trust and all the other things I mentioned, but there'd have to be something special that drew me to him, that kept us together in the face of so many obstacles."

"What would that be?"

"Love."

"But what is love? People are always talking about it, but they never say what it is."

How could she answer that? She was certain her father had loved her mother, but men didn't talk about their feelings, especially to their children. Her mother had always said her husband was a wonderful man, but she had been one of the beautiful Brown sisters. She could have married anyone she wanted. Why had she chosen their father?

Maybe it didn't matter what her parents' feelings for each other were. Colby has asked what *she* thought, but despite having reached the age of nineteen, she hadn't given it much thought. She'd been too busy taking care of her family after her mother's death, she hadn't met any man who appealed to her, and she'd seen her cousins make unhappy marriages. With the war swirling around them and then the nightmares, love wasn't something she had time to think about.

So what did she think? Didn't she have some idea about what she wanted? To her surprise, she knew exactly what she wanted.

"There would have to be a strong physical attraction. I know some people would say that's shallow, but I think a woman needs to think her husband is the most attractive man in the world, even if only to her. She needs to want to be near him, to feel his presence, to enjoy the intimacy of touching him. She has to enjoy his kisses, his embrace." She could feel herself blush. "Being with him, becoming part of him, has to be more rewarding to her than parental approval or the acceptance of friends. She will place his interests above her own even if she couldn't be sure he'll do the same for her." She stopped, at a loss for what to say next.

"Do you think it's possible for a woman to feel all that?"

"Only if a man is worthy of it."

"You can't find one man in a hundred that close to perfect. What about everybody else? Don't they deserve love, too?"

She noticed he had said *they*, not *we*. She didn't understand why he valued himself so little. "The man doesn't have to be perfect any more than the woman. That's how a woman would have to feel to marry a man in the face of so much opposition. She'd want to feel that way even if everybody was enthusiastic about her choice." Colby didn't look as though she'd answered his question. "What did you want me to say?"

"It's not that."

He didn't get to say what it was because Ben came running up.

"They've got a committee and Norman isn't on it," he announced. "They want to talk to you right now."

"I'll go in just a minute."

"Papa said I was to get you. You gotta come now."

"Go," Naomi said. "We can finish talking later."

Colby hesitated before following an impatient Ben. He looked over his shoulder at Naomi just before they disappeared around the corner of a wagon.

Naomi wondered what had raised the questions in Colby's mind. Had she given him the right answers, or was she as confused as he seemed to be?

She wasn't wrong about trust, honesty, or any of the other things. Anybody would list those. It was the attraction element that was hard to understand, impossible to pin down. Exactly what made him so attractive to her? He wasn't the most handsome man she'd ever met. He was taller than anybody in the wagon train and more muscular than anybody except Morley Sumner, but she'd never been overawed by physical size and prowess. He said he didn't have enough money to replace his worn uniform with decent clothes, but that didn't appear to bother him. He didn't try to ingratiate himself with people, yet everybody liked and trusted him. He was kind, thoughtful, and willing to help anyone if he could.

That couldn't be the whole answer. She was attracted to him before she knew that.

It had to be more than mere physical attraction. She had known almost immediately he was a man who would stand by his word, who could do whatever he put his mind to, who a woman could depend on. What other kind of man would jeopardize his life to save a bunch of strangers? She thought of many more traits and characteristics, but none of them held the answer. Yet something had to be there because she thought about him constantly. The desire to be with him, to know everything about him, was impossible to stem. Why?

Maybe love was something that couldn't be described in words. Maybe it was something that had to be experienced to be understood. It was an indefinable melding of the physical, emotional, and intellectual—a combination a rational person might tell you couldn't possibly exist.

Yet she was certain it did. Otherwise, how could she explain her deepening attraction to Colby, and the feeling that it had already grown to more than that?

❧

The next day Naomi and her father were eating their midday meal when a frightened Paul Hill came running up to their wagon.

"Wilma's labor pains have started. You gotta come."

"It'll take several hours," the doctor said. "I'll come as soon as I finish eating."

"You gotta come now," Hill insisted. "She said she's been having pains since sometime during the night. She didn't want to say anything because everybody was so upset."

"Naomi will go with you. I'll come as soon as I get my bag."

"I told her to tell me as soon as anything happened," Hill said to Naomi as they hurried to his wagon, "but she said she didn't because it was going to take a long time."

"Are the pains sharp yet?"

"Yeah. That's why I noticed. She went white and couldn't hide her groans."

Naomi had helped her father with several deliveries. Groans didn't necessarily mean the baby was ready to make its appearance. She'd known labors to last most of a day. She wondered what Colby would decide when he found out. Surely he wouldn't leave them behind to catch up later.

When they reached the Hill's wagon, Wilma's sister-in-law, Flora Hill, was with her. Several women had gathered around to keep the curious at bay. In a way that was characteristic of all small villages, everyone knew everything without having to be told.

"One contraction is hardly over before the next one starts," Wilma told Naomi. "Where is your father?"

"He'll be here in a minute." Naomi knelt down where Wilma was lying on a pallet under the wagon out of the sun. "How are you feeling?" she asked.

"Like this baby is going to be born any minute."

Naomi turned to Paul Hill. "Do you have some

sheets you can hang around the wagon to give her some privacy?"

Mothers dispatched children to wagons to gather the needed sheets. By the time Naomi's father arrived, the wagon was draped in sheets of various sizes and colors.

"I need to examine you," he said to Wilma. "You can wait outside," he said to her husband. "You can make yourself useful by telling Colby what's happening."

Paul Hill looked both reluctant to leave and relieved to be spared his wife's ordeal.

"Why didn't you call me sooner?" the doctor asked Wilma after his examination. "I can see the crown of the baby's head."

"I didn't want to"—Wilma stopped when a contraction caused her to go white—"say anything until I was sure this was a real labor."

"It's real all right," the doctor said. "If you can press down hard, this labor might be over quickly."

Naomi had often wondered how a woman who'd had one baby could be willing, even anxious, to go through the ordeal of having more. Wilma's body was soaked with sweat and gripped by agonizing pains.

"It's coming," her father said. "Push. It shouldn't be long now."

It took more than one push, but minutes later the baby's shoulders emerged from the birth canal and it slid into the doctor's hands. The baby took its first breath and let out a cry.

"You've got a fine baby boy," he said to Wilma. "You can be proud of yourself."

"Can I see him?"

"As soon as I make sure he's all right."

It took several minutes before Naomi had the baby clean enough to be placed in his mother's arms.

"What have you decided to name him?" she asked. Wilma was too exhausted to talk.

"She said if it was a boy, she was going to name him after his father," Flora said, "but Paul doesn't want another Paul in the house."

"There'll be plenty of time to decide," the doctor said. "He won't be responding to his name any time soon."

Wilma gazed at her baby with a sense of wonder and happiness. "I think he looks exactly like his father."

"Why don't you go put his father out of his misery," the doctor said to Flora. "The poor man has been jumpy as a frog on a hot stove the whole trip."

"He didn't want to try again after I lost our first baby," Wilma explained, "but I insisted." She gazed down at her son. "We would never have had this beautiful baby if I hadn't."

She had barely finished the sentence when her body was wracked by pain.

"What's happening?" Flora cried. "She's not going to die, is she?"

The doctor took the baby from Wilma's slackened arms and handed him to Naomi. "I've suspected all along she was too big for just one baby."

The second birth came quickly. A little girl made her appearance with less fuss and bother than her brother.

"Paul isn't going to believe it." Flora was so excited she stammered. "Two babies at once."

"You want to tell him?"

"Let Naomi go. I want to stay with Wilma."

"Take his son to him," the doctor said.

The crowd was still gathered around when Naomi crawled out from under the wagon. "It's a boy," she announced. "And he has a twin sister."

Everybody wanted to hold the baby, but Naomi told them they had to wait until the father had seen his son. But when Naomi tried to hand the baby to Paul, he was so nervous he backed away.

"I don't know how to hold a baby," he protested.

"It's easy."

"That's because you're a woman. All women know about babies. Men don't."

Naomi was about to respond to what she thought was a stupid remark, but Colby forestalled her.

"Let me take him."

Naomi hesitated.

"If I could handle Little Abe, I can handle Paul, Junior." He held out his arms, and Naomi placed the baby in them. It took a moment before he had the baby situated so he was comfortable. "See," he said to Paul. "If a clumsy man like me can do it, so can you."

There was nothing clumsy about Colby. But what struck Naomi forcefully was that he looked so comfortable, so natural, holding the baby. He actually seemed to like it. Could it be that he would have liked children of his own?

"The baby's not crying," one of the children remarked. "Are you sure it's all right?"

"It's fine," Naomi said.

"But all babies cry."

"Why should he cry?" Pearl Sumner asked. "He's

in the strong arms of a man who can do anything that needs doing. He couldn't be more safe."

Naomi was dismayed at the stab of jealousy that Pearl's remark caused. Had her feelings gotten so far out of hand that she was jealous of any woman who admired Colby, even one who was happily married?

"Why don't you try to hold him?" Colby asked Paul.

Paul shook his head, but he didn't back away.

"Just hold out your arms," Colby said.

"I'll drop him."

"I won't let you. Now hold out your arms."

Paul looked like he was about to faint, but he complied. Colby placed the baby in his father's arms then positioned Paul's arms until he held the baby in a comfortable and natural position.

"See, it's easy," Colby said.

Paul looked in shock.

"You'd better get used to it," Pearl advised. "With two of them to feed, Wilma's going to need a lot of help."

Every woman and half the children volunteered to help Wilma at any time, but Naomi doubted Paul heard a single word. He stood there, stiff as an icicle in January, staring at his son like he'd never seen a baby in his life and had no idea what he was to do with one. Flora emerged from under the wagon with the baby daughter in her arms.

"Here is your daughter," she said to Paul. "Isn't she gorgeous?"

Paul looked so close to fainting, Pearl took the baby from him. He managed to collect his wits enough to ask after his wife.

"The doctor says she's fine," Flora informed him. "She's a little tired, but she's eager to have her babies with her."

"I made a bed for her in our wagon."

"You can't drive the wagon and help with the babies," Elsa Drummond said. "We have only one wagon so we don't need Polly. She'll be glad to help you."

Renewed offers of help came from every corner.

"I don't want to rush anyone," Colby announced, "but we need to get underway as soon as the doctor says Mrs. Hill is ready to travel."

The women assured him they'd be ready then turned their attention back to the babies.

"I hope their husbands aren't this fond of babies," he said to Naomi, "or we'll never leave."

"You don't have to worry. They're all like Paul. Why aren't you uncomfortable with that baby?"

"Why should I be? He's too small to hurt me."

Naomi laughed. "I don't mean that. You held him like you were used to it."

"I figured it couldn't be that difficult if every woman and child could do it. Besides, Paul has wanted that baby—those babies—for so long it would be a shame if he was too afraid to hold them. He just needed someone to show him how."

"Why couldn't he have learned from watching me?"

"Because he figured it was different for a man."

Naomi stared at him for a moment. "How do you know all of this?"

"All of what?"

"Everything. Horses, snakes, babies, *everything*."

"I don't know. I guess I just watch and pay attention.

And now I'd better pay attention to getting these wagons moving, or we'll still be here at nightfall."

Naomi watched him walk away completely unaware that he'd done anything unusual.

Then maybe it wasn't unusual for him. Maybe he didn't think of anything as being too hard, just as a problem to be solved. She'd have to start doing that. There was no going back to Kentucky. The rest of her life would be unfamiliar, an unending series of problems to be solved.

It would be a lot easier if Colby were there to help her.

❧

Colby was grateful to have reached the Upper Springs of the Cimarron before dark. A small spring flowed into a ravine four miles from the river. It was a lovely spot surrounded by towering cliffs, craggy spurs, and deep-cut crevices winding through thickets of greenbrier, wild currant and plum bushes, grapevines, and wild gooseberries. The trail passed over a ridge a quarter of a mile from the stream, but before making camp, he'd turned aside so everyone could fill their barrels with its refreshing water.

The new leadership under Dr. Kessling, Vernon Edwards, and Morley Sumner had managed to smooth over some of the antagonism between the factions while Wilma's safe delivery was a cause for general celebration. Colby was making a last-minute check with Ethan, who'd volunteered for night guard duty in place of Paul Hill who wanted to stay with his wife and new babies.

"Everything's quiet," Ethan said from his perch on a mound above the small valley where the animals grazed. "Some of the oxen have lain down."

"You shouldn't have to worry about a stampede, but don't doze off. There are pumas around here, and they love mule meat."

"I have my rifle. I'm a good shot."

"Who's your relief?"

"Norman."

"Let me know if he doesn't show up."

"I'm not afraid to go get him."

"I know, but you'll need somebody here while you do it."

Ethan grinned. "You don't like him, do you?"

"I don't like what he's done. He might be a decent man if he wasn't so wrapped up in his money."

"He'll never be decent. I don't know why Sibyl married him. I mean, I *know* why she did it, but Naomi nearly had a fit. Sibyl wouldn't listen to anything she said. That upset Naomi because they'd always been close."

Colby was uncomfortable hearing details he didn't want to know. "It's time I head off to bed. I want to get moving early tomorrow."

It was a short walk back to the circled wagons, but Colby was tempted to pause and enjoy the night. It could hide many dangers, but could set everything else at a distance, leaving him able to see himself more clearly than he could in the daytime with so many demands on him.

He had hoped to have more time to talk with Naomi. He needed to sort out the feelings she aroused in him, needed to find a way to get over feeling he wasn't in control, that he was careening toward a place he couldn't see and didn't know anything about. He didn't like that. Ever since he ran away, everything had been about control because he could depend only on himself. Elizabeth had been the only time he'd put himself into the position of being dependent on someone else. He didn't mean to repeat that mistake.

He was certain he wasn't in love with Naomi. Yet he couldn't ignore the feeling that something significant and powerful was happening. Otherwise, why would he keep pursuing an explanation of love when he'd already decided it didn't exist? Was he trying to convince himself that he was wrong, that it would be different with Naomi?

It *would* be different, but that didn't mean it would be right. Did he believe what he wanted was possible? If he was certain, would he recognize it when he found it…*if* he found it?

Why was he driving himself crazy? He had started by attempting to enjoy the night before going to bed, but he'd ended up beleaguering himself with questions he couldn't answer. Time to bid the night good-bye and put himself to bed.

The camp was quiet. After so much activity earlier, the stillness was almost eerie, like it was a ghost camp. He wondered when he'd started to be so fanciful. He never used to think of things like that. It would be better to make the rest of the trip as quickly as possible, but they still had about one hundred and fifty miles to go before they reach La Junta. The sooner he got away, the sooner he'd start feeling like he was in control again.

He tossed his bedroll on the ground and spread it alongside the Kesslings' wagon. He could hear the sound of Ben's soft breathing, but no sounds came from inside the wagon. He wondered how he could be so aware of a woman he could neither see nor hear that he had difficulty sleeping. It didn't make sense, but so much about his feelings for Naomi didn't make sense.

He dropped down on his bedroll and started to remove his boots. He didn't undress, but he couldn't sleep in his boots. Once they were off, he removed his socks. It felt good to wiggle his toes in the cool, night air. He and the boys had taken quick baths once they were well away from the camp so he felt fresh and clean. Having accepted one set of clothes from Morley, he'd let himself be talked into accepting more. It felt good to wear clean clothes even if they had been washed in the Cimarron.

A sound from inside the wagon caught his attention. It sounded like Naomi had turned over. He didn't hear anything else so his thoughts returned to his bed. When he lay back, there was a rock right where his left shoulder rested. With a silent curse, he sat up again.

Naomi must be restless tonight. She was moving about again. Maybe she was still keyed up from helping her father deliver the babies. He could still see the stunned look on Paul's face when he held his son. Would he have felt like that if he'd been able to hold his own child minutes after its birth? The question was so painful he forced it from his mind. That chance had been gone years ago. It was pointless to revisit it.

He was relieved when Naomi went quiet again, and he returned his attention to the stone. It wasn't very large, but it was sharp. Unsure of where to put it so it wouldn't cause injury, he carried it to the river and tossed it in. He was halfway back when he heard the first scream.

Fifteen

COLBY REACHED THE WAGON AND WAS TEARING AT the flap before Ben came awake. When he climbed inside the wagon, Naomi threw herself at him.

"I know what happened," she sobbed. "I saw it."

He wrapped his arms around her. "What did you see?"

"I saw the man I killed."

Colby didn't believe Naomi had killed anybody, but there had to be an explanation for this dream. Something she'd seen, something she'd heard, maybe even something she'd imagined. "You didn't kill anybody," he said, hoping to soothe her fears. "You just think you did."

"I did. I know I did because I saw it."

Ben stuck his head in the wagon. "Is she having her nightmares again?" He was so sleepy it was hard to understand his words.

"It seems so."

"I wish she'd stop having 'em. She scared me half out of my wits." Ben looked too sleepy to feel anything beyond fatigue.

"Get your father. If anybody else asks what happened, just tell them she had a bad dream."

"Everybody already knows," Ben complained. "She's been having them forever. The first time she woke practically everybody in Spencer's Clearing."

"I don't want to be arrested," Naomi pleaded.

"You won't be arrested. It was only a dream."

"No, it wasn't. It was real. I know it." She was insistent, frantic.

"It won't be as frightening if you tell me about it."

Naomi shuddered. "I'm not sure I can. It's too horrible."

"Why don't you start at the beginning, before anything happened?"

Naomi sat up, pushed her hair out of her eyes. "All the women were at a quilting bee. It was coming winter, and people can always use an extra quilt."

"Where were you quilting?" He hoped if he asked questions, she'd start to relax.

"We were at Norman's. His was the biggest house."

"Where were the men?"

"They'd gone hunting. Pearl couldn't quilt because she was making apple butter. She said the younger children could stay with her if Polly would help look after them."

"Why did you leave the quilting?" she asked.

"How did you know I left?"

"Nobody else has these dreams so you must have been somewhere else when it happened."

Naomi held her head in both hands. "The ladies decided one of the quilts should be for Papa. I had some scraps from a dress my mother used to wear that I wanted to put in the quilt. I thought he would like that."

"Where did you go?"

"I was going to our house, but I had to walk past Grandpa's house to get there. He had wanted to go hunting, but he had a cold in his chest, so Papa made him stay home. I heard a noise when I was walking past. It sounded like a grunt or a cough. Then I heard a crash and another grunt. I knew Grandpa kept a shotgun by the back door, so I ran around the back, went inside, took down the shotgun, and tiptoed to the front room."

When she didn't continue, Colby asked, "What did you see?"

A sob shook Naomi's body, and Colby realized she hadn't continued because she was weeping. He held her a little tighter.

"Grandpa was lying on the floor covered with blood. A man stood over him clubbing him with the stock of his rifle. Grandpa didn't move, but the man kept hitting him with his rifle and muttering awful oaths."

"What did you do?"

"I must have made some noise, a gasp, a groan, something. The man turned and saw me. He said a horrible blasphemy and pointed his rifle at me. I must have shot him because the next thing I knew he was lying on the floor." She shuddered. "There was blood all over him."

"What did you do then?"

"I don't know. I don't remember anything until I woke up in my bed at home. Papa said I'd had a fever for three days and had been delirious. He said Grandpa had died the night I found him. He said the fever must have been the result of shock, that the fever must have caused me to dream the rest."

It didn't sound to Colby like something that would happen to a strong-minded woman like Naomi, but shock could do terrible things to the mind. He'd seen soldiers go berserk who saw their comrades shot or blown to pieces. Some even turned their guns on themselves.

"It was a few days before I was well enough to see people. At first I thought everybody was the same. Then I realize they were upset. I figured it was because of Grandpa. Everybody liked him. But after I got better, I noticed they weren't acting like themselves."

"How?"

"Some acted confused, like they were waiting for something to happen but didn't know what. Others were nervous and tended not to look me in the eye. Conversations were broken off when I approached."

"Did you ask why they had changed?"

"They said it was just my imagination. Gradually everything returned to normal so I forgot about it. Until the first dream."

"What was it like?"

"Just lots of blood. I didn't see anybody and couldn't tell where it was. Gradually the dreams got worse. I could see a room and then bodies. Papa said I must have gotten Grandpa's death mixed up with my aunt and uncle. I tried to believe it, but the dreams got clearer until tonight when I realized it was Grandpa on the floor and the man had killed him."

"Are you sure that's what you saw?"

"It was so clear I couldn't be mistaken," Naomi insisted. "I saw Grandpa and a soldier. I know he was a soldier because he was wearing a Union Army uniform."

Now Colby understood. "Is that why you thought the army had sent me after you?"

Naomi nodded.

"Do you think you killed that soldier?"

"I had to. There was nobody else there."

"What happened to the blood?"

"I cleaned it up."

At the sound of her father's voice, Naomi jumped and gave a small gasp. Her father stood at the open end of the wagon.

"How long have you been listening?" Colby asked.

"Long enough."

"Tell us what really happened. I think you owe your daughter that much."

Dr. Kessling lifted the flap and climbed into the wagon.

"Why did you try to convince Naomi it was a dream?" Colby asked.

"To spare her the knowledge that she'd killed a man. And then to keep her safe. If she didn't remember, she wouldn't have to lie to anyone later."

"I knew it!" Naomi gasped. "I knew it."

"Tell her what happened. I know Naomi well enough to know it wasn't her fault."

"It was a strange event for which we have no explanation," the doctor began. "Apparently this soldier had deserted. I don't know why he decided to rob people in Spencer's Clearing. I can only guess that my father-in-law came upon the soldier after he'd broken into the house."

The army had had its share of deserters during the first years of the war, but most of them had just wanted to go home. They hadn't expected the war to last more than a few months. They had crops to tend and families to feed.

"When the man turned his rifle on Naomi, she shot him. The recoil must have thrown her against the wall. When we got there, she was unconscious and both men were dead."

"Did you tell anyone in the army what had happened?"

"No," Dr. Kessling said.

"Why?"

"There had been several bloody skirmishes in the area between the two armies, and neither side trusted us. After the trouble in Kansas, the Union Army watched everything we did. It was only our word that one of their soldiers was killed trying to rob an old man."

"Did anyone look for him?"

"Yes, but by the time the troops arrived, all they found was a town in mourning for the death of a well-loved old man."

"What happened to the soldier's body?" Naomi asked.

"We buried him in the bottom of your grandfather's grave."

Colby thought they'd made a poor decision, but he couldn't blame them. "What did you do with his horse?"

"One of the men, I don't know who, released him a long way from Spencer's Clearing. We heard later that they had found the horse even farther west."

Colby didn't like what he heard, but they were used to living in a town where there was no such thing as crime. "Is that why the whole town decided to move west?"

"Yes. He must have told someone he was coming through Spencer's Clearing because they sent a colonel to question us a few months later. He said it was strange that they should find the horse but no sign of the soldier. Another soldier had deserted, one who had courted one of our young women, and the colonel suspected we knew something about his disappearance. He nosed around asking a lot of questions. We figured once the war was over, they would come back again. Only this time, they might do more than ask questions."

"Like what?"

"I'm a doctor. I don't know what you do to people when you try to force information out of them. We didn't have any information we could give without incriminating ourselves, and we weren't willing to see our wives and children frightened, so we decided it was best to leave."

The story was plausible, but it still sounded weak. However, that wasn't Colby's problem. His job was to see that they got to La Junta.

"I wish you'd told me," Naomi said to her father. "I could have stood the truth better than these nightmares and the doubt."

"I wish I had, too, but we made the decision for the safety of the whole community. If you didn't know anything, you couldn't divulge anything by accident. Nor would you act guilty. It wasn't just that. I knew how much you loved your grandfather. I thought you'd be happier if you didn't know how he died. Nor did I want the weight of that soldier's death on your conscience. I may not have made the right decisions—*we* may not have made the right decisions—but we did what we thought was best for everybody."

Colby's decisions had always been easy and clear-cut because he'd never had to make decisions for anyone but himself. He wondered how he'd react if he were forced to make the wrong decision for the right reasons. The doctor's dilemma forced him to see how narrow his thinking had been. At some point, he'd opted to take the easy way out. He hadn't thought of it that way at the time, but that's what it looked like now.

Naomi turned to Colby. "What are you going to do?"

"What do you mean?"

"You're in the army. I killed a soldier."

"I'm *not* in the army so I have no responsibility to it. In any case, I'd have done what you did. It doesn't matter that he was wearing a uniform. He was a thief, deserter, and a murderer. If you hadn't shot him, the army would have hanged him. You should have gone straight to the nearest army headquarters and reported what had happened. As it is, they've probably written him off as a deserter and forgotten about him. The army is much more concerned about Reconstruction in the South."

"You don't think anyone will come after me?"

"There's no way to connect you with the disappearance of the soldier. Do you know his name?"

"Vernon may have discovered his name before they buried him," the doctor said, "but the shotgun blast tore him up pretty badly. They buried him in the blanket they use to carry him out of Papa Brown's house."

"No one will come after you," Colby told Naomi, "but it wouldn't matter if they did because you were within your rights. Now I hope you don't have this dream again."

"Do you think you can rest now?" her father asked. "I need to get back to Wilma. I'm not happy with the way she's doing."

"I'll stay with her," Colby offered.

"Nobody needs to stay with me," Naomi insisted. "I'm fine now."

Colby wasn't sure, but he didn't argue. "I'll be outside. All you have to do is call."

"I know."

There didn't seem to be anything to do but leave.

"Keep an eye on her," the doctor asked Colby when they were outside once again. "She may think she's happier knowing what happened, but she adored her grandfather. To see him die like that must have been awful."

"She's a strong young woman," Colby said. "It may take a little while, but she'll handle it."

"I know that, but she went through so much with her mother's death I try to spare her whenever I can."

"Is she going to scream again?" Ben asked when Colby slipped back into his bedroll.

"I don't think so."

"Good."

Colby thought Ben had gone to sleep, but he spoke again moments later.

"I didn't know about Grandpa." He didn't sound the least bit sleepy. "If I'd been the one to shoot that soldier, I wouldn't be having any bad dreams."

"Killing somebody is a hard thing, even when they need killing."

"Have you killed anybody?"

This wasn't a conversation Colby wanted to have, but it couldn't be avoided. "Yes."

"Was it hard for you?"

Was it hard? In the beginning he'd been so full of anger he looked for excuses for violence. Later it was forced on him in order to survive. During the war, he was told it was his patriotic duty to kill enemy soldiers. Had it been hard? No, but it had changed him.

"Sometimes we have to kill to protect those we love."

"Like the Indians?"

"A lot of people are bad, not just Indians. But no matter who it is or why we do it, it should never be easy. You lose a little bit of your soul, and that ought to hurt."

"I didn't know a soul could hurt."

"It can hurt worse than a bullet or an arrow."

"I'm glad my soul doesn't hurt."

"I am, too. Now you'd better get some sleep. We're behind schedule so I want to make a long drive tomorrow."

"Can I ride Papa's horse?"

"You'll have to talk to Naomi."

Ben groaned. "She won't let me. She's already told Papa he has to buy her a horse when we get to Santa Fe. I want one, too. Will you pick it out for me?"

"I'm not going to Santa Fe." Ben didn't need to

know he'd been driven out of Santa Fe and told not to come back.

"Where are you going?"

How could he answer that when he didn't know himself? "I don't have an exact location, but I know where I want to start looking."

"Can't you look where we're going? When we find a place, will you come see us?"

"A lot can change between now and then."

"But you'll come, won't you?"

"Why do you want to see me? You hardly know me."

"If you hadn't come, the Indians might have got us."

The idea that he might be a hero in Ben's eyes caused the bottom to fall out of Colby's stomach. He didn't want anybody looking up to him or thinking they owed him anything. "You'd have held them off. They just caught you by surprise."

"It was you and your rifle that made the difference. Otherwise, we'd all be dead."

Colby hadn't realized Naomi had been listening.

"I've never understood why you would endanger your own life by coming to the aid of strangers," she said.

"Survival is hard. We help other people so that when we need help, they'll help us."

"Go to sleep," Ethan called from under the neighboring wagon. "Some of us have to work in the morning."

From inside the wagon, Naomi called, "Good night."

"Yeah, night," Ben echoed.

Troubling thoughts kept Colby from falling asleep until sometime later.

❧

Two days of steady travel had brought them to a campsite at McNees Creek, about fifteen days and more than two hundred miles from Santa Fe. Colby proposed that they camp early so they could celebrate the 4th of July. The Hill brothers had killed a young buffalo cow, which meant fresh meat for the celebration. Wilma had invited Cassie and her baby to join them while Pearl Oliver insisted on sharing their meal with Colby. Only the Drummond wagon separated the Hills and the Olivers so they ended up all together. The children gathered fresh berries for pies, a welcome treat.

As twilight approached, most of the adults were content to relax around their wagons while the younger children roamed about climbing over pieces of equipment left by Armijo's army thirteen years earlier. Ted Drummond flirted harmlessly with Amber Sumner while Polly tried to convince Cato Johnson to challenge Ted for Amber's affections. Laurie and Sibyl Spencer sat talking quietly while their husbands smoked expensive cigars.

Colby had talked Naomi into taking a walk with him. They found a break in the brush along the river where rocks formed a bank about a foot above the water. At this point, the Cimarron had widened into a shallow stream moving lazily around a gentle bend in the river. A crane waded through the shallow water looking for frogs hiding among the reeds that choked the far bank.

"This is a lovely, peaceful spot," Naomi said. "It's hard to believe we could be attacked by Indians at any moment."

"There's not as much danger here as on the open plains."

"I can believe people will live here one day. I can see a snug, little house built on the rise behind us, and children playing on the bank of the river. Large trees would shade the house with a fruit orchard and a large garden."

"You're imagining a home like you had back in Kentucky."

"What's wrong with that?"

"This is a different land."

"So I've found out." Naomi moved out onto the rock at the edge of the river.

"Do you want to go for a swim?"

"No," she said with a laugh, "but I do want to dip my feet in the water. Are there any vicious fish that will try to bite my toes?"

"I think your toes are safe. Let me take off your boots."

He knew he was asking for trouble, but he did it anyway. Her boots were high-topped, heavy, clunky, not at all feminine but necessary for walking through high grass and uneven land. He wondered what kind of shoes she had worn back in Kentucky. Elizabeth had worn a flimsy shoe that wouldn't have lasted more than a week outside her house. But Elizabeth never left the house. He couldn't imagine Naomi being so confined. There was too much spirit in her, too much energy, too much will to meet any challenge that came her way.

He wondered what she would think of him if she knew he'd given up facing his challenges. No, that wasn't quite right. He'd backed away from his challenges because he'd decided the reward wasn't worth the effort.

"Are you going to take off my boot, or are you going to keep on daydreaming?"

Colby came to himself with a start. Getting caught up in thoughts of another woman and forgetting Naomi was no way to deal with his fascination for her. But then he hadn't forgotten her. She had been the impetus behind most of his thoughts for the last week.

"I was thinking of how your foot would look in the dainty slippers worn by ladies in Santa Fe."

Naomi looked at her boots with disgust. "Don't tease me with thoughts of pretty slippers. Anyway, it's improper for you to be thinking about my feet or my shoes."

"It's hard not to when I'm about to remove your boot."

"Then close your eyes and pretend it's your own foot and your own boot."

Colby laughed. "That's probably the most ridiculous thing you've ever said."

"If you knew me better, you wouldn't say that. Now are you going to remove my boots, or shall I? I'd hate for it to become so dark the snakes couldn't see my toes."

"We don't have water moccasins out here, and rattlesnakes don't like water. Hold still, and I'll unlace your boots."

By making a concerted effort, he was able to focus his gaze on her boot rather than her leg, but he couldn't do anything about his thoughts. What was so erotic about a foot?

The laces were thick, grown stiff with ground-in dirt. The boot itself was coated with dust and plant fibers. Ugly and bulky, it was an insult to the limb it enclosed. Removing both was a form of liberation. Her socks were thick cotton pressed flat from hours inside the boots.

Naomi sighed and wiggled her toes once he had removed the last sock. "If I ever get to Santa Fe, I'll never wear a boot again."

"What will you wear?"

"Slippers like the ones Norman buys for Sibyl. You should see them."

Colby couldn't force himself to pay attention to her description of Sibyl's shoes—not just because he had no interest in what Sibyl chose to put on her feet, but also because he was fascinated by the sight of Naomi's feet splashing in the water. They weren't the tiny, feminine feet one might expect, but long and slender with delicate bones and skin that was nearly translucent. He tried to keep his gaze from her ankle, but to no avail. He'd never paid particular attention to the ankles of any of the women he'd been with, but he was certain he'd have done so if they'd been as beautifully formed. He couldn't say what made Naomi's ankle beautiful, only that it was.

It connected the foot to the leg, and there Colby's imagination ran rampant. Once the leg was breached, the whole body lay open to speculation. A tightened feeling in his pants was proof that Colby's mind had gone in a direction that wasn't conducive to his comfort or his peace of mind.

"You're awfully quiet," Naomi said.

"I was thinking."

"About what?"

"You."

Had he intended to say that, or had the word just slipped out? He didn't know, and that bothered him. He'd always known what he intended to say before he said it.

Naomi's gaze followed a cottonwood leaf as it floated down the river. "What were you thinking?"

"Lots of things."

"Like what?"

"How much I'd like to kiss you."

"Then why aren't you doing it rather than just thinking about it?"

Sixteen

NAOMI HAD TURNED TO FACE HIM, LEANED IN SLIGHTLY. It was an invitation he had no desire to refuse.

Colby had believed that their kisses during the storm held everything he could possibly hope to find. They had been angry, their emotions at fever pitch, the weather adding to the atmosphere of heightened sensibilities. Could a kiss shared on a quiet summer evening by a placid river hope to reach the same level of intensity?

Their lips had barely touched, and he knew he hadn't been mistaken. The intensity, the excitement, the magnetism that was so strong it threatened to pull him under. It was more than a meeting of lips, more than physical closeness, more than rampaging lust. Whatever it was—he didn't have the mental energy to explore that question—it was something completely beyond his experience, beyond his expectations, something that reached all the way to the slagheap of his abandoned hopes.

He pulled Naomi into his arms. She was neither small nor fragile, but the way she melted into his embrace made him feel strong enough to battle the world in her defense. She didn't resist when his arms tightened around her or when his kiss deepened. She seemed to encourage his embrace, even to welcome it. Every part of his body was on the alert, every sense heightened, a whole world of possibilities speeding through his mind.

A soft groan distracted his thoughts.

"I would never have guessed you could kiss like this."

"Like what?"

"Gentle yet strong. Possessive yet giving."

He meant to ask what she meant, but he got distracted by another kiss. When he came up for air, he asked, "How did you think I would kiss?"

She leaned against his chest, tucked her head under his chin. "I never thought you'd kiss at all. I figured you'd growl a command, then go out and kill a bear or something."

He'd have laughed if he hadn't been so bewildered.

"I wasn't sure I believed you when you said you'd fallen in love." She raised up long enough to give him a quick kiss on the lips before resting her head against him once more. "I wondered if you were using it as an excuse to avoid women altogether."

The excitement, the desire for another kiss began to fade. Reality was such a bitch. Still, he didn't pull away. The trip wouldn't last much longer. It would be good to have some pleasant memories to look back on. Winters could be a long, lonely time.

"What was she like?" Naomi asked suddenly.

"Who?"

"The woman you fell in love with."

Why were women always so curious about other women? Even when they weren't in competition with each other, they wanted to know every detail.

"She wasn't the woman I thought she was," he said. "I *thought* I was in love because I couldn't stop thinking about Elizabeth. I wanted to be with her all the time, to look at her and see nothing else, to touch her hand or cheek, to hold her and never let go. I couldn't stop telling her how happy she made me or talking about our future together. I got a new job and picked out a place for us to live. I even chose a church and date for the wedding."

"What did Elizabeth say to all of this?"

"She said any plans I made were fine with her."

"What did her parents say?"

"We didn't tell her parents. She said they wouldn't understand, and she was right. As soon as they knew about us, they told me never to come to the house again. We decided to ignore them. I took a job out of town that promised to give me enough money for us to marry. When I got back to Santa Fe, I was told she'd married someone else. Her father had me escorted from the meeting by armed guards."

That had been the worst day of his life. Thinking about it now almost five years later had the power to bring the hurt back as though it had never left.

"What happened? Were you able to see her alone?"

"I climbed through her window to convince her to run away with me. She was shocked, didn't want to see me, and tried to make me leave immediately. At first I thought she was worried about my safety, but she didn't care about me, only that her husband would be upset when he learned I'd broken into their house. I tried to tell her I could support her, that I'd work two jobs, even three, but she said she couldn't run away with me, that she was married and nothing could change that. Then she insisted I leave." He had started to tell Naomi that Elizabeth had been pregnant with his child, but it was too painful.

"What did you do?"

He'd felt like killing someone, would probably have tried if her father had been there. "I said a lot of other things I don't remember. It was enough to bring the servants in, several of them holding guns. They forced me to leave."

"You said you won't go to Santa Fe. Why?"

"Her father convinced the army commander to throw me into jail. Elizabeth sent me a letter begging me to leave Santa Fe and never come back."

"Is that when you went into the army?"

"As soon as I got out of jail, I headed straight for Elizabeth's house. I was pounding on the door when a mounted guard rode up. I was escorted to the gates and told not to come back. That's when I joined the army."

It had been a way to work off his rage without being hanged for it. It also gave him time to accept that Elizabeth had never been in love with him, that to her it had probably been nothing more than an exciting adventure. "Does that answer your question?" He hadn't realized he'd pulled away from Naomi until she took his left hand between both of hers.

"I think she must be a heartless, unfeeling woman. She must be very beautiful to have blinded you to her character."

He had thought it would be easy to forget a child he'd never seen, but it had proved impossible to put it out of his mind. It was a dull ache that never let up. At times the loneliness, the feeling of isolation, hurt as much as a physical pain. It had been so bad on occasion he'd even entertained thoughts of going to see his parents. They didn't love him, but they were family.

"What did I miss?" he asked. "What should I have looked for?"

"That's hard to say."

He brought his right hand up and gripped her hands. "Don't back out on me now."

"I think you were right about what you felt for Elizabeth. That you never stopped thinking about her, that you were never happier than when you were with her, that you wanted to stare at her for hours, touch her, hold her, protect her. You didn't use these words, but you didn't feel complete without her. A part of you was missing, and you thought you'd found that part in her. But she was never in love with you, or she'd never have left you for another man."

"Would you marry a poor man when you had the chance to marry a rich one?"

"If I loved him, it wouldn't care if he was poor. Two people who love each other can build a good life together without being rich."

"Even a man as poor as I am?"

"You're not poor. You have a magnificent stallion, a fancy saddle, and an amazing rifle. You just don't have any clothes."

Colby tried to stifle a laugh, but it escaped anyway. "You have a funny way of looking at things."

"You're rich in all the things money can't buy. That's what a woman looks for first. Everything else can come later."

Colby leaned forward and gave Naomi a quick kiss. "Not every woman. Just a woman like you."

"There are lots of women like me."

He kissed her again. "I haven't found them. Where are they hiding?"

"I told Papa you were probably in the bushes smooching." The sound of Ben's voice was so unexpected, so much a shock, they sprang apart.

"We weren't *smooching in the bushes*," Colby told Ben. "Your sister said something very nice about me, and I was just showing my appreciation."

"Then give her a flower," Ben suggested. "You keep kissing Naomi, and people are going to think you want to marry her."

"What do you want?" Naomi asked. "I know Papa didn't ask you to spy on me."

"I wanted to ask if I could ride the horse tomorrow. I'm tired of driving the wagon."

"I'll make you a deal," Naomi offered. "You do all the cooking and cleaning up, and I'll drive the wagon."

"I knew you'd pull a dirty trick like that," Ben complained. "No one would eat anything I tried to cook."

"How about this? You ride in the morning and I'll ride in the afternoon."

Ben's face lit up. "Do you mean it?"

"Of course I do. If I didn't, you'd never let me forget it."

Ben pushed Colby aside to give his sister a hug. "You can smooch all you want. I won't tell anybody."

Colby thought Naomi blushed.

"I gotta tell Ethan. He said you wouldn't let me ride because you liked being with Colby. He said you two were sweet on each other."

"You can tell Ethan for me—no, it's time for us to go back. I'll tell him myself—that in the future he's to keep his opinions to himself."

"Nobody listens to Ethan. He thinks Cassie is the most beautiful woman he's ever seen. That's dumb because everybody knows Sibyl and Laurie are prettier. I think you are, too."

"Thanks for the compliment," Naomi said, "but Ethan is right. Now before you say anything else you shouldn't, take yourself off to bed. It takes more energy to ride than it does to drive the wagon."

"I'll be asleep before you get back to the wagon." With that, Ben turned and ran off.

Naomi pulled on her socks. Colby helped her with her boots. "There are times I wish I'd been an only child."

Colby took her by the hand and helped her to her feet. "The whole time I was growing up I wanted brothers. I would have been happy to take Ben."

"I love him dearly, but he can be a trial."

"Is that part of love, loving somebody even though you want to hit them?"

Naomi chuckled. "I guess so."

❧

Naomi woke to the sound of raised voices, jingling harnesses, and squeaking wagon wheels. She sat up too quickly and bumped her head on the underside of the wagon. She looked around, but her father's and Ben's pallets were empty. Rubbing the sleep from her eyes, she scrambled to her feet and crawled from under the wagon.

"I was about to wake you." Her father sat near the remains of a small fire enjoying a cup of coffee.

"Why did you let me sleep so long?"

"You looked so comfortable, and there was no need to wake you."

"What about breakfast?"

"Colby made it. He's quite handy with a campfire."

"Where is he?"

"He and Ben have gone to the *ciboleros* camp."

"Who or what are *ciboleros*?"

"As near as I can gather, they're Mexican buffalo hunters."

"What are they doing here?"

"I have no idea."

"Why didn't you go with Colby and Ben?" she asked.

"My desire for coffee was greater than my curiosity." He took a swallow and sighed contentedly. "Colby makes the best coffee I've ever tasted. If he were a woman, I'd marry him."

Naomi walked over to the Dutch oven nestled in the dying embers and lifted the lid.

"Bacon and beans," her father informed her.

Naomi found a plate and filled it. "Did you leave me any coffee?"

"It was a struggle, but my love for you is greater than my love for coffee. But just barely," he added with a grin.

Naomi poured herself a cup of coffee and sat down

to eat. The beans and bacon were good. The coffee was even better.

"You might want to join them," her father said.

"Why?"

"According to Colby, they sometime have things to sell."

"We don't need anything. I'd rather save our money for later."

"Then go out of curiosity. Colby says they're colorful fellas."

"How does he know so much about everything?" She wouldn't have let her irritation show if she hadn't felt so off balance. She'd lain awake half the night thinking about what Colby had said two nights earlier. Possibilities had battled with improbabilities until her head ached.

"He hasn't spent his whole life in a tiny village like the rest of us. Still, I get the feeling he's paid a heavy price for all that knowledge."

"And now we're paying a heavy price for the lack of it."

"That's not why we're paying it, but that's no longer worth worrying about. What we need is a man like Colby to join us. He has the skills and knowledge we need. I think we could give him the family he's missing."

"How?"

"You could marry him."

Naomi slowly lowered the spoon she'd been about to bring to her mouth. She was relieved to know her hand didn't shake because her insides did. She put her plate down and forced herself to take a swallow of coffee before meeting her father's gaze. "What makes you think that's possible?"

His gaze seemed to intensify "Why do you think it isn't?"

"I don't love him."

"But you do. I can see it in your eyes when you look at him. I can hear it in your voice when you talk about him. If I didn't believe you loved him, I'd be very disappointed to know you were kissing him down by the river."

"If Ben told you—"

"Not Ben. I could see it in your eyes when you came back. You had that vacant stare, the one that comes from being in a world all your own. I'm forty-nine years old. I've seen that look too many times not to know what it means."

Naomi didn't know what to say. She didn't believe she was in love with Colby, but neither could she say she wasn't. It was hard to be in love with a man who stayed at a distance, who swore love didn't exist, who didn't *want* to believe in it.

"Colby isn't in love with me."

"He could be."

"He fell in love with a woman who swore she loved him. Yet she married another man. When he tried to see her, he was driven out of town and told he would be shot if he returned. That and abuse by his parents have turned him against any emotional relationship. He's determined to isolate himself."

"All the more reason for you to convince him he's wrong. He's much too fine a man to lose."

"What makes you think I have him to lose?" She

had never expected this conversation. She wasn't prepared for it. She got to her feet. "I think I'd like to see these *ciboleros*. Where is their camp?"

Her father smiled the way he did when she was a little girl and needed comfort. "I won't ask any more questions. Finish your breakfast. Afterwards, we'll go together."

She had to force herself to eat the last of her food. It didn't taste good anymore. She wiped her plate and swallowed her coffee. She would have tossed it away if she hadn't worried her father might consider it a worse crime than not admitting she was in love with Colby.

The *ciboleros* had camped on the far side of Rabbit Ear Creek. It was a bewildering mix of colorfully dressed men with plain women and children. The forest of tents was interspersed with heavy oxcarts with solid wood wheels. Long strips of drying meat hung from wires or ropes strung between poles, oxcarts, and even tent poles. Bags of what looked like hard, coarse, brown bread hung from the sides of carts. A large herd of horses could be seen grazing in the distance. She spied Colby and Ben in the midst of a group of men wearing brightly colored jackets, close-fitting leather trousers, and flat straw hats who gestured excitedly and all spoke at once. Several people from the wagon train were standing a little apart, apparently awaiting the outcome of the discussion. The moment Ben spied them, he came running.

"You gotta come," he cried. "Colby says they're trying to cheat us, and he won't let anybody buy anything."

Naomi's gaze swept over the campground with its shoddy tents, shabby women, and children before asking, "What do they have to sell that we would want to buy?"

"Dried buffalo meat and bread," Ben replied. "Colby says the bread is as hard as adobe, but he says it's really good when you dip it in coffee." Ben took hold of Naomi's hand. "Come on. You're missing all the fun."

Naomi didn't see anything that made her think of fun. The camp was barely habitable, the women and children had a neglected look, and a diet of dried buffalo meat and hard bread was barely better than living off cornmeal mush. She had no idea what kind of agreement was being hammered out, but apparently one had been for the *ciboleros* stopped shouting and broke out in smiles. Expressionless women went away and came back with strips of dried meat while grinning children scampered about hawking bags of bread. A dirty little boy ran up to them and said something she didn't understand.

"He's offering you his bag of bread," Colby explained.

"We don't want any."

"Yes, we do," her father said. "We'll have some buffalo meat, too."

Colby said something to the boy who dashed off and came back with a woman holding strips of dried meat about a yard long.

"How much do they want?" her father asked.

Colby managed the negotiations and explained how many pesos were in an American dollar.

"That was very cheap," her father said after Naomi was loaded down with bags of bread and Ben was draped in strips of dried meat.

"They hunt to support their families," Colby explained. "Once they've sold what they don't need, they'll head back to Mexico."

Naomi indicated the bread and meat. "What are we going to do with that?"

"Eat it," her father said. "I haven't had bread in so long I've almost forgotten what it tastes like."

"And the meat?"

"I'll show you how to cook it," Colby offered.

Just what she needed, one more thing Colby could do better than she could. She was surprised at the need to compete with him, to prove she was just as capable despite the fact that she knew she *wasn't*. It didn't make it any easier to tell herself that she was in a part of the country Colby had known since birth. She was still annoyed, sometimes to the point of being angry with him. She knew that was wrong. If she had to be angry with anyone, she should be angry with Norman and the other men who'd forced them to leave Spencer's Clearing.

Now everything had changed. The rules would be different. At home the men wouldn't have invited a woman to take part in their decision making, wouldn't have listened to her if she'd given her opinion. Colby was different. He was irritatingly capable and just as domineering at times, but he listened to her opinions, encouraged her to do things she'd never tried, and had made it clear he expected a woman to play an important role in her family's life. It was a point of view that was new to her, one she wasn't quite sure she could accept on face value, but she found it exciting.

❧

"I don't know why I let you talk me into climbing this mountain," Naomi said between gasps for breath.

"It's not a mountain," Colby said. "It's hardly a thousand feet tall."

"It would be a mountain in Spencer's Clearing."

"Wait until you see a real mountain."

"I won't mind *seeing* it. I just don't want to *climb* it."

They had ridden ahead so Colby could decide whether to camp at Round Mound or Rock Creek. He had put off the decision until after they climbed the beautiful, round-topped cone. Though it wasn't looking as beautiful now as it had been when Naomi was standing at the bottom looking up.

"Don't give up now," Colby encouraged. "We're close to the top."

Naomi grabbed hold of a scrawny sapling and pulled herself several feet up the slope. "Who said anything about giving up? After a thousand miles of flat prairie, I'm thrilled to find a mountain." She was pleased Colby didn't repeat his insistence that this *wasn't* a mountain.

After ten more minutes of stumbling over roots and crawling around boulders, they reached the nearly flat summit. To Naomi, the view was stunning. The country to the south was rolling or level, dotted with mounts and hills. The vast plain stretched to the north with occasional peaks and ridges.

"What's that?" Naomi asked, pointing to a silver stripe above an azure band.

"That's the snow-capped peaks of the Rocky Mountains."

"They look bigger than this mound."

"At least ten times bigger." Colby moved next to her, put his arm over her shoulder. "You ought to see them someday. They're magnificent."

Naomi was more interested in the arm over her shoulder than she was in any mountain. Colby had placed it there casually, almost as though it belonged there, certainly in a manner that indicated he didn't expect to be rebuffed. She didn't want to rebuff him, but she wanted to know if the casualness of it—a familiarity that felt almost like a possessive quality—had anything to do with the kisses they shared so recently. His words said one thing, but his actions were clearly leading in another direction. Thoughts, ideas, hopes, dreams, even idle longings had been swirling around in her head for days in a kind of aimless meandering—not seeking a solution but unable to ignore that answers needed to be found—but her father's words had brought them into focus. She had reached a point where she needed to know what Colby's intentions might be. She'd never indulged in an idle flirtation or a momentary fling, but she was sure it wouldn't feel like this.

"You're awfully quiet," Colby said. "If you think the Rockies are impressive now, wait until you see them up close."

"I wasn't thinking about mountains."

"What were you thinking about?" he asked.

When she turned to face him, he let his arm slide off her shoulder, down her arm, until her hand slid into his.

"I was thinking about you," she said. "About us. About the future."

He looked as though she'd suddenly started speaking in a language he didn't understand.

"Don't act like you don't know what I'm talking about," she demanded. "You've made a point to seek out my company. We've been alone together. We've climbed this mountain together. We've kissed and held each other. I think I have a right to ask if you intend to ask me to marry you."

Seventeen

COLBY'S THROAT THREATENED TO CLOSE ON HIM. HE'D never pretended he wasn't attracted to Naomi, but neither had he expected his interest would last beyond the time he left the wagon train. Her father inviting him to travel with his family had made it inevitable they would be thrown together. They ate together. They rode together. They even argued together. It was inevitable that a close relationship would develop between them.

But that didn't mean he was going to ask her to marry him.

He didn't want to marry just for companionship, for a helpmate, for the mother of his children. Least of all did he want to marry for a convenient way to take care of his physical needs. He found it difficult to say exactly what *would* be sufficient to make him fall in love, but he hadn't found it despite the strength of his feelings for Naomi.

Suppose he did ask her to marry him and she changed her mind? He'd nearly killed Elizabeth's father when she jilted him. What would he do this time? Naomi had said all he had to do was look at Paul and Wilma Hill or Haskel and Pearl Sumner to see that love was real. Observing them had added to his conviction that what he wanted from marriage, what he *needed* to take the risk, didn't exist. He wanted fire. He wanted excitement. He wanted to feel desperate just thinking of losing her. He wanted her touch to ignite a desire in him that was unquenchable. The mere sight of her should drive every other thought from his mind. He should feel that her every breath was *his* breath, that her heartbeat was his heartbeat. Separation from her should be agony, while being with her was sheer bliss. He wouldn't waste a second glance on another woman no matter how beautiful, fascinating, or alluring because, to him, *she* was the most beautiful, fascinating, and alluring woman in the world.

That wasn't how he felt about Naomi. There was no desperation, no fear, no bone-crushing need.

"I'm never going to marry, but if I were, you'd be the woman I'd want to be my wife."

"What kind of answer is that?"

"A less hurtful way of saying no. I don't believe in love. Without it, I'd rather live alone."

"You mean you would deny yourself friendship, companionship, even children because you haven't found a kind of relationship you're convinced doesn't exist?"

"Yes." It seemed unnecessary to say more than that.

"One day in the company of Pearl and Haskel or Wilma and Paul, and it's impossible to imagine them being married to anyone else. What more is there?"

If she didn't know already, it was impossible to explain. It was something she had to feel as deeply and intensely as he did. It had to come from within her. It couldn't be learned. It had to have been there since the day she was born.

"I can't put it into words, but I'd know if I found it."

"If you can't put it into words, you don't know what it is." Naomi pulled away. "We'd better go down. If the others arrive and you still haven't decided on a place to camp, they won't be happy."

Naomi started down without waiting for Colby. He wanted to call her back, but what could he say that hadn't been said already? He didn't want their time together to end so quickly, but hadn't he been the one to effectively end it? There was something between them that was unfinished, but he didn't know what it was. He *did* know that in turning away from him, she was leaving a big hole in his life. He would miss her as he hadn't missed anyone since Elizabeth. This was the end.

But the end of what?

❧

Naomi woke with a headache that wasn't improved by the smell of cooking grease and the sound of rain on the canvas covering. In an ironic reflection of the situation between her and Colby, it had rained for the better part of three days during which they had hardly spoken. Her father had cocked a curious eyebrow but said nothing. Ben hadn't been as tactful, but he'd been too happy for the chance to ride each day to push the issue. Ethan was too involved with Cassie and Little

Abe to notice anything that wasn't shoved under his nose. The rest of the caravan was too concerned with keeping dry and preventing the wagons from getting mired in mud to have time or energy to be aware of the death of a romance.

Had it been a romance, or had she been deceiving herself from the start? Colby had told her from the beginning he didn't believe love existed. He'd had twenty-seven years to be confirmed in that opinion. Why should she think she could change his mind in two weeks? Had she been trying to change his mind, or had she wandered into this blind?

Her father, who'd slept next to her, sat up. "Drat," he said when he realized it was still raining. "I guess it's cold breakfast again." He sniffed the air, a puzzled expression on his face. "I must be dreaming."

"You're not," Naomi assured him. "I smelled it, too."

"It smells like beef. Where can it be coming from?"

"I don't know, but I'll find out."

"You can't go out there. It's still raining."

"I won't dissolve."

Neither of them had to leave the wagon because the flap at the end of the tent opened to reveal Ben's grinning face.

"I thought you two would never wake up, but Colby said it was okay if you overslept in this weather."

"It's not oversleeping when it's still dark outside," Naomi pointed out.

"Colby fixed breakfast for us," Ben announced.

Her father, less interested in the weather or whether they'd spent too long in bed, asked, "How did he manage it in this rain?"

"He cooked underneath the wagon."

Naomi wondered where he found dry wood, but she wasn't surprised. Colby could do anything except communicate with his heart.

Colby's rain-soaked face peered around the flap at the front of the wagon. "Are you ready to eat?"

Naomi wondered why water dripping from the end of his nose only served to make Colby more handsome. It wasn't fair. His face ought to be so unattractive that a silly woman like herself wouldn't fall in love with him. Yes, she'd admitted she loved him. She'd had two days with little more to do than try to convince herself that she *wasn't* in love with him. She had failed miserably.

"We'll eat only if you eat inside the wagon with us," her father said to Colby.

"I can eat under the wagon."

"No, you won't." Naomi was determined no one, especially Colby, would think she was nursing a broken heart. "You'll eat with us, or none of us will eat. That includes you, too," she said to Ben before he could lodge a protest.

"I agree with Naomi," her father said. "Now come on in. There's nothing in here that won't dry."

It was a tight fit. The bed of the wagon had been filled to the height of five feet with furniture, trunks, and boxes. The mattresses had been placed on top. There was enough room for three people to sleep side by side, but hardly enough space to sit up. Ben climbed up with his sister and father. After handing up plates of steaming beef stew, Colby chose to stand just out of the rain.

"Thank you," her father said to Colby. "This is a real treat."

"I confess I had a reason," Colby said.

"It's the river," Ben interjected.

"What about it?" their father asked.

"It has risen overnight," Colby said. "With all the rain we've been having, it's going to rise still higher."

"Can't we wait until it goes down?" her father asked.

"It could take a week or more," Colby said. "We don't have enough food and clean water to last that long. But there's another danger."

"Indians," Ben intoned.

"Indian attacks aren't as prevalent here as they are a hundred miles back," Colby said. "Being backed up against the river, we could be surrounded and cut off."

"Is the river really high?" Naomi asked.

"It's normally only a few yards wide with a rocky bottom that makes crossing easy. Now it's so high we'll have to swim the stock across."

"That doesn't sound hard," her father said.

"It's the rapid current that we have to worry about."

"Well let's not worry about it yet. I want to enjoy my breakfast."

Warm sunshine and a trickle of water in the river wouldn't have been enough to enable Naomi to enjoy her breakfast, not as long as Colby was only inches away. His presence made the air crackle with energy that reached out to everyone around him, an energy that had an especially powerful effect on her. It was like something tangible that wrapped itself around her making it impossible to ignore him. And she needed to ignore him. She *wanted* to ignore him. It was cruel that he had accomplished so easily what she couldn't despite her struggles.

How could three of the most important men in her life act like nothing had happened to her? Men were usually blind to emotional turmoil, but how could they not realize the significance of the silence, of the distance between them?

Maybe the rain was a godsend. Sibyl or Laurie would have known immediately something was wrong and wouldn't have been satisfied until they forced it out of her. Naomi didn't like the prospect of having to explain that she'd lost her heart to a man who told her he didn't believe in love. How stupid could she be? Had she been hoping her love would change his mind?

No, because she hadn't intended to fall in love. She hadn't even thought it possible. Which just went to show that being intelligent didn't mean you had common sense.

"Thank god you made coffee," her father said as he took the last swallow from his cup. "Now I feel like I can face anything."

That *anything* proved to be quite formidable. Everyone had gathered to stare at the torrent of water that should have been a quiet stream.

"Wouldn't it be better to wait?" Norman asked.

"Colby has already explained why we can't wait," Morley Sumner said. "I say we get started before the river gets any higher."

"Are there any strong swimmers in the group?" Colby asked. "I only need one other."

Several men glanced at the river, others at the

ground, but his question was met by silence until Ethan stepped forward.

"Do you think you can swim against that current?" Colby asked him.

"If you can, I can."

Naomi struggled to keep from raising a protest. Ethan was a good swimmer, but he was tall and thin, nothing like Colby's powerfully muscled body.

"We have to swim ropes across," Colby explained. "Once we attach them to something solid, we can start with the stock. In the meantime, collect all the empty barrels you can find. We will need those to help float the wagons across."

Naomi hated the feeling of helplessness, but there was nothing she could do as she watched the men tie lengths of rope together while Colby and Ethan stripped down. Clothed in nothing but underwear, the contrast between their bodies was even more apparent. Her body tensed, words of protest primed to leap from her tongue when her father spoke.

"Colby won't let anything happen to Ethan," he assured her.

"What if Colby can't take care of himself?"

"I haven't seen anything yet that man can't do."

That's because he hadn't tried to swim a rain-swollen river. Colby was still human, which meant he had limits. Much to her embarrassment, she found herself thinking about the breadth of his shoulders and the muscles that rippled across his back, rather than the dangers of the swim. She should be thinking about her brother's safety rather than the powerful arms that had held her in a tight embrace. And the last thing that should cross her mind at this moment was the generous mouth that had kissed her into surrender. What was wrong with her that she had let a man who didn't believe in love cause her to tumble head over heels? She was almost relieved when the two men waded into the churning water.

Will they make it?

The question thundered in her brain, but she was determined to remain confident regardless of the difficulty. It wasn't easy to do when the current swept both men off their course.

Ben grabbed for his father's hand. "The river's carrying them away, isn't it?" Fear made his voice weak and unsteady.

"The current will make it harder and take them longer to cross, but they're already making progress. The ropes will keep them safe."

Naomi was grateful for her father's calm reassurance. It enabled her to tell herself her father had a much better understanding of the situation than she did, that if he felt confident Colby and Ethan were safe, then she needn't worry. Still, it was hard when Ethan was swept farther down the river than Colby.

"The current is strongest in the middle," her father explained. "It'll get easier as they get closer to the far bank."

If they got closer. Their strength would give out while the river flowed on relentlessly. Colby's hands knifed through the water with a rhythmic precision that changed only when he had to dodge a piece of floating debris. As the minutes rolled by, the current fought them to a standstill. Naomi moved closer to her father until he took her hand in his. His fingers gave her a squeeze of reassurance, but neither of them took their eyes off the swimmers.

"Colby's out of the worst of the current," her father announced.

"What's he doing?" Ben asked.

Rather than continue across the river, he turned downstream.

"He's going to help Ethan," their father said.

"How?" Ben asked.

Ben didn't have to wait long for an answer. Upon reaching Ethan, Colby swam next to him.

"He's blocking the current," their father explained. "It's easier for Ethan to swim in Colby's wake."

Their progress was slow, but their approach to the far bank was steady. Everyone sighed with relief when Colby waded out of the river. Naomi thought he looked like some kind of god emerging from the water. Ethan's safe arrival was cause for spontaneous applause.

Naomi wanted to sink down to the ground and cry with relief. It was the realization that this was only the first step in a difficult and dangerous crossing that stiffened her back and hardened her resolve. This was not the life she'd expected, definitely not the life she wanted, but she wouldn't let it defeat her. Thousands of other women had succeeded. There was no reason she couldn't as well.

Once Colby had secured the ropes to a large cottonwood tree, he waded back into the water and swam across. Once out of the water, Colby came directly to Naomi.

"I want you to swim Shadow across," he said to her.

Naomi was too surprised to speak, but her father wasn't.

"She's not an experienced rider, and she's never tried to cross a flooded river."

"All she has to do is hang on. Shadow knows what to do. I'll be on your horse next to her. I'd rather she be safe on the other side before we start taking the wagons across."

Once Shadow was saddled, Colby lifted Naomi into the sidesaddle. "Hold on to his mane. Whatever you do, don't pull on the reins. Don't worry about the current. The ropes will keep you from being swept downstream."

Naomi had never learned to swim, and she'd only started riding a couple weeks ago.

She struggled to hide the fear that was making her nauseated. The other women would be watching from the bank. None of them knew how to swim, and most had never sat on a horse. If Naomi showed fear, it would make it more difficult for them when they had to cross the river in their wagons.

"I'm ready." She'd never uttered a greater untruth.

Shadow waded into the river without hesitation while Colby had to force her father's horse to brave the current. She felt a moment of near panic when Shadow started to swim. Only his head remained above water. The force of the current hit her with stunning impact, and she groped blindly under water to keep her hold on Shadow's mane. Her leg curled around the pommel hardly seemed sufficient to keep her in the saddle. She was in up to her bosom in the cold, angry river.

"Lean into the current,"

Colby's presence reassured her, but her father's horse was fighting to return to the bank. By the time they were in the swiftest part of the current, she and Shadow were several yards ahead.

She was on her own.

The current repeatedly carried Shadow against the ropes, but each time the powerful stallion found the strength to pull away. Naomi kept looking back to see how Colby was doing. That's why she missed seeing the tree branch headed toward her.

"Watch out!"

Colby pointed upstream at what looked like a small tree branch.

"Most of it is underwater," Colby called out. "It could be a whole tree."

Naomi's breath caught in her throat. There was nothing she could do to stop the branch—or tree. Could Shadow swim fast enough to get ahead of it, or should she try to stop him and hope it would pass ahead of them?

"Get on the other side of the ropes," Colby told her. "They'll hold the tree long enough for you to get past it."

Shadow swam with powerful strokes toward the shore, his eyes straight ahead. He didn't see the tree branch or respond when she tried to nudge him back toward the ropes. When Naomi leaned forward to reach for the reins, she nearly lost her balance. Holding on to Shadow's mane with all her strength, she managed to catch up the rein. Once she regained her balance, she pulled to the left. When Shadow didn't respond, she pulled harder. He moved closer to the rope, but it was still out of reach.

"Pull harder," Colby shouted.

Over the noise of the rushing river he sounded far away. She was going to have to do this herself.

She pulled on the rein, keeping the pressure up until Shadow came up against the ropes. With a sigh of relief, she reached over, grabbed hold of the double ropes, and pulled.

Nothing happened. The weight of the ropes plus the weight of the water they'd absorbed combined with the pull of the current made them too heavy for her to lift. The ropes might as well have been made of iron.

"Try again," Colby called from behind her.

"They're too heavy."

"I'll lift it out of the water back here. That'll help."

Colby had brought his horse up to the ropes. He leaned over and grabbed hold of the ropes. For an instant she thought he wouldn't be able to lift them, but with a grunt, he raised the ropes about two feet out of the water.

"Now you try."

The branch was almost upon her. If it was attached to a tree underwater, it would tangle Shadow's legs and both of them would drown. She grabbed the rope and pulled with all of her strength. After a moment's hesitation, the water released its grip, and she was able to lift the rope.

"Hold it over your head and push Shadow downstream."

It was all she could do to hold the rope out of the

water. She didn't have any strength left to force Shadow to change direction, but the branch was headed directly toward her. She had only seconds left. Using both hands and summoning all her strength, she lifted the ropes over her head and Shadow's. She immediately dropped the ropes and pulled hard on Shadow's rein. He pulled downstream just as the limb caught on the ropes.

Before she could breathe a sigh of relief, Shadow started to struggle.

"His feet are caught in branches underwater," Colby shouted. "Pull him farther downstream."

She tried, but Shadow's head went underwater, and she was swept away by the current.

Eighteen

NAOMI DIDN'T KNOW IF MOST PEOPLE'S LIVES PASSED before their eyes when they were about to die, but hers didn't. Instead, she was furious that something as temporary as a swollen river and a submerged tree could take away her chance to live, marry, and grow old watching her grandchildren. It was a senseless waste, and she didn't intend to accept it.

She thought Colby was shouting something, but she couldn't hear because her head kept going underwater. The weight of her clothes was pulling her down.

"Grab Shadow's tail."

That didn't make any sense until she realized Shadow hadn't drowned but was swimming several yards down river. She didn't know how to swim, but she had watched Colby and Ethan cross the river and had seen how they used their arms. Doing her best to imitate them, she started toward Shadow.

The river swept her closer to Shadow but not near enough to grab the tail she could see floating on the water behind him. Colby was too far away to help.

She knew what she had to do. The only question that remained was *could she do it?*

She was *not* going to die in this muddy river. If Colby could cross it three times, she could cross it once. Focusing all her energy, she forced her arms to cleave the water as she'd seen Colby do. Muscles that had never been called upon for such strenuous activity screamed under the strain. Each breath was more painful than the last. The frigid river leached the heat from her body and turned her fingers numb. She choked on mouthful after mouthful of muddy water, but she didn't give up. Her only chance was to get close enough to latch on to Shadow's tail before she was swept down the river to a cold, wet grave. The weight of her waterlogged clothes pulled against her, but she fought back, kicking with all her strength. Calling upon the last of her strength, she pushed through the swirling water and reached for Shadow's tail.

She was able to grasp a few hairs, but she needed a firmer grip if she expected him to pull her out of the river. Going hand over hand, she reached a point where she had a secure grip on his full tail. Now all she had to do was hold on until Shadow reached the shore.

But they had been swept past the open spot on the opposite bank. Now the bank was lined by trees with floodwaters swirling several feet up their trunks. If her skirt got tangled in the trees before her feet could reach ground, she'd be stranded.

She didn't know what caused her to look around. When she did, she saw Colby swimming toward her. What had happened to his horse? Why wasn't he headed toward the shore instead of toward her?

She could hardly believe it when she realized Colby was catching up with her. He came up to her on the downstream side.

"Let go of Shadow's tail and hold on to me."

"Why?" Fear told her not to let go.

"He's going to avoid the trees and wait until he finds an opening downstream. We need to get out as soon as we can."

Her hands felt like they were locked onto Shadow's tail. They refused to respond to her signal to let go.

"You can let go now," Colby urged. "The current will bring you to me."

It took all her willpower to release Shadow's tail. Almost immediately the water carried her up against Colby.

"Grab my waist, and don't let go until I tell you."

That wasn't easy because he was a big man and he was kicking with his feet. She grabbed hold of his long underwear and hoped they didn't rip.

Oddly enough, now that she started to feel safe, events from her past flashed through her mind. She remembered her mother's smile, a sunny day when the whole family went berry picking, the time her mother made her a bright yellow dress to wear to church, the time by the creek when Colby kissed her, her father's look after her mother died. She had no doubt her father had loved her mother the way she loved Colby. If she only knew how to make him believe.

When they reached the trees, Colby guided her to one with a small trunk. "Hold on. I'll look for a place to climb out."

She felt silly hugging a tree as though it was her

best friend, but under the circumstances it was. Colby hadn't gone far before he turned back.

"I was able to get a footing," he told her. "Take my hand."

Colby pulled her through the trees and the swirling current until she felt her feet touch ground. It was soft mud, but she didn't care. She had made it across. She was safe.

They had been washed more than a quarter of a mile down the river before they had been able to climb out. The cold rain and her wet clothes drained her body of warmth. Yet it was easy to forget her misery because Colby wore nothing but his wet long underwear that clung to him like a second skin. Naomi had been around her father and brothers too long to be unfamiliar with the male anatomy, but it took on a different significance when it came to Colby.

She couldn't remember paying attention to a man's backside or legs. That changed when she followed Colby out of the river. His underwear clung to his butt and thighs. She could see the muscles move as his butt cheeks and thighs swelled and contracted as he waded ashore. It was like an erotic dance. It appalled her that she could be so fascinated by his body, but she couldn't take her eyes off him. It was all she could do not to reach out and touch him. She was climbing out of a flooded river, for goodness sakes. How could she be so fascinated by a man's backside? She ought to be shouting hallelujahs for her deliverance. Instead, she was lusting after a man who'd endangered his own life to save her.

Maybe lust, love, and thankfulness were all part

of the same package. It certainly was for her when it came to Colby.

❧

It took several hours to complete the crossing, but by midafternoon all the wagons were scattered along the riverbank. Everything from clothes to bedding would need to be laid out to dry when the weather cleared. Minor repairs were underway while the livestock grazed on fresh grass. There was an extra bustle in activity from knowing that the last river had been crossed with no loss of lives and only minor damage to property.

"I don't know why we couldn't have waited until the river went down," Norman complained to anyone who would listen. "We were lucky nobody drowned."

"That's because we had Colby," her father said. "Without him, we wouldn't have gotten this far."

"I still say—"

"You've complained enough, Norman. Everybody's tired of hearing you. For the first time in your life, you don't know any more than the rest of us. In fact," the doctor continued relentlessly, "if you don't start paying attention instead of thinking you already know the answers, even the children will know more than you."

Naomi was shocked to hear her father speak to Norman like that. It didn't matter that he had only put into words what everyone was feeling. He was never rude to anyone.

"Why don't you help Sibyl with the wagons?" Vernon Edwards said to his son-in-law. "Getting everything reorganized in three wagons is too much for one person."

Norman looked like he wanted to argue, but Naomi's father made a shooing gesture. Rather than infuriate Norman as she had expected, he stiffened then turned and walked off.

"I wouldn't be surprised if you wind up in Hell for forcing your daughter to marry that man," her father said to Vernon. "I'd rather Naomi die an old maid than marry a man like Norman."

"Who my daughter marries is none of your business."

Naomi thought Vernon looked uncomfortably guilty before he turned and left.

Still, it could be exhaustion. The crossing had been long and difficult. The animals had been forced to swim across in a group, but they had brought the wagons over one at a time. The swift current had nearly capsized two of them, but the rocky bottom at the ford made getting out of the river easier.

"I'd better thank Colby for pulling you out of the river," her father said to her.

"You've thanked him every time he's come within shouting distance. I think he knows how you feel."

"He can't," her father said. "*I* didn't know how I felt until I saw you go under. I think I aged a hundred years before you grabbed Shadow's tail."

Shadow had come back, but her father's horse was still missing. Colby had apologized for abandoning the animal, but her father had said his daughter's life was worth more than a thousand horses. Morley Sumner had cut the tree loose from the ropes, and everybody had crossed without having to dodge any more debris.

"Colby says we don't have any more big rivers to cross," she told her father.

"Roy Greene told us the Rio Grande is on the other side of Santa Fe. We won't have Colby when we have to cross that."

Naomi didn't want to be reminded that the time was fast approaching when Colby would leave them. She'd overheard him telling Norman that it was about three day's travel to where the desert trail crossed the Mora River and hooked up with the route from Bent's Fort. Since there was only one trail from there to Santa Fe, Colby said they'd have no trouble traveling the last ninety miles on their own.

"Have you had any luck convincing him to stay?"

Naomi resented being made to feel it was her fault that Colby was leaving. He'd always been clear that he would leave them at La Junta. His partiality for her company probably led everyone to expect he would change his mind, but he hadn't.

"Colby rarely changes his mind." She looked down at her feet.

"Anybody can see you'd make him a perfect wife."

"He's running from something that had a powerful effect on him. Until he comes to terms with that, he's not going to be happy or able to make anyone else happy."

Her father gave her a comforting hug. "And I thought the man was intelligent. I'm sorry, sweetheart. I know how you feel about him."

She loved him and was certain he loved her in return. She didn't understand why he couldn't see that. She didn't know what Elizabeth was like, but just because one woman had betrayed him didn't mean she would, too. But he wasn't going to give her a chance to prove she was different. He'd closed his mind to all other possibilities. She had the horrible feeling she'd done the same in that she could never love another man as she loved him. She would be doomed to live her life alone.

The restraints that had been holding back the dammed up emotions inside her burst. She flung her arms around her father's neck and burst into tears.

❧

The camp was filled with excitement. After crossing the Mora River—a fast-moving, muddy little stream—they had met up with a group of traders who had agreed to escort them the rest of the way to Santa Fe. For the first time since crossing the Arkansas River, they were no longer alone. Paul Hill put everyone's feelings into words.

"I thought living in a small village like Spencer's Clearing was lonely," he'd said. "I didn't know what loneliness was until we crossed the Arkansas River. For a while I was convinced we were the only people in the world."

Naomi didn't need anybody to explain why, instead of feeling relieved to be joining a large train, she was feeling lonelier than ever. Colby was taking leave of everyone in their little group. He was saving his good-byes to her for last.

"I wish Colby wouldn't leave," Cassie said to Naomi. "I feel safer with him around. I'm sure these people are nice, but we don't know them."

Naomi had joined Cassie in her wagon because she couldn't bear to be alone at this moment. It was almost impossible not to see or hear Colby saying good-bye to someone. It was like having the fact of his leaving pounded into her head time after time. She had prepared herself for one leave-taking. She couldn't endure a dozen.

"I'm sure we'll be safe. Colby said he has worked with some of the men in the group."

Cassie cuddled her baby. It was hard to believe how much Little Abe had grown since leaving Independence, Missouri, nearly two months ago. Naomi hoped Cassie would find a good father for him. He was such a sweet, cheerful baby; every woman in the train had done her best to spoil him.

"I thought he was going to marry you," Cassie said. "Didn't you?"

Not for the first time had Naomi wished that people in a small community didn't know everything about everybody else. She also wished Cassie could learn a little subtlety.

"I guess it's no secret that I'm fond of Colby," Naomi confessed. "Unfortunately, he's not equally fond of me."

"Anybody can see he's in love with you," Cassie insisted. "What did you do to him to make him leave?"

She supposed it was only natural that everyone would believe she'd been the one at fault. After all, if she'd given him what he wanted, he would have stayed. She had. He just hadn't recognized it.

"He said from the beginning that he would leave when we reached La Junta."

"But that was before he started liking you."

"Like is not love. If you're going to hold me responsible for his not falling in love with me, I guess that's what I did wrong."

The baby stirred. "He's hungry, the greedy little fella," Cassie said fondly. "If Ethan hadn't made me eat, I wouldn't have had enough milk for him."

Being made responsible for Cassie had had a maturing effect on Ethan. He'd need it wherever they ended up. She couldn't help wondering where Colby would end up. According to him, there were thousands of empty places in the West. He just had to pick one.

Ethan appeared at the end of the wagon. "Colby has come to say good-bye to us."

Cassie handed her baby to Naomi then climbed out of the wagon. "I wish you'd stay," she told Colby. "I feel safe with you."

"You've got Ethan to look after you, and everybody else in the train to make sure you have everything you need. You'll be perfectly safe with the new folks."

"It won't be the same," she pouted.

"We'd never have survived without your help," Ethan said, shaking Colby's hand.

"You can't be sure of that," Colby said. "There are a lot of good men in this group. Now I want to say good-bye to Naomi. The traders are getting ready to leave, so I don't have much time."

"We can say good-bye here." Naomi knew it was cowardly, but she wasn't sure she could keep her composure otherwise.

"Don't be silly," Ethan said. "Give Cassie the baby.

He's hungry and needs to be fed. Besides, I'm sure Colby doesn't want us hearing what he has to say to you."

She didn't want to hear it, but it looked like what she wanted didn't matter. She waited until Cassie was back in the wagon before she reluctantly handed over the baby. Then she allowed Colby to help her down from the wagon. Without a word, he led her toward a maple tree where Shadow waited saddled and ready. Unable to wait any longer for him to speak—fearful of what he might say when he did—Naomi decided to go first. Though when she tried to speak, her throat choked off the words.

"I'm sorry I have to leave."

"Then why don't you stay?" The words exploded from her before she could stop them. Before she could mortify herself further by begging him to stay, pride came to her rescue. "You don't have to answer that." She was relieved her voice sounded steadier than she felt. "You've told me over and over."

Colby put his hand under her chin and raised her head until she was looking into his eyes.

"You have so much to give. Warmth, kindness, caring, even love. You deserve that and more in return. I know you think I can give it to you, but I can't."

She was tempted to argue, but she knew nothing she could say would make him stay. Silence would allow her to keep what was left of her pride.

"You're a very special person."

But not special enough for him to love, not special enough for him to give up spending the rest of his life as some kind of hermit.

"You'll thrive out here. You've got the courage and the intelligence to meet all kinds of challenges."

She'd failed in the challenge of getting him to admit he loved her. Not a very auspicious beginning.

"I've given your father the names of a few men to look up when you get to Santa Fe. You can trust any one of them to help you find a place for your town and make sure you get there."

That was more than she could endure in silence. "Why do you care where we go or what happens to us? You'll be hundreds of miles away. You'll never see us again."

"During these past weeks, I've gotten to know and like nearly everyone in the train. Why wouldn't I care what happened to them?" He paused before adding, "You know I care what happens to you."

She was *not* going to cry. This leaving-taking couldn't last much longer. The traders had already hitched up their teams. The call to start would come at any moment.

"I'm sorry you're leaving, too." It was difficult, but she forced herself to look him in the eye. "You're mistaken about love and your inability to give it. You're crazy to plant yourself in some godforsaken corner of this wilderness and waste your life. Most important of all, you're a coward not to face whatever it is that has driven you to isolate yourself. You're a wonderful man who could make some woman a marvelous husband and some children an incredible father. No matter what happened to you in the past, it's stupid to waste all of that. Now I've said too much, and the traders are ready to leave. I wish you the best on your journey, and hope you find what you're looking for. Good-bye."

She stood on her tiptoes to give him a kiss on the cheek. Without waiting for him to speak or return her kiss, she turned and walked away praying he wouldn't say anything more.

He didn't, and that broke her heart.

❧

It had been two days since Colby left the train, and Naomi hadn't been able to think of anything else. Where was he? What was he doing? Why had he left? Would he have stayed if she'd tried harder? She was so desperate to get her mind off Colby she'd begged Noah to let Laurie travel with her. He hadn't wanted to, but Norman had said Naomi needed some diversion so she'd stop moping over a man who didn't want her. Not content with insulting Naomi, he added that they were well rid of a man who was too much like an Indian. Naomi was sorry Frank Oliver had failed in his attempt to murder Norman. She considered shooting him herself, but decided against it only because of the distress it would cause her family.

"Ignore him," Laurie had said.

"I've been ignoring him for years, but it hasn't gotten any easier."

It had taken two days, but Laurie had relaxed enough that they could talk like they had before her marriage. Naomi had forgotten how much she missed those talks. And it did help to take her mind off Colby.

"Have you noticed that man who keeps looking at

you?" Naomi asked Laurie. They had finished their midday and were back on the trail.

"No one's been looking at me," Laurie insisted.

They were riding in the wagon, Naomi driving and Laurie sitting next to her

"I've seen him," Naomi insisted. "He looks at you like he'd like to swallow you whole."

Laurie colored. "You're being ridiculous."

"No, I'm not. His name's Jared Smith. He was in the army."

"How do you know?"

"I asked. You can't think I could fail to find out anything I could about such a handsome man, especially when he was staring at my cousin?"

"If you think he's so handsome, why don't you go after him?" Laurie was immediately penitent. "Sorry. I know you can't think of anybody but Colby."

"Well, Colby's gone so we might as well concentrate on Mr. Smith. I might consider giving him a smile or two, but he's clearly not interested in anyone but you."

"I hope that's not true. Do you think Noah would let me stay here another minute if he thought another man was looking at me?" Laurie looked as though it was all she could do to keep from crying. "I really want to stay with you all the way to Santa Fe. It's practically the first time in a year I've been able to take a deep breath."

Naomi was sorry she'd teased Laurie about Mr. Smith. She adored her cousin and knew how miserable she had been since her marriage. She did everything she could—including wearing tent-like dresses—to insure Noah didn't believe other men were looking at her, or that she was trying to attract attention.

"Do you want me to say something to him? He really has been quite obvious."

"No. I don't believe he's been staring at me. But if he has, asking him to stop would only make it worse. We'll be in Santa Fe in about three days. I'm sure we'll never see him again after that. I can't imagine that he'll be going to some remote corner of the Arizona Territory." Laurie sighed. "I wish Colby were still here. I'm sure your father and the rest of the committee will do their best to find us a good guide, but doubt he'll be half as good as Colby."

Everyone in the train had told her how much they missed Colby and how difficult it was going to be to find anyone they trusted as much. Naomi appreciated how they felt, but she wished they'd express their discontent to someone else. *Anyone* else. Their unhappiness was nothing when compared to hers. It was hard on her when they insisted on reminding her of his good qualities and the thoughtful things he'd done. She knew better than anyone the extent of the loss they'd suffered.

But Colby was gone, and it was time everyone accepted that.

Even if she couldn't.

∽

"This is the weirdest town I've ever seen," Ben said. "All the houses look like they're made of mud."

"It's called adobe," their father said.

"It looks like mud to me."

Naomi agreed, but she had little thought to spare for the city. It had been three full days since Colby had left. Three days during which—rather than think of him—she'd tried to fill her mind with thoughts of reaching a town, even a small one, that had streets, businesses, churches, homes, and people. She had envisioned a place not very different from Spencer's Clearing. Santa Fe wasn't like that.

Adobe homes were scattered along the trail coming into town. Some were modest dwellings of one story high. Others possessed courtyards enclosed by adobe walls. Still, others had large fields behind. Timbers used to support the roofs protruded from the walls like fingers, some casting shadows on the walls like the bars of a jail cell. A church built of the same brown material towered above the town. She wondered if its two stumpy, square towers contained bells. The open fields beyond the houses were populated mainly by sheep and goats.

They followed the traders' wagons across a small river to a plaza that appeared to be the center of town. A busy flow of traffic had churned the streets to dust. Traders' carts lined the streets in front of businesses, one of which advertised stoves for sale. A long building with a spacious portal flanked another side. From Colby's description, she knew it had to be the Palace of the Governors. Burros carrying wood and what looked like cornstalks were everywhere, some standing, others lying down under the weight of their load. Men who appeared to be local citizens drove open carts with solid wood wheels pulled by spotted oxen.

The inhabitants appeared to be friendly. Some were

obviously wealthy, but most appeared to be wretchedly poor. Yet, they seemed quite happy and content. Roy Greene had said it was a city mired in vice and degradation, but it looked peaceful, even slumbering, to Naomi.

"Now that we're here, what are we going to do?" she asked her father.

"Once we find a place to camp, we'll meet and decide what to do next."

Ben pointed to the square. "I want to say here."

"I doubt they'll let us camp in the middle of town," their father said. "We have nothing to sell and little money to spend."

The plaza was surrounded by a white picket fence. Several trees inside offered shade from the relentless sun. From its empty state Naomi supposed it was primarily used on festival days.

"We'll probably park the wagons outside of town," her father said. "The main thing we have to do is decide on a location for our new town and hire a guide to take us there."

"Will that take long?"

"I hope not. Arizona is a long way from here."

"What are we going to do now? It's nearly dark."

"After we eat, I'm going to find a hotel. I want one night when I don't have to sleep on the ground or sandwiched in between the two of you."

Naomi hoped a real bed would make a difference. She hadn't been able to sleep since Colby left.

❧

Colby had been calling himself a fool for the last six days, but that hadn't made any difference. He had still followed the trail into Santa Fe, though he kept his distance. At least twice a day he'd ridden close enough to be able to catch a glimpse of Naomi's wagon. He knew they would have no difficulty getting to Santa Fe, but he had to *know* she was safe. Now he was camping on the slopes of the Sangre de Cristo Mountains close enough to see the lights of the town. He was locked in place, unable to go forward or backward.

Forward would have been to a remote valley where he could spend the rest of his life in a mostly solitary existence. Yet what had once seemed so necessary to his peace of mind had lost its appeal. Going backward meant going down to Santa Fe and finding Naomi.

If his parents couldn't love him—what was more natural than that parents would love their children regardless of their differences—maybe it wasn't possible for *anybody* to love him. That would explain why Elizabeth's love didn't last.

Naomi's love wouldn't last either.

He poured his coffee over the dying embers of his fire. It was cold and tasteless, pretty much how his life felt just now. He ought to saddle up and ride north. He'd already accepted that cold and tasteless was how things were going to be. Naomi said she loved him, but so had Elizabeth. How could he be sure now when he thought he'd been so sure before?

Enough! It was time to leave. He scooped a bucket of water from a nearby stream and doused his campfire. Five minutes later Shadow was saddled and he was ready to ride. He mounted up. With a gentle nudge in Shadow's flanks, he was on his way.

Headed down the mountain toward Santa Fe.

❧

"I feel selfish having a hotel room all to myself," Naomi said to her father.

"It's not your fault that neither Norman nor Noah would let your cousins share your room. I don't know what trouble they think the three of you might cause."

Naomi knew that wasn't the reason. Norman didn't trust her influence on his wife. Noah was too jealous of Laurie to let her out of his sight.

"It seems only fair that you have a room when I do," her father said as they climbed the stairs to the second floor.

Ethan said he had to stay with Cassie, and Ben had jumped at the chance to be on his own for the night.

"Can we really afford it?"

"I'm using part of the money Paul Hill paid me for giving him two healthy babies."

Naomi smirked at her father. "I thought his wife did that."

Her father grinned back. "She did the preliminary work. I was responsible for the part that counted."

They had reached the second floor landing. Her father was staying on the first floor, but he'd insisted upon seeing her safely to her room.

"Sleep well," her father said. "We can't afford to stay in a hotel every night."

Naomi unlocked and opened the door to her room. "After sleeping in the wagon or under it, I might not be able to sleep in a real bed."

"Give it a try." Her father kissed her cheek and handed her the lantern. "See you in the morning."

"Night."

Naomi closed and locked the door before placing the lantern on the table beside the bed. It didn't take long to wash her face and change into her nightgown. Too keyed up to lie down just yet, she walked to the window and looked out.

The cloudless sky provided enough moonlight to illuminate the street below. It seemed there was almost as much activity as during the day. Several boys were playing a game in the square that involved kicking a ball, but it seemed too random to have an objective. An occasional cart moved through the street while two couples strolled through the park. People filled the boardwalks conducting business they'd put off during the heat of the day. Others were just starting to look for a place to eat. Naomi couldn't imagine waiting until after nine o'clock to eat supper. She wondered if Colby would eat so late. He never seemed to have any trouble eating his meals on their schedule while he was with them.

She came away from the window. She wondered where he was now. She couldn't imagine living alone in any of the places they'd passed since leaving Independence. Where would he live? What would he eat? What would he do?

She had to accept that none of that concerned her any longer. She had to put him out of her mind just as she was certain he had put her out of his. She was headed toward a new life, one that would need all the attention and effort she could give it. It wouldn't do her or anyone else any good to have her mooning over a man who'd turned his back on her.

She walked over to the bed and settled on the

edge. The mattress wasn't soft, but it was better than sleeping on the ground.

The problem that faced her now wasn't the mattress but finding a way to fall out of love. It would have been so much easier if Colby had been cruel, thoughtless, or dishonorable, but he was the opposite of all that. How could he have held her like he did, kissed her senseless, if he hadn't loved her at least a little bit? He was an honest and straightforward man.

It wouldn't do any good to keep thinking of all the reasons why he should have stayed. He was gone and that was that. She got in bed, and pulled the covers over her. The sheets smelled freshly laundered. Now if the mattress had only felt a little less like a board, she might be able to drift off to sleep.

She was aware of voices coming from the street. They were a mixture of English, Spanish, and dialects or languages she'd never heard. That seemed so strange after living her whole life among people who spoke only English and with the same accent, but in some way Colby had made it seem almost normal.

She turned on her side and pulled the pillow over her head. She had to stop thinking about Colby. Maybe it would help if she could block out the voices from the street below. She would try to imagine she was back home in Kentucky in her own bed. She would make a list of the chores she had to do the next day, arrange them in order of importance, and decide what she needed to complete each job. By the time she did all of that, she'd always been on the verge of falling asleep.

Only it didn't work anymore. She wasn't in Kentucky,

she wasn't in her own bed, and everything was so different she hardly knew where to begin. The future was a huge blank. How could she sleep when she couldn't stop thinking about it? The worst part was that she felt terribly alone. It didn't seem to matter that she had her father and two brothers, or that the rest of the community would be with her. Colby had a way of making sense of this new and daunting world, a way that made it seem less frightening and threatening.

A knock on the door broke her train of thought. What could her father want, and why was he knocking so softly?

She sat up, shoved her feet into her slippers, and then got up. There was enough light coming through the window that she didn't need to light the lantern. The soft knocks came again followed by a whispered request to open the door. Thoroughly confused, Naomi decided not to open the door just yet.

"Papa, is that you? What's wrong?" When the answer came, it left her so weak she wasn't sure she could stand.

"It's Colby. Let me in."

Nineteen

NAOMI'S HAND SHOOK SO BADLY SHE COULD BARELY work the key in the lock. The moment the door was open, Colby rushed in and closed it behind him. She opened her mouth to say something—she had no idea what—but he took her in his arms and kissed her until any thought seemed superfluous. Colby was here, and she was in his arms.

"What are you doing here?" The answer seemed obvious, yet the deeper meaning was not.

"I love you."

She had been certain those words would answer every question, banish every doubt, but they didn't.

"Why have you come sneaking into my room like you're afraid someone will see you?"

They hadn't moved. Colby still held her in an embrace, and the room remained in shadows.

"If they find me, they're liable to try to hang me. I didn't tell you this before, but I set fire to Elizabeth's father's house. That's why they won't let me back in Santa Fe."

Naomi never doubted that Colby could be a

dangerous person when provoked, but she hadn't expected anything like this. "That was horrible."

"I know." He kissed her. "Now I don't want to talk about that anymore. I came here to tell you that I love you, that I was a fool to think I could leave you, and that I want to marry you."

Naomi disengaged herself from Colby's embrace and stepped back. She needed light. She had to be able to see his face, look into his eyes. She lit the lamp, adjusted the wick, and motioned for Colby to sit on the edge of the bed next to her. "What made you change your mind?"

Colby sat next to her, took her hands in his, looked into her eyes. Even in the limited light of the lantern, she could tell he was seeing her with different eyes. There was a warmth there she'd never seen before, a softness—and a vulnerability. She'd always felt he'd been honest with her, but despite the kisses and the embraces, he'd managed to maintain a distance. That had disappeared. He was here now, all of him.

"I was camped on the foot of the mountains just outside of town. I got on my horse intending to ride away. Instead I turned toward Santa Fe despite knowing I would be jailed if I was caught."

"How did you find me?"

"I have my ways."

"You still haven't told me what happened to make you change your mind about love," Naomi said.

"I couldn't stop thinking about you. It's like we're connected. I know this doesn't make a lot of sense, but when I left I felt like a part of me was missing.

Everything I saw reminded me of you in some way. Everything I did—saddle up, light a fire, top a rise—reminded me of times we did them together. You were all I dreamed about."

She could see his expression soften.

"You would grin at me like you knew a secret you wouldn't share. Other times you'd disappear, and I wouldn't be able to find you. There were times when I would wake up in a terrible state."

Naomi didn't need an explanation of what happened in those dreams. She was thankful for the dim light that hid her blushes. Yet if what Colby said was true, why had he shown no signs of that attraction when he was with her?

"You were always a gentleman with me."

"Do you think it was easy? You are a beautiful woman, Naomi."

He reached for the lamp and pulled Naomi to her feet. By holding the lamp close to the window, he was able to cause the glass pane to reflect Naomi's image. "Look at yourself and tell me what you see."

Naomi felt rather foolish staring at herself. Everything looked the same, her nose, her eyes, her skin, her hair. She wasn't ugly, but she wasn't beautiful, especially when compared to Sibyl. Nor did her body have Laurie's curves. She wasn't even as pretty as Cassie.

"I see an ordinary face that shows the strain of enduring nightmares, leaving my home, and traveling through a wilderness to a land I know nothing about. I used to think I still had a bit of my youthful look. Now it's gone."

"I see a woman, not a girl. Someone who has experienced life and knows something of its joys and sorrows, someone who's able to appreciate the present without forgetting the past or ignoring the future."

Naomi peered at the shadowy image before her. Where did he see any of that? In her eyes? In her expression?

"I see a woman of principle who knows what she wants from life and won't settle for less."

He was making this up. How could she show on the outside what she couldn't figure out on the inside?

"I see a woman who will rise to any challenge, conquer it, and then ask for more."

He was wrong there. She had wanted to go back to Kentucky from the moment they left.

"I also see a woman of strong passions and great determination who doesn't know that she's capable of much more than even she imagines."

She turned around to protest, but he guided her to back to the window.

"I see a woman who is beautiful in the eyes of everyone else even if not in her own. Your eyes are always alive. At times they sparkle with excitement or mischief, but they're always welcoming."

"Nonsense. Ben says my eyes scold him more severely than my words."

Colby ignored her interruption.

"I'm particularly fond of your lips, and not just because I like to kiss them. When you smile, they make your eyes shine brighter. I especially like them when they pucker because you're trying to keep from laughing."

This was ridiculous. Whoever talked about lips like they were a separate part of the face?

"I especially like your hair when you're not wearing your bonnet and it falls over your shoulders."

He was exaggerating. Her skin was chapped and sunburned, her hair as dry as straw.

Colby slipped his arm around her waist and drew her to him. "You would make any man hunger for you. You can't know how many nights I couldn't sleep because you were so close I could reach out and touch you. Just having my arm around you is making me want things."

Much to her surprise, Naomi felt an unfamiliar stirring in her belly, a kernel of warmth that was expanding much too rapidly. Could this be the kind of warmth Colby was feeling? If so, did it mean for her what it meant for him? She had felt a physical attraction to men before, but it had been a kind of excitement, maybe giddiness, but not this heat that was invading every part of her body. What she felt for Colby was much more than physical attraction. She was in love with him. She wanted to marry him. She wanted to sleep next to him and bear his children.

That meant she wanted to endow him with her body as well as her heart.

She had known this in an abstract way, but there was nothing abstract about Colby's arm around her or the nearness of his body. There was nothing imaginary about the emotions stirring inside her nor, she was certain, the feelings stirring inside Colby.

Colby placed the lamp back on the table and took her in his arms. "I've been thinking about holding you and kissing you practically every minute since I left. I kept thinking I would never see you again."

"I didn't think I would see you again, either."

"Did you think of me?"

She couldn't repress a smile. "I opened the door for you. I'm in a hotel room alone with you. What do you think?"

He returned her smile. "I was afraid you'd be so angry you wouldn't want to see me. I wouldn't let myself believe that because then I really *would* bury myself in some remote valley."

"I want to marry you, too, but I can't leave my father and brothers. I don't know where we're going or what we're going to do when we get there. Norman is looking for—"

"I know the perfect place in Arizona. I was thinking about going there myself. I'll talk to your father and the others tomorrow."

"Are you sure? I don't want you to go somewhere just because I'm there."

"I can't think of a better reason. Now stop worrying about the future and concentrate on the present."

That was an invitation that had profound implications.

Naomi didn't trust herself to speak. His declaration was all she had hoped for and more.

"I'll follow you wherever you go," he said to fill the silence. "I'll make a nuisance of myself by asking you to marry me at least once every hour. I'll waste away so badly your father will have to take me on as a permanent patient."

"Stop!" Naomi couldn't repress a chuckle. "I'm not marrying anybody just so they won't starve themselves to death."

"I can think of lots of other things to do."

"I'm sure you can, but they won't convince me to marry you, either."

"What will? Tell me, and I'll do it."

She leaned forward and kissed him.

Colby embraced her. Their kiss was long and heated. Having finally removed the barriers to admitting their love, they couldn't get enough of each other. Being seated made it awkward so Colby stood and pulled her into an embrace. If his kisses had seemed intense before, they were overwhelming now. She couldn't imagine how a man full of such passion could have thought he could hide. One day all of this warmth, this unused heat, would have burst into flame and destroyed him.

She was more than willing to share his heat. She loved her family, but she'd always felt a little lonely, different, out of step. No man had appealed to her. Certainly none had awakened the fire that Colby stoked with so little effort. The intensity of what she felt for him scared her, but she was eager to embrace it. Her future was full of unknown challenges and nameless dangers, but she wouldn't hesitate to face it as long as Colby was by her side. She found it almost miraculous that such a man could have fallen in love with her.

She felt naked in his embrace, the thinness of her nightgown hardly a barrier against the hardened muscles of his body. It was merely a tissue separating her warming skin from his rough hands as they wandered over her back. It was easy to imagine it didn't exist, that he was caressing her flesh. The feel of his hands on her body was as unsettling as it was impossible to resist. Never before had she wanted to share herself with a man. She'd always insisted on keeping a distance between them.

Now that had changed.

It was almost impossible to feel too close to Colby. She had tried so hard to convince herself this would never happen that she was finding it hard to believe. A sliver of fear that all this might still be snatched from her caused her to hold him tighter. Being in his arms was more wonderful than she had ever imagined. She wanted to sink deeper and deeper into his embrace until they had become inseparable. She held him tighter, kissed him harder, but more wasn't enough. They were still separated. She wouldn't be content until each had been absorbed by the other, until they became one in spirit if not in body.

The hardness pressing against her thigh left no doubt about the effect of their closeness on Colby. When his hands moved from her back to cup her breasts, she had no question about the effect on her. She wanted him as badly as he wanted her.

With a moan muffled by their kiss, she pressed against him. She suffered a shock when his hands left her breasts, but it lasted only until she realized he was loosening the tie that secured her nightgown. When he pulled the gown off her shoulders and let it slide down her body and pool around her feet, she shivered from the chill of excitement, of anticipation. Colby lifted her in his arms and lay her on the bed. She held out her hand beckoning him to join her.

"In a moment."

Watching him undress was an erotic experience. She had already seen him in his underwear, the wet cotton clinging to his body, but this was different. She could watch the play of muscles along his shoulders, over his back, through his thighs with the certainty that she would soon feel these muscles against her skin, under her fingertips. The heat coursing through her body increased so rapidly she squirmed in anticipation. He unbuttoned the top of his long underwear to reveal a scattering of dark brown hair. She barely had time to take that in before he lowered his clothes below his thighs and his erection sprang free.

She snapped her eyes shut. The thought of having to accommodate him inside her body threatened to turn her chills of anticipation to shivers of apprehension.

She opened her eyes when the bed sank under his weight. He lay down next to her and pulled her to him. "You know I'd never hurt you, don't you?"

"Yes." Her voice was only a thread.

"If I do anything that hurts or upsets you, promise you'll let me know, and I'll stop."

She nodded.

Rolling up on his elbow, he took her in his arms and kissed her. Welcoming his embrace, she threw her arms around him. A network of fine welts across his back reminded her of what she'd seen the day her father treated his injury. She broke the kiss. "Where did these welts come from?"

"It's not important."

He tried to kiss her again, but she pushed him away. "It is important. I have to know."

He sighed. "My father thought he could make me

into the son he wanted by beating what he disliked out of me. Now let's not think about it anymore."

How could she *not* think about it? Her brothers had been punished, but never in a way that would cause scars. What kind of man had his father been? She had to know what he had done to warrant such brutal punishment.

But Colby sabotaged her by turning his attention to her breasts. When he teased her nipple with his thumb, it made it hard to remember what she wanted to ask him. When he took her nipple into his mouth and nipped it with his teeth, she forgot his father, the scars, everything. Nothing mattered except what he was doing to her body. She found it hard to believe any part of her body could so completely dominate the rest of her.

Squeezing gently, he alternately laved her nipples with his tongue and nipped them with his teeth until she writhed under him, moaning in appreciation of exquisite sensations she hadn't thought possible. When his mouth forsook her breasts, wove its way down her belly until it reached her navel, she was positive she'd reached the height of decadence. Surely God would never approve of anything so deliciously marvelous. No sooner had that thought crossed her mind than she decided she was mistaken. No one else could have made such a wonder possible.

It was so wonderful she didn't realize Colby's hand had moved down her side and along her thigh until it slipped between her legs. She tensed. She didn't mean to, but she couldn't help it.

"I won't hurt you," Colby said.

"I know." She concentrated on making herself relax, but it wasn't easy. Colby resumed his attention to her breast, but his hand remained between her legs, touching, caressing, probing. She felt hot and moist. Even though her father had explained how a man and woman made love, it was an unfamiliar sensation, one he'd failed to mention.

"Open for me. Your knees are pressed together."

She hadn't realized her body was so rigid. Yet when she did manage to relax, the shock of Colby's hand moving inside her nearly caused her to tense again. She knew this was supposed to happen, but talking about it and having it happen weren't at all the same. Sensations that had only moments before centered on her breasts, now clustered around Colby's probing fingers sending shock waves of pleasure rocketing through her from one end to the other.

Papa hadn't mentioned that, either.

It seemed incredible that anything could feel so powerfully wonderful. Waves of pleasure washed over her. She felt encased in a cocoon of sensations, each more powerful, more encompassing than the last.

Then Colby touched something inside her that lit up her entire being like a flash of lightning. It was impossible for anything to be that overwhelming, but the waves kept coming until they seemed to rush from her like a stream bursting from its banks. Before she could recover enough to utter a sound, Colby had entered her.

She didn't marvel at how easy or painless it felt, but how natural. She didn't know why she'd been so apprehensive.

She didn't have much time to think about that because the sensations that radiated to every part of her body had taken over all conscious thought. Everything was the same as before but only more so. She had always thought Colby was a marvelous man, but she'd had no notion he could give her such incredible pleasure. And it was all the sweeter because it was Colby who held her, who loved her, who was bringing her to a sexual peak that was as unlooked-for as it was gladly received. She was barely aware that she had begun to move with Colby, rising to meet him, falling away, then rising again. But as the fetters of rapture encircled her more tightly, she wrapped her legs around Colby trying to draw him deeper and deeper into her.

Without any warning, her body went rigid and she felt she was about to explode. Then the dam broke and the tension flowed from her like water in a turbulent stream.

❧

Naomi woke with a feeling of well-being that was so convincing she was certain there were no difficulties ahead she and Colby couldn't conquer together. She couldn't tell what time it was, but if the night sky was anything to go by, dawn was still several hours away. She could hardly wait for the chance to see Colby in the daylight, to tell her father that Colby did love her and they were going to be married. He knew the perfect place for their new town and he would take them there. He was a perfect man, and she a fortunate woman to have found him. She intended to make sure he felt so well loved he would forget about his parents and Elizabeth. He would have the family he'd been denied, a community that admired and respected him. He would have the home he'd always wanted.

Unable to wait for him to wake up, she tapped him on the shoulder. He opened his eyes immediately. When he turned to face her, he smiled.

"Morning, beautiful."

"Let's start by promising never to lie to each other. I can't possibly look beautiful with my hair a mess and my face unwashed."

"You're beautiful to me."

She couldn't argue with that because, even rumpled by sleep, he was breathtaking to her. "I'm going to skip over the fact that it's dark and you can barely see me, because I like the idea that you find me beautiful. I've never felt that way before."

Colby rolled up on his elbow and kissed her. "I'm going to do my best to make sure you feel beautiful for the rest of your life."

"And I'll make sure you know you're the most wonderful man in the world. I want to give you lots of sons who will grow up to look just like you."

Even in the dark, it was evident that something she said had caused Colby to undergo a change. He stilled, his body stiffened.

'What's wrong? You do want children, don't you?"

"Very much."

"Then why did you act like that?"

"I already have a child."

Twenty

IT TOOK SEVERAL MOMENTS FOR NAOMI TO PROCESS what Colby had just said. She repeated the words in her mind, but the meaning always came out the same way.

Colby had a child. He was already a father.

She didn't know why it should be such a shock. He was twenty-seven. Cassie was twelve years younger and she was a mother. But it was a shock. That changed everything.

She sat up and turned away from him toward the open window. The streets were silent. A cool breeze stirred the curtains. The deep velvety blue of the cloudless sky was pricked by a dozen points of light. It should have been a comforting sight, but it made her feel cold and very much alone.

"Who is its mother?" She didn't want to know, but she *had* to know.

"Elizabeth."

Her worst fear was realized. Elizabeth hadn't been consigned to his past. She was very much a part of his present and his future. Naomi knew enough of Colby to know he could never ignore the existence of his child or its mother. She didn't doubt that he loved her, but he hadn't come to her with his whole heart. A good portion of it was allocated elsewhere.

It was hard to tell what she was feeling. She felt numb. It was like floating among the clouds then plummeting to earth with such force you couldn't move, couldn't think. All you could do was feel the pain.

"Is it a boy or a girl? What's its name?"

"I don't know."

"You don't know the name of your own child?"

"I don't know if it's a boy or a girl. I've never seen it. I don't even know when it was born."

She turned to face him. He was sitting up now, leaning against the pillow. "Light the lantern. I'd rather not have to tell you about this in the dark."

She would rather have kept the mantle of night wrapped around her. It would have been easier to endure the collapse of her dreams without Colby being able to read it in her face, but she lit the lamp. Since she couldn't avoid this truth, it was better to face it and start figuring out how to live with it.

She lit the lamp, then turned to Colby.

"I was twenty when I met Elizabeth. She was seventeen. I was poor and without any family. She was beautiful and her father was rich. I couldn't believe anyone like her could fall in love with someone like me, but she did. I didn't get to see her often because I was traveling between Missouri and Santa Fe, but when we were together, it was like the first time all over again. I know now that being apart so much and knowing her father wouldn't approve were part of what made it exciting, but I was too young to see that then. I only saw that for the first time in my life someone loved me. We planned to wait to marry until I had saved enough money."

Naomi couldn't understand how Colby must have felt because she'd always had a family who loved her, a community where she belonged. She could only try to imagine how desperately he wanted to be loved.

"I scrimped on food, clothes, every way I could until I saved what I thought was enough for us to get married. I sent her a message as soon as I got back to Santa Fe. I knew something had changed when she invited me to meet her at her house. I didn't need to see her flanked by her parents and the son of another wealthy family to know what she was going to say."

The pain was still in his voice.

"She told me that with time and maturity she'd realized she'd mistaken infatuation for love. While I'd been away, she'd fallen in love with the young man standing next to her. They married a month earlier."

Naomi couldn't begin to imagine how cruelly that must have hurt.

"I didn't know what had caused Elizabeth to change her mind, but I knew she wouldn't have if she hadn't been forced. I suppose I went crazy. I don't remember much of what happened, but when I woke up in jail, they told me I'd attacked Elizabeth's father."

Naomi reached out to rest her hand on Colby's arm. "Did you ever find out why she changed her mind?"

"Not right away. After the last time I tried to see her, they escorted me out of town and told me not to come back. I might not have gone back—Elizabeth was married. There was nothing I could do to change that—but I overheard two traders talking about her husband saying he would be a father soon. They were snickering over the fact that it would be a seven-month baby. I didn't need anybody to tell me it was my baby, and that her father had forced her to marry when he found out she was pregnant."

"Did you talk to her? Did you find out for sure?"

"I tried, but her father had talked the governor into keeping a guard around her house. That's when I set fire to his house. I was arrested and beaten. When I got well, I was escorted out of town and told I'd be shot if I came back."

So he didn't know that a child had actually been born, but it was an open question that had to be answered for his sake if not for hers. He wouldn't belong to her completely until he faced that part of his life. Once he did, he might not feel about her as he did now. Forcing him to find answers might cost her his love, but she couldn't marry him knowing there was a part of him that could never be hers.

"How did you get here tonight?"

"It's been almost five years. They're not looking for me now. I took advantage of the dark."

"You have to see Elizabeth and find out about your child."

"It's not *my* child. It's his."

"It's his legally, but it's yours in your mind. Elizabeth, the woman you loved so deeply, is its mother. Are you sure you're not still in love with her?"

Colby jerked away from her. "How could you think I could still love a woman who betrayed me like that?"

"Love isn't an emotion that can be controlled. You didn't want to fall in love with me. I tried not to fall in love with you, but both of us failed. You can't think that after all your talk about wanting a family, that I'd believe you'd forget you had a child."

"It's not my child!"

"You're its father. Nobody can change that."

"No, but I can forget it. I haven't told anybody but you."

"Why did you tell me?"

"Because I don't want any secrets between us."

"It's because you know you'll never be able to forget about that child."

"Maybe, but that doesn't change anything."

"It's unfinished and will stand between us for the rest of our lives."

"Not mine."

"It will for me. I'll always wonder what if you'd seen Elizabeth again, what if you'd seen your child, what if her love for you had never changed?"

Colby reached for her. "None of that would make any difference. I'm in love with you. I want to marry you. I want us to have a family."

Naomi tried to believe him, but she couldn't say none of it mattered. It did. Even if Colby no longer had any feelings for Elizabeth, he would grieve for the child he'd never known. That would affect her and any children they might have. That was something she couldn't endure.

"You have to see Elizabeth and your child. I can't marry you until you do."

❧

Naomi had endured two days of misery such as she'd never known. It was made worse because she couldn't confide in anyone. She hadn't heard from Colby since he left her hotel room. She didn't know if he was in jail, still camped out on the mountain, or if he'd mounted up and ridden away. She had punished herself emotionally for insisting she wouldn't marry him until he'd seen Elizabeth, but she couldn't have done anything else. She couldn't commit to being his unless he could do the same. She couldn't imagine how she could just forget a child of hers, so she couldn't believe Colby could.

"What's wrong with you?" Cassie asked. "You've been looking like you were somewhere else ever since you got back from that hotel."

Naomi had been eager to get back to the wagon train and her friends. The night spent with Colby remained too vividly in her mind, was associated too closely with the hotel. Being back restored some sense of order in her life, helped steady her emotions. There were times it felt like she'd dreamed that night in his arms.

"I'm worried about where we're going, what we're going to do when we get there."

She had volunteered to watch Little Abe for the afternoon, but Cassie had said she wanted company more than help. They were sitting under the shade of a tree that didn't look like any tree Naomi had seen back in Kentucky. The women and children were enjoying a sunny day made pleasant by a cool breeze from the Sangre de Cristo Mountains while the men were in town trying to find a guide.

"There's no point in worrying," Cassie said. "We'll do whatever the men decide."

"Doesn't that bother you?"

"What?"

"Doing what *men* decide without having any say in what happens to you or your children?"

"I don't want to decide what happens to everybody else. Do you?"

"No, but I'd like to be asked what I think."

Cassie laughed. "Men don't care what women think. Besides, we have enough to do taking care of children and running the house. Why would you want more work?"

Cassie would never understand. She had accepted her place in the world and was happy with it. The other women in Spencer's Clearing had done the same. Why was she different? Had being different cost her Colby? Why hadn't she heard from him?

"Do you ever think of Colby? I thought you liked him."

Naomi looked down at the baby who had gone to sleep in her arms. "Everybody did. Even you."

Cassie laughed again. "You know what I mean."

Naomi decided it was useless to pretend. "I liked him very much."

"I wonder where he is."

Naomi was almost bursting to tell somebody what had happened, but she held her tongue.

"Are you tired of staying with the wagons doing nothing?" Cassie asked. "I want to go into the town, go in the shops, eat at a restaurant, hear some music, go dancing."

"I'd rather they found a guide so we could be on our way. I can't wait until we have a house again."

"Ethan says we won't have houses like we're used to. He says we'll have cabins with dirt floors. He says—"

"Ethan doesn't know any more than the rest of us."

"He's been into town and talked to people. He says they don't have sawmills where we're going."

"Are you going with us?" Naomi hadn't given much thought to Cassie lately, but she hadn't forgotten the girl's intention of marrying the first man to ask her.

"Ethan says I can't marry just anybody. He said he'll take care of me until I can find a good husband."

At that moment, the paragon of thoughtfulness came riding up. Naomi wasn't surprised when he headed toward them. She was surprised when he turned to her rather than Cassie.

"Colby is in jail. He says he needs you to do something for him."

⁓

"Are you sure you should do this?"

Ethan had tried to persuade her to wait for their father, but Naomi had insisted on leaving at once. "Colby wouldn't have asked me to come to him if it weren't important." She hadn't expected the prison would be the military barracks.

"You don't even know why he's in jail. Maybe he got in a fight and killed someone."

"He wouldn't do that."

"How do you know?"

Naomi didn't answer. They had reached the court-rooms that were part of the governor's palace.

Once they were inside, Ethan said, "Wait here." Then he disappeared.

The stern and disapproving faces of the men in the room did nothing to calm Naomi's nerves. However, once they sensed she wasn't going to interrupt their various activities or require anything of them, they ignored her. Naomi had never been so happy to be considered of no consequence. After what seemed like an unreasonably long time, Ethan returned accompanied by a soldier.

"They weren't going to let you see Colby," Ethan said. "I talked them into it, but this soldier has to accompany you."

Naomi wished the soldier would smile rather than look as though he'd rather be facing combat.

"He's in the barracks jail," the soldier said. "It's not a place for a woman."

"I'm sure I'll be perfectly safe as long as you're with me."

"I'll be there too," Ethan said. When she looked surprised, he said, "You don't think I'd let my sister go into such a place without me or my father, do you?"

It seemed that being responsible for Cassie had matured Ethan. He'd never worried about her safety before.

The soldier led them out of the courtroom, through two smaller rooms, then out into a courtyard. They crossed a street and entered a low adobe building of no beauty or redeeming aspects. The inside was like a rabbit warren. She was lost after the third turn. They stopped before a door that was reinforced by iron straps.

"This is the jail," the soldier said. "If anyone speaks to you, act as though you didn't hear them."

"There's nothing but drunks, thieves, and cutthroats in here," Ethan said. "I tried to get him to let you meet Colby in one of the empty rooms, but he wouldn't agree."

"When we reach his cell, you've got five minutes," the soldier told Naomi. "Don't waste it."

The moment Naomi passed through the doorway, the man in the cell opposite leapt to his feet with a shouted profanity that caused Naomi to flinch. "I don't know whether I've gone to heaven or hell, but that's a woman I see, and a pretty one at that."

Every man in the jail started shouting or banging on something. After hearing what the next man said—something she didn't understand and didn't want explained—she hummed to herself to block out the din. Colby was standing at his door when she arrived.

"Thank god you're here," he hollered so she could hear. "I was afraid they wouldn't let you come."

"Tell her what you want," Ethan shouted. "I want to get her out of here as soon as possible."

"I tried to do what you asked," Colby yelled to her, "but Elizabeth's father still has a guard posted at night. It took me a full day to convince the guard to get a message to you. It cost me every cent I had with me."

"Can you shut them up?" Ethan yelled to the guard. "She can't hear what he's saying."

"It's not my concern," the guard replied.

Naomi turned on the man. "Colby *paid* you for these five minutes. That may be a common practice here, but I doubt you'd like me to complain to one of the judges that you took a prisoner's money then cheated him of what he'd paid for."

The guard gave her a furious look, then turned and started down the hall that fronted the cells.

"Shut up, you sons-of-bitches!" he shouted. "Get back to your beds and shut your mug holes. If you don't, not one of you lying, cheating bastards will get supper. If just one of you makes another comment while this lady's here, I might forget to close the door. You know how fond the rats are of visiting these cells."

Apparently both threats had been made good in the past because the noise stopped almost immediately. There was some low grumbling, then silence.

"Get on with it," he said to Naomi when he came back. "Your time's almost up."

"I'll ask Papa for the money to get you out," Naomi said to Colby.

"I don't want your money. I want you to go to Elizabeth."

"I can't do that."

"You must. It's the only way I'll get out of here or see my child."

"I don't know her. I don't know what to say. I don't even know where she lives."

"Time's up," the guard said. "You have to leave now."

"I haven't finished."

"You leave, or he gets no supper and rats to keep him company."

"She lives on San Francisco," Colby said. "Anyone can show you her house."

Ethan was already pulling her away from the cell.

"She married an American named Haman Stuart," Colby shouted after her.

❧

Naomi stared at the white-washed adobe wall that surrounded the home of Elizabeth Stuart, a woman she didn't know, had never seen, and yet had to convince to help the man she jilted. She not only didn't know what to say, she didn't know what she *wanted* to say, but she had to think of something. At any moment, Colby could be brought before a judge. She had no idea what punishment he might receive.

She pulled the rope and heard a bell ring in the distance.

She wished she had brought her father with her, but she felt certain a strange man would have been denied a meeting with Elizabeth unless her husband or father was present. Naomi was certain of only one thing: The success of her mission depended on meeting Elizabeth alone.

The gate swung open to reveal a young woman. "May I help you?"

Naomi was relieved she spoke English. "My name is Naomi Kessling. I wish to speak with Mrs. Elizabeth Stuart."

"She is expecting you?"

"No, but tell her it's urgent I speak with her on behalf of Colby Blaine. He's in jail and needs her help to avoid serious punishment."

"You may wait in the courtyard while I take your message."

From the outside, the adobe building appeared little different from others. However, once inside the court-yard, it was obvious this was the home of a wealthy woman. The ground was covered in paving stones. Benches lined the walls decorated with mosaic designs. Comfortable chairs were grouped in the shade of a low tree with spreading branches. In a sunny corner, clothes had been hung out to dry. The house itself was made of adobe that had been white washed recently so that it was almost blinding in its whiteness. Naomi had made several circuits of the courtyard before the door opened.

"Mrs. Stuart says she will see you."

Naomi entered a wide hall that extended the length of the house and was interrupted only by a staircase. Though clearly the home of an American, Naomi could see the Spanish influence in the heavily carved chairs and tables as well as pictures in gilt frames. Rugs scattered along the hall showed patterns unfamiliar to her. She was ushered into a room immediately to the right.

She didn't know what she had expected Elizabeth to look like—Colby had never described her—but the woman seated on an embroidered settee couldn't be the woman Colby knew. The signs of youthful loveliness were still present, but she looked more than forty. Her skin appeared dry and taut over the bones of her face, her hands almost skeletal. Her meticulously groomed hair was streaked with gray. Her extreme thinness gave her the appearance of one who was recovering from a grave illness.

"There must be some confusion," Naomi said.

"I asked to see the Elizabeth Stuart who knew Colby Blaine."

"I understand your confusion, but I am indeed the Elizabeth who knew Colby." She pointed to a chair next to the settee. "Won't you have a seat and tell me what I can do to help him?"

Despite her physical appearance, her voice sounded young and vibrant. Her eyes were steel gray and brimmed with the energy that seemed to have deserted the rest of her body.

"I'm not entirely sure where to begin."

"Why don't you start when Colby left Santa Fe?"

"The last time Colby was released from jail, he was told to leave Santa Fe and not come back or he might be shot."

Her gaze didn't falter. "My father is very unforgiving. We were both imprisoned for what we did."

Her meaning couldn't be misunderstood yet Naomi felt no sympathy for her. "Colby served in the Union Army during the war. He was on his way to visit his parents' graves when he kept our small wagon train from being massacred in an Indian attack."

"Now tell me why you're here. I can see you're in love with him, but you don't need my help with that."

"Actually I do." All the words she'd rehearsed went out of her mind. "Colby has asked me to marry him. I very much want to be his wife, but he has to settle with his past before he can be the husband and father I know he can be. He can't forget you bore his child, a child he's never seen."

Elizabeth seemed to turn to ice. "What does he want from me?"

"Ask your father to see he's released then grant him one interview. After that, he'll never bother you again."

Elizabeth thawed perceptibly. "How can you promise that?"

"Because I will be the wife he needs and provide him with the family and sense of belonging he's never had."

After several moments during which Elizabeth neither moved nor spoke, she reached for a small bell on the table next to the settee. When a servant answered her summons, she said something to the woman in Spanish after which the woman withdrew.

"I'd never met anyone like Colby." Elizabeth seemed to be remembering out loud rather than talking to Naomi. "He was so handsome, so full of energy, practically bursting with life. I was swept away by him." She met Naomi's gaze with a faint smile. "I expect you understand that."

"I was determined not to like him."

"I don't think it's possible for any young woman to dislike Colby when he makes up his mind to be attractive."

"I think he thought of me as a challenge. Before we knew it, both of us were lost."

"But you don't feel lost now, do you?"

"No. I don't understand anything about this country, but I'm never worried when I'm with Colby."

"That's how I felt when I was with him. Unfortunately, I wasn't with him when I learned I was going to have a child. My father gave me an ultimatum. Either I marry a man of his choice, or I would go into a convent and give up the baby. I'm not a strong person, but I couldn't give up my baby.

My husband is a good man, but I don't love him and he doesn't love me. Nor does he love my children."

Before Naomi could ask for an explanation, the door opened and two children entered. The girl went straight to their mother, but the boy stopped to stare at Naomi. She didn't need anyone to tell her Colby was the father of both children. She could see him in the face of each child.

It was morning and they hadn't been expecting a guest, but both children were formally dressed. The boy wore long pants, a white shirt with a tie and a coat. The child looked like a miniature man. He couldn't play in those clothes.

Elizabeth spoke to the servant. "Caroline, tell Louis I need him immediately." She then turned back to Naomi. "This is Peter and Esther. They're twins. Children, I'd like you to meet Miss Naomi Kessling."

Esther smiled and said hello from the safety of her mother's side, but Peter walked over to Naomi and extended his small hand. "How do you do? It is very nice to meet you."

Naomi's heart melted. She could see the youthful Colby in this child. "How old are you?" It sounded stupid to ask that of a child she'd just met, but her thoughts were in chaos.

"We are four," Peter said, including his sister. "We had a nice birthday party."

He sounded so grown-up. She wondered what Colby was like at that age, what he would have been like if he'd been in a good home with loving parents. Maybe he would have been like this little boy, bright, confident, and secure in his mother's love.

"Did you have cake and get lots of presents?"

"Grandpapa said we got too many presents."

Naomi glanced at Elizabeth, expecting her to comment, but a male servant had entered the room and she was speaking to him in Spanish.

"I don't think it's possible to get too many presents," Naomi told Peter. "Did you have fun opening them all at once?"

"Grandpapa said I could open only one each day."

"That's like having a birthday every day."

"Esther cried."

All was not well in this house despite the money and the servants. This little boy acted like an adult, not a child of four. His sister depended on the protective presence of her mother.

"Peter, come here and sit down," Elizabeth said to her son. "You'll tire our guest."

"Not at all," Naomi hastened to assure Elizabeth. "I think he's a charming little boy. I would love to have one just like him."

A strange look came over Elizabeth's face, almost like she'd discovered the answer to some problem and was relieved yet fearful.

Peter settled himself on the settee next to his mother. "Grandpapa says I'm a young man. He says I must not act like a little boy."

"Are you very busy today?" Elizabeth asked Naomi.

"I have nothing to do except get Colby released from prison."

"I have a plan, but it will take much of the day. Will you stay and have lunch with me?"

"Do the children eat with you?"

Elizabeth seemed surprised by the question. "They can if you wish."

Naomi looked at the brave little boy and the blushing little girl and wondered why anyone would be separated from them a moment more than necessary. "I would like that very much."

"Peter, go find Caroline and tell her we will have a guest for lunch." She patted her son's leg. "Tell her you and Esther are to eat with us today."

Rather than jump up and run from the room as Naomi expected, Peter slid down from the settee and walked to the door like a small mannequin. Naomi itched to take him outside and let him play until his clothes were dirty and tattered beyond saving.

Elizabeth put her arm around her daughter. "Tell me about your journey," she asked. "It must have been quite exciting. How did you meet Colby?"

Over the next half hour, Elizabeth's questions made it obvious she was more interested in Colby than the trip itself so Naomi talked more about him. She was describing their crossing the flooded river when she heard a slammed door and raised voices in the hall Almost immediately a man burst into the room. He was tall, thin, dressed impeccably, and in a towering rage.

"What the hell do you mean by sending Louis with a demand that I come immediately? What in hell has gotten into you? Have you lost what little sense you have?"

Naomi wasn't so absorbed by the visitor that she didn't notice Esther trying to bury herself in her mother's embrace. Peter didn't move, but his face lost all trace of animation.

"Father, I'd like you to meet my guest. This is Naomi Kessling. Naomi, this is my father, Elijah Davies."

"I don't want to meet any guest. I do want to know what this is all about."

Naomi heard a door open and voices.

"That's Haman. Now we can get to the bottom of this."

It took an effort, but Elizabeth rose. "Miss Kessling, please excuse me while I talk with my father and my husband. I'll send the children back to their room."

"Please, let them stay," Naomi asked. "I enjoy talking to them."

Mr. Davies turned to her. "Children don't have anything worth saying, and anybody who thinks so is a fool. Out," he shouted at the children. "I don't want to see you again."

Peter slid off the sofa, took his sister's hand, and the two of them walked from the room.

Naomi was so angry she couldn't hold her tongue. "That is the cruelest thing I've ever witnessed. You don't deserve such beautiful grandchildren."

He rounded on her, his face a mask of fury. "You don't know what you're talking about."

"I know you're a bully and a tyrant."

"I don't want you in this house. Get out."

Elizabeth squared up to her father. "She's my guest, not yours. She can stay as long as I wish. Now let's go see Haman." When her father didn't move, Elizabeth said, "I'm willing to have this conversation in front of Miss Kessling, but you will be unhappy if she hears what I have to say."

"What has gotten into you?"

"I'm dying, father. That's what has gotten into me. I'm no longer afraid of you." She turned and left the room leaving her father to follow.

For the next twenty minutes Naomi listened to voices raised in anger. She didn't know what Elizabeth was saying, but judging by her father's language, it was unwelcome news. Finally, after a series of thumps and banged doors, the house fell silent. Moments later Elizabeth returned. She looked near exhaustion, but her eyes were gleaming and she was smiling. There was even a hint of color in her cheeks.

"If you're ready, we can have lunch with the children. Colby should be here by the time we're finished."

Twenty-one

COLBY HAD PACED HIS CELL UNTIL THERE SHOULD HAVE been a rut in it. He cursed himself for asking Naomi to come to this cesspool, for asking her to see Elizabeth in his place, yet what other options did he have? He had several. He just hadn't used them. He could have asked her father. He could have asked Ethan or any of the other men in the train, but he never considered them. Naomi had been his only choice. He needed to see her, to know she still loved him. If that had changed, he wouldn't have cared whether he ever got out of prison.

What could Naomi say to Elizabeth to make her want to help a man she'd jilted? She would have to go against her father. If she couldn't do that for the man she thought she loved, why would she do it for a man she hadn't seen in almost five years? It was a futile errand.

But he *had* to see Elizabeth. That was the only way Naomi would marry him. It might be a month before they released him from jail. They would certainly tell him never to come back, but he'd find a way to talk to Elizabeth. Nothing was going to stop him from marrying Naomi.

The door at the far end of the corridor opened. He wondered who was being released. He hoped the man wasn't going to the gallows.

The guard stopped in front of his cell. "You must have some powerful friends," he said to Colby, "or your lady friend is mighty persuasive. I'm ordered to escort you to the house of Haman Stuart. Can't understand what they would want with a rat like you."

Colby didn't waste time responding to the guard's invective. He was shocked to learn he wouldn't be handcuffed and would be accompanied by a single guard.

"How do you know anybody as rich as Mr. Stuart?" the guard asked.

"He's a trader," Colby said. "Before the war I knew all the traders." He didn't know Haman Stuart, but the man's father didn't have a good reputation.

"Fancy neighborhood," the guard said. "I don't get over this way much."

Not many people did. People like Elizabeth's father and her husband's family jealously guarded their street.

The closer Colby came to the house, the more tense he became. When he asked Naomi to see Elizabeth, the most he'd hoped for was a message. It never entered his mind that he might be summoned to her home. The servant who admitted them to the courtyard told the guard to wait outside. When the guard started to argue, the servant stated that Elijah Davies had given the order. Such was the man's influence that the guard subsided immediately.

On entering the parlor, four individuals faced him from across the room. Elizabeth sat on a settee with Naomi beside her. Her father and the man Colby remembered as her husband stood at either end of the settee.

"Come in, Colby," Elizabeth said. "Please have a seat."

Her appearance shocked Colby. "You aren't well," he said. "Have you seen a doctor?"

"I appreciate your concern, but I see my doctor regularly."

It was a surreal experience, Elizabeth acting like they were old friends rather than former lovers, Naomi sitting next to Elizabeth, their hands clasped, the father and husband standing on either side glaring at Colby, one with dislike and the other with open hatred. The drama was on hold. He was a mere distraction.

"Now that the war is over, what do you plan to do with yourself?" Elizabeth asked.

"What he's always done," her father snapped, "work as a hired hand. That's all he's fit for."

Colby ignored her father. "Naomi's family is looking for a place to settle and start a town. I plan to take them to Arizona."

"Naomi tells me that you two have fallen in love and want to marry."

Colby turned to Naomi. "If she'll have me, I plan to settle down and raise a family."

"You'll never settle down," her father exploded. "You're a shiftless nobody. I don't know this woman," he said, pointing at Naomi, "but I couldn't give her any better advice than to look for another man to marry."

Ignoring her father, Elizabeth rang the small bell on the table next to her. Almost immediately the door opened and two small children entered the room and went directly to their mother. When she turned them to face Colby, he thought his heart would stop beating.

"Who…Are they…?" His power of speech left him.

"This is Peter and Esther," Elizabeth said. "They're twins. Children, this man is Mr. Colby Blaine. Say hello to him."

Esther spoke from the safety of her mother's arm, but Peter crossed the room and extended his hand to Colby. "How do you do?" he said. "I'm very glad to meet you."

Colby was so choked up he couldn't speak. He could hardly believe that the small hand tucked in his belonged to his son, that the little girl who eyed him with curiosity was his daughter. How was he supposed to leave this room and pretend he'd never seen them, that he wouldn't ache to hold them in his arms, to shower them with the love he'd been saving up ever since he was a small boy?

"What do you think of them?" Elizabeth asked.

Colby was too overwhelmed to find words to express his emotions. Even if he had been able to speak, he doubted there were words with sufficient power to describe the wellspring of emotion that the sight of these two children had unleashed. He felt weak, drained, so helpless he was unable to speak. Naomi spoke for him.

"I think Colby would like to say he's never seen two finer children. They're exactly the kind of children he'd want for his own."

Peter's big, nearly black eyes gazed up at Colby from under a stray lock of chestnut hair. "Grandpapa says we're misbegotten. Do you know what that means?"

Colby knew it was unchristian to hope Elizabeth's father met a slow and painful death, but he didn't care. "It means you're very special," Colby told Peter.

"Would you like to take a walk with Mr. Blaine?" Elizabeth asked Peter.

"Where would we go?" Peter asked.

"Anywhere you and your sister would like."

"Esther won't go," Peter said. "Grandpapa says Indians will get us."

"There's not an Indian brave enough to come after you as long as you're with Mr. Blaine," Naomi said. She turned to Esther. "I'll go with you. You can hold my hand the whole time."

"Children, why don't you take Naomi to your room? She can help you decide what to wear."

The door had hardly closed behind Naomi and the children before both men turned on Elizabeth. Colby sprang to his feet, crossed the room, and placed himself between Elizabeth and the two men.

"Not another word!" he shouted. "I'll hit the next one who says a cruel word to Elizabeth. My god, can't you see she's not well?"

"You're the one who'd better shut up!" her father shouted back, "or you'll rot in jail."

"Ignore him," Elizabeth said to Colby. "I've finally gotten the better of him, and he can't stand it."

Colby didn't move. "What do you mean?"

"I told him I'd tell everyone in Santa Fe that Peter and Esther are your children. I'm not sure that he doesn't hate you more than he fears a scandal, but Haman can't afford scandal or gossip. It would ruin his plans to marry a very pious Spanish lady after I die."

"You can't be dying. You're too young."

"I've seen every doctor in Santa Fe. They all say the same. The only question is how long it will take."

It was hard to believe Elizabeth was dying. It was impossible to remember the young woman she used to be and not feel it was a terrible waste.

"What will happen to the children?"

"I'm going to give them to you if you're married to Naomi and have a house by the time I die."

Colby wasn't sure he could handle any more shocks, but this was so wonderful, so beyond his wildest dreams, that he didn't dare let himself believe it could be possible.

"What about your father, your husband?"

"My father hates you, but he hates me more for refusing to go to a convent where I could give birth and put them up for adoption. He'll be glad to have them disappear. Haman will say he's too overcome with grief to give the children proper love and attention so he has sent them back East to his family. After a period of time, he will marry his Spanish bride and they will start a family. There'll be one reason or another why the children can't, or don't want to, return. After a while, everyone will forget about them."

"How could you have done all of this in the few hours since Naomi got here?"

"I've been thinking about it ever since the doctors told me I was going to die."

Colby was ashamed of all the years he'd spent

blaming Elizabeth for his unhappiness. She had braved her father's wrath to put his children's welfare before everything else.

"I've made a will," Elizabeth told Colby, "but I don't trust my father. I will have papers drawn up and signed by him and Haman giving them to you and Naomi."

"You can't force me to do that," her father said.

She turned to her husband. "Maybe not, but Haman will."

Haman's gaze shifted to his father-in-law then back to his wife before he nodded his agreement.

"You need to leave Elizabeth to rest," Colby said to the two men. "I have a few things to say to her before Naomi and I take the children for a walk."

The men were reluctant to leave, but Elizabeth surprised everyone by saying she'd seen enough of both of them for one day.

Colby couldn't forgive Elizabeth for jilting him and denying him four years of his children's lives. He knew it must have been difficult to withstand her father's pressure, but if she had loved him as deeply as she said, she could have withstood anything.

"I can tell from your silence you're having difficulty forgiving me. I don't expect it. What I did was too terrible to forgive. I'm weak, Colby. I don't have Naomi's strength. I could never have loved you the way she does."

"You're too hard on yourself."

Elizabeth shook her head. "Not nearly hard enough. If you'd married me, you'd never have met Naomi. You do love her, don't you?"

"More than I thought possible."

"More than you ever loved me. I can see it in your eyes when you look at her, and I'm content. You gave me four years with two wonderful children. That was the one time I *was* strong enough to stand up to my father. I've always been grateful for that, but they would grow up stunted if they remained here. I want them to run and shout, laugh and cry. I want them to fall down and get up again more determined than ever. I can't do that for them, but you and Naomi can. If dying is the price of making it possible for my children to grow up to be happy, wholesome, positive adults, then I'm willing to pay it."

Colby wanted to say something, but his throat was too tight to allow it.

"I think I hear Naomi and the children approaching."

"I haven't had time to say anything."

"I'm the one who needed to speak, to try to make right what I did."

"I need to thank you for giving me my children. You didn't need to do that."

"But I did. I love them as I've never been able to love anyone else. It's for *them* that I'm giving them to you. Had it been best for them to stay here, you'd never have set eyes on them."

Colby found himself smiling at the determination in that tired, sad face. "If you'd only felt like that five years ago—"

"We'd have made a mess of both our lives."

He wanted to say more, but Naomi and the children entered the room. He was pleased to see Esther didn't appear quite so timid. Rather than seek the comfort of her mother's arm, she remained standing next to Naomi, her small hand in Naomi's.

"May we go to the square?" Peter asked. "Caroline says men play ball there. I've never seen men play ball. I want to see how they do it."

"I'll do more than that. I'll teach you to play."

"Caroline says the men run. I'm not allowed to run. Grandpapa says only peasants run."

"Well I run and so does Naomi. You don't think we're peasants do you?"

"I don't know. I've never seen a peasant. Are they like people?"

Colby's gaze met Elizabeth's over the child's head. "They're very much like people. In fact, they're not very different from you and me."

"Grandpapa says—"

"I think you can forget what *Grandpapa says*. We'd better get started. It's a long way to the plaza."

"Are we going to walk?"

"Yes."

"Grandpapa says…" Peter stopped in midsentence and thought for a minute. Then he looked up at Colby and said with great seriousness, "I think I would like to forget what Grandpapa said."

❧

"Are you ready, Mrs. Blaine?"

"Yes, Mr. Blaine. I've been ready almost from the day I met you."

"It won't be anything like Spencer's Clearing."

"I'm not the person who used to live in Spencer's Clearing. You've managed to turn me into someone else entirely. Now it's your responsibility to find a place for the new me."

"Will you two stop acting like newlyweds and get moving? Everybody is waiting on you."

Naomi thought her father sounded a bit jealous. She'd never stopped to think that he might be lonely. Her newfound happiness as Colby's bride made her hope her father might find someone to make him equally happy.

"Up you go."

Colby lifted Naomi onto the wagon seat and climbed up to sit next to her. Her father was riding the horse he'd bought in Santa Fe. Ben was astride Shadow and so eager to get started he could hardly contain himself. They were ready to begin their journey from Santa Fe to their new home in Arizona. When Colby cracked the whip over the oxen's heads, the six sturdy beasts put their shoulders into their yokes, and the wagon rolled steadily down the streets of Santa Fe and out into the wilderness beyond.

"Are you sure you want to become the mother of two four-year-olds?" Colby asked.

"Will you stop asking that?" Naomi responded. "I've told you a dozen times I think both children are adorable, and I can't wait for them to come live with us. Why can't you believe me?"

"I feel like I've put you in a position where you'd feel guilty saying you didn't want the children. Elizabeth wouldn't let me have them unless you married me."

"I was going to marry you, Colby Blaine, if I had to follow you through every remote corner of Arizona.

Those children are a bonus. I want them as much as you."

"But you want them because of me."

"Yes, I want them because I know they're yours, but I want them because I've fallen in love with them. I hope I'll be able to give you children, but none of them will ever be more special to me than Peter and Esther. Now stop worrying."

"I'm trying, but I want this so much I live in fear that something will go wrong."

"Many things will go wrong, but nothing will change how much I love you or the children. Everything else we can deal with."

Naomi was pleased when rather than voice any more doubts, Colby decided to use his energy kissing her. Being married had introduced her to many new experiences, but being taken into the powerful arms of her husband and kissed ruthlessly was one of the ones she enjoyed most. She was looking forward to many years of the same.

"I hate to interrupt," her father said, "but unless you want to end up in the river, you'd better spare some attention for your oxen."

Colby was embarrassed, but Naomi didn't mind the laughter. She'd already crossed a flood-swollen river in pursuit of Colby. The river ahead was only the Rio Grande.

Epilogue

A year later

THE BARE OUTLINE OF THE TINY SETTLEMENT THAT WAS Cactus Corner came into view around a bend in the Verde River in the Arizona Territory.

"Is that where we're going to live?" Peter asked his father.

"Yes, this will be your new home," Colby told his son.

Colby didn't know when he'd anticipated anything as eagerly as welcoming his son and daughter into his home. Only his wedding day and learning Naomi was pregnant with their first child merited comparison. It had been an arduous journey of over six hundred miles from Santa Fe in a covered wagon, but Colby wouldn't have traded a minute. Having his children to himself for nearly seven weeks had been a terrifying experience, but he would always cherish the memory of the evenings by the campfire, an arm wrapped around each child, telling them stories and answering questions about their new life.

His only regret was that Naomi hadn't been able to accompany him.

As the first houses came into view, Esther said, "They don't look like Mama's house."

The buildings were constructed of raw wood that hadn't had time to weather. Only a few had been painted.

"Which one is ours?" Peter was scrutinizing each house as they passed. "Will I have my own horse?"

The transformation of the children had been gradual, but it was now complete. Each wore floppy hats to protect them from the sun and heavy shoes to safeguard their feet. Esther's dress was of calico while Peter's pants were of denim and his plaid shirt cotton. Both children ran rather than walked, jabbered constantly, played noisily, laughed aloud, and viewed their strange new world with endless curiosity. The two large trunks containing their clothes hadn't been opened after the first day.

"Our house will be the white one in the middle of town," Colby said. "Naomi will be on the porch waiting for you."

Colby had had no way of letting Naomi know when he and the children would arrive, but he had met Reece Hill's boys gathering wood about a mile back. By now the boys had had time to alert everyone in town to Colby's arrival. When his house came into view, it was surrounded by nearly everyone in town.

"Who are those people?" Peter asked.

"These are people who've come to welcome you to your new home."

Bert Hill ran up to the wagon. "I told everybody

you were coming," he shouted to Colby as he ran alongside. "Mama said Peter could come over whenever he wants."

Esther pointed to Naomi who had walked out of the house and down the steps to greet them. "Is she going to be my new mother?" she asked.

"Yes," Colby answered as he pulled the wagon to a stop. He jumped down and held out his arms to Naomi who folded into his embrace.

"I thought you'd never get here," she whispered. "The last two months have seemed liked two years."

"I've missed you, too. How are you doing?"

Naomi put his hand on her belly.

"Papa says *we* are doing just fine. How are the children? How are you?" She laughed. "I wasn't sure you'd survive the trip."

Colby glanced back at the children. "Except for missing you, I wouldn't have cared if it *had* lasted two years. I've never been so scared yet had so much fun in my life. Come on. They're waiting to meet you."

Peter jumped down from the wagon. "I'm Peter," he announced as he extended his hand to Naomi. "I remember when you came to our house."

"I've been waiting ever since to welcome you to our home," Naomi told the boy.

"Mama said I would like you. Esther will, too, but she's afraid."

"Maybe you and I can make her unafraid."

"I'm not afraid," Esther insisted. "Mama told me young ladies should wait until they're spoken to. Boys don't have to wait. I don't think that's fair."

"I agree with you," Naomi said. "Let Colby help

you down, and we can meet all the people who've come to welcome you to Cactus Corner."

"I can get down by myself," Esther announced. "Colby taught me how. He said young ladies have to know how to drive buggies and ride horses. He said he's going to teach me."

"Let me give you a hug," Naomi said when Esther had climbed down from the wagon. "I've been wanting to do this for a long time."

"Have you been wanting to hug me?" Peter asked.

"Very much," Naomi said.

"Now that we're all welcomed and hugged," Colby said, "it's time to meet your new neighbors."

Bert Hill swaggered up. "I'll introduce them," he offered. "Mama says after being gone for so long, you won't want to let go of Naomi for any reason."

Colby could imagine Flora's embarrassment over her son's statement, but she was right. He didn't want to let go of Naomi ever again. But he wouldn't have to now. He finally had his family with him. *All* of his family.

He watched as Bert took the children around to each family, introducing them to the children first and the adults afterward. Soon they were surrounded by a gaggle of kids making plans for enough entertainment to occupy the children through most of the summer.

"Did you ever imagine anything like this could happen?" Naomi asked Colby.

"Never in a thousand years. But never in a million years would I have imagined I'd be standing here with my arms around you watching those two amazing children become part of the rest of our lives."

It came as an unbidden afterthought.

The only thing that could have made it better would have been if his two brothers could have been standing here with him.

Author's Note

The Santa Fe Trail is probably the most storied trail in U.S. history and the one in operation for the longest time. Captain William Becknell took the first wagons over the Trail to Santa Fe in 1821. It remained a major artery of commerce until the railroad reached Santa Fe in 1880. I have found two books to be of great help in doing research for this book. The first, Stanley Vestal's *The Old Santa Fe Trail,* was invaluable for its meticulous description of the various places along the Cimarron cutoff, the condition of the land and the rivers, and its stories of colorful episodes in the life of the trail.

The second book, *The Prairie Traveler*, was written by U.S. Army Captain Randolph B. Marcy as a guide to anyone contemplating a journey across the prairie from points in Texas, Arkansas, and Missouri. It covers everything from relative merits of mules and oxen to the choice of desiccated and canned vegetables, methods of purifying water, repairing and circling up wagons, and any kind of equipment needed for such an adventure. It was from this book that I found the treatment for rattlesnake bites.

Another book of great interest, but not used directly for this book, is *Down the Santa Fe Trail and into Mexico*, the diary of Susan Shelby Magoffin, 1846–1847. Her description of each day's travel was colorful and remarkable for its detail. It also makes clear that even with the proper equipment, preparation, and leadership, the journey over the trail was a challenging experience.

About the Author

Leigh Greenwood is the author of the popular Seven Brides, Cowboy, and Night Riders series. The proud father of three grown children, Leigh resides in Charlotte, NC. He never intended to be a writer, but found it hard to ignore the people in his head, and the only way to get them out was to write. For more information visit www.leigh-greenwood.com.

Heart of a Texan

by Leigh Greenwood

In the wrong place...

Roberta didn't mean to hurt anyone. But the night that masked bandits raided her ranch, it was hard to tell friend from foe. She didn't know Nate Dolan was only trying to help when she shot him in the chest. And when he offers to help her catch the culprits, she only feels guiltier. The absolute least she can do is nurse the rugged cowboy back to health...

with all the right moves

Nate has been on the vengeance trail so long, he nearly forgot what a real home looked like. And Roberta is mighty fine incentive to stay put for a while—even if she has a stubborn streak as wide as the great state of Texas. She might be convinced she's healing the wound in his chest, but neither of them know she's also soothing the hurt in his heart.

"Readers will enjoy the battle of wits between these two stubborn protagonists." —*RT Book Reviews*, 4 Stars

"Strap yourself in for a wild ride with this cowboy and the stubborn love of his life." —Fresh Fiction

For more Leigh Greenwood, visit:

www.sourcebooks.com

Texas Pride

by Leigh Greenwood

A Prince Among Men

Carla Reece had never met anyone more infuriating in her life. The blond giant who swaggered up to her door had no right to take over half her ranch—no matter how stupid her brother had been gambling it away in a high-stakes poker game. Her new foreman claimed to be some foreign royalty who promised to leave in a year. Still, a year was way too long to spend with a man who made her madder than a wet hen and weak in the knees all at the same time.

A Hellion Among Women

Ivan may have charmed everyone in town into thinking he was the perfect gentleman, but Carla knew better. There had to be a chink in his armor—a red-hot passion under that calm, cool gaze. But once she finds it, she may be in for more than she ever bargained for...

Praise for Leigh Greenwood:

"For a fast-paced story of the Wild West, Leigh Greenwood is one of the best" —*RT Book Reviews*

For more Leigh Greenwood, visit:

www.sourcebooks.com

Paradise Valley

by Rosanne Bittner

Maggie Tucker has just gone through hell. Outlaws murdered her husband, looted their camp, and terrorized Maggie before leaving her lost and alone in the wilds of Wyoming. She isn't about to let another strange man get close enough to harm her.

Sage Lightfoot, owner of Paradise Valley ranch, is hunting for the men who killed his best ranch hand. But what he finds is a beautiful, bedraggled woman digging a grave. And pointing a pistol at his heart.

From that moment on, Sage will do anything to protect the strong-yet-vulnerable Maggie. Together, they'll embark on a life-changing journey along the dangerous Outlaw Trail, risking their lives…and their love.

Praise for Rosanne Bittner:

"A wonderful, absorbing read, with characters to capture the heart and the imagination… it's a romance not to be missed." —Heather Graham on *Outlaw Hearts*

"Power, passion, tragedy, and triumph are Rosanne Bittner's hallmarks." —RT *Book Reviews* on *Wildest Dreams*

For more Rosanne Bittner, visit:

www.sourcebooks.com

Thunder on the Plains

by Rosanne Bittner

In a land of opportunity

Sunny Landers wanted a big life—as big and free as the untamed land that stretched before her. Land she would help her father conquer to achieve his dream of a transcontinental railroad. She wouldn't let a cold, creaky wagon, murderous bandits, or stampeding buffalo stand in her way. She wanted it all—including Colt Travis.

All the odds were against them

Like the land of his birth, half-Cherokee Colt Travis was wild, hard, and dangerous. He was a drifter, a wilderness scout with no land and no prospects hired to guide the Landers' wagon train. He knew Sunny was out of his league and her father would never approve, but beneath the endless starlit sky, anything seemed possible...

"Bittner has a knack for writing strong, believable characters who truly seem to jump off the pages." —Historical Novel Review

"I hated having to put it down for even one second." —Romancing the Book

For more Rosanne Bittner, visit:

www.sourcebooks.com